# RED LIGHT
# WIVES

# RED LIGHT WIVES

## MARY MONROE

Dafina Books

KENSINGTON PUBLISHING CORP.
http://www.kensingtonbooks.com

DAFINA BOOKS are published by

Kensington Publishing Corp.
119 West 40th Street
New York, NY 10018

All Kensington Titles, Imprints and Distributed Lines are available
at special quantity discounts for bulk purchases for sales promo-
tions, premiums, fund-raising, and educational or institutional use.
Special book excerpts or customized printings can also be created
to fit specific needs. For details, write or phone the office of the
Kensington special sales manager: Kensington Publishing Corp.,
119 West 40th Street, New York, NY 10018, attn: Special Sales Department, Phone: 1-800-221-2647.

Dafina Books and the Dafina logo Reg. U.S. Pat. & TM Off.

ISBN-13: 978-0-7582-5401-6
ISBN-10: 0-7582-5401-6

First hardcover printing: September 2004
First trade paperback printing: August 2005
First mass market printing: October 2010

10  9  8  7  6  5  4  3  2  1

Printed in the United States of America

# ACKNOWLEDGMENTS

Thanks to David Akamine and Sheila Cunningham Sims for the emotional support. Thanks to Maria "Felice" Sanchez and Anita "Wuzzle" Sanchez for being my friends and for keeping me grounded.

Ann Agnew, you still owe me lunch but I'll mention you anyway.

Thanks to my literary agent, Andrew Stuart (The Stuart Agency). I wouldn't trade you for the world.

When I prayed to land the best editor for me, God sent me Karen Thomas. Much love and respect to everyone at Kensington Books. I couldn't have asked for a better publisher.

Thanks to Black Expressions Book Club for featuring my novels as main selections. Thanks to the reading book clubs, bookstores, magazines, radio stations, newspapers and everyone else for supporting my work. Thanks to Peggy Hicks for organizing my book tours and to the many wonderful people I met as I dragged myself from one city to the next. A very special thank-you to the nice folks in Nashville who stuffed me with so much good food!

# Chapter 1

# LULA HAWKINS

Sex was one thing I could always count on to cause trouble in my life.

The nightmare that led me from Barberton, Mississippi, to San Francisco began last April. In each city I had allowed the wrong man to control me with sex. I went from being a naive, lovesick country girl to a high-priced call girl.

Larry Holmes must have gotten his wife and me pregnant the same night because nine months later, she and I ended up in the same hospital on the same day to give birth to his babies. But that wasn't bad enough. I didn't even know that the man I'd been sleeping with for more than a year had a wife, until she coldcocked me in the parking lot at Jupiter's Discount Department Store one afternoon five days ago.

Other than that vicious assault, there was nothing unusual about that day. It was a Friday, the chosen day of my workweek that I usually called in "sick," so I could start my weekend early. I did this about every eight weeks. My high-maintenance relationship with Larry required a lot of my time. And even though I needed my mundane job at the Department of Motor Vehicles, I couldn't let it interfere with my plans. It had taken me too long to find happiness and true love. Except for death, nothing was going to stand in my way. I was not just a woman in love; I was a fool in love.

But at thirty-three and still single, you would have thought that I was blind, too. Because, so far, I had refused to acknowledge the red flags that Larry frequently waved in my face. Like him never taking me to his apartment or even letting me know where he lived. And, he would only allow me to call him at work or on his cell phone.

Larry had me right where he wanted me: in the dark. I couldn't see the light even though it was right in my face. It was a sad position to be in at my age. But like I said, I was a fool in love.

One of the reasons for my condition was Larry made me feel special. He'd missed a day's work without pay to paint my apartment, he worked on my car for free, and he often accompanied me to movies I knew he would hate.

"Girl, we are the only Black folks sittin' up in this theater," he'd complained with a chuckle and a loud yawn, the night I dragged him to see *My Big Fat Greek Wedding*.

"We can sneak into that race car movie next door," I said, pouting.

"Uh-uh, baby. This is the movie *you* wanted to see. All I care about is pleasin' you. Just wake me up when it's over."

That's the kind of talk he used to keep me in my place. And it worked.

It took a lot of energy to make a relationship work, and I was one hardworking woman. I figured that if I put a lot into it, I'd get a lot out of it. I didn't even mind lending money to Larry because he always paid me back when he said he would. Even though he often borrowed the same amount of money the next day! I had girlfriends who did even more for their men, so I didn't think that I was doing anything out of the ordinary.

Not long after I'd made the well-rehearsed call to my supervisor's voice mail, complete with a weak voice and a hacking cough, Larry had come by my apartment on his way to work for a "wake-up call." Our sex life was so good we'd named it. I looked forward to our wake-up calls, which, by the way, sounded a lot better to me than the crude and overused term "booty call" that so many of the people I knew used. And I didn't wait for Larry to approach me; I requested wake-up calls as often as he did.

Since Larry had stopped trying to talk me into getting an abortion, and was now helping me choose a name for our baby, I thought he was as happy as I was about me being pregnant. He didn't care how bloated and lopsided my face was, or how swollen my ankles were as I splashed around naked in the shower with him that morning.

"Lula Mae, uh, I don't know if I can make it back this evenin' for dinner. My . . . uh . . . cousins from D.C. are still at the house, see," Larry told me, tapping my navel and then rubbing the base of my belly with the palm of his hand. "They wanna go out to dinner again before they leave."

Since Larry made so many sacrifices for me, I didn't like to badger him too much. But when he disappointed me, I felt I had a right to let him know.

"Don't you want me to go with y'all?" I whined. "I would like to meet some of your relatives."

Larry tickled my chin and kissed my forehead. Then he spoke to me in the same slow, controlled way I'd heard him speak to foreigners who didn't fully understand our language. "Now, baby, you better stay home and get some rest. Me and my cousins are drivin' all the way to Biloxi, and you know how carsick you get these days. After you have the baby, I'll take you up to D.C., honest to God." I felt like a docile immigrant when he added, "Do I make myself clear?"

I gave Larry a weak nod, but with my bottom lip poked

out. A slight grin decorated my face as I slid my hand between Larry's hard, soapy thighs. I started giving him a hand job, something we often had to settle for lately. My backaches, cramps, spotting, and other discomforts associated with the advanced stages of pregnancy had temporarily stopped us from fucking like dogs.

"If you don't want me to go, why don't you bring your cousins over here? I got enough food to feed an army. And, like I said, I would like to meet some of your family," I suggested, praying that Larry would at least offer to come back to my place after taking his cousins to dinner.

As much as Larry liked my cooking, I often ended up alone, eating elaborate meals that I had prepared to share with him. Those were the most miserable nights of my life. But I wouldn't get mad at him; I'd just get drunk. Then I'd eat everything I'd cooked and sit by the telephone waiting like a lovesick tiger in a tree for him to call.

I never knew what was going on in Larry's head, but marriage was on my mind after our first night together. It was a subject he avoided like the racist cops who got their kicks by harassing Black men for no reason at all. Whenever I brought up marriage, Larry wasted no time changing the subject, but not before giving me a list of excuses. Even though we had been together more than a year, he had decided that we didn't know each other well enough, he couldn't afford a wife, and he was not ready for a lifetime commitment.

I turned off the shower and repeated my last question with a slight variation.

"Can't you bring your cousins over here for dinner to eat some of my mustard greens, gumbo, corn bread, and pork chops?" I held my breath and waited.

For a moment I thought I had him hooked, the way his eyes froze. Then he came out of his trance, shaking his head so hard his wet hair whipped the side of my face. The water from the shower and his sweat made his face look like it had been glazed. I wanted to lick him dry, but I didn't because the red flag he waved this time was so big I could have used it for a towel.

"That's all right!" Larry said, talking so fast he almost choked on his words. He stumbled away from me, forcing my hand to slide away from his crotch. "Uh, I don't want you to go to all that trouble." He started groping for a towel, his eyes on everything in my bathroom but me. His erection had disappeared within a matter of seconds.

"Well, if you change your mind, y'all can all come over anyway. And I'll go ahead and cook this evenin', after I get back from the mall. Just in case y'all do make it over here," I decided. I was so disappointed, my head began to ache. But that didn't stop me from arousing Larry again. I finished him with my tongue. He held my head in place with both hands, moaning like he was the one with the headache.

He was still moaning when I dried him off. "Lula Mae, I swear to God, you so good to me, girl," he said, smacking his lips and patting my crotch. I followed him to my bedroom and watched him slide back into his work clothes. "You sure know how to make a man feel like a man. *Mmph!*"

"And I can be even better to you, if you'd let me," I purred, grinning so hard my cheeks ached. "My daddy is scared to death he won't live long enough to see me get married," I confessed.

Larry sat down on the side of my bed, grunting as he wiggled his feet into his shoes. I squatted in front of him and tied his shoelaces. Except for the large beach towel draped around my shoulders that I had used to blot Larry dry, I was still naked. A cool breeze coming in from an open window in my bedroom made me shiver.

Larry's warm body suddenly felt cold and rigid, but not

from the breeze. His eyes stopped moving. It seemed like a very long time for a person not to even blink. Then he let out a deep breath and finally shifted his eyes, blinking so hard it almost made me dizzy. "Girl, how many times do I have to tell you, I ain't ready for no family?" I had never seen him so upset.

"Well, the only difference between us and a married couple is we don't live together," I whined. "I don't want to end up like my mama." Larry stood from the side of my bed so fast, I almost fell. Stumbling up, I followed him to the mirror behind my bedroom door, watching him rake his fingers through his damp, curly brown hair. "And if we lived together, we'd save money on rent," I added.

I couldn't ignore the look of contempt on Larry's face as he glared at me in the mirror. "Look, woman, I didn't come over here this mornin' for you to be naggin' me like a fishwife," he told me, still raking his hair. "Why you wanna spoil things by bringin' up marriage all the time? Shit. All my married friends that ain't already divorced, they miserable as hell." He grunted, whirling around to face me. With his voice humming with rage, he went on. "I couldn't love you no more, if we was married, than I do now. So let's leave things the way they are. Besides, it's more fun this way, ain't it?"

I nodded, even though I didn't agree.

Larry sighed and looked around the room. Then he sniffed and looked back at me with his eyebrows raised. The smile that usually brought me to my knees popped up on his face. "A cup of coffee sure would be nice," he hinted in a soft voice, tickling my chin and kissing my forehead again.

I sniffed and trotted to the kitchen. Like an obedient servant, I returned a few minutes later and handed Larry a cup of coffee. It was black and strong, the way he liked his women. I didn't feel so strong anymore. I plopped down on the bed next to him, lying on my side, looking like an over-turned cement truck. My swollen belly was hanging off the side of the bed. Larry reached over and rubbed my stomach.

"Put on some clothes, woman," he ordered. "I can't have you catchin' pneumonia while you carryin' my baby."

I snatched my robe off the foot of the bed and wrapped it around me as I walked Larry to the door. He kissed me long and hard before he left. I cracked my front door open just far enough for me to watch him until he reached his car parked in front of my building. Without looking back, he jumped into his dusty blue Thunderbird and shot off down the street.

I stood in my doorway a few more minutes, with the cool air teasing my face, wondering why I was feeling so apprehensive. I had used all of my paid sick leave, so I was missing a day's work without pay. Normally, when I played hooky from work, Larry would slip away from his job two or three times that day to spend a little time with me. The thrill of doing something so sneaky kept me from getting bored. But I was also being careless and jeopardizing my job. One day as Larry and I waltzed out of a trendy café on the boardwalk, holding hands like newlyweds, we bumped into Gloria Fisher, one of my meddlesome coworkers on her lunch hour. She greeted me with a loud, snide remark. "Lula, you better go home and get in the bed before you get even sicker!" That little incident caused me to be more discreet. Larry and I decided to spend our time in my apartment making love, eating snacks, watching music videos, and drinking.

I cursed Larry's cousins from D.C. These creeps had begun to pay him surprise visits once or twice a month, and it had gotten on my last nerve. Since Larry had refused to let me meet them, they had begun to sound like phantoms. I didn't know their names, what they looked like, or how many of these mysterious demons I was dealing with. I didn't even know if they were male or female. I made up my mind right then and there in my doorway, with my bathrobe open and my naked body getting colder by the minute, that when I saw Larry again, I'd insist on meeting these greedy intruders. I had too much time invested in Larry to let somebody I didn't even know throw a monkey wrench into my life.

After I left Jupiter's, the only department store at the only mini mall we had, I entered the parking lot with two shopping bags full of items for the nursery I'd fixed up in my apartment. Three cars over, two Black women in their mid-twenties crawled out of a dark brown van that reminded me of those coffee-colored UPS trucks. And that reminded me of Larry, because he worked for UPS. Every time I thought about my man, I smiled.

I was smiling when the two women started strutting toward me as I struggled to load my packages into the backseat of my Toyota. They were both nut-brown, with the same big, shiny black eyes, but the scowls on their faces were so severe, I couldn't tell if they were pretty or not.

"Yeah, that's her! That's that whorin' Black bitch!" one of the women hollered, pointing in my direction as I closed my back car door with my foot. Naturally, I thought she was talking about somebody else so I proceeded to open my driver's door. "I'm talkin' to you, slut!" the woman added. Like an angry soldier, she marched toward me, the heels of her clogs click-clacking against the hot concrete.

My head whirled around so hard and fast my neck made a popping noise. "What—are you talkin' to *me*?" I asked, wide-eyed and annoyed, pointing at my chest with my finger. My pregnancy was responsible for all kinds of unattractive surprises and I noticed for the first time that my fingers looked like bloated Vienna sausages. A sharp pain that started at the base of my neck shot all the way down to the bottom of my back. I felt dizzy as I leaned back on my legs, breathing through my mouth.

"Yeah, I'm talkin' to you, tramp," the woman yelled with a husky voice. Her companion, as pregnant as I was, and looking like she wanted to cuss out the world, handed her friend her purse and waddled in my direction. Her huge belly rode high on her body. *She's carrying a girl,* I thought. Baby girls rode high in the belly, baby boys rode low. The old folks I knew had been telling me that for years. I was carrying a boy, but I was going by what my sonogram had revealed, not what old Reverend Dixon's grandmother had told me at church a few weeks ago.

"So, bitch, we finally meet!" the pregnant woman yelled, standing in front of me with her thick, ashy brown hands on her hips. An ugly red rash covered half of her face and both of her hands. She looked like a spotted piñata. People going in and coming out of the store slowed down to watch. I recognized a couple from my neighborhood, and a nosy woman from the church I used to attend. The woman addressing me didn't seem to care about the attention she was attracting. "You done fucked up, you skanky whore!"

It was the middle of April. In Barberton, Mississippi, our sleepy, dusty little town near the Delta, that meant the weather was warm enough for females to be prancing around in shorts. And wearing shorts was something most of the women I knew didn't think twice about doing, no matter how ridiculous they looked. The woman standing in front of me couldn't have looked any worse if she'd tried. Neither could her companion. Each had on cheap, ugly, well-worn shoes and flowered shorts, revealing hairy brown legs that looked like logs. The one who was not pregnant had the nerve to have on a silver ankle bracelet. It was wrapped so tight around her stout ankle it looked like a tattoo. The pregnant one had on a sleeveless, faded plaid maternity top that would have slid off her body if she hadn't had so many safety pins holding it together. There was a white scarf—no, a diaper—wrapped around her head. A diaper! And it didn't even cover all of her frayed cornrows. Both of these sisters were screaming for a makeover.

Even with all of the confusion going on, I was still smiling. I held up my hand and took a few steps back. On top of everything else, I could feel sweat forming in my crotch. It rolled down my thighs, making me feel like I was peeing on myself. "Look, ladies, I don't know either one of you sisters, and y'all don't know me, so I advise both of y'all to get the hell out of my face," I said. My smile finally disappeared. A small, excited crowd, with amused and anxious looks on their faces had gathered a few cars over.

"You just a low-down, sleazy Black bitch!" the pregnant woman's companion screeched at me. "Goin' around fuckin' other folk's man." Each time she opened her mouth to speak, a huge silver stud clamped in the center of her tongue bobbed up and down.

"I . . . what did you say?" Larry Holmes was the *only* man I had been with lately. "Are you talkin' about Larry . . . Holmes?" Instead of answering me, Mrs. Holmes sucker-punched me in my stomach. I stumbled, then fell to my knees. My head slapped the side of my car. I didn't see stars, but I blacked out for a split second. Before I stood back up and opened my eyes, I saw colors that I didn't know existed.

One of the few things that my busy daddy had taken the time to teach me was not to take anybody's mess. "Lula Mae, if you goin' to go down anyway, go down fightin'." Daddy had told me that more times than I could count.

Something told me that I wasn't going to get out of this parking lot until I duked it out with this beastly woman, so I dropped my purse and sucked in my breath. There was a foul taste in my mouth. I could feel the sour bile rising in my throat. I was not at that time, nor have I ever been a big woman. Even almost nine months pregnant, I weighed only a hundred and thirty pounds. The woman who had jumped me was about my size, maybe half a size larger. With the same hand that I had jacked off Larry with in the shower, I socked the side of my attacker's face as hard as I could, knocking her to the ground. The palm of my hand stung like I'd been scalded. It was just like that scene in *The Color Purple* when Oprah knocked out the mayor with one punch.

Popping up like a weed, my attacker brushed off her clothes and told me, "I'm goin' to put somethin' on you a doctor can't take off."

Out of the corner of my eye, I could see that the number of drooling spectators had doubled. I heard a few disembodied voices comment about some "dude's wife" and "his whore" having a showdown.

Then a heavy fist landed along the side of my face, making me see stars for sure. Since my hand was already in a fist, I did what I had to do. Larry's wife seemed surprised when I punched her in the nose. Blood squirted, her eyes widened, and she started kicking at my legs. Within seconds, my calves and ankles felt like they'd been run through a wringer. Just as both women tried to pin my arms behind me, a hefty security guard came running out of nowhere and pulled us apart.

I was too angry to feel any more pain. Even with all that was going on, I realized the truth. But I still needed to hear it. And I heard it loud and clear. "This bitch has been fuckin' my man!" the pregnant woman hollered, spit flying out of her mouth like fireworks.

"Look, I didn't know the man was married," I managed, my fist still balled and ready to strike again. "If you knew

about him and me, his ass is the one you need to be kickin,"
I snarled. I think I was more upset with Larry than I was
with his wife because for the first time I realized what a pig
in a poke he really was.

"Oh, don't you worry none about my husband, bitch. His
butt is mine. You better worry about yourself and that bastard you carryin'!" Mrs. Holmes yelled. She rubbed the
spot on her face where I had hit her.

The way my baby was kicking, it seemed like he had
joined the fight. But I was not interested in continuing something I'd already lost. All I wanted to do was get home, compose myself, and maybe pay an emergency visit to Dr. White's
office to make sure my son was still okay. But every time I
tried to get in my car, both of the women blocked my way,
still cussing at me and trying to hit me in my stomach again.

The security guard was practically useless. He got scratched,
punched, knocked down, and kicked by all three of us. The
crowd roared with laughter. Some instigating teenagers chanted,
"fight, fight, fight." Then, while Mrs. Holmes and her fero-
cious friend stood there entertaining the crowd, cussing and
calling me out of my name, a beefy-faced policeman showed
up to sort out the mess.

To add insult to injury, Larry's vicious wife attempted to
have *me* arrested for assault! But the nosy sister from the
church I used to attend was the first of several people to
speak up in my defense. They told the sweaty cop who had
really started the fight.

"Ma'am, do you want to press charges?" the cop asked
me, wiping sweat off his face with his cap. The battered and
bruised security guard was peeping from behind the cop.

For a moment I considered this option. I would have been
getting back at Larry's wife and Larry, but after thinking
about it for a minute, I decided it wasn't worth it. I was bet-

ter off just getting Larry out of my system for good. This was the last straw.

I shook my head, limped back to my car, and drove like a bat out of hell. As soon as I got home, I started pacing my living room floor like a tiger, waiting to get my hands on Larry. I called his job; he was "unavailable." I called his cell phone, he didn't answer. And he didn't call me or come to see me that day, or any other day.

The next time I saw Larry was at the hospital when I gave birth to his son. When he came to see his wife in the room across the hall from mine, he glanced in my room with a blank stare, like I was a stranger. It was hard for me to accept the fact that he was the same man who had told me over and over that he loved me.

Words could not describe the pain I was in. Physically, I felt fine. But my mind felt like it was on fire. I had never been so betrayed and used before in my life. The rage I felt was so severe, every man in that hospital looked like Larry to me. I glared at the husbands of all the other women sharing the room with me. Even old gray-haired Dr. White's presence upset me. I almost bit his head off when he came to see how I was doing.

"Lula, you seem awfully tense," the kind old man said, backing away from my bed.

"And I'll be this way from now on," I hissed.

# Chapter 2

# ROCKELLE HARPER

I'd been on five job interviews in the last week. So far, not a single person had called me back. I could type, but I hadn't passed any of the typing tests, and I didn't know shit about all the new office software. Until I improved my skills, getting a job in an office didn't seem like a possibility.

The restaurants wanted waitresses with experience. And the pocket change that the department stores offered was not enough for me to support a cat, let alone me and three kids.

*Interview* was a fancy word for what I was about to do. Thanks to Joe running out on me and the kids, I was about to involve myself with a man who made his money setting up dates for horny men with desperate women like me. At least three hundred dollars a date, I'd been promised. I told myself that nobody I knew would ever know. And I swore that I would only do it until I got on my feet, or until Joe came back.

San Francisco is one of the most exciting and glamorous cities in the world. It is a haven for everyone from the rich and famous to the lost souls who wouldn't fit in anywhere else. When you grow up the way I did, on welfare in a Section Eight apartment located in a neighborhood that the press calls a war zone, you miss out on a lot of things that this city has to offer.

I was born and raised in San Francisco, but I'd never been to Fisherman's Wharf until today.

I'd been in a few fancy restaurants with Joe, so I knew how to behave. I had on my most expensive-looking outfit. I'd spent an hour putting on my makeup and fixing my hair. And the way the waiters and male patrons in the restaurant were smiling and blinking at me, I knew I was looking good. What man wouldn't want to pay me a few hundred dollars for a date?

"You must be Rockelle." The voice didn't fit the man. I turned around, expecting to see some slick-haired brother with a mouth full of gold teeth, a neck draped with gold chains, and a ring hanging off the side of his nose. He was older than I'd expected. On the telephone he'd sounded like a man in his late twenties. With the deep lines crisscrossing his high forehead and the crinkles around his small black eyes, he had to be at least forty. He was tall and trim. His thick short hair was coal-black, but I knew a dye job when I saw one. Even though he was smiling, there was a sad, tortured look about him. He was good-looking, but not what I would call handsome. I would not have noticed him in a crowd. In his expensive-looking black suit and maroon tie, with a smile dividing his caramel colored face, he could have passed for a banker or a funeral director, depending on how you wanted to interpret the situation.

"And you must be Clyde Brooks." I smiled as he helped me remove my cashmere sweater in the lobby of Alfredo's. I held on to my sweater, draping it across my arm so it wouldn't get wrinkled or soiled. The price tag was still pinned inside, and I planned to return it to Macy's, like I did with all of the new clothes I bought lately. That scam, one I'd learned when I lived in the projects, made it possible for me to look like I belonged on the cover of a fashion magazine.

"I got us a booth so we could have some privacy," he said in a strong voice with a hint of a southern accent. He led me past a few dozen hungry patrons sipping fine wine and munching on fancy Italian food.

"Thank you," I mumbled, so nervous my voice cracked.

From a huge window I could see the yachts hauling the people who could afford them across the bay as great white birds flapped across the sky. I loved Italian food, but I'd never been inside a restaurant as elegant as Alfredo's, even though my mother had spent many of her years scrubbing and waxing its floors. A sad feeling came over me, and I suddenly wished I was anywhere but where I was. But I knew before I even left my house, that if I made it this far, it would be too late to turn back. Clyde cleared his throat and rubbed his smooth hands together.

"Well now. Let's talk business." He paused as we slid into a booth in a corner. "My girl Carlene tells me you want to make some money," he said in a low voice, sitting down across from me.

I hated booths and had always avoided them. The fifty extra pounds, most of it stacked up on my hips and ass, which I had to haul around like a sack of flour, made it hard for me to sit comfortably in a booth. There wasn't even enough room for me to cross my nervous legs.

"Uh-huh. But just until I get myself straightened out. That's all," I insisted, quick and low.

Clyde nodded, but his smile was gone. "I feel you, sister. And I'm fin to help you do just that, if you do like I tell you." He paused to drink from a large glass of red wine, diffusing a belch with a monogrammed handkerchief. "Now, how old are you?" he asked, neatly folding his handkerchief and dropping it on the table. He had nice black eyes with long black lashes to die for; a waste on a man.

Shuffling in my seat and blinking hard, with my cheap mascara stinging my eyes, I tried my best to sound like a young girl. "Twenty-three." My voice came out sounding squeaky and weak. Minnie Mouse trying to sound like Tina Turner. Clyde turned his head to the side and gazed at me out of the corner of his eye, tapping the top of the table with a long neatly manicured finger. "Twenty-five," I said firmly, coughing. He wasn't going for that either, so I told the truth. "Twenty-eight."

His smile was back on his face. "What's your background?"

"Huh?"

"Where you from? You look kinda exotic."

"Um, I got a little Irish blood, Italian, Indian on my mama's side. My daddy's great-grandfather was French. I got a lot of mixed blood."

He nodded. "You and every other Black person in America. Shit!" he grumbled, speaking like somebody from the ghetto. He gave me a hard look and tapped my hand. "Let's get one thing straight right now, *sister*. That biracial shit don't mean nothin' to me and it ain't goin' to get you no more money than my girl Rosalee, and she black as the ace of spade. I'm lookin' for women with class. I'm lookin' for women who know how to deal with men and make 'em feel good. I know girls who look like Biggie Smalls and they got regular tricks lined up like ducks. The men I deal with, all they care about is gettin' . . ." he paused and lowered his voice, "you know . . . gettin' took care of. They ain't lookin' to marry you so your pedigree blood don't mean no more to them than it do to me. Shit." Clyde snapped his fingers and a young waiter in a tuxedo rushed over and refilled his glass with more wine. "What you drink?"

"I like red wine," I managed, waving my hand in the air, balling it into a fist when I noticed three chipped nails. As soon as the waiter poured wine into the glass in front of me, I took a long swallow, pleased that I got an immediate buzz.

"Tell me a little bit about yourself, Rockelle," Clyde suggested, blotting his juicy lips with a napkin.

I shrugged. "What do you want to know?"

"What do you like to do in your spare time? I like to get a handle on my girls. I need to know what kind of women I'm dealin' with."

"Well . . . I like to read, watch movies." I shrugged again.

"You into men?"

"Huh? What do you mean by that?" I asked stupidly, shuddering.

He laughed. "This is San Francisco, the gay capital of the world, and you are kinda husky. Some dykes make the best workin' girls." He sniffed and winked. "I ain't got no problem with that."

I frowned, insulted because nobody had ever questioned my sexuality before. "I love men," I snapped. "But I've never . . . uh . . . *fucked* men for money." I paused and took another swallow of wine. "Other than what I've seen in the movies and what I've read in books, I don't know how all this works," I whispered, looking around to make sure none of the waiters or other patrons were listening. My ears couldn't believe the words sliding out of my mouth. I fanned my face with a napkin, hoping I wouldn't sweat too much and stain my clothes. I wanted to return the blouse and skirt I had on back to Macy's, too.

Clyde gave me a surprised look, holding up his hand and shaking his head. "I ain't said nothin' about you fuckin' nobody for no money now. Don't you be puttin' words in my mouth," he said, giving me a look that could have meant just about anything. I couldn't tell if he was teasing me or testing me. Maybe he was being cautious. And in his business, I could understand why. He had just met me. I could have been anybody—from the wife of one of his clients to a vengeful relative of one of the women who worked for him. But I was the last person in the world he had to worry about. And with the financial mess I was in, I needed him more than he needed me.

"But Carlene said . . ." I muttered, groping for words.

"Carlene's a fool. She's from the old school. Spent her best years humpin' for a old battle-ax in Ohio of all places. If she was as smart as she thinks she is, she'd have been out of this business ten years ago with a million bucks stashed away in a Cayman Islands bank. Shoot."

"What about the cops?" I mumbled, clutching my wine-glass with both hands.

"What about 'em?"

"I don't want to get arrested. I would just die if that ever happened."

"Girl, that's the last thing you need to be worryin' about. Ain't none of my girls never had no problem with the cops. Hell, I play cards with half of the dudes on vice. In a city like 'Frisco, they got a lot more important things to be investi-gatin' than a man and woman hookin' up to have a little fun. As long as you do like I tell you, you ain't got to worry about no cops. Now if you a hardheaded fool like Carlene and try to break the rules, you just might have a run-in or two with the man. You got any kids? You look like a breedin' woman."

I nodded so hard, the curls on the hair weave that I had spent so much time trying to tame, came undone and fell across my eyes. "Three. Two boys, six and seven, and a girl just turned ten," I told him, tucking my hair back behind my ears. I hadn't had enough money to make an appointment with my hairdresser so I had to pray that none of my loose fake hair would fall off my head. "I like to spend as much time with them as I can."

"What about Daddy? He know what you fin to do?"

"He's long gone. That bastard." Just thinking about Joe made my blood boil. I had no idea where he had run off to with his bitch and all of the money from our savings account. He was from Canada and had relatives everywhere but on the moon. He could have been just about anywhere. And as corrupt as he was, I was sure that wherever that dog was hiding out, he was working under a fake social security number so the welfare folks couldn't track him down. "He was never much of a daddy anyway," I wailed, trying to hide the pain in my voice with a dry laugh. I blew out a weak breath and hunched my shoulders. "It's just me and my kids now. I love them, and I want to give them everything they need. That's why . . . that's why I came to see you."

"Well, if you a good mama to them kids, you ain't goin' to do nothin' that'll fuck you up with the cops. And, you'll behave yourself so I won't have to get ugly with you." Clyde yawned and cocked his head to the side, staring at me out of the corner of his eye as he handed me one of the two menus on the table. "All I want you to do is make that money, honey." He sniffed and gave me a mysterious wink.

"Uh, what else do you do?" I asked, smiling the same anxious way I'd done during my other interviews. My confidence level was pretty low, so I had to fake my way to the very end. I was ready to lie, kiss ass, act like I was interested, and do whatever else I had to do. "You are nothing like what I expected."

"Say what?" he drawled, raising both eyebrows.

"I mean, don't men like you have jobs on the side, too? A

front job to keep the IRS and the cops off your back? Or do you pay people off?"

Clyde leaned sideways and glanced around the room before responding. "In the first place, you been watchin' too many movies. In the second place, let's get one thing straight right now: *I* ask all the questions," he said firmly, giving me a cold, hard look.

"Okay," I croaked. I rubbed my nose and gave Clyde a curious look. "How many other girls work for you?"

"That ain't none of your business!" he snapped. "Didn't I just tell you that I was the one to ask all the questions, woman? A nosy woman is a woman lookin' for trouble." He grinned, and that kept me from getting too upset over his outburst. As odd as it seemed, there was something charismatic about Clyde. I liked a man who was in control, even if it meant that I was one of the things he controlled. "I pay the cost to be the boss." I had no idea what he meant by that and I didn't have the nerve to ask him to explain. "Do you hear me?"

I nodded and fixed my eyes on the top of the table.

"Order whatever you want, Rockelle." He took out a pair of dark glasses and held them up to his eyes and shook his head. "I can see you like to eat."

"I'll just have a small salad. I'm tryin' to lose a few pounds," I said, sucking in my stomach.

Clyde shook his head again and sniffed. "You ain't got to be losin' no weight. I got enough bean poles in my garden. You a fine, healthy-lookin' sister. A lot of men like that. They want to ride a horse that they ain't got to worry about buckin'."

I gasped so hard I hiccupped. "I thought you said I wouldn't have to sleep with any of these men."

Clyde clapped his hands together and laughed, shaking

his dark glasses in my face. "Girl, what you do on a date I set up is up to you and that man. I ain't askin' you to do nothin' you don't want to do."

I looked around again then I looked straight in Clyde's eyes. "Are you telling me that these men pay your women three hundred dollars just to talk?"

An amused look appeared on Clyde's face. "I don't know what my girls do behind closed doors. That's the beauty of my game. I don't tell 'em what to do. Like I said, what you and your dates do is up to y'all." He pursed his lips and gave me a thoughtful look. "I want you to dress with some class. None of them cheap Lycra frocks and none of them tight, see-through blouses."

"I don't own any clothes like that," I said quickly. "All of my stuff is tame."

"I hope it ain't too tame. I don't want you goin' to my clients lookin' like no old maid librarian. That frock you got on now, that'll work just fine. Men go for that college-girl look."

I nodded.

"Good," Clyde said, grunting. "Now that we on the same page, let's get that waiter over here so we can get us some of that lasagna before them greedy tourists eat everything up."

# Chapter 3

# LULA HAWKINS

"I feel like a five-dollar streetwalker," I mumbled, struggling to sit up in the hospital bed I'd been confined to for the past two days. My hair was long, but so tangled and matted, it looked and felt like a skullcap. My lips were dry and my eyes so red and puffy, putting on makeup had been a waste of my time. I frowned at the lipstick and compact on the stand next to my bed. I had never been in a hospital before in my life.

The grim-faced doctors and stern nurses swishing in and out of the room dressed in white from head to shoes, looked like sheep. I had given birth to a huge baby, almost ten pounds. Delivering him had been rough, almost splitting my crack in two. I'd been stitched up so tight, I felt like a virgin. And a dumb one, at that.

"And you look like one of them five-dollar wenches, too." Agreeing with me was Odessa Hawkins, my best friend for the past six years and my stepsister Verna's lover. "I told you to leave that lowlife motherfucker alone last year when he disappeared on you for two months. Not to mention all the money he borrowed from you."

A lot of people thought that Odessa and I were related, and the way my daddy got around, that was a strong possibility. She and I had the same dark brown skin with a few black freckles across the nose, thin lips, and large slanted brown eyes. Cute, maybe even pretty to some people, but not without a little help from our friends at the cosmetics counter. Every time I looked in Odessa's face, it was like looking in a mirror.

"Larry always paid me back—"

"Girl, don't you be defendin' that cheesy-ass bastard to me, 'less you wanna spend another few days stretched out in this hospital bed. I won't be as gentle with your black ass as Mrs. Larry was. Me and Verna both tried to tell you that that young-ass punk wasn't good for nothin' but a good fuck. And if that's all he was, you didn't need him. All the money you loaned him, you could have invested in a good vibrator until you found yourself a real man," Odessa said, growling, hovering over me like a vulture.

I sighed and glanced around the long, narrow room, looking from one bed to the other. There were ten beds, ten women—five beds, five women on each side of the room facing each other. It was hard to have a private conversation, but none of the other women seemed to be interested in anything Odessa and I had to say. They were too busy nursing their newborn babies and bragging on the telephone about how happy they were.

As far as I knew, there was only one other Black woman in the maternity ward, and that was Larry's wife. That bitch from hell. I found out a few hours after our scuffle in the department store parking lot, that her name was Belinda. Odessa knew her from her old neighborhood and had tangled with one of her older sisters over a man. But that was during Odessa's teen years before she realized women lovers were more to her liking.

Belinda Holmes was in a private room across the hall. I think that if we both hadn't been so weak, we probably would have duked it out some more right in the hospital. I had a feeling that she wanted to kick my ass some more, the way she glared at me every time I ran into her in the hallway. But I was through with that weak drama. Larry was not worth it. He had not even checked to see how I was doing, ask about his son, or even acknowledge my presence when I encountered him in the waiting room. After all I'd gone through with that man, this was my reward.

"A twenty-eight-year-old man ain't out for nothin' but a good time. A thirty-three-year-old woman ought to know that," Odessa said with a smirk, giving me a stern look and adjusting a pillow under my head. She had on a man's shirt, unbuttoned over a T-shirt and a pair of baggy flannel pants.

"Since when do you know so much about men?" I teased my best friend about being a lesbian as often as she teased me about being a fool.

Odessa rolled her eyes and tugged at the limp ponytail hanging off the side of her head. "I know more than you think, Lula. I've had more than a few dicks in my life to know they ain't all they cracked up to be. And, you don't grow up in a house with six brothers and not learn everything else you need to know about men. Shit." We both laughed.

"I should have known somethin' wasn't right when Larry tried so hard to make me get an abortion," I said lamely, sipping cold water from a plastic cup. My throat was so dry, it hurt when I swallowed. I felt like I hadn't eaten in days. The hospital food tasted like paper, but Odessa had smuggled me in some fried chicken. I couldn't wait to gnaw on it. I was anxious for things to get back to normal, but I knew that was something I wouldn't experience for a long time.

"Well, was that all you was suspicious of? What about him not lettin' you know where he lived?" Odessa snapped. With a grunt, she rolled up the sleeves of her plaid shirt and folded her arms.

I sighed. "I didn't need to know. I know where he works. I've called him there dozens of times. He likes havin' his space as much as I like havin' mine. I was the one with an apartment all to myself. He lives way across town somewhere, and he has four roommates—"

Odessa gave me a stern look, shaking her finger in my face as she talked. "Four roommates that turned out to be a wife and three kids. Don't you defend that punk because he ain't worth it." She had nosed around like Shaft, gathering more incriminating evidence than I needed to get Larry out of my system. "He played you like a piano, girl. Oh, that nigger had him a good thing goin'."

"I know, I know. You don't have to rub it in. Anyway, I'm glad this is all over," I said sadly, rubbing my stomach. "Givin' birth sure ain't what it's cracked up to be. I feel like holy shit between my legs."

Odessa lowered her head and leaned closer toward me, looking at me through narrowed eyes. "Uh, you seen his other newborn? The nursery is right around the corner if you want to take a peek."

"I don't want to," I said, sniffing so hard the insides of my nostrils burned.

"Well, I peeped in the nursery. You had the cuter baby. That other one looks like a Peking duck. And bein' a girl, she goin' to catch hell the rest of her life."

"But that other baby lived, mine didn't." A dark shadow slid across my face and my chest started aching. My son who had looked just like Larry had lived only two hours. A congenital heart defect had returned him to God.

Odessa touched my forehead and said in a soothing voice, "I know, sugar. I know. But the sooner you get over that, the better. If he was goin' to die anyway, it's better that it happened now, before you got too attached to him. You still young enough. You got a few more years to have babies. But first, we got to find you a new man. A real man."

"Don't you start up that mess about me hookin' up with one of your recently divorced brothers." Another man was the last thing on my mind. My life needed a complete makeover. A new location was what I needed. I just didn't know where to go, and even if I did, I didn't have the money to go too far.

Odessa shook her head. "Bo, my brother that's here from San Francisco, he ain't never even married."

I had never met Odessa's middle-aged brother, Bo. But she talked about him so often, I felt like I had. He was an independent musician who roamed around the world blowing a saxophone with whatever band would have him. He had performed with some of the most famous people in the business. I had seen pictures of Bo. Not only was he plain, but he was cross-eyed, too. It was no surprise to me that the man had never been married.

I certainly had no interest in Odessa's brother. He was a sorry specimen of a man compared to Larry. Then she said something that did peak my interest, and that same cross-eyed brother suddenly sounded like the man I'd been looking for all of my life.

"Bo's goin' to be movin' back to San Francisco in a few weeks to find work with another band. If I was still into men and Bo wasn't my brother, I'd go after him myself," Odessa said smugly, giving me a sideways glance.

I perked up right away. It was like a lightbulb lit up inside my head.

"Your brother is movin' back to California?" I asked.

"Uh-huh. Next month. Me and Verna goin' to give him a little goin' away party, and you better come."

"I will," I said, so tired and confused I said the first thing I could think of.

"If y'all do hit it off, maybe he'll ask you to go back with him. I hear San Francisco is one happy town."

I looked at the wall behind Odessa, all kinds of thoughts going through my head. "And I just might go with him," I said.

# Chapter 4

# ROCKELLE HARPER

"Where you goin' this time, Miss Rocky?"

"Uh, just to visit a sick friend."

"The same one you went to visit last night?"

"Uh-huh."

"What's wrong with your sick friend?"

"Look, Helen, I'm in a hurry, and I don't have time to stand here talking a lot of nonsense. Where are the kids?"

"Oh, you don't have to worry about them little dudes. I tucked 'em all in the bed, and they are sleeping like logs. Can I go watch music videos on BET now?"

"Yeah, yeah, go on," I ordered, snapping my fingers. "There's soda and chips in the kitchen. And you stay away from my beer! Your mama would have a cow if she knew about you drinking over here."

"Yes, ma'am."

I closed my bathroom door as soon as Helen stumbled out, pouting like she usually did when I hollered at her. Helen Daniels was a good friend to have. She came in real handy. A lot of it had to do with the fact that she was mildly retarded. At nineteen, she was more like ten or twelve. But she was mature enough to run errands for me and baby-sit when I didn't have to be away from my house for too long.

It was convenient having Helen living right next door. Her elderly parents eagerly allowed Helen to help me with the kids. Even before Joe took off with that bitch of his, Helen spent a lot of time at our house. In addition to keeping an eye on my three little monsters, she loved doing the things around the house that I didn't want to do.

One of the few good things I could say about Joe was, he liked to live well. We had rented a nice big house in a safe, quiet neighborhood. He'd let me spend as much money as I wanted to decorate the house. I'd spent a fortune on black leather couches, smoked-glass coffee tables, an entertainment center, and carpets so thick and shaggy, it felt like walking on cotton. My house on Joost Street was a long way from the cheap, gummy walls and linoleum floors in the run-down Bayview neighborhood I'd escaped from. I was willing to do whatever I had to do to keep some distance between myself and that jungle.

Now that I was "escorting" lonely men who Clyde Brooks had set me up with, I needed Helen more than ever.

*Just a few dates. Just until I get my bills caught up.* I'd told myself that at least a dozen times since my meeting with Clyde at that Fisherman's Wharf restaurant a week ago. But what I said and what I did were two different things.

It would take more than a few dates to get me out of the hole that Joe had left me in. I'd been hiding my Honda two blocks and one street over from my house, because I was three payments behind. And a damn repo man had already come banging on my door, twice in one week. I didn't know how long I could hold him off with the lie about my brother taking the car to L.A.

Right after Joe's disappearance, I'd applied for welfare, planning to stay on it only until I found a job. But anybody who knows anything about welfare knows that money is not enough to live on and live the way you should. It covered my rent, and we got food stamps, but I couldn't handle other necessary expenses like utilities, clothing, gas, and maintenance for my three-year-old Honda. Without a decent job, or a generous man in my life, my only other option was to move back to that run-down ghetto that I'd married Joe to get away from! My welfare check could cover me and my three kids there, but living in the rough areas meant other necessary expenses. That included things like bullet-proofing and putting bars on your windows, replacing items in your house that some bold thief had helped himself to, and worst of all, unexpected funeral expenses. I hoped that life was behind me for good.

Tonight's date, Mr. Bob, lived in Marin County. It was my second date in two days. My first date, with a nervous little man from Philly, had only involved dinner and a little fondling on the bed in his hotel room. After admitting that he was slightly impotent and had just wanted some female company, that trick had dismissed me after stuffing three hundred dollars into my bra.

"Mr. Bob's an older man, so you'll be out of there in ten minutes if you treat him real good. I been hookin' him up for years. He's one of my best clients," Clyde told me over the telephone. Clyde was a very "private" person or so he claimed. He only dealt with his "business associates" in person when he had to. The regular clients would call him up and put in an order for a woman, just like they would for a pizza. Like a secretary, Clyde called up a woman and rattled off a list of instructions. After each date, he'd meet the woman in a designated spot to collect his fee.

Clyde went on with relish. "And my girls just love Mr. Bob. He'll want a few drinks before anything else. And if you get him good and drunk, that's all you'll have to put up with. You behave yourself now. Don't steal nothin' from his house, flush your condoms down the toilet, and don't leave no other mess—like rank panties or cum-soaked tissue. If you do, I'll hear about it," Clyde informed me, talking in a fast, eager voice. I felt like a teenager being groomed for my first date.

It was the easiest money I ever made in my life. I had no trouble getting Mr. Bob to drink three shots of bourbon to my one. Within an hour of my arrival, he was so drunk he couldn't even stand or sit up, let alone do much of anything physical with me. He passed out on top of me. When he came to, I told him how great he'd been and how much I'd enjoyed his lovemaking, and how sorry I was to have to charge him for my services. My lies backfired. Mr. Bob wanted me to stay a little longer so that he could make me feel even better.

After it was over the second time, while sitting on Mr. Bob's living room couch with his head on my shoulder, I did something I should not have done: I told him all about Joe running out on me and the kids, draining our bank accounts, and leaving me with a ton of bills. After a few more drinks, he felt so sorry for me, he gave me an extra three hundred dollars.

"This is just to show you how much I appreciate you gals," Mr. Bob croaked. His limp gray hair slapped against the side of my face and his hot, foul breath almost melted my ear. Somehow I was still able to smile through the entire ordeal.

I didn't know what kind of arrangements the other women who worked for Clyde had with him. As a matter of fact, I hadn't even met any of them in person yet. When I'd returned a call to Clyde's apartment to get the details for my first date last night, a woman with a young, high-pitched voice named Ester answered the telephone. She introduced herself, with a Spanish accent, as Clyde's "first wife." She didn't explain her role any more than that, and I didn't ask her. And when I tried to pry more information about Ester out of Clyde, he told me the same thing that this Ester woman had told me, "She's my *first* wife."

Since I didn't plan to be involved with Clyde and his shadowy business too long, his relationships with the other women he dealt with didn't mean a thing to me. The main thing on my agenda was getting paid.

When I got home from my date with Mr. Bob, Clyde was sitting in his shiny black Range Rover in front of my house. I crawled into the passenger seat and handed him a hundred dollars, a third of what he'd told me that Mr. Bob was good for. For every date Clyde arranged for me, I agreed to give him a third of everything I earned.

"How'd it go?" he asked, giving me a mysterious look, a toothpick dangling from his lip, a baseball cap turned sideways on his head. He looked nothing like he did when I'd first met him. His *GQ* look was gone. He had on a denim jacket and denim pants, and a T-shirt. I could smell marijuana smoke on his breath, despite the huge wad of gum on which he was chewing.

"Just like you said it would. I didn't have to do much of

anything after he got drunk." I looked toward my house, annoyed to see my ten-year-old daughter, Juliet, and my babysitter peeping out the window.

"See there. I told you. On a dull night, all he'll ever want to do is lick your pussy."

"Well, tonight was a dull night," I said, sighing.

"Why that old dog." Clyde laughed, making a slurping noise with his tongue. "That old peckerwood ain't got no shame."

It embarrassed me to think about what Mr. Bob had done to me. For five minutes I'd sat splayed on a plush red sofa, watching his head bob up and down between my legs. "Yeah, that was all he did," I mumbled, my face burning. My husband, Joe, was the only other man who had ever touched me in such an intimate way on such an intimate part of my body. I couldn't help thinking about him while I was with Mr. Bob. As hard as it was for me to believe, I missed Joe. If he had returned to me that night, I would have accepted him with open arms. And open legs, too, for that matter.

Clyde leaned back and narrowed his eyes. "Now where's the rest of my money?" he asked, cracking his gum.

"I thought we agreed on you getting a third?" I wailed, my eyes still on my house.

"We did. What you gave me ain't no third of what Mr. Bob gave you," Clyde grumbled, his lips snapping brutally over each word.

I turned to face Clyde. The angry look on his face made me nervous. "How do you know what Mr. Bob gave me?"

Clyde removed his cap and scratched the side of his face and shook his head. I didn't have to ask to know that he'd spoken to Mr. Bob after I'd left Mr. Bob's house.

"If you think for one minute you goin' to play me, you

better get out of this business right now. You came to me, girl, I didn't come to you."

I handed Clyde another hundred dollar bill.

My date tonight was with a grumpy old man in Pacific Heights. According to Clyde, this old goat had more old money than he'd ever be able to spend in his lifetime. He sent for a woman a few times a month just so he wouldn't forget what fucking felt like. He called himself Prince Harry. He had a wife who was just as old as he was, and the last thing she wanted to do was fuck.

"Dude's wife goes to bed at the same time every night. And once her head hits her pillow, she could sleep through the eye of a hurricane," Clyde told me. "But that don't mean you can go out there and act like you ain't got no class. Be a lady."

Unlike Mr. Bob, and the impotent man from Philly, old Prince Harry had as much stamina as a teenager. His body resembled a prune, and his breath smelled like a hog trough. He was so disgusting that I was having second thoughts already about going on any more dates. But another date with Mr. Bob the same night made me change my mind. And if that wasn't enough to seal my fate, Clyde let me keep the five hundred dollars that Prince Harry had paid me.

"I seen that sucker naked at the gym, so I know what a trauma it was to do him. You deserve to keep every penny . . . this time," Clyde told me with a mysterious gleam in his eyes. "Now give *me* some sugar." Clyde hauled off and kissed me so hard I trembled. I knew then that Clyde Brooks was a man who knew how to work a woman's mind.

Like with that first date, and with any others I planned to go on, I wanted everything to be over with as soon as possible. I wanted my life to be back to normal, the way it was before Joe left. If I had known that night that my life would never be the same again, I probably would have cut myself off from Clyde right then and there.

But I didn't.

# Chapter 5

# LULA HAWKINS

As mad as I was with Larry, I *still* had feelings for him. One of my problems was that I loved too hard and I suffered because of that. Because everybody I loved eventually deserted me.

Mama was the first.

I don't remember much about Mama's family. I hadn't seen them since I was six. My grandfather was a huge, red-faced, wild-haired, fire-breathing preacher of whom everybody was afraid. When he preached his sermons, the older sisters danced out of their shoes and fainted. The church even shook. Other kids were afraid of him, but I just laughed and hid when he yelled at me for misbehaving. Because as fierce as he was, he was also a gentle and loving man. I would end up being sorry that I had not appreciated him when I had a chance.

My grandmother was a petite, attractive, but overbearing woman who was always telling Mama how she was going to go to the devil and take me with her if she didn't "get right." There were other relatives on my mother's side, just as judgmental and sanctified as my grandparents, but they all stopped coming around because Mama embarrassed her family by fooling around with married men.

Mama was only sixteen when she had me, but she had been fooling around with my daddy since she was fifteen, and that's something her folks reminded me of every day. We lived with her parents and half a dozen other relatives in an old house in Barberton, Mississippi. Barberton was a sleepy little farm town known for its cotton fields, fishing creeks, churches, juke joints, and peanut patches. People had to drive all the way to Biloxi, fifty miles away, when they wanted to experience the "big city" life.

My grandparents' house on Pipe Street looked like a wide, sad face at the front from the outside. The windows had shades that were always half drawn, looking like half-closed eyes, and the front door looked like a grim mouth. There was a big peach tree with a crooked trunk in the front yard shading two lawn chairs. That's where Mama and I could be found most of the time, sipping from glasses of lemonade (half of hers was vodka) as we basked in the sun.

I could play with the other kids in the neighborhood, but I didn't do that much because I got tired of defending my mama's name. Which was Maxine and not "that slut" or "that tramp" like the other kids called her. The thing about all that was my mother was not the only "shameless hussy" (another name the people called her behind her back) in our neighborhood. But most of the other loose women tried to hide what they did. My mother didn't.

For Mama, life was all about having a good time, and she did that in three shifts. She would leave me alone with my grandparents for days at a time. Then she'd stagger into the house looking like she'd been mauled by a grizzly bear.

"Lula Mae, don't you be lookin' at me like you crazy, girl. I'm young. I'm goin' to enjoy myself while I can. Help Mama to bed, baby."

When Mama was home, she spent most of her time in the bedroom she shared with me, lounging up under one of Grandma's goose-down quilts or getting dressed to go back out again. I got used to her shenanigans fast. Some nights I'd even help her put on her makeup then I'd lie awake most of the night waiting for her to come home.

When my mother's behavior got to be too much for her family and their constant put-downs got to be too much for her, Mama found us an apartment across town on St. James Street next door to a convenience store.

"Now we can worry about your whorin' behind day and night," my grandmother said, crying hard as Mama ran around our bedroom, snatching our clothes out of drawers. As much as Mama and I irritated my grandparents, they didn't want us to leave.

"Y'all ain't got to worry about me and Lula Mae. I'll be takin' care of myself and my child by myself from now," my mother shot back, adjusting one of the many headbands she wore to hold her unruly dyed brown hair in place. Like my grandmother, my mother was a petite and pretty woman. With her big brown eyes and dazzling smile, she didn't have to do much to make herself attractive. But that didn't stop her from wearing the tightest, shortest dresses she could squeeze her sexy body into. It was no wonder men couldn't keep their eyes and hands off her.

"Ha!" my mama's daddy screamed, stumbling into the room on his thick, crippled legs. "You mean that other woman's husband'll take care of y'all. This girl," he pointed at me with the cane that he needed to get around with, "she'll end up just like you, if you was to take her away from here where we tryin' to set her a good example."

Mama snapped one of our suitcases shut and then folded her arms, looking from her mama to her daddy. "Well, it didn't do me no good livin' all these years with y'all. All them preachin' sessions and Scripture readin' about somebody in the Bible begattin' this or that, and chattin' with a God they couldn't see just made me want to do the opposite. Lula Mae, go empty your bladder and your bowels, so we can get up out of here. I'll go crazy if I stay in this house another minute."

As I ran to the bathroom down the hall, I heard my grandmother say to Mama, "Lula Mae is gwine to end up just like you. Layin' up with men for money. Mark my word."

It would be more than twenty-five years before my grandmother's prediction came true. But a lot of other things happened along the way that drove me to that point. Things that I had tried to do to make sure that I didn't end up laying with men for money like my mother.

My daddy, George Maddox, was married to a woman named Etta. Etta was not a bad-looking woman. She had a nice body for a woman her age, smooth high-brown skin, bright hazel eyes, and thick black hair she always wore in a braid wrapped around her head. She read her Bible every day and had a few good qualities, but people overlooked all that because most of the time, she was mean and hostile to people she didn't care for. Like me.

Etta Maddox knew all about my mama and me. But she left us alone as long as we stayed out of her way. I don't know what she would have done if she had known that every time she went to visit her relatives in Philadelphia, Daddy brought me and Mama to the big white house she guarded like a palace.

I knew about some of the nasty things Etta said about me and Mama. One day I passed her and one of her friends on the street. I overheard Etta talking about me like a dog.

"Look at George's little jungle bunny . . . only thing missin' is a spear."

I liked going to my daddy's house when Etta was gone. I rooted through her things like a thief. That's how I got back at her for talking trash about me and Mama. My revenge included me snapping her necklaces in two, tying her belts and scarves into knots, ripping holes in her gaudy underwear, and peeing in her cold-crème containers.

The apartment that Daddy moved Mama and me into was furnished and in one of the best parts of town. For the first time, I had a room to myself. Daddy bought me my own television set and more toys than I knew what to do with. He also bought us new clothes, a stereo, and a nice little car for us to get around in. Mama had him wrapped around her little finger, but she didn't let that stop her from adding more men to her collection. The old man who owned the store next door to our apartment was always giving us something free. And, as far as I knew, all Mama had to do for him was smile and flirt.

Our landlord, a blind albino man named Mr. Green, couldn't even see how pretty Mama was. But that didn't stop him from coming around grinning like a Cheshire cat, scaring me like a ghost with his white hair, white skin, and haunting eyes. Some months when Daddy gave Mama the money to pay our rent, Mama would spend most of it and give Mr. Green the change, and it didn't even bother Mr. Green. He would still grin every time he heard her voice. I never could figure out why Mama's mercenary habits didn't rub off on me until after that fiasco with Larry Holmes.

That first year away from my grandparents' house was all good. But one day I came home from school and there was an ambulance in front of our house. I found out later that Mama was already dead when I'd left for school that morning. During the night, she had had a brain aneurysm. My grandparents, my daddy, and our landlord's wife, the woman who had found my mama dead, were all in the apartment weeping and wailing when I got home. Before that day, the worst thing that had happened to me was the car wreck that had damaged my grandfather's legs. Mama's death was ten times worse.

I don't know how I got through Mama's funeral. There must have been a thousand things going through my head. I sat there on that hard pew, my body as stiff as a tree, listening to Reverend Newton go on and on about what a "wonderful daughter and mother" my mother had been. As much as I had loved and was going to miss my mama, the main thing on my mind was: what was going to happen to me? I didn't have to worry about that too long, because right after the funeral, my daddy packed up all my stuff and took me to his house.

It was a big house with four bedrooms and a lot of corners and closets for me to hide in when I wanted to get away from my stepmother. I had a bedroom to myself, but it was more like a well-furnished prison. Every time I misbehaved, I got locked in my room.

While Daddy was at work, his wife treated me the way I'd always heard that stepmothers treated their stepchildren. She gave me all kinds of chores to do, and when I didn't do them the way she thought I should have, she slapped, pinched, bit, and even kicked me. The one time that I did tell Daddy, she attacked me for doing that as soon as he left the house.

Back then, Daddy and his wife didn't have any kids together, but Etta had a daughter from her first marriage. Verna was ten years older than me, and in some ways she treated me more like a daughter than Etta.

Even though Verna was her real daughter, Etta was often mean to her, too. It took me a while to figure out why. Verna

was a lesbian, but that was not the word I heard. Both Daddy
and Etta always referred to Verna as being "confused."

"Confused hell! I ain't confused. I know what I am. I just
like to eat me some pussy," Verna said to her mother, with
me standing right there in the living room listening. It was
my ninth birthday. The way Etta's eyes bulged out, with her
mouth open, I thought she was having a stroke. But all she
did was shake her head and stomp out of the room, dropping
pieces of my birthday cake all over the floor. "Lula Mae, the
sooner you learn about life, the better off you'll be. I ain't
never goin' to hide nothin' from you, girl. You done already
seen more than a child your age should anyway," Verna told
me, a serious look on her face. Even though I was still a
child, sassy and disruptive most of the time, Verna treated
me with respect and affection.

She was a gentle person. But with her big moon face,
beady black eyes, shaved head and barrel-shaped body, she
looked like a truck driver. As a matter of fact, Verna *was* a
truck driver. Daddy co-owned a trucking company with another man and Verna worked for them. Most of her jobs only
took her across town to help somebody haul something to
the junkyard, every now and then, she had to drive out of the
state or to some other city in Mississippi to haul fruit or live
chickens. I hated the days when Verna had to go out of town
overnight.

Daddy was old, almost as old as my mama's daddy. So,
like most other older people, he slept a lot and was out of
touch with a lot of things. Verna was the only person in my
life at the time with whom I felt comfortable. When she was
gone, I felt like I was all alone in a world that was so big and
unfair, I never knew if I was coming or going. Attention
seemed to be the one thing of which I could never get
enough.

As old as Daddy was, he still had enough juice in him to get my stepmother pregnant with twin boys.

I was fourteen when Etta gave birth to Logan and Ernest. She wasn't so young herself, so when her health started to fail, she took me out of school so that I could stay home and help her with the twins.

"Lula Mae needs a education," my daddy said weakly. "I want her to be able to fend for herself."

"Like her mama did? Either Lula stay home and help me with them babies, or you hire me a full-time nurse," Etta told Daddy, from the bed she rarely left anymore.

"I can always go back to school, Daddy," I said, peeping around the door to the bedroom he shared with Etta.

With a surprised look on her long, evil face, Etta lifted her head off her pillow and glared at me. "You so triflin' you don't care nothin' about no school nohow," she insisted with a smirk. "I got a lot of things for you to do around this house," she declared, laying her head back down on her pillows so hard the bed's headboard shook.

I hated school, and as far as I was concerned, I'd learned as much as I could anyway. As bad as it was being in the house with Etta and her two squawking brats, it was better than being in the school I attended. Barberton had a lot of small-minded people with big ugly attitudes, and I suffered because of that. Etta was on the school board so she knew every one of my teachers and had managed to poison most of them against me. I was glad to be away from mean old Miss Windland. That heifer used to make me stand in a corner just for having a "stupid look" on my face or for being disruptive. I got violent when kids said something nasty about my mother, so I had to get "disruptive" a lot. And Miss Windland never failed to remind me that when she'd taught my mother, my mother had been just like me.

Every time a teacher punished me and sent me home with

a note, Etta made me snap a switch off a tree for her to whup me. But there was more to it than that. When she whupped me, it was for a lot of reasons. The worst one was, I was a constant reminder of my daddy's infidelity and weakness for younger women. She couldn't take it out on him, so she took it out on me. Even though I knew I would suffer, I was glad when the rumors started flying around the neighborhood about Daddy's relationship with yet another sweet young thing over in Meridian. I was even happier when Verna told me that it was more than a rumor. She'd seen Daddy with his new piece.

"I love my mama, but she can be a bitch," Verna said, right after she'd told me about Daddy's newest mistress. I was perched on a pillow in the passenger seat of the eighteen-wheeler she was driving to deliver some live chickens to a poultry store in Alabama. "She ain't never goin' to accept me for what I am, and I ain't never goin' to accept her for what she is. You, Lula, you keep your eyes and ears open and don't let nobody make a fool out of you. Not even my mama."

By this time, Verna had moved into her own place, and I spent as much time there as I could. Even when I had to drag my two knotty-headed half brothers along with me, with them kicking and screaming all the way. The twins were afraid of Verna and her big, hairy, husky female friends. Etta stopped me from taking my half brothers to Verna's house when Logan came home one day and asked her why Verna looked and acted like a man. He also revealed the fact that Verna and her female lovers got very affectionate in front of him and his brother.

"Lula, if you carry my babies over there again, you better start lookin' for you someplace else to live," Etta warned me. Daddy had all but moved in with his latest girlfriend, so I had to deal with Etta by myself most of the time.

I was seventeen, but I felt more like somebody twice my age. I enrolled in night school and I got my diploma anyway.

"Lula, as soon as you turn eighteen, I advise you to get the hell up out of that house," Verna told me.

When Etta found out that I was planning my escape, which meant she would have to take care of her own kids and her house herself, she finally started treating me like a human being. She would crawl out of her bed and drive me all the way to Biloxi to shop. She bought me things that I'd never been able to get her to buy me before. She even hired a woman from her church to come help with the twins and that big house. But it was too late. I had landed a job in the mail room at the Department of Motor Vehicles. With my first paycheck, and money from Daddy and Verna, I moved into my own apartment.

It was nothing to brag about, but it was my place, and I could do as I pleased. Daddy helped me furnish my apartment, and he came by a few times a week to give me money. I saw more of him after I moved out of his house than I did when I lived with him. But Daddy had his own motives. He had yet another young thing on his agenda. Honey Simms was just a couple of years older than me and still lived at home with her mama. When Daddy didn't feel like taking her to a motel, they'd rendezvous at my place. And when that happened, I left them alone and I went to Verna's where I slept on her living room couch. When she and one of her lovers wanted to let loose, I slept on a pallet on the floor in her garage.

I spent so much time at Verna's apartment, I got to know all of her friends. Odessa Hawkins entered our lives and became my sister's live-in lover and my best friend. She was a few years older than me, but we had a lot in common. We both liked the same movies, books, clothes, and food. One night after one of the monthly parties Verna and Odessa hosted, Odessa lured me to the kitchen and hugged me. It startled me so bad, I stumbled against the refrigerator.

"Don't even go there. You are my sister's . . . uh, friend," I said, dizzy from drinking four beers.

"Girl, don't you go there," Odessa said, guffawing. "I know you don't swing my way, and even if you did, you ain't my type." Odessa hugged me again and this time she kissed me on the lips. "See there. You don't even taste good to me. Sour lips mean a sour pussy, and I ain't goin' *there*." Even though I was horrified, I laughed with her when she pinched my cheek.

"Girl, you better not let Verna catch you actin' like a bitch in heat," I said, wiping my mouth off with the back of my hand.

"If Verna don't like what I do, she can lick my pussy! And before the night is over, I hope she will," Odessa said, swooning.

My first boyfriend dumped me for one of his mother's friends. And the few after him, well, it didn't take me long to forget them after they dumped me. I never considered myself a raving beauty, but people were always telling me how attractive I was. I was medium everything. Height, weight, color. I had enough hair to wear in some of the best styles, and I knew how to dress. Why I couldn't get involved in a good relationship was a mystery to me. And then I met Larry Holmes.

Larry worked for UPS and delivered packages to the DMV two to three times a week. Working in the mail room, I saw him every time he came. His long legs, light brown skin and curly brown hair made me drool. He was the best-looking man I'd ever seen. There was only one other Black woman working in the mail room. But Emma Lou Hanks was in her fifties and all she talked about to anybody who would listen was her husband, her kids, and her grandkids.

I was thirty-two and managing the mail room, and I knew that Larry was younger than me. But I didn't know just how young. As it turned out, he was five years younger, but that didn't stop him from asking me to go out for a drink with him. It was to celebrate my promotion from the mail room to the front counter to process vehicle registrations. The pay was pretty good, but it was a boring job, and I hated it. Larry brought some long overdue excitement into my life.

One thing led to another, and before I knew it, I was in a committed relationship. Larry took me to bars and to parties where he introduced me to some of his friends, so I knew our age difference didn't bother him. Since my experience with men was so limited, a lot of the things he did didn't seem odd to me, but they did to Odessa and Verna.

"Girl, that brother is hidin' somethin', if he don't even want you to know where he lives," Verna told me. "If he's as crazy about you as you think he is, he'd take you to his place at least once."

"Well, I've asked him to plenty of times. I can't keep nag-gin' him and run him off," I protested. I never liked discussing Larry with Verna or Odessa. When his name came up, I usually changed the subject or made myself scarce. That kept the peace, and it kept me happy.


Daddy had slowed down a little and didn't need to bring his girlfriends to my apartment as much, so every time Larry asked to come over, I said yes. Even though he often spent the night, I never questioned him about why he showered and left so early every morning.

Working for the DMV, I had access to a lot of confidential information. All I had to do was nose around on a computer. I was surprised when I found out that Larry lived in the low-income Noble Street Projects on the outskirts of town. Even

I found that odd. The man made decent money and he had several roommates. He could have afforded something better. Again, that was just another mystery about Larry that I didn't spend much time thinking about.

For Larry's twenty-eighth birthday, I arranged for a singing telegram to go to his apartment and sing "Happy Birthday" to him. It was a Saturday morning and he had just left my apartment. When he spent the night with me, he always left the next morning at exactly the same time. He'd call me as soon as he got home to tell me how good I'd made him feel. He always called at the same time, whispering into the telephone so he wouldn't disturb his roommates. He called me when he got home on the morning of his birthday, too. But not to whisper sweet words in my ear.

"Girl, what's wrong with you? You crazy? What the hell do you mean sendin' some fat-ass, white-ass bitch to my house?" Larry was sizzling with rage.

I was stunned. "It's your birthday," I said, pouting.

" 'It's your birthday,' " he mimicked. "Who gave you my address? You been followin' me?"

I could not believe my ears. I was in such a state of shock, it was a struggle for me to speak. "I got it off the computer at work." My voice was so low and squeaky, I could not believe it was me talking.

"Well, you better lose my address and I mean you better lose it quick. That fat-ass, white-ass bitch, screechin' like a owl, woke up the whole building with her bullshit singin'!"

"Well, excuse me. It won't happen again," I barked, my teeth grinding.

"It better not." Larry hung up on me.

He didn't come around for two months. Since I no longer worked in the mail room, I didn't see him when he made his deliveries. Then like nothing had ever happened, he showed up at my door one night with whiskey on his breath. I was glad to see him and he was glad to see me, but he was not glad about the news I had to share with him. Since he was already tipsy, I fixed him some coffee, as he stretched out on my couch. He waved the coffee away and ordered me to get him a beer.

"Where yours at?" he asked as I handed him his drink.

"I don't think I should be drinkin' in my condition," I said sweetly. "It wouldn't be good for the baby." I held my breath and stood back, bracing myself for his reaction.

Larry stood so fast he dropped the bottle of beer, spilling it all over the carpet I'd just steam cleaned the day before. "Pregnant? Girl, I ain't ready to be no daddy!" he hollered, rotating his arms like a windmill.

I gasped and rubbed my stomach. "What are we goin' to do then? I'm pregnant and I can't get unpregnant."

When Larry got nervous, he raked his fingers through his hair. With both his hands working his hair, he looked at me, raking and blinking. "I know this doctor over in Gulfport. He'll fix you up. . . ."

I sucked in my breath so hard, my tongue flapped. "You want me to have an abortion? I thought you loved me." In addition to telling me that he loved me, Larry had talked like we had a future—even though he had never mentioned marriage, unless I brought it up. But since he loved me, I thought that things would fall into place sooner or later. Some of his clothes were at my apartment, he borrowed money from me, and he did things for me that some of the women I knew couldn't get their husbands to do. What else could I think?

He started to talk with his back to me. "Listen," he began. He stopped and shook his head. "I'm sorry, Lula Mae, I do love you, girl. It's just that . . . well, a baby is a big responsibility. And I'm still a young man."

I didn't like it when age came up in our discussions.

"Well, yes, you are still young and I am, too, compared to some people. But I am in my thirties and that's pretty old to be havin' my first baby or gettin' married." Larry gave me an exasperated look but that didn't shut me up. "Havin' a baby won't change things between us. I mean, you can still live where you live, if you don't want to get married." I let out a mild sigh and looked at the floor. When I looked back up, Larry was still standing there, his hands on his hips, looking at me like I'd just flung a dead bird at him. "I've already looked at a bigger place, and it would be fine for me and the baby."

With a hiss, he moved closer to me, his eyes looking as hard as ice and just as cold. "What's wrong with you, girl? It takes a whole lot of money to raise a baby!" His hands were on my shoulders, gripping me so hard I could feel the tips of his fingers pressing against my shoulder blades. I pried his hands off and stepped back.

"It's not like I don't have a good job. I can take care of my baby by myself . . . if I have to," I said wearily. Confrontations tired me out, and that was why I avoided them whenever I could. That was hard to do with a man like Larry.

He sighed real long and hard, shaking and scratching his head on both sides. "Double shit," he muttered.

"Look, Larry, I don't have much family and there ain't much love there anyway. At least not for me. I want this baby."

He shook his head some more.

"What about a name for . . . it?" he asked gruffly, narrowing his eyes.

"If it's a boy, I'm goin' to name him Richard."

"That ain't what I meant." He waved his hand so hard, it made a swishing noise. "What you goin' to put on the birth certificate?"

"What?"

"If you put my name on the birth certificate, the man'll come after me for child support," he said, shifting his weight from one foot to the other.

I gave him an incredulous look. "Why would I have to go to the man on you? You sayin' you won't help me support this baby?" I touched his arm, and he promptly snatched it away, wincing like I'd jabbed him with an ice pick. "I want this baby, Larry."

He threw his hands up in frustration. "Look, if you want this baby, go on and have it. I-I can't promise you nothin'. Things could change any day. Uh, I . . . my cousins want me to move up to D.C. and help them run their limo business." This was the first time I'd heard of cousins in D.C. with a limo business. "Now, if I was to move to D.C. . . ."

"You could take me with you. I'm desperate to get out of Mississippi anyway."

The look on Larry's face went from frustration to absolute horror. "Girl, you workin' both sides of the street, ain't you? I can't take you with me, if I do decide to go."

I slid my tongue across my teeth and backed over to my couch. I plopped down with a thud. By now I was really worn out, physically and emotionally. "Well, why don't we worry about that if and when it happens. Like I said, I want my baby, and I'm havin' it, no matter what you decide to do. While you in Barberton, if you still want to be with me, fine. If you don't, well, that's fine, too. I got along without you before I met you, I can get along without you if you leave me. We Black women are used to bein' deserted by our men anyway . . ."

After a deep sigh and a reluctant smile, Larry held open his arms.

"Aw, now you makin' me feel real bad. My mama used to say that same shit after my old man took off. I ain't nothin' like my daddy. I'm a real man. And, girl, you know I'm crazy about you. Come here, baby . . ."

It made me feel good about myself, knowing that I had the patience and insight to recycle a hardheaded man like Larry. I felt sorry for the women I knew who didn't. He continued to come around, and we went on with our relationship. He even brought over some clothes for the baby.

"Uh, these ain't new. My nephew grew out of these things. Ain't no use in buyin' too many things for no newborn since they grow out of everything so fast." He sniffed as he handed me two shopping bags of freshly washed items. "Now you better be carryin' a boy. I put too much into this thing to end up with a girl," he teased. It was so nice to see him in such a good mood. He had gone from one extreme to the other, proving to me that just about any man could be turned around.

I didn't tell Daddy and Etta that I was pregnant until I could no longer hide it. Daddy slowed down from his numerous affairs long enough to give me a hug and a pat on my stomach.

"And you better do everything that doctor tells you to do. I don't want my first grandchild to come here with no water head or nothin'," Daddy told me, a proud look on his face, glancing at his watch before he dashed out the door less than a minute later.

A few moments after Daddy's abrupt departure, Etta looked me up and down, shook her head, then let out a deep sigh. "I sure hope that baby don't come into this mean world with them big boat-ass feet like you got," she said, smirking. Her eyes were on the doorway that Daddy had just trotted through. Etta's harsh words didn't bother me as much as they used to. If anything, I felt sorry for her now. It had to be hard being married to a man who led so many women around town like the Pied Piper.

Larry got really excited when I told him that the doctor said I was having a boy. And even though he continued to drop off used clothing that his nephew had outgrown, I spent a lot of money and time at the mall, buying things for the baby. And that's exactly where I was when my whole world came crashing down around me.

Dr. White released me on a Saturday afternoon, three days after I'd delivered my son. "Lula, I see you're still just as tense as you were the other day," he said, standing a safe distance away from me.

I didn't even respond, even though I had cooled off a lot. I felt bad about being such a bitch to other men because of Larry. And I did manage to give Dr. White a big smile before I left the hospital.

My great big, baldheaded, fierce-looking stepsister, Verna, drove me home from the hospital in her huge truck. She fussed all the way about how I'd let Larry make a fool out of me. "If I didn't love you so much, I'd drag you outta this truck and beat your brains out. I'm spendin' the night with you, to make sure you all right—and to make sure that punk-ass Larry don't show his face. 'Cause if he do, I'm goin' to raise so much hell, they'll put me on the cover of *The Enquirer.*" Verna sucked her teeth, glanced at me and shook her head. "I ain't never understood you straight women when it comes to men. I didn't even know Larry that well, but I had his number. All them fairy tales he told you about havin' four roommates, no money, blah blah blah." Verna paused and rolled down her window. "That shit makes me hot just thinkin' about it," she said, fanning her face with her hand.

I was too weak to argue with Verna. It never did me much

good anyway. I was glad that she was looking out for me. I sat there like a mute, all the way home.

I returned to work a few days later, like nothing had happened. But Larry was gone from my life forever, and so was my son. Verna had taken care of the burial of my baby. She had arranged a memorial service at the funeral home and to my surprise, my mean stepmother, Etta, showed up with flowers. The word *mean* didn't describe her on this emotional day. She cried almost as much as I did. That meant a lot to me, and it had a lot to do with my quick recovery. I knew then that not every "bad" person was all bad.

A day after I returned to work, I got a call from Odessa while I was on my lunch break. Even though Odessa wasn't that much older than me, I'd allowed her to take on a maternal role in my life. The same as I'd done with my stepsister, Verna. My mother had not been much of a mother to me, and I'd ignored the rantings of my grandmother. Etta had shown me in more ways than one that she didn't care anymore about being a mother figure to me than she would a duck. Her behavior at my son's memorial didn't make up for all the years she had mistreated me. But when I had to be around her, I treated her with respect. It took too much energy to be angry. Besides, I wanted to use it all on Larry and any other man who dogged me.

Even though I sometimes protested, I liked it when Odessa jumped into her position of authority with me. "Now you see here, Miss Girl, you been mopin' around long enough. You comin' to that party me and Verna's throwin' for my brother if I have to drag you by the feet." Odessa blew her nose and cursed under her breath. She had a mild cold she had contracted while sleeping with her bedroom window open the night before.

Odessa worked for the welfare department, processing

applications for people in need of welfare assistance. Like me, she hated her job. She had shared dozens of horror stories with me about irate welfare recipients calling her up and threatening her with physical violence every time their check was late. When her job got to be too much for her, she called in sick, whether she really was or not. Her recent cold had nothing to do with her taking off sick this time. She would have done it anyway, just so she could be on call for me if I needed her.

Even though Odessa was already my best friend, I still went out of my way to stay on her good side. "Party for your brother? All right. I'll be there," I said in a meek voice.

Odessa's brother, Bohannon Hawkins, was forty-eight, twelve years older than Odessa, and almost old enough to be my daddy. But I liked him right away. Even though he looked his age, he was not a bad-looking man. He wasn't that much taller than me, and most of the limp hair on his peanut-shaped head was gray. He had nice, shiny black eyes and a smile that seemed to light up the room. And since he was the only male at the party of more than a dozen folks, he really stood out.

"Baby sister tells me you lookin' for a new friend," he said, talking loud enough to be heard over Grace Jones blasting from the CD player.

"I wouldn't mind that at all," I replied, following him to the corner in the small living room where we could have more privacy and a better view. We watched Odessa, Verna, and their husky female friends party their butts off. They danced, drank, and smooched like it was their last chance. It was entertaining, and I was glad to be present. I had the best time that night than I'd had in years. And I had Bo Hawkins to thank for that.

Bo was likeable. There was no doubt about that. His cross

eyes, wandering all over the place when he looked at me, didn't bother me at all. It was a while before I noticed his other flaws. Like his crooked mouth and stained teeth. Still he had a nice smile. After a few dates, I knew I could never love Bo Hawkins. At least not the way I'd loved Larry. And, I think he knew that. But he was the nicest, most charming man I had ever met. I felt bad about my mild feelings for him. However, I made up for that by always being available when he wanted to see me. I had nothing else to lose but time.

Bo was a convenient man to have around. He offered to do my laundry, buy my groceries, and clean my apartment when I had cramps or was too lazy to do it myself. He worked on my car when it needed to be worked on and he cooked for us when I didn't feel like doing it. Larry had done the same things for me. There were times when I wished that Bo wasn't so quick to do so many nice things for me, because it reminded me of Larry. And sometimes when I was with Bo, I found myself wondering what Larry was doing. Even when I was in Bo's arms.

I felt kind of bad about wallowing in the same bed with Bo that I'd been in with Larry. It didn't help when Bo served me breakfast in bed one Sunday morning, but I appreciated it.

"Bo, you spoilin' me," I told him, feeling sad, but forcing myself to sit up and smile. He handed me a tray with grits, bacon, and toast on it. When I was with Larry, I served him breakfast in bed. I would have done it for Bo, too, but serving me pleased him more.

"I'll spoil you sure enough, if you let me," he offered, plopping down on the side of my bed, giving me looks of love no man had ever given me. Not even Larry.

"Uh, you still thinkin' about movin' back to California?"

I asked, stirring the overcooked eggs with my finger. It had been a month since I'd given birth. I had made love with Bo a few times. I didn't know if it was because my mind wasn't in it, or because what I felt for Bo was more pity than passion. But making love with Bo was even more boring than my job. If he hadn't made so much noise while he was on top of me, I probably would have slept through it. One thing I had learned after my disaster with Larry was, there was more to a good relationship than good sex. As much as I hated to admit it to myself, that was all I'd really had with Larry. I tried to force myself to be passionate with Bo, but it was no use. He couldn't turn me on with twenty thousand volts.

Bo was not rich and he didn't have much of anything to offer. But he offered me the one thing I needed the most right now: a chance to escape. Oh, I knew that I could have done that on my own eventually. All I had to do was save up the money. But on my salary that could have meant staying in Barberton at least another six months. I had to get out of town before I ran into Larry or his wife. I was angry with them both, and I knew that if I encountered them again in public, I wouldn't be responsible for my actions.

"Just as soon as I get that muffler fixed on my car," Bo told me, snapping off a piece of bacon and chewing it so hard his cross eyes were straight for a minute.

I gave him a surprised look. "You drivin' all the way to California?"

Bo nodded. "I don't travel no other way no more. Not after them lunatics of Bin Laden's started blowin' up planes and buildin's that September."

I laid my fork down and looked in Bo's wandering eyes. "If you take me with you, I can help you drive."

Bo had never refused anything I asked for and this time was no different. I quit my job, sold my car to one of my half brothers, gave Odessa and Verna all the stuff we couldn't squeezed into Bo's Ford station wagon, and just like that Bo and I left Mississippi.

With both of us driving, it took three days to get to San Francisco. Our only major stop was Reno, Nevada. That's where I married Bo, even though he admitted to me when he proposed that he knew I didn't love him.

"It takes more than love to make a relationship work, Bo," I told him. "You're good for me and I appreciate that." I don't know where my mind was. I never thought I'd see the day that I'd marry a man I didn't love. It had to be because I hadn't got my mind back together yet. I wanted romance and excitement. I didn't expect that from a man I pitied more than I loved. "I'll be a good wife," I promised.

One thing I could say about myself was I was loyal to the people who treated me well. I could never forgive myself if I ever hurt a person the way I'd been hurt by Larry. And anyway, Odessa assured me that she would crucify me if I mistreated her brother.

Bo and I had a little more than three thousand dollars between us, but he was determined to get a job blowing that horn of his with the first band that would take him. I planned to work, too, until I got pregnant again. That was something I hoped would happen right away. I thought that a child by Bo, even one with Bo's cross eyes and plain features, would strengthen my feelings for him.

Bo had kept in touch with a few of his old friends in San Francisco. The man who had agreed to put us up until we found a place had suddenly been offered a job in Alaska. He was gone by the time we arrived so we had no choice but to check into a motel. To save money, we chose the cheapest one we could find. From the looks of the run-down neighborhood, I could see why the tacky motel we'd picked was so cheap. We were in the heart of the ghetto.

There was a lot of mess going on outside in the motel parking lot when we checked into The Do-Drop Inn. Aggressive homeless people wandered around demanding money. Angry-looking people screamed at other angry people, while young boys walked around hugging huge radios blasting music that sounded like nothing but a lot of noise. About an hour after we checked in, Bo offered to go get us something to eat and drink from an all-night convenience store at the corner.

"Wait for my hair to dry and I'll go with you," I said, walking out of the dank bathroom with a towel around my head.

"No, you stay right here and warm the bed until I get back," he insisted. "I ain't goin' to set around waitin'," Bo snapped, nodding toward the bed. "Now you just get in that bed and be ready for me when I get back." That was the last thing he would ever say to me.

The eleven o'clock news had just gone off. I clicked off the shit-box of a television, because it kept going off by itself anyway. The noise from my blow-dryer kept me from hearing some of the noise outside, but it didn't drown out the yip yip of a siren that seemed to be getting closer and closer.

I looked at my watch. Bo had only been gone a few minutes. I finally cracked open the door and looked out. I couldn't see what was going on because a huge, rough-looking crowd had gathered in the parking lot. In addition to an ambulance, several police cars were present. Feeling that I would be safe with a bunch of cops running around, I went out to investigate. And that's when I saw Bo on the ground, with blood trailing behind him. He was on his belly, crawling like a snake, trying to get back to me.

I froze in my tracks. As long as I live, I will never forget the look in Bo's eyes when he saw me. He smiled and blinked, as a huge tear rolled down the side of his face like a marble. Then he closed his eyes and went to sleep. I was still standing in the same spot, unable to move when the paramedics covered Bo and slid him into the back of the ambulance. Bo's impatience had saved my life. If he'd waited for me to go with him, both of us probably would have died.

The hardest telephone call I ever had to make in my life was to Odessa to tell her that her brother had walked in on a robbery in progress and had been shot dead.

# Chapter 6

# ESTER SANCHEZ

Cops was everywhere, but nobody was telling 'em shit. I wasn't worried about them cops; they never scared me. And they never bothered me 'cause I never gave them no reason to. Me, I seen that dude shoot that man, but I couldn't say I seen it. Oh well. Too many of them thugs out there knew where I lived.

My man wouldn't have been too happy if he knew I was somewhere I wasn't supposed to be, so I had more than one reason to keep my mouth shut. I was still supposed to be at the Mark Hopkins Hotel, spending the night with a trick from L.A. A thousand dollars for a whole night was a lot of money to me. Five Benjamins for me, five for my man. That's the way we planned it. Usually, he only took a third of what I got from every trick. Lately, he was having a lot of expenses. And, so was I. I had to be cool if I wanted to stay hot. And staying hot meant I couldn't be wasting valuable time with a trick that's gonna sleep like a dead man.

That's why when the trick at the hotel passed out, I tippy-toed out. I had to get back on the job. I figured I'd hop a cab over to Capp Street in the Mission, pick up one more trick before I had to meet up with my man and bring the trick to the motel that me and some of the street girls used. And that meant more money for me that I didn't have to share with my man. I believed that the most important person to "get paid" for my hard work was me.

I felt kind of bad for not telling them cops what I seen. I seen everything through the window in the front of that mini-mart store. The trick did, too, but he wasn't talking. He ran out to his car like somebody was shooting at *him*. I'm lucky he paid me first. The dead man was probably real nice. Him and his lady was checking into the room next door to me and my trick when we checked in. Their ride had Mississippi license plates.

Since the room was paid up for the whole night, I decided to stay and get some sleep. It had been a long day for me. That was my problem with being popular. A lot of tricks wanted to give me their money. And I'd been hella popular lately. But I needed to stay put until the cops left. I needed some rest. I needed to think.

The motel clerk was cool. He was a Mexican with no papers and he had crooked cops and drug dealers looking for him back in Tijuana. To make sure he stayed cool with me, I slapped a fifty in his hand every time I seen him, and he looked out for me. Besides, we spoke the same language. I never had to remind him that we Latinos had to stick together.

Clyde didn't expect to see me until eight in the morning, in front of my apartment. By then, I'd have forgotten about seeing that man get shot. Death was one thing I didn't want to deal with until I had to. I'd been hiding from it since the day I was born.

"Ester, you my best girl. I'll take care of you." My man, Clyde, told me that all the time, and it made me feel good. Even though I knew he was a liar. Him being a man, he couldn't help that. He told all of his women the same thing he told me. I knew that because me and them other women talked about the things Clyde said to us. Clyde was also a stupid man. He had to be if he didn't know that his women got together to rat him out to one another. But I was his first wife, so when he told me I was his best girl, it meant something to me.

In a way, Clyde and his wives was my only family. He ain't married to none of us, he just called us his wives. He said it had more class than some of the things other people called women who slept with men for money.

I don't know where I would be if it wasn't for Clyde. I never thought that I would grow up to sell pussy. I never thought that I would grow up at all.

The woman who gave birth to me had better things to do with her time than to raise a baby. A few hours after I was born, my mother left me in a Dumpster in an alley behind a bar in the Mission District. Me, a little baby, was left there with the trash and hungry rats.

It was Clyde who found me. It was Clyde who saved my life and even though I lie to him, I would do anything for him. Well, not anything, but a lot.

I just wanted to forget all about seeing that man get shot to death. Besides, I needed to come up with a good lie in case I had to tell one to Clyde about tonight.

# Chapter 7

# LULA HAWKINS

Daddy begged me to come back to Mississippi after I called to tell him about Bo getting killed.

"I'll pay your way home and you can move back into your old room 'til we find you another apartment. Why in the world you went runnin' off to a hellhole like California in the first place is beyond me. Girl, what was you thinkin'?" Daddy's voice sounded like it was a million miles away.

Etta's voice was the next one I heard. It was a boom that sounded like it was coming at me from all different directions. "I tried my best to raise you right after your mama up and dropped dead. I see now that I didn't do too good a job. You done quit your job, run off and married some musician, and now look at the mess you done got yourself into. I'm surprised that the devil who shot Bo didn't shoot you, too."

"I don't want to come back to Mississippi," I whimpered, spit oozing out of my mouth, greasing the telephone in my hand.

"Well, what do you plan to do, besides worryin' everybody to death? Did Verna and them confused friends of hers put you up to runnin' off the way you did? You ain't got a lick of sense, but it ain't like you to be runnin' off. You ain't smart enough to come up with a clumsy scheme like that on your own. Didn't you shame yourself enough by gettin' pregnant by that woman's husband? You headed for trouble, girl. Bring your tail back on home before it's too late," Etta said, growling.

"I'm not comin' back to Mississippi. Bye, Etta. I'll talk to you and Daddy later." I hung up and dialed my stepsister's number. She picked up right away. "Verna, I might need you to send me a little more money until I find a job and a place," I said dryly. I had cried all the way to the police station when they took me downtown to get my statement. To add insult to injury, by the time I got back to the motel, somebody had stolen Bo's car! I didn't even call the police back to report that. I knew that I wouldn't be able to drive Bo's car anymore so it didn't matter. It was in its last days anyway. We had spent a lot of money during our journey on that car, so that it would get us all the way to California. And we'd made it by the skin of our teeth. I was glad it was gone. It was one less thing I had to worry about.

"Baby, don't you worry about a thing. Me and Odessa'll be out there as soon as we can get a flight," Verna assured me. "I'll give you every dime I got."

"Thanks, Ver. I knew I could count on you. Let me . . . let me speak to Odessa."

"She standin' right here. Don't keep her on the telephone for too long. She ain't doin' so good."

I heard some muffled moans before Odessa spoke.

"Lula, you doin' all right, girl?" Odessa sounded like she had a frog in her throat.

"I'll be fine," I lied. I felt like I was going to fall apart any minute.

"I'm comin' out there to bring my brother home and you, too, if you want to come. You can stay with us."

"I think I'll stay out here for a while. The motel manager said I can stay here for a while. He'll let me stay in the room, if I help the maid. And he'll pay me minimum wage. That'll do until I can do better."

"Well, you be careful out there. You ain't in no country town no more, and all kinds of shit be happenin' in California. Get some rest and we'll get out there as quick as we can."

The first day was the hardest. As much as I hated cleaning motel rooms, it kept me from thinking about what had happened to Bo. The motel manager seemed just as shady as some of the people who checked into the musty rooms, which some of them rented by the hour. Even though the shifty-eyed motel manager promised to pay me under the table and let me pay a lower rent, it seemed too good to be true.

And it was.

It was a Saturday night. I'd spent most of the day helping the regular maid mop up the motel's filth. "Hurry up, hurry up so I can get up out of here," the testy old Black woman insisted, waving a mop handle at me. "I gots to get away from here before it gets dark. And if you smart, you won't go out your door after it gets dark." When the maid left, trotting off toward a bus stop with a can of Mace in her hand, I felt all alone in the world. It was hard to tell what time it was from one hour to the next, because there was always a ruckus going on in the parking lot and in the rooms on both sides of me. With all of the moaning going on, it sounded like somebody else was being murdered in the parking lot and in the other rooms.

Not long after the maid's departure, I crawled into the sad-sack of a bed, almost rolling to the floor when the mattress flattened out under my weight. I had just dozed off when a thumping noise woke me up. Somebody was coming in my door! I sat up and clicked on the dim lamp, clutching my heart and breathing through my mouth. It took me a moment to focus.

Jose, the motel manager, a sly grin on his wide, homely face was walking toward me, limping like one leg had suddenly grown longer than the other. I couldn't tell which was more frightening, him or his huge shadow on the wall. His shirt was unbuttoned, showing off a belly the size of a watermelon you would only see in Texas. He stopped in the middle of the floor and smoothed back his long, oily hair with his slow hand.

"What the hell—what in the world are you doin' in here?" I hollered. I was so scared and shaking so hard, it felt like I was in a vibrating bed. I was surprised that I was even able to get my words out. "What do you want, Jose?"

"Don't get up, *mami*. You right where I want you to be," he said, growling under his breath, sliding off his cheap flannel shirt as he moved toward me. I could smell his foul body odor from across the room. "You just relax. I know what you want . . ."

I rubbed my nose and tried to come up with the meanest look I could. "What do you want?" I yelled, not taking my eyes off his, which were so bloodshot I could barely see the whites.

"You know what I want. Shit, you want it more than I do. I seen the way you looked at me today."

"You bastard!"

"Keep your voice down," he ordered, holding up his hand. "As it is already, seems like these walls talk," he added with a suggestive sneer. Then he humped the air with his wide hips.

He jumped on top of me, covering my whole body like a fleshy blanket. His dusty, hard, greasy hand covered my mouth. He slapped me when I bit his fingers, drawing blood.

"You Black bitch. If that's the thanks I get for helpin' you out, you can get the hell out of here!" he roared, shaking a fat fist in my face.

I kicked Jose to the floor. I was amazed to see a man his size jump up as fast as he did.

"I'll leave first thing in the mornin'," I said, pulling the musty bedcovers up to my neck.

"No, you're leavin' *now* or I'll call the cops and tell 'em you tried to rob me. Bitch." The angry man slammed the door so hard on his way out, a velvet picture of Jimi Hendrix caressing a snake fell off the wall.

I got dressed and tried to call Odessa and Verna back to let them know that I was checking out of the motel, but the telephone was dead.

I'd met a little Spanish girl earlier when I'd gone out to get something to eat. She had checked into the room next door. She seemed friendly enough, so I knocked on her door.

"What?" she barked, cracking open her door just enough for me to see the body of a naked White man sprawled across the bed snoring.

"Excuse me. I don't mean to bother you, but I was wonderin' if I could use your telephone. The one in my room don't work."

"Come on in. You gotta be quiet," she said, snatching open the door and pulling me inside by the sleeve of my blouse. She had on jeans and a halter top. "I got company. Who you want to call?" She seemed rough and cold to be so petite and pretty.

"Uh, I need to call somebody out of state. Is that all right? I'll pay you."

"I don't need your money. I got plenty. Go use the telephone." She waved me to the telephone on the nightstand next to the bed. I hesitated when the naked man on the bed rolled over and coughed. "Go on. He's dead drunk. He won't wake up until mornin'." The pretty little Latin woman laughed. I could see that she was getting impatient. She started tapping her foot on the floor and breathing real hard.

Then she strolled over and stood next to me, chewing on a vine of licorice as I dialed Verna's number. The phone rang four times before she answered.

"Verna, I'm goin' to have to leave this motel right away," I blurted in a voice rattling with fear.

I heard my stepsister gasp and curse under her breath. "Somebody fuckin' with you now?" she asked, breathing hard and loud.

"Somethin' like that. I just had a, uh, disagreement with the motel manager and he said I had to leave tonight."

"The one who gave you a job?" she said, wailing. "I thought he wanted to help you."

"He wanted to do more than that."

"Well, where you gonna go now?"

"I don't know yet. I'll call y'all as soon as I get to another motel." I hung up before Verna could say anything else. I knew that if I stayed on the telephone long enough, she would have broken me down and made me agree to come back home.

The girl folded her arms and looked me up and down, nodding.

"That Jose is the biggest scumbag I know. He would fuck his own ass, if his dick was long enough," she told me.

"Thanks for lettin' me use your telephone. Is there another motel around here? Real cheap?"

"You got money?"

"Some. I think I have enough to last me about a month. My sister and my husband's sister are comin' out here tomorrow and they'll be bringin' me some more money."

With a concerned look on her face, the girl mumbled something in Spanish under her breath. "So, you ain't got nobody out here?"

I shook my head. "Me and my husband just got out here yesterday. He got killed last night. He walked in on a robbery in progress at the mini-mart at the corner." I stared at the floor. Strange unrelated thoughts started to flow through my head like hot water. Like how old the carpet was on the motel floor and how musty it smelled. I even thought about a comment that the maid had made earlier in the day about an operation she needed on her foot. I was trying to think about anything and everything that would keep me from thinking about the latest mess I'd got myself into.

"I know all about that. Uh, I heard some dudes talkin' about it in the parkin' lot," my new friend said, crossing herself and mumbling in Spanish again,

"I want to stay out here." I sighed. "There's nothin' for me to go back to in Mississippi."

"Listen, I can help you if you want me to. I'm Ester Sanchez." She held out her hand to me and I shook it. I was amazed at how soft and smooth her skin was.

"I'm Lula," I paused then added, "Hawkins." Even though I'd only been Bo's wife for a little while, I wanted to honor him by keeping his name and I planned to use it until the day I died. I'd never liked the name Lula Mae Maddox anyway.

"Lula, welcome to California." Ester smiled and made a sweeping gesture with her hand.

"Thanks, Ester." I didn't have to ask Ester what she did

for a living. How she got paid was obvious. What she did was her business, and it wasn't my nature to judge people anyway.

"I got a real nice place on Athens Street. I live there all by myself. You want to come home with me? You can wash up there. And we can kick it for a little while. Then I can help you find a place and . . . maybe a job, too."

"Oh, that's all right. I don't want to put you to no trouble. You don't even know me."

"If it was trouble, I wouldn't be askin' to do nothin' for you. And you ain't got to worry about me tryin' to do nothin' freaky to you. You almost twice my size anyway." Ester laughed.

"What about your friend?" I nodded toward the bed. The naked man was in a fetal position, looking like a big white whale.

"Who, Henry? He can take care of hisself." Ester waved her hand, dismissing the subject. "He's a guard at San Quentin. If a big booger like him let somebody come in here and kill him, he deserves it."

"That's all right. I'll just get my things and call a cab. Cabdrivers know where all the cheap motels are." I sniffed, walking toward the door. I didn't want to leave my purse and other belongings alone in my room too long.

"Girlfriend, if you can get a cab to come out here this late, I will give you a hundred dollars," Ester said sharply, running to stand in front of the door, blocking my way. "And the bus stop is too dangerous. Especially for a pretty girl like you. If you don't want to end up like your husband, you better listen to me."

I was too weak to argue with this woman. "How are we goin' to get from here to your place?"

"Someone is comin' for me in a hour anyway with my car. My homegirl name Rosalee. I'll just call her up and tell her to come now. We'll go to her place instead. She's Black and maybe you need to be with your own people right now. My man is Black, so I know all about Black folks. Relax and have a drink," Ester said, strolling across the floor to a sorry dresser where she snatched up a bottle of tequila and a glass. "I think you need it." She filled the glass and handed it to me so fast, tequila splashed on my foot, leaving a stain the shape and size of a silver dollar.

The alcohol burned as it slid down my throat. I didn't wait for Ester to offer me another shot, I got it myself.

# Chapter 8

# ROSALEE PITTMAN

I usually turned off my telephone ringer as soon as I was in for the night. Once I had finished doing whatever I had to do outside my apartment, I liked to leave all that madness right where it was. I hated selling my body to men who saw me as nothing more than a piece of warm meat. But that's exactly what I'd been reduced to. The long, hot baths that I took every night when I got home didn't wash away the shame I wore like a second layer of skin.

I was very stingy when it came to my downtime. I didn't want to see or talk to any human beings when I didn't have to. I didn't even leave my answering machine on once I turned off my telephone. Clyde knew that. And the other girls knew that, too. The only people who knew that I turned my telephone back on after midnight were Ester Sanchez and the people at the old folks' apartment complex where I'd dumped Mama when she got too nosy about my activities.

Mama had been asking way too many questions and making comments that made me uncomfortable when I visited her. "Rosalee, how come I ain't never seen none of your modelin' pictures in the magazines or newspapers or even on the television? You just as pretty as that Tyra Banks and all the rest of them Black models I see grinnin' and posin'," she'd said.

"It takes time, Mama," I told my mother, searching my mind for other subjects to bring up. "Did you record Bernie Mac last night?"

Mama ignored my question. "Time? Well, honey, time ain't somethin' you got too much of to waste. Clara, the White lady from across the hall, said you was kind of long in the tooth to just be startin' out modelin'. Them girls always start out when they teenagers."

"Not in San Francisco. And, I do not look my age. A lot of people think I'm still in my teens."

"But you ain't! You a twenty-four-year-old woman—with a husband."

Mama had a way of making me sigh and hold my breath to keep from saying the wrong things. "Mama, things are different in California."

Mama rolled her eyes at me and screwed up her lips. "And another thing Clara said was, maybe you was posin' for them nasty man magazines. Butt naked. Girl, I sure enough hope you ain't caught up in none of that ponygraphic mess. Your daddy would explode in his grave."

"I'm not."

To keep Mama off my back, I went out the very next day and had a portfolio put together with shots of me wearing a different outfit in each one. Clyde had snapped the pictures himself. I gave the bogus model evidence to Mama, and she shared it with all of her friends right away. That shut her up for a while about that subject, but she still called me up every day to whine about other things. Everything from losing the generous monthly allowance I gave her at the blackjack tables in Vegas to her fear of getting raped by one of the elderly men in her building. No matter what it was, I could count on it upsetting me more than it did Mama.

I had just talked to the woman I paid to look in on Mama from time to time. Other than complaining about a few new ailments, Mama was doing fine, so I knew it had to be Ester calling me exactly one minute after midnight. I was convinced that she'd been sitting by the clock with her telephone in her hand, counting the seconds to the minute she could disturb me.

Ester was a fast-talking Latino who had eased her way into my life and now called herself my homegirl. But I didn't have any close friends, and hadn't for a long time. The women I dealt with were "business associates" and I wanted to keep it that way. It made what I did to get paid seem less shameful and painful.

I didn't have a naturally deep or strong enough voice to sound threatening, like some of the Black women I knew. I had to fake it. I swallowed hard, cleared my throat, and gave my best imitation of a growl. "Ester, this better be good. Shit."

Ester let out an exasperated sigh then mumbled something in Spanish. Knowing her, she was cussing me out. But it didn't bother me because I was used to it. "Doggie shit, girlfriend," Ester grumbled, loud and clear. "Listen up, I need your help. Come pick me up at the motel. You know which one. *Rapido,* fast!" Everything this girl wanted, she wanted fast. But I didn't do nothing *rapido*, for her or anybody else.

I fired up a joint first and took my time responding. "Aren't you supposed to be at that party in North Beach with them horny dudes from the airlines?" I was stretched out on my bed, still in the leather skirt and silk blouse I had worn to "work." My head, throbbing from the six shots of tequila I'd swallowed earlier, was propped up on two pillows. Every light in my bedroom was on, but a cloud of thick, sweet smoke oozed out of my nose and mouth, blinding me for a few seconds.

"I done that already. I done everything for them guys but ride a white horse. And I got the sore pussy and achin' mouth to prove it. Come on, girl. You owe me some favors anyway." Ester's voice was ringing in my ear. "I never ask you for that much nohow."

I rubbed my nose and ground out my joint in the dirt of a droopy fern sitting on the corner of the nightstand next to my bed. "My night is over. I told you that when I talked to you a little while ago. You with Clyde?"

"Fuck no, I ain't with Clyde. I don't have to see him until in the mornin'. You know that." Ester paused, sucked her teeth, and let out a long, deep breath before she continued. "I tried to call Rocky, but that retarded girl who babysits her kids told me Rocky was still with you."

"Yeah, Rockelle is still here with me. We had that bachelor party tonight, remember?" I looked up at Rockelle, standing over me with her thick arms folded, fanning smoke I'd blown in her direction. Rockelle didn't smoke weed. She didn't even smoke cigarettes, claiming she cared too much about her health. But that didn't stop her from gobbling up every greasy, fatty thing in my refrigerator. She was gnawing on a pig foot now.

"Well, tell Rocky to come pick me up. If she don't wanna drive that rattrap of hers, give her the keys to my Jetta. *Rapido!*"

"Rockelle is restin', Ester. She's got to sober up, shower the funk and slime off her big ass, then get up out of here so I can get some sleep. A horny judge over in Oakland is sendin' a limo for me tomorrow mornin'.'" I winked at Rockelle. She rotated her thick neck and gave me a dirty look. Rockelle was not my best friend, just my wife-in-law and a "business associate." We tolerated each other because of our relationship with Clyde, a man who treated us like he'd bought us by the pound. "You know Rocky can't leave her kids for too long with that slow-witted girl."

Why Rockelle trusted her precious babies with a retarded girl was beyond me. I'd left my old cat, Callie, with that same girl one night when I had to fly to Vegas for an all-night date and I haven't seen that cat since. I winked at Rockelle again.

Nodding and chewing hard, Rockelle rolled her eyes at me and waddled toward my kitchen.

Ester gritted her teeth, her impatience at its highest level. "Stop bitchin' me around, bitch. Don't punk out on me tonight. Rosalee, I don't ask you for much. I never say no when you ask me for a favor. I wouldn't be callin' you if I didn't really need you. Come on now. There's this girl, a Black girl, and she got some trouble. She need our help. Real bad."

"Ain't she got a man to help her out?" I had my own problems. I didn't want to have to deal with somebody else's, too. Especially some strange woman I didn't even know.

"Not no more. Remember that man I told you got shot to death in that corner store by our motel last night? Dude was this girl's husband. She from out of town and ain't got nobody to help her out, see. Come on now. You always tellin' me that you Black girls look out for each other."

I sat up straight on my bed and crossed my legs. I kicked off my stilettos and was massaging my feet when Rockelle wobbled back into my bedroom. There was a bucket of cold Kentucky Fried Chicken in her hand.

"Oh. That girl," I mumbled, giving Rockelle a look of pity as she chomped on a chicken wing. Ester had told me the night before how she'd witnessed the brother walking into that store and getting shot, and I'd felt bad about it. Death had already claimed most of my family, so it was one subject that was always on my mind. "Where is she now?" I asked, waving Rockelle to the wing chair facing my bed. She ignored me and left the room again hugging that chicken container against her chest like it was a baby.

"She's right here with me. Believe me, you gonna like this girl. Uh, *everybody* gonna like her . . ."

"I'll be there in a little while," I said, sighing.

My apartment was the only place I felt comfortable in anymore. There was nothing in it to indicate what my life had become. I had tried to decorate my bedroom so that it would look as much like my old room back in Georgia. So many years ago. Plain, cheap items from stores like Wal-Mart and Target were everywhere. Thin, stiff plastic drapes covered my bedroom windows. Large, gaudy plants, not as green as they were when they were new, leaned out of crooked planters. My bed was a mattress on the floor with a vomit-colored bedspread and pillows so flat I had to use two at a time. Pictures of Mama and all four of my dead siblings, and my dead daddy, sat on my bedroom dresser in frames that I'd picked up at a yard sale.

I didn't want to be like Rockelle. She went out of her way to hide what she really was: a Black American Princess wannabe. Everything for her and her kids had to come from the most expensive stores in town, and she tried her best to buy herself some class and intelligence. But she was too stupid to realize just how stupid she really was. Her bear-claw nails, a hair weave that looked like she'd been flying, blue contact lenses, makeup that looked like she'd slapped it on with a spatula, and a bookcase filled with cheap paperbacks in her house said it all.

Rockelle had returned to my bedroom balancing some barbecued ribs on a paper plate in one hand and a paperback copy of *Jaws II* in the other. Girlfriend wasn't as highbrow as she wanted folks to believe she was, so I never expected to see her reading *Roots* or *The Grapes of Wrath*. But, *Jaws II*? Hello? California had some strange birds and most of them didn't have any feathers.

I knew that Rockelle thought I was an odd egg, too, just because I didn't have a lot of fancy shit in my apartment like she did. She wouldn't even sit on any of my chairs without covering the seats with some newspaper first. And I didn't appreciate the fact that she wouldn't even sit on my toilet seat. She would hover to do her business at my place. And as big as she was, that was a sight to behold. I didn't care enough about her attitude to put her in her place. She was the one with the problem, not me. But I knew that I could always count on her when I needed her, and that was enough of a reason for her to be my girl.

I could afford to decorate my place like it belonged to a princess, a real one, if I wanted to. Even though I hated having sex with a bunch of strange men, it was hard to turn my back on three hundred dollars to suck dick for a few minutes, or to do whatever else I had to do to get paid. As an escort, I made more money in a week than I used to make in a month at that cashier's job I had in Detroit. I'd moved there after leaving Georgia. I got homesick all the time for both places, but I preferred to keep those thoughts to myself. I needed to focus my attention on my present situation.

I didn't rush to go pick up Ester. That hussy was a spoiled-ass bitch and expected too much from everybody. But she was the "baby" of my new "family" so to speak. She expected everybody to cater to her, and everybody usually did.

In some ways, I used to be just like her. But that was a long time ago and a long way from the mean streets of San Francisco.

# Chapter 9

# LULA HAWKINS

I couldn't figure out why I was feeling so light-headed and paranoid. The women I'd just met had all been very nice to me, so far. Ester's friends Rockelle and Rosalee seemed just as nice as Ester. Besides, I'd already lost my husband and almost been raped. What more could happen to me?

We left that damn motel with the suitcases containing everything I owned in the world, including Bo's clothes and the beloved saxophone he'd never play again, in the trunk of Rockelle's Honda. During the tense ride to Rosalee's apartment, the women listened as I poured out my whole story. And I left out nothing. They groaned when I told them about me coming home from school to a dead mama. They cussed when I told them how Larry had played me and agreed that he was a "hound from hell." They didn't say anything, but they shook their heads and moaned when I told them about my son dying and me hooking up with Bo then losing him, too, so fast and in such an awful way.

"It seems like a black cloud's been followin' me around all my life," I complained. I glanced out the backseat window, wondering how I could be feeling so miserable in a place as beautiful as San Francisco. We drove through the downtown area. The huge office buildings scraping the sky looked like big toys. But San Francisco was no toy box, and I was not Alice in Wonderland. However, I did believe that things had to get better for me. I was praying that my new "friends" would help make that happen. I just couldn't bring myself to return to Mississippi. "Things have got to be better for me out here."

"Honey child, you got to make things get better," Rosalee said, turning around to look at me from the front passenger seat. "If you can't do that in this city, you can't do it nowhere. That thing that happened to your husband, that could have happened to anybody anywhere. This is a nice city as long as you watch your step."

"I sure hope so," I muttered. "I sure hope so."

The first thing I noticed when we entered Rosalee's living room on the third floor of the cold brick building she lived in, was how cheap everything looked. In the center of a hardwood floor was a faded plaid couch with a brick holding up one leg. There was a matching love seat facing the couch that was just as faded. A coffee table lined with cigarette burns and cluttered with old issues of *Cosmopolitan* magazine had two end tables that didn't match. A small television set was on top of a wooden orange crate. There was a hole big enough for a horse's head to fit through in the wall next to the door. It was hard to believe that a woman like Rosalee, who claimed she made hundreds of dollars per date, lived in such a shabby place.

"Sister, you been in the storm too long," Rosalee told me. "You need somebody to fall back on . . ."

There was something conspiratorial about the way the women looked at one another and nodded in agreement.

"Well, I tried that and look how I ended up. I thought Larry Holmes was my soul mate. I don't want to go back home because if I see his face again too soon, I won't be responsible. A job and my own place is what I need now," I said, sharing the couch with Ester and Rockelle.

"How much money you got?" Rosalee asked, handing me a bottle of ice-cold beer. She stood in front of me with her arms folded. She was tall and thin, but she had curves in all the right places. Her body looked better than all the other women's in the room, including mine. And, she was the prettiest. Her big brown eyes and full lips took the attention away from her long, narrow face.

I clutched my purse. "Uh, maybe enough to last me about a month. A little over a thousand. I sold my car before I left home and Bo had a little money," I told her. I drank the beer, wishing it was something stronger.

Ester groaned. Rockelle and Rosalee looked at each other then back to me.

"A thousand dollars ain't gonna get you nowhere in San Francisco," Ester hollered, waving her hand. "That wouldn't pay half of my rent."

"Well, I don't need a fancy place. And I do plan to get a job," I said defensively.

"What kind of work can you do?" Rockelle asked in a steely voice. She looked at her watch then gave Ester and Rosalee a mysterious shrug.

"Whatever I can find, I guess. I was workin' on the counter at the Department of Motor Vehicles back home." I shook my head and laughed. "It was the job from hell." I looked from one woman to another and said, "I want a job now that pays big money, is easy, and involves dealin' with some fun people."

Rosalee clicked her teeth and snorted. "Other than a hit man, a star, or a gangster, ain't too many jobs like that."

"A pretty woman like you can make a lot of money," Ester advised, tapping her fingers on the battered coffee table, giving me a strange look. Her eyes were wide and shiny, making her look like a Spanish doll. And she was as pretty as one with her apple cheeks, upturned nose, and long dark hair. She couldn't have been more than five feet tall, but she had a tight, round little body that jiggled when she walked. "I bet you—"

"Shhhh," Rockelle cut Ester off. Rising and buttoning her jacket, she looked at her watch again. "Uh, you look tired, Lula," she noticed. "Ester and I'll haul ass before you pass out." Rockelle beckoned for Ester to follow, and they strutted out the door.

Rosalee gave me another beer, a blanket, and two flat pillows.

"Try to get some sleep. You'll feel better in the mornin'," she predicted, squeezing my shoulder. "You got somethin' to sleep in?"

"Yeah." I nodded toward my suitcases sitting on the floor by the door. "I'll sleep in my clothes tonight, if you don't mind," I said, sliding off my shoes. "I appreciate you lettin' me stay here. I won't give you no trouble," I mumbled as I stretched out on the couch.

"Oh, I ain't worried about you givin' me no trouble," Rosalee told me, heading out of the room. "I'll leave the light on. You can turn it off when you want to."

I glanced at the suitcases Bo and I had brought with us. Tears rolled down the side of my face. I didn't sleep at all that night.

# Chapter 10

# ROSALEE PITTMAN

I didn't feel comfortable with a strange woman in my place. In this day and age, who would? There seemed to be just as many maniacs outside of the nuthouses as there were inside. It was times like these that I wished I had not watched so many stupid movies with people running around chopping up people for no good reason.

With Lula on my couch, with God only knew what she had in her purse and on her mind, I reminded myself that there was also a lot of mayhem happening every day in real life. I was having some grim thoughts for a woman in my line of work, but that was a whole 'nother story. I didn't want to spend too much time thinking about that, too.

I locked my bedroom door before I crawled into my bed. And I made sure that the baseball bat I kept for protection was close enough for me to grab if I had to.

But something told me I didn't have to worry about Lula. She seemed like a nice enough person. I liked her because I felt sorry for her and I could relate to her. What she'd been through sounded almost as bad as my situation. I was surprised that she was holding up as well as she was. If some thug had shot and killed my husband, I don't think I would have been doing as well as Lula seemed to be.

I don't know what kind of impression I made on her. But I didn't just drop out of the sky and land in San Francisco on my back, although sometimes it seemed like it had happened that way. If things had been different, I would never have left Georgia in the first place. Because at one time, I had a real good life.

I grew up in Homeworth, Georgia, a sleepy little farm town that wasn't even on the map. Everybody knew everybody, and all their business, and we didn't even have to lock our doors. When I was around thirteen, my daddy started managing a popular grocery store in town. We lived about a mile away from the store, down a dirt road with cornfields on both sides. Even before the grocery store, Daddy was already a tired old man. He had worked hard, doing whatever jobs he could find to take care of a wife and five kids. He'd worked on the railroad and cooked in a prison. Before all of that, he'd dug graves. That was the only job he'd ever complained about. He'd done it so long and hard, he had developed a hump on his back.

Daddy didn't own the store he ran, but you would have thought he did. The real owners, a childless old White couple, liked Daddy so much, they let him run the place like it was his. He made all the rules, and he did all the hiring and firing. After a while, everybody who worked in that place was related to me. My oldest brother, Marvin, was the bookkeeper. My other brother, Tyrone, and my older sister, Maybelline, worked behind the counter. My only other sister, Dorothy—Dot we called her—ordered everything. Daddy's main job was to keep his eye on us and make sure we didn't fuck up.

I was the baby of the family, spoiled as hell, so I spent most of my time driving my siblings and Mama and Daddy up the wall. I only hung around the store when I wanted something, and I ran every time they tried to put me to work.

I'd been to Mississippi where Lula came from. I still had a few distant relatives there. My deceased uncle Doobie had lived in Mississippi with a mysterious woman named Pearl Carl during the early nineties. Miss Pearl was this itty-bitty, light-skinned woman with reddish hair and moles on top of moles on her face. Nobody ever told us where she came from, but she had an accent. Somebody said she came from Haiti, another somebody said it was New Orleans. Wherever she came from, she was heavy into voodoo.

By the time Miss Pearl entered our lives, Black folks had already come a long way as far as voodoo was concerned. But there were a lot of Black folks in the south still living in the Dark Ages. They believed in things that science couldn't explain. Spooky things like spells and ghosts. Back then and, I am sorry to say, to this day.

I had never talked about this subject with anybody else in California but Clyde. I would share this information with the other girls eventually. I had already told Clyde, mainly because he'd come from one of the same types of little southern towns with some of the same kind of people I grew up around. He knew all about this stuff. "I ain't scared of nothin'," he told me one time, waving the nine millimeter Glock he carried all the time and slept with under his pillow. " 'Less it's somethin' I can't see . . ."

I never believed in anything I couldn't see, either. But I experienced something strange after a girl I used to hang with fell off a roof and died when we were fourteen. Her name was Annie Mae Proctor and she had been my best friend. One of the things that Annie Mae had always liked about me was my long braids. Since she'd been practically bald, I could understand why. Every bald-headed Black girl I ever knew had major issues when it came to hair. I felt sorry for Annie Mae, when people would mistake her for a boy because of her smooth head. However, I hated the way she used to sneak up behind me and tug on my hair.

Well, a week after Annie Mae died, I was in the kitchen standing over the sink washing dishes. The kitchen door slammed, but I didn't look up right away to see who it was. Then somebody yanked on my freshly braided hair. When I turned around, nobody was there! I forgot about it until it happened again, while I was in the bathroom standing in front of the mirror washing my face. And there was Annie Mae in a white gown, standing behind me, grinning with her gapped teeth sparkling like diamonds. But the girl was dead! I'd attended her funeral and watched them plant her in the ground.

Annie Mae came to visit me two and three times a week. She never said anything, and I wasn't scared the first few times. But after a while I did get scared. I wanted Annie Mae to go back to wherever it was she was supposed to be. So I finally told Mama.

Mama didn't even look surprised or scared. She just let out a deep breath and shook her head. "Sister Pearl over in Mississippi knows how to deal with these things," Mama told me, whispering so the rest of the family wouldn't hear us talking on our back porch. "We better pay her a visit." Even though almost everybody I knew had some kind of fear or interest in the supernatural and it was no secret, it was something talked about behind closed doors. Even then, it was usually discussed in low voices or whispers.

The very next day, Mama drove me to Mississippi to "shoo off the spook" that was harassing me. In Miss Pearl's kitchen, a congested little room that always smelled like a just-baked cake, Miss Pearl sprinkled some green stuff on my head that looked like green meal. When my head looked like I had on a green cap, Miss Pearl closed her eyes and mumbled some gibberish. After that, she prayed for about five minutes, massaging my head the whole time. Then she had me drink something from a cracked cup. It was a foul-smelling concoction that looked like something you might expect to see in a toilet. When I gagged and threw up on the kitchen floor, Miss Pearl filled the cup again. She poured that slimy mess down my throat like it was a funnel and held my mouth shut until I swallowed every drop. I felt totally ridiculous the whole time.

After Miss Pearl made me mop my puke up off her floor, Mama slapped a few dollars in her hand and we left. That was the one and only time I had to seek Miss Pearl's "professional" services, because Annie Mae never came back from the dead to bother me again.

When my uncle died, and since Miss Pearl didn't have anybody else in Mississippi, Daddy encouraged her to move to Georgia so she could be near us. "Pearl ain't got no family and she gettin' on in years," Daddy said in his gruff voice. He'd made a few visits to Miss Pearl himself, and she had literally straightened him out. The hump on his back had been reduced to a slight curve. Another thing that I'd noticed about my father after his visits to Miss Pearl was that he looked so much better. When he was cleaned up, he was one of the most attractive older Black men in town. He was dark and well-built from working so hard for so long. He had gray eyes like a cat, that more than one woman had admired. And now that he could stand up straight, everywhere I went with him, women with roving eyes gave him looks that made me uncomfortable.

A lot of people we knew took to Miss Pearl right away. She didn't work and she didn't have a check coming in the mail like a lot of the older Black folks I knew back then. But

Miss Pearl didn't need a measly check from Uncle Sam or anybody else. She made good money "helping" folks, the same way she had helped me. It seemed like every time I eavesdropped on a conversation between my mama and one of her friends, they were talking about some divine thing that Miss Pearl had done for somebody. She had located a beloved dog that had been missing for a month, and she even helped a childless woman get pregnant. I don't know if Miss Pearl really had any divine powers, but she solved a lot of people's problems. That had put her in a very high position in our little town.

Eventually, things took a sinister turn as far as Miss Pearl was concerned. It didn't take me long to figure out that supernatural power was a double-edge sword and could cut both ways.

I started hearing rumors about people going to Miss Pearl to put spells on somebody. Now, as ridiculous as it sounded, I was real skeptical about all that shit (even though I'd had my own experience with something that couldn't be explained), and it scared the hell out of me. Especially when healthy people suddenly got sick, or somebody lost a job they'd had for umpteen years.

Mama and Miss Pearl were good friends so Miss Pearl "helped" us a lot. She even took credit for getting Mama through menopause in one piece. Then things went in an ugly and frightening direction. People started calling our house leaving messages for Mama saying Miss Pearl was fooling around with Daddy. When Mama confronted Daddy and Miss Pearl, they both denied that they were having an affair. But a few nights later, my brother Tyrone caught Daddy fucking the hell out of Miss Pearl on a desk in a back room in the store. Daddy was supposed to be at choir practice and Miss Pearl was supposed to be at home in bed with a severe case of grippe.

All hell broke loose. That same night, with me and all the rest of my siblings riding shotgun, Mama drove Daddy's truck to Miss Pearl's fancy red-brick house. Mama had come from a long line of feisty country women. When she got angry, even voodoo didn't scare her. Her own mother had spent the rest of her life in prison for burning down some racist man's house after he'd raped her.

Anyway, Mama cussed Miss Pearl out and batted her head a few times with a two-by-four plank. She told Miss Pearl, "Heifer, I ain't scared of nothin' you *think* you can do. I got Jesus on my side! He got a whole lot more power than you got!"

Before we left Miss Pearl's place, my brother Tyrone punched Miss Pearl in the chest so hard, her wig and glasses flew off. My sister Dot crushed Miss Pearl's glasses with her foot. Then she kicked Miss Pearl in the side while she was already on the floor of her kitchen squawking like a chicken. "Bitch, you don't fuck with my family," Dot hollered. "I don't care what kind of power you think you got, you can die like anybody else."

Mama didn't waste any time turning a lot of people against Miss Pearl. The people who were too scared to piss off Miss Pearl stayed out of the mess. But Mama had a lot of friends, and when they stopped going to Miss Pearl to locate a lost ring or to get a child's ringworm cured, Miss Pearl's generous income went way down. She had to get a job cleaning houses. She also lost her brick house and had to move into a trailer.

I'll never forget the day Miss Pearl called our house while we were having dinner. She left an ominous message on our answering machine. And it was a warning that chilled me to the bone: "You block-ass neegers'll weel be sorry you evere fucked weed me."

"That crazy bitch don't scare me," Mama snapped,

spooning more greens onto my plate. She gave Daddy one of the meanest looks she could come up with. "Alex, I hope you happy with the mess you done stirred up."

All Daddy did was bow his head and keep chewing.

I was eighteen. I had a lot of other things on my mind, like finishing school and marrying Sammy Pittman. He was the cutest boy I'd ever seen. I was so damn crazy about that boy, with his big brown eyes and neat little Afro, I didn't have time to be worrying about some old witch's threat.

A month after our attack on Miss Pearl, Daddy had a heart attack and died while he was taking a bath. We found him floating in our claw-foot bathtub. There was nothing strange about Daddy having a heart attack because he'd smoked five packs of cigarettes a day most of his life and had always had trouble with his heart.

Then my sister Maybelline died a week later. That morning she had complained about a severe pain in her stomach and by noon she was in the hospital. She died that night. The doctor couldn't figure out what had killed her, so all we ever heard was "unknown causes." Tyrone was next. A month later he got into a fight with somebody in a card game over ten dollars. He got stabbed in the neck and died on the spot.

A week after my graduation, which Mama was too nervous to attend, Sammy and I got married. We moved Mama in with us in a little house on a hill behind the church we went to. My sister Dot moved in with her boyfriend and a year later, they got into a fight. He beat her to death with a brick.

Mama didn't mention Miss Pearl's curse until after Dot's funeral.

"We got to get out of this town away from that crazy woman," Mama told me. The fear in her voice was so thick, I could have sliced it with a knife.

"Mama, you are the one actin' crazy. Miss Pearl didn't kill Daddy, Maybelline, Dot, or Tyrone."

Mama gasped and shot me a look full of contempt and disappointment. "How many other folks lose so much family in so little time, girl?"

"What about the Hardy family? Nine of them died in that church bus crash last year. Miss Pearl responsible for that, too?"

"I ain't worried about no other family but my own. I know more about these things than you do. I seen all kinds of shit when I was growin' up. Them roots women can do just about anything they set out to do."

"If you think Miss Pearl did somethin' evil, you need to go see her and set things straight," I insisted.

Mama did try to talk to Miss Pearl, but it was too late. Miss Pearl had put the word out that she would never forgive Mama for ruining her life and that Mama would pay for it. A year later my brother Marvin caught pneumonia and died. Mama seemed to turn into a dried-up old hag overnight. Her soft light brown skin looked like leather. Her delicate features looked like they had melted and slid halfway down her face. And she rarely smiled anymore. A slight noise would make her jump up like a rabbit and she lost so much weight, none of her clothes fit.

I didn't get really nervous until I ran into Miss Pearl at the Laundromat one night. She gave me a look that was so cold, I shivered. Then, as she was walking out, she told me with a smirk, "You and your mommee, y'all ain't nevere goin' to have no peace. I weel see to eet."

I didn't tell Mama about my run-in with Miss Pearl until a month after we'd buried my last brother. The fact that I'd waited so long to tell her upset Mama almost as much as Miss Pearl's threat. By now my mother already looked so grief-stricken and old, what I told her didn't make her look any worse. But I knew she was scared and she couldn't hide it. She started going to church more, she burned candles, and, she even went to see another woman in Fayette, who also practiced voodoo.

Every time Mama heard me cough or complain about cramps or any other ailment, she started watching me like a hawk. Then she rubbed me with some greasy red oil that the other voodoo woman had given her. She made me promise that I wouldn't eat anywhere but at home. And she insisted that I sleep with a Bible under my pillow and wear a cross around my neck at all times. I wasn't surprised when Mama started talking about us moving away.

Mama had a friend in San Francisco, a retired school-teacher who used to go to our church. Sister Curry had tried to get Mama to move to California to live with her right after Daddy died but Mama had refused. Now Mama was begging that old lady to extend the invitation again. But by that time Sister Curry was sick herself and hinting that she would eventually move to Arizona for her health.

Mama decided to try Detroit where she had a distant cousin. Sammy had relatives in Detroit, too, so we went with her. Sammy didn't want to quit his job supervising workers at a peach orchard, and he wasn't that wild about moving to another state. But after I begged and pleaded with him, threatening to go whether he went or not, he gave in. One of the things I loved about Sammy was the fact that he had always let me have my way. I had told him before we got married that my mama would always come before him in my life. He'd accepted that and married me anyway.

Detroit didn't work out for any of us. Sammy couldn't find a decent job, and it made him cranky. He had dropped out of school in the tenth grade and worked on farms most of his life. There was not much farm work in Detroit. I took whatever jobs I could, but we were still having a hard time

making ends meet. We couldn't even afford our own place
and had to live in Mama's cousin's basement.

In addition to all of that, the cold weather was bad for
Mama's health. Mama and I insisted on staying in Detroit
anyway, but Sammy wanted to move back to Georgia. His
former boss was still holding his old job open, hoping
Sammy would return. Because Sammy had accepted me
under my conditions, he wouldn't argue too much with me
when it came to my mama. He shut up about moving back to
Georgia real quick.

Less than six months after the move to Detroit, Mama decided it was time for us to move on again! After begging and
pleading with her friend in California, her friend said that
we could stay with her. My mama was old and so scared, I
thought she'd keel over from a heart attack or a stroke if she
got any more upset. She was the only close relative I had
left. I knew I would never forgive myself if she went off to
some strange state and died alone. I had to do what I had to
do. I told Sammy we were going with Mama. His reaction
shocked the hell out of me.

"Rosalee, I done had enough of this foolishness. If you
leave Detroit, you'll be leavin' here without me. I finally got
a job, and I ain't about to leave it," Sammy told me, whispering in bed that night because Mama was on the other side of
the room on a rollaway bed. With Mama so close by every
night, we couldn't even make love. We had to sneak and do it
in the bathroom or on the garage floor. Every now and then
we went to a cheap motel. It was a young married couple's
worst nightmare. Especially a couple who liked to make love
as loud and often as Sammy and I did. And, I could no longer
admire my man walking around naked in front of me. "I
ain't goin' to spend the rest of my life runnin' from a goddamn witch's curse," Sammy said, not even trying to hide his

anger. I was horrified. He had never talked in such a bold way to me before.

Like me, Sammy didn't really believe in that voodoo shit. But he'd grown up with family members who did, too. He just went along with it because he knew how serious it was with some people.

I sat up in the weak bed and glared at my husband. The glow from the lamp on the crate we used for a nightstand was dim, but I could still see the pain in my husband's eyes. I decided that I was in more pain than he was. Sammy still had all of his siblings and a healthy mother who didn't need anybody to look after her. Besides, I was spoiled and used to getting my way with everybody except Mama.

"Now you see here, I'm your wife," I hissed. "You came to Detroit with me so we could both look after my mama."

Sammy sat up, his face so close to mine I could feel his breath. "I married *you,* Rosalee. I didn't marry your mama. It's supposed to be me and you, not me, you, and Mama."

I heard the springs on Mama's bed squeak. *"Shhhh!"* I covered Sammy's mouth with my hand. In a dry whisper, I continued. "If that's the way it's goin' to be, that's the way it's goin' to be. I'm all my mama's got now and she needs me more than you do," I insisted, hoping that Sammy would see things my way. He used to!

"Rosalee, I have been more than patient with you. I have tried to make you happy. As long as you feel that you should put your mama ahead of me, we ain't never goin' to be happy. If you don't grow up, you goin' to be a miserable woman for a long time. And, you'll be miserable by yourself, because ain't no other man in his right mind goin' to put up with what I done already put up with."

For the first time in our relationship, Sammy Pittman had stood up to me. He refused to quit another job and run away with me and Mama. The strange thing about that was, I was glad he did. It gave me hope that someday I would be strong enough to refuse my mother's unreasonable demands, too. As much as I loved my husband, and as proud as I was of him, I couldn't choose him over my mother. It would have killed her, and I knew I'd never be able to live with that. And, I would probably hold Sammy responsible for it until the day he died. I didn't feel good about the way I treated my husband. But it made me feel a little better when I reminded myself that a woman could only have one mother; a husband could be replaced like a pair of shoes.

When Mama packed up and climbed on a train to California, I was right behind her. We stayed with the retired schoolteacher, Sister Curry, until she moved on to Arizona to live with her son.

"Mama, I'm tired of runnin'. If you want to go off somewhere else, you'll be goin' without me. I'm stayin' in California," I told her when she started dropping hints about following Sister Curry to Arizona.

"I'm tired, too," Mama told me. "And you ain't got to stay out here with me. You can go on back to that husband of yours. I'll be fine." Mama knew which buttons to push on me. "I got enough money to last me for a while and enough to bury me . . ."

After Sister Curry moved away, we stayed on in her apartment. But she had been living there on some kind of agreement where she didn't have to pay but a hundred dollars a month. The apartment owner wouldn't let us take over that same agreement, so the rent went up to a thousand dollars a month! I took whatever temp jobs I could get, but even with Mama's pension, we couldn't make it. Bill collectors started calling, we couldn't keep our utilities paid, and we ate a lot of Spam and peanut butter.

Then I answered a newspaper ad. Within two months

after moving to California, I landed a job answering telephones for an escort service. The cramped little office was on the first floor in a big brick building on Howard Street, in downtown San Francisco. That's where I met Carlene Thompson. As a go-between for the man who owned the service, she was the one who'd interviewed me for the job. I didn't need any experience, but I was told to my face in no uncertain terms that I had to be discrete and dependable. My job was to take names and numbers, not to set up dates and certainly not to quote prices. If a caller brought up sex, I was supposed to play dumb, tell him it was an escort service, not a brothel. A lot of teenage boys called up acting the fool. If the caller sounded too young, I was to hang up. If the man was not a regular, Carlene had to check him out by calling his place of business and in some cases, going to visit him there.

There were two other women, alcoholic hags who couldn't get work anywhere else, who helped me take the calls. But when they were too wasted or hungover to work, Carlene helped when she wasn't going on dates herself.

"Rosalee, you can expect just about anything to happen in this line of work. One customer who's into watchin' a woman do crazy shit called up and asked me to come to his mansion, get out of my car, go into his backyard and masturbate for ten minutes. Then I was supposed to knock on his back door so he could pay me. I did everything I was supposed to do—but at the wrong house!" Carlene laughed until she cried.

There was never a dull moment. Between calls, Carlene entertained me with one off-the-wall story after another. Some were funny, but then there were a few that were downright scary. Like the story about the man who'd hog-tied her, then passed out for three hours before he turned her loose.

I didn't like what I was doing, but it was the first job I had been able to get that had flexible hours and paid good money. And, I got paid under the table so Uncle Sam couldn't get his pound of flesh from me. I was able to afford to do nice things for Mama, and that kept her happy.

Carlene seemed to enjoy telling me about all the years she had slept with men for money. "Girl, back in Ohio, I lived with this old madam we all called Scary Mary. That sister taught me most of everything I know about men and their money and how to get it. It ain't that hard. Especially for a pretty woman like me," Carlene bragged. She was in her late thirties, and looked it, even with her long dyed black hair and petite body. Being light-skinned, and always boasting about it, she thought mighty highly of herself. "Me, even at my age, I can still make as much money as a girl your age."

I rolled my eyes and yawned, knowing it would irritate Carlene. "I know I need money real bad, but I don't think I want to start walkin' the streets yet," I told her. "I think more of myself than that," I added with a sneer. I'd enjoyed such good sex with my husband, every time I saw a man now who looked like him, my crotch itched. I couldn't imagine getting that close to any other man. Even for money.

Carlene's eyes flashed and she shot me a hot look. "Who said anything about walkin' a damn street?" she said, huffing. Carlene swatted the top of my head with a folded newspaper. "The women we set up on dates, don't do none of that, if they don't want to. Ain't you learned nothin' by workin' here? These women we send out get three hundred dollars just to go have dinner with some lonely man from out of town." The telephone rang and Carlene's voice suddenly seemed like it was coming from another woman. She sounded sweet and soft, purring and giggling as she processed the call. "No problem, sweetie. How's your back? Uh-huh. Well, I'm sure Ester will be glad to hear she didn't hurt you too much last week. You better start takin' better care of yourself before you get hurt even more. Yes, baby. I'll pay you a visit myself next week." As soon as Carlene completed the call, she turned to me again and said harshly, "You better get the spirit, sister. That call just now," she tapped the telephone, "that old goat is good for five hundred dollars. He's fat as fuck and comes like that," she giggled, snapping her fingers.

"Five hundred dollars?" I almost choked on the words. "What-what would I have to do to get that kind of money?"

Carlene shrugged, blew on her long nails, and spoke in the same sweet voice she used when she took calls from the tricks. "That's up to you."

"Well, I'm not stupid. I know enough about men to know that they are not goin' to be handin' over no hundreds of dollars just to have somebody keep 'em company durin' dinner. Is talkin' all you do when *you* go out with these men?"

Carlene shrugged again. "Sometimes. But it don't matter to me because I love to fuck anyway." I was stunned that a woman who hardly knew me shared so much intimate information about herself.

"Well, I'm not that desperate." I paused and looked around the office. "Yet."

For the rest of that day, the telephones rang off the hook. One regular trick called from his cell phone. He was parked in his Mercedes in the alley behind us. In a desperate voice, he claimed he was so horny, he had to see a woman "at once." Carlene literally ran out the door and was back within twenty minutes, waving three hundred dollars in my face.

It seemed like every month my bills got bigger. Mama needed more medicine and better clothes. Then she wanted a big-screen color television set. Our apartment in the shabby neighborhood we lived in got broken into so many times I stopped counting. One day while I was at work, a bold burglar broke into our place while Mama was taking a nap and made off with a clock radio I had just bought. I knew I had to do something drastic to get us into a safer place.

It didn't take long for me to get desperate enough to go out on a few dates that Carlene set up. She made me agree to give her a thirty percent cut. At first, it was easy. Almost fun. Carlene and I didn't tell Clyde Brooks, the man who was behind the escort service, about me going on dates, too. I had not met him in person yet, but he sounded pretty scary over the telephone so I didn't want to piss him off. Besides, Carlene went out on a few dates herself that she didn't report to this Clyde, so she had my back and I had hers.

I was twenty-four and the only man I'd ever had sex with was my husband. Sammy had never asked for anything too extreme or out of the ordinary in bed. I had a lot to learn about what men wanted. And because the ones I was dating were paying for it, they expected to get whatever they wanted. Even something as outlandish as me pissing on them! I was surprised, and pleased, to occasionally run into a man who was happy just to have me give him a hand job in the front seat of his car on his lunch hour in the alley behind our building.

I'd been dating strange men for about a month before I actually had to fuck one. And he made it worth my while: four hundred dollars and some new clothes from the boutique he owned. I just didn't like all the lies I told Mama about where all the money was coming from.

"Baby, I am so proud of you. A thousand dollars in one day just for modelin'. I always knew your good looks would pay off," Mama told me, admiring the new furnished apartment we'd just moved into. We even had a view of the San Francisco Bay, a fireplace, and an alarm system. "That Naomi Campbell better be watchin' her back." Mama grinned, running her brand-new vacuum cleaner over the thick carpet on our living room floor.

I smiled and agreed with Mama.

"Rosie, I want to go to Vegas. Book me a suite at that Mirage this time. I might run into Gladys Knight. Besides, them drinks at that Bellagio place was too weak, and I didn't see nary celebrity."

The more extravagant Mama got with her demands, the more dates I had to go on. "Mama, I just sent you to Vegas last week. You lost more than three thousand dollars playin' those slot machines."

"So what! I wanna go again. We rich. What good is it for me to have a supermodel for a daughter if I can't enjoy it!" Mama roared. Then her voice got real low. She coughed and rubbed her chest. "I mean, how many more times will you be able to do nice things for me?"

I sent Mama to Vegas the very next day and she lost another two thousand dollars.

When the building we lived in was sold a month later, I started looking for us a new place. It was Carlene's idea for me to put Mama in an apartment complex for seniors and get a place of my own.

"You'd make even more money if you had a place where you could take tricks," Carlene advised. "You wanna share my place with me? I live in the same neighborhood as Robin Williams."

I declined Carlene's offer to be roommates, but I did move into my own apartment on Silver Street. No movie stars lived on this block, but it was a nice, quiet, and safe place for a single woman. However, I couldn't bring myself to bring tricks to it. Fucking in the same place I lived in didn't appeal to me.

I furnished my apartment with odds and ends that I picked up secondhand, because I didn't plan to stay in it long. For some reason I believed that eventually Mama and I would return to Detroit. I missed Sammy, and it was so painful I couldn't even bring myself to call him up. But I did send him notes every now and then, with no return address. I just prayed that he would still be there for me when I straightened my life out.

I don't know who tipped that Clyde man off about Carlene and me going on dates with some of his wealthy tricks and keeping all the money. One of the drunken women, Carlene assumed.

Clyde stormed the office on Howard Street cussing a blue streak. Carlene just laughed and told Clyde to lick her pussy, but she promised to give him all the money she made on her next five dates. After he cooled off, he started raving about how pretty I was. Instead of firing me, he "offered" to "manage" my "career" for a third of my trick money. Since I had already wet my feet, it wasn't hard for me to accept his offer. Especially since I was already giving Carlene thirty percent of the money I made.

"And just to show you what kind of man I am, I ain't goin' to ask you for none of the money back that you got from my clients," Clyde told me with a cheeky grin. He followed that with a mysterious threat. "If you decide you wanna work as a outlaw, you just might get yourself into all kinds of the trouble with the man. I play cards with everybody on vice." Turning to Carlene, he said, "Don't I, Carly?"

"He sure do, 'cause I seen him do it." Carlene nodded, blowing on her nails.

To this day, I don't know if Carlene had set me up so that I would feel I had to work for Clyde. She didn't seem too upset with him and was acting mighty casual about Clyde finding out our dirty little secret.

I went on my first date for Clyde that very night. To make

sure I had a good time, he sent me to Mr. Bob, the easiest trick in San Francisco and one of the wealthiest. He spent thousands of dollars each month on women. And since he preferred Black women, Clyde took full advantage of that. Once a month, he would let this Mr. Bob have the woman of his choice for free. But the joke was on Clyde. Carlene told me that even when Clyde sent Mr. Bob his freebie, Mr. Bob paid the woman anyway. "And Clyde don't see nary penny of that money," Carlene told me. "See, it's all good."

It was hard to dislike Clyde, even though he had cussed me out and called me a crook. But he had a sense of humor, and he was generous. He would let me borrow his Range Rover to haul Mama back and forth to the expensive stores she liked to shop at. I found out he was also a sensitive man when I told him about losing most of my family. He pretended he had something in his eye, but I had already seen the tears. Also, Clyde resembled my late brother Tyrone. The minute Mama met him, she started treating him like one of the family. Not only did Mama start inviting him to dinner and church, she encouraged him to get me as many "modeling" assignments as he could.

But when Clyde came around too often, Mama got suspicious. "Rosie, you ain't tryin' to date that man, are you? Is he doin' more than managin' your modelin' career?"

"Oh, you don't have to worry about me and Clyde gettin' together like that. He only likes White women."

Mama sniffed and smiled. "I figured that. He seems like the type. Tell him to come have dinner with us this Sunday."

Clyde showed up the following Sunday evening with a bottle of Mama's favorite wine. I couldn't tell which one did the most grinning: him or her.

"Sister Vaughn, you ain't got to worry about your baby girl. Modelin' is a cutthroat business, but I ain't goin' to let nobody take advantage of her," Clyde told Mama, his eyes on me as he smacked on some of Mama's honey-dipped fried chicken. "She's in good hands now."

"Thank you, son," Mama purred. Then she turned to me with a scowl on her face. "And I don't care what he do to you, you better stay with him."

Clyde had been managing me for more than a year when Ester brought Lula to him.

# Chapter 11

# LULA HAWKINS

Verna and Odessa arrived the evening after I moved in with Rosalee. They checked into a Travelodge motel instead of taking Rosalee up on her offer to stay at her apartment and sleep on pallets on her living room floor.

"It's bad enough that you sleeping on that woman's couch," Verna said with a frown. "A queen like you ought to be sleepin' on a bed of feathers."

I didn't remind my stepsister about all the times I'd slept on her garage floor when she had her lovers spend the night.

"You can still go back home with us," Odessa told me, looking around Rosalee's sloppy living room. They had already inspected the rest of the apartment.

Rosalee and Ester were somewhere in Nevada. They were helping out some madam in one of the legal brothels that their man Clyde had a relationship with.

"I'm stayin' out here. Rosalee said I can stay with her and split the rent," I insisted.

Verna, wearing a pair of bibbed overalls, blinked. "Somethin' is strange about that Rosalee," she said, giving me a dry look. "That sister seems sneaky. She wouldn't even look me in the eye when I talked to her. Like she hidin' somethin'. Mmmm huh," Verna muttered, rotating her thick, ashy neck.

"Girlfriend, you know them models gots to be strange to put up with all the shit they have to put up with. Men lookin' at 'em half naked and shit. But they do make some serious money," Odessa said, waving her hand. She had gained at least twenty pounds in the last few months. Her hand looked like a brown cow's hoof. "If I wasn't such a big moose, and fifteen years younger myself, I might try to pose for a few pictures."

"Don't let Rosalee's behavior bother you. She's got bad nerves and is just gettin' over a nervous breakdown." I had learned that the right lies kept people from asking too many questions. "Modelin' is all she can do right now. All she has to do is look pretty, and she can work her own hours. Her psychiatrist says she's makin' progress."

"Is modelin' what you plan to do? You done had a few traumas yourself recently. And you prettier than she is," Odessa added, walking around Rosalee's living room, being nosy. She fixed her eyes on an address book on the floor next to a pair of dirty panty hose. "This place looks like a polter-geist got loose in it." Odessa kicked the panty hose to the side, snatched up the address book and started leafing through it. "Well, I'll be damn. Ain't nothin' but men's names and phone numbers in this damn thing." Odessa pursed her lips and gave me a strange look.

I snatched the address book out of Odessa's hands. "Uh, I don't know yet if I will do some modelin', too. Um, these men," I said, waving the address book, "they are mostly pho-tographers, bookin' agents, businessmen with clothin' stores and showrooms, and gay hairdressers. They hire girls like Rosalee." That seemed to satisfy Verna and Odessa. They blinked and sniffed, but I could see that they were both still uneasy and curious. "I got a job interview lined up already."

"When did you have time to be lookin' for a job?" Odessa asked. "And where at? I thought you told us you ain't been out of Rosalee's apartment since you got here."

"When the police took me down to the precinct to get my statement right after Bo got killed, I met a sister who works in the personnel office. She told me they had an openin' for a receptionist. Don't y'all worry about me. I'll be all right. And if I won't be safe workin' with cops, I won't be safe nowhere." I laughed.

"From what I read in the newspapers, these cops out here is just as corrupt as the thugs they arrest," Verna said with a sneer.

"I'm stayin' out here," I protested in as firm a voice as I could manage.

Verna shook her head and sighed. "Well, if and when you change your mind about comin' back home, all you got to do is let me and Odessa know. Your daddy's gettin' older, and his health is failin'. You need to be there for him anyway," Verna said with a concerned tone of voice.

"I think your mama and the twins can take care of Daddy. I did as much as I could for him, Etta, and them twins when I was back there, and now it's time for me to do some things for myself," I said firmly.

As happy as I was to see Odessa and Verna, I was glad when they climbed back into their rental car and returned to the Travelodge. But it was hard and sad to deal with the fact that Bo's body was going back on the same plane with them in a box. I didn't have the strength to go back to Mississippi for my husband's funeral. It was hard, but I had to put all of that out of my mind. I had prayed for Bo's soul, and I knew that if he could, he would understand my actions. That was the kind of man Bo had been. I was so grateful that I had had the chance to show him how much I had cared about him by running off with him and becoming his wife.

That night when Rosalee got back from Nevada, she ha
so much money it wouldn't fit in the shoe box she tried t
store it in. Even though she looked tired and worn out, sh
still went out with Ester and Rockelle on another date a fe
hours later.

Just before dawn, Rosalee rolled back in with anothe
huge wad of cash. She tossed all of the money toward me o
the couch, and it landed smack-dab in my lap. Somethin
strange and exciting came over me. My face got hot, and m
hand started itching as I caressed the money. That mone
represented all kinds of things to me—security, freedom
maybe even another chance to be happy. It had not been sai
outright, but I knew that from the very beginning, Este
Rockelle, and Rosalee had been wooing me to join them i
their escapades.

"Rosalee, do you think your man, Clyde, can hook m
up?" I asked, squeezing the money like it was already mine

Clyde's apartment was all the way across town in a bi
brooding stucco building on a street lined with exotic pal
trees and expensive vehicles. It looked like Beverly Hills.
felt as out of place as a goat in a jewelry store.

I didn't like the fact that he had insisted on meeting m
alone, but I had agreed to it anyway. I was just that despe
ate, and I must have been crazy, too. Never under normal ci
cumstances would I have agreed to sleep with men for mone
I had to have lost my mind. After losing Larry, my son, an
Bo all in such a short period of time, how could I not t
crazy? That seemed to be the best way to rationalize my d
cision. I was not responsible for my actions. I was more lik
a puppet. Yeah, that made me feel better. So, what happene
to me in San Francisco wasn't my fault.

Ester and Rosalee had dropped me off on their way to a double date, explaining to me that all the sharp-nosed White men standing in front of Clyde's building belonged to the Russian Mafia.

"If any of them communist motherfuckers ever try to get in your face, just tell 'em you are one of Clyde's wives," Ester advised, waving and grinning to the same men she'd just warned me about. I smiled at the Russians, but they gave me a hard, mean look anyway.

Clyde buzzed me into his building. As soon as I got inside his apartment door, he stood back and looked me up and down. "How old are you, twenty-four, twenty-five?" All he had on was a navy blue terry-cloth bathrobe and a pair of black suit pants. The butt of a gun was sticking out of the waistband.

"Twenty-eight," I said, praying he wouldn't ask to see the ID that showed my age as thirty-three.

He smiled. "You sure don't look that old," he told me, waving me to a couch. "You could have lied and told me you was twenty-four, and I wouldn't have doubted you."

"I know. But I didn't want to start off tellin' you no lies." I sniffed. For a moment, our eyes locked and that made me nervous.

"Lula. Now that's a fine old southern name you got you, too. You lucky your mama didn't stick you with a countrified name like Mae Alice or Alice Mae."

"My middle name is Mae," I admitted, feeling shy for the first time in my life.

"Well, don't tell nobody," Clyde said, laughing. He took the sweater I'd borrowed from Rosalee and draped it on the back of a plush blue wing chair.

Clyde's place was nothing like the one I shared with Rosalee. He had expensive leather furniture, thick dark green carpets, a gigantic fish tank full of exotic fish, a huge television set with a CD player on top and a mountain of CDs stacked up on the floor. There was not an empty spot on one wall of his living room. It was covered with pictures of him posing with some of the most famous people in the world— Mick Jagger, Nelson Mandela, and even Mickey Mouse. Next to a poster of him hugging Halle Berry was one of him with a light-skinned young girl with blond hair. Despite a severely lopsided face, one bulging eye, and a scarred cheek, the girl was still beautiful.

"Uh, she work for you, too?" I asked, nodding at the picture of the blond girl.

Clyde blinked and cleared his throat. "That's my baby. My baby girl, Keisha. She's twenty-eight now," he told me in a sad, soft voice. The girl in the picture didn't look twenty-eight and Clyde didn't look old enough to have a daughter that age. He cleared that up right away. "I was sixteen when she was born. She was sixteen when we took that picture." That made him forty-four, but he looked ten years younger. Clyde was as dark as I was. The girl in the picture was obviously biracial. He seemed like the type to be into White women, but that didn't bother me. I'd dated a White boy in high school. My only concern was business.

"Oh. She live here with you?"

"Oh, no. She live in Oakland with my grandmother. See, my baby got all kinds of physical problems. She ain't responsible and need to be looked after twenty-four seven."

"Oh. I'm sorry to hear that." I sniffed and glanced around the room some more. There was a rose-scented fragrance in the air. The ceiling was so high, I felt like I had stepped into a glamorous cavern. "You from Oakland?"

Clyde shook his head. "I grew up there, but I'm from Mississippi."

"So am I!" I gasped, feeling more at ease after hearing that piece of information. I took the flute of wine that Clyde handed me and sank down onto his huge leather couch. He sat on the arm next to me, looking me over like I was something for sale, which I was.

"So they tell me. Well, you in a whole 'nother world now. 'Frisco is a long way from Mississippi, and it's a whole different ball game out here. This city is one big-ass cash cow. You got to milk this cow 'til it can't be milked no more. With them juicy lips and pretty face, you'll do real good."

"I hope so," I muttered. My common sense was getting pushed farther and farther back in my weak, confused mind. "I really need to make some quick, easy money—but just until I find a real job."

"Uh-huh. I know all about that."

Clyde tilted his head and stared at me, making me squirm in my seat. I didn't want to squirm too much and wrinkle the pretty denim skirt I'd borrowed from Rosalee, so I steered the conversation in a different direction.

"You lucky to have your grandmother livin' so close," I said, feeling sad because I couldn't say the same thing about myself.

"Oh, but that old sister is a real piece of work. I tried to get her to move over here to a nice house in the Sunset District where she would be a lot safer. But you know how impossible old folks can be. She raised me in that house out in East Oakland, and all her friends still live in that same 'hood. Girl, them ignorant-ass niggers and spics out there be just fightin' and fightin'. Next to the drug dealers, the richest folks in Oakland is the undertakers. I ain't about to deal with all that mess. And as much as I like my old 'hood, I ain't about to live out there and let them motherfuckers steal all of my shit!"

"Don't you worry about your grandmother and your daughter livin' in a bad neighborhood?" I took a sip of my wine, enjoying the strong tingle it gave me.

"I do. But I can't make 'em leave. I tried to do that for years and years. Granny Effie done told me that the only other address she's goin' to have is Heaven. I send Keisha to a camp for them handicapped folks when I can, but she don't like it. She wants to be right there in that old house with her granny." Clyde paused, took a drink from his glass, and stared at the picture of his daughter. "The old folks in the 'hood help look out for Keisha."

Clyde set his wineglass on the coffee table and rubbed his palms together, giving me a wide grin. "All right now. Enough of that small talk. Let's cut to the chase." He paused and sniffed, looking at me with his head tilted back a little. "You a pretty woman, Lula Mae. Ray Charles could see that much. And, I like you." He shook a finger at me. "You be good to me, I'll be good to you. My girls, they done told me all about your . . . uh, situation. You broke, done lost your husband, new in town. Girl, you need help."

"Well, I just need to make some money real fast. A lot of it. I don't want to do . . . uh, date any longer than I have to. I just don't want to get myself into somethin' I can't get out of." I couldn't figure out why I was almost whispering and looking around like I was expecting somebody else to pop into the room. I knew I was alone with Clyde. "Rosalee and Ester, and that fat woman Rockelle, they all said you would look out for me. Help me out. And that you wouldn't let nobody hurt me." My eyes got big when Clyde removed that gun from the waistband of his pants and placed it on the coffee table. A narc I'd once dated had carried the same type of gun, so I knew Clyde's was a Glock. Verna thought that *Glock* was a stupid name for a gun. She figured that some macho man, preoccupied with his own cock, had chosen that ridiculous name because it rhymed.

I glared at the gun and scooted farther away on the couch. The barrel was aimed right at me.

"Could you put that thing away, p-please," I stammered.

"You ain't got nothin' to worry about. Not no more," Clyde told me. "Not as long as I'm packin'."

He lifted the gun and waved it anyway.

# Chapter 12

# ROCKELLE HARPER

I don't why, but I had a strange feeling about that Lula. There was something about her that gave me the creeps. I *knew* she was going to be trouble. Not just to Clyde, but the rest of us, too. She gave me odd looks when I tried to get more information from her about herself.

Nowadays, I wanted to know as much as I could about the people I had to deal with. I didn't trust too many people anymore, and if I was smart, I never would again. I had trusted Joe Harper, and he'd made a fool out of me.

Mama—like she would know—had tried to warn me about Joe when I first brought him home. I was seventeen; Joe was twenty-eight.

"Rocky, that man is goin' to make a fool out of you," she told me so many years ago. "You need to finish school, get a job, and find you a real man."

"Like you did?" I shot back, rolling my eyes at Mama as she stumbled around the tacky living room in the tacky apartment we lived in in the projects.

"No, I want you to do better than I did. I didn't have no choice. When I got pregnant with you, my daddy made

Booker marry me. I knew it was goin' to be rough and I wasn't goin' to be happy. When your brothers came, I knew I was stuck with Booker and livin' in this flophouse for life. But your daddy is a good man, and I love him."

I hated living in the projects. I deserved so much more. I couldn't stand to look at my daddy in his filthy janitor's work clothes and Mama with her greasy aprons and limp hair. Her hands seemed to be covered with flour or grease all the time—even when she wasn't cooking up one of her pecan pies or frying a slimy-ass catfish. And I was way too embarrassed to invite my friends to our apartment. I didn't want them to see how much damage poverty could do.

Daddy had divorced Mama before I was born. Her own mama and the rest of her family lived in a pigsty in Fresno, so she couldn't get any help from them. She had no choice but to go on welfare.

When things didn't go the way Daddy thought they would, he moved back in with Mama when I was two. And Mama being the fool she was, let him get her pregnant two more times. When we moved from our first apartment into one that Section Eight covered, you would have thought that we had all died and gone to Heaven the way Mama carried on. I couldn't understand how a woman could be so happy with so little.

"We are truly blessed," Mama insisted, while at the same time the people in our neighborhood were killing and robbing one another on a regular basis.

I refused to babysit for my younger brothers when Mama had to leave the house. But I still ended up doing other things that I didn't want to do. Like going to buy groceries with food stamps! I thought I would die that time when Gail Hawthorne, the biggest snob I knew, walked into a Safeway supermarket and caught me paying for some generic items with food stamps. Her daddy was a lawyer and she was the

one girl in my school with whom I went out of my way to try
and be friends. I was willing to do whatever it took to make
myself look like I had some class. Reading a lot of books
and watching educational programs on television helped me
a lot. My looks and intelligence were the only things I had to
fall back on. I looked at that as my ticket to a better life. I
had even forced myself to speak better than the ignorant
people who lived in my depressing neighborhood.

"Rocky Nicholson, is that you?" Gail asked, her big
brown eyes blinking at the food stamps in my hand. "What you
doin' with Monopoly money?" Standing there in her designer
jeans, so new and expensive the crease was still in the legs,
Gail narrowed her eyes and gave me a look that made my
skin crawl.

"Oh, hi. Uh, these are food stamps," I said lamely, balling
those damn things up in my sweaty hand. I could not have
been more disgusted if I'd been clutching a cow's tongue.
There was a grocery store closer to our apartment, but I'd
walked eight blocks to the Safeway located in Gail's neighborhood.

"Food stamps!" Gail made the words sound like profan-
ity. "What you doin' with food stamps?" An amused look appeared on her face.

"I was, uh, doing a favor for this old lady who lives next
door to us. She's all crippled up with arthritis and can't do
her own grocery shopping," I lied.

"Yeeow! I wouldn't be caught buyin' stuff with food
stamps—for nobody!" Gail exclaimed, giving me a smug
look. "Well, if you got a lot of stuff to carry home, I'll help
you. That way I'll know where you live."

I almost swallowed my tongue trying to get the words out
so fast. "That's all right! Uh, my mama's real sick and I can't
have no company." I almost peed on myself. I hurried out of
that store as fast as I could, hoping that Gail had believed my

lie about the arthritic old woman. She must have, because eventually we started hanging out together, but just at school and her house. There was no way in hell I was going to let a lawyer's daughter see the way I really lived.

My brothers were just as much of an embarrassment as my parents. Carl, three years younger than me, was a slow learner and was in a special class. The one that all of the other kids made fun of. Sid, who was four years younger than me, was a wannabe thug. He hung out with the roughest kids he could find. I didn't have to worry about him embarrassing me in school because he'd dropped out in the eighth grade. And on top of all that, both of my brothers were fiercely ugly. They had real dark skin, and hair so nappy it looked like they had barbed wire on their heads. I didn't even want them touching me.

"Girl, you need to get up off that high horse you been ridin' all your life. You ain't no better than the rest of us," Sid snarled. He was mad because I'd covered a chair that he'd just got up from with some newspaper before I'd sit on it.

"Well, I *know* I'm better than your Black ass. I can't wait to get out of school so I can get away from all of this mess," I yelled, waving my hand around the room. Mama trotted out of our forever smoky kitchen and stood in the living room doorway, looking as tired, old, and greasy as ever. She spent a good deal of her time breaking up fights and arguments between my brothers and me.

"There's a lot of folks got a lot more than what we got, and they ain't half as uppity as you. I don't know who you got your ways from, but it sure wasn't from me or your daddy," Mama told me, shaking a greasy spoon at me.

"And you expect me to be happy? What's wrong with wanting something better than what we have now?" I shot back. "You and Daddy are so ignorant, you never even tried to go back to school or get better jobs. There is no excuse for anybody to get on welfare and stay on it these days," I wailed. My voice was shaking so hard it sounded like I was singing.

"If you don't like the way things is here, you can leave now. You ain't got to wait 'til you turn eighteen."

I knew that Mama didn't mean what she said by the weakness in her voice and the tears in her eyes. But I challenged her anyway.

"You don't think I'll go?" I asked.

"If you wanna go . . . so," she muttered, looking away. "I'm too tired to stop you, and I'm tired of tryin' to make you happy."

"And I plan to. Joe said I could work at his gas station and he'd pay me under the table so I wouldn't have to pay taxes," I announced.

"Well, you go right ahead, Miss Rocky-*feller*. You got so much class, you want to up and run off to work in a greasy fillin' station that gets robbed once a month, and work under the table. That's real class," Sid scoffed, folding his arms. His anger made him look even darker and uglier.

I looked at Mama. Sweat was dripping off her face onto her gummy blouse. Her long, flat breasts hung down her chest and stomach like a second pair of arms. She sighed and gave me a look I could only describe as hopeless. "Girl, Joe Harper done already gone through a dozen women that I know about. And accordin' to his own mama, the courts in three states is lookin' for him so they can collect back child support for God knows how many babies he done made." Mama started walking back to the kitchen with me right behind her, almost stepping on the heels of her ashy bare feet.

"I don't care about none of that. That's Joe's business. He loves me and wants me to work for him, and I plan to. If I'm lucky, he'll eventually marry me," I snarled, with the fingers on both of my hands crossed.

Mama whirled around and shook her spoon at me again. Sid had followed us to the kitchen and was standing in a corner snickering.

"Rockelle, Joe Harper ain't nothin' but a shady fool that ain't good at nothin' but makin' babies. Is that the kind of man you want?" Mama asked with a snort.

"It was good enough for you!" I hollered, immediately wishing I could take my words back. I'd never seen my mother look as sad and hurt as she looked at that moment. But I didn't want her to know how I felt, thinking that she would see me as being weak. Like her. "Joe takes care of his business."

"And overchargin' folks for gas is one of 'em," Sid said, smirking.

I gave Sid an evil look, talking with my teeth clenched. "Well, at least Joe would make some pretty babies. I wouldn't be stuck with a bunch of dog-faced monkeys like—" Mama cut me off by slapping my face.

"You don't look so hot yourself now. That yellow skin can only get you so far," Mama said in a gentle voice I rarely heard, looking at her hands, turning them over twice. It was as if she couldn't believe how bad they looked. She'd gotten darker over the years, but she was still almost light enough to pass for white. "And just 'cause you and Joe both got light skin, that don't mean your kids'll turn out that way."

"You let me and Joe worry about that," I snapped, rubbing the spot on my face where she'd slapped me. I couldn't wait to call up Joe to beg him to come get me. I only had two months to go before graduation, but I couldn't stand one more night in the same house with my family. I attempted to leave the room. Mama grabbed my arm and spun me back around. Except for when I was a toddler, I'd never been this close to her body. It was only then that I noticed just how many wrinkles she had on her face and how deep they were.

"Rockelle, I done the best I could with you and your brothers. It wasn't much, but it was the best I could do. I don't like the way you behave toward us, never did. Even when you was a little bitty girl, you had a real nasty attitude. I thought that you would mellow out as you got older. I see now I was wrong. But I am your mother, and I do love you. No matter how bad you treat me, that ain't goin' to change."

I pulled away and started walking toward the congested bedroom I shared with my brothers. We had only two bedrooms. Mama shared the smaller one with Daddy. I glimpsed him sitting on the side of his unmade bed. It was the middle of the day and he was still in his pajamas. He and I rarely interacted. We could go for days without speaking. I had never forgiven him for leaving Mama in the first place. He flashed the gold tooth in the front of his mouth that I hated so much. Daddy avoided confrontations by spending most of his time in the bedroom watching the hot television set that he'd purchased from some thug on the street.

The room I shared with my brothers was divided by a thin sheet hanging from a rope. No matter how much I sprayed that foul-smelling room with Glade, I couldn't get rid of the lingering, unholy stench of my brothers' frequent farts and filthy tennis shoes. I kept the window above my sorry bed open at all times, but it didn't do much good.

"I bet one thing," I said over my shoulder as I plopped down hard on the lumpy rollaway, tossing a soiled jockstrap off my bed to the floor, "when I have a daughter, she won't have to live the way I do."

Mama had followed me. She stood in the doorway, wiping off sweat that always seemed to be on her face. She looked at me with eyes so weary, I wondered how she was able to keep them open.

"When and if you do ever have a daughter, I hope you

have one just like you, Rocky. Then you'll know the kind of pain you caused me."

That was the last thing Mama said to me that day. The next day I moved in with Joe Harper. That weekend I started working the cash register part-time at the service station he managed. Things were looking up for me.

My arrangement with Joe came with a high price. Sure, I had to fuck him that same night I moved in with him. And it was hard to think of Joe as being romantic with his buck-teeth. But even though I was a virgin and didn't know shit about sex, I enjoyed it. I just wanted to be with somebody who had more ambition than my parents. All I had ever wanted was a better life and I didn't care how I got it.

As soon as I graduated, I started working full-time for Joe. When I got pregnant with Juliet, I gained fifty pounds in less than three months. But I was still happier than I'd been living with my crude family. However, my happiness was weak, and it got weaker by the day. Joe had a lot of friends, and he liked to spend time with them, usually without me "breathing down his neck." There were times when he came home with another woman's perfume on his body, but I let that slide. It was enough to have him come home to me.

"You need to learn how to cook better if you want me to come home for dinner more often," Joe told me as he tossed a scorched pork chop into the trash. "And another thing, *big mama,* you need to pay Jenny Craig a few visits." The look on his face made me feel as big as a moose.

As insensitive as Joe was, he had some good qualities. He was generous with his money. "As long as you pay the bills, I don't care what you spend my money on," he told me. He doled out thousands of dollars at a time.

To keep my mind off Joe and his outside activities, I shopped with a vengeance. I bought unnecessary knick-knacks for the house and clothes I didn't need. And I spent tons of money every month at Marcus Books, the premiere Black-owned bookstore in the Bay Area. Even when I went in just to browse, the sister who ran the place, Blanche Richardson, always had a shipment of new books that I couldn't leave the store without. The characters created by E. Lynn Harris, Carl Weber, Eric Jerome Dickey, and all the other African-American authors had become my new best friends. I always enjoyed reading. When I'd lived with my family, it had been the only way I could truly escape. Now I had to do the same thing with Joe.

But lying around the house pregnant with nothing but food and books to keep me occupied, I gained even more weight. The money I gave to Jenny Craig was a waste. I would eat that Jenny Craig shit and still gobble up a whole pizza by myself the same day.

I gave birth to a beautiful baby. Like I had hoped for, Juliet had my light skin and Joe's straight hair. I treated her like a Black American princess and so did Joe. Because of my daughter, I was so happy with my new life that I rarely thought about where I'd come from. One thing that helped put my past behind me was I never visited the projects, and I never called anybody who still lived there. Not even my family. There were times when I wanted to, because I did love and miss them. But I couldn't give Mama the satisfaction of knowing that she'd been right about Joe all along. If I was nothing else, I was stubborn. That was something I hoped I could correct someday. I just didn't know when and how.

My kids were all school age the first time my family saw them and that was by accident. It was at Stonestown Mall one Saturday afternoon.

Like dazed sheep, Mama, Daddy, and my brother, Carl,

strutted over to where my kids and I had stopped in front of a bakery. It was a tearful "reunion," at least for my family. Mama cried and hugged and kissed on me and my frightened kids like she'd just rescued us from a death camp. Juliet, eight at the time, wiped off her face after Mama kissed her on her cheek. Barry, my six-year-old slapped Daddy's hand when Daddy tried to pick him up. Five-year-old Michael giggled.

"They're shy," I managed, slowly walking away. The last thing I wanted was for somebody I knew to see me talking to such a group of vagabonds.

"Rockelle, our telephone number is still the same. You could call us sometime, just to let us know you all right," Daddy yelled. He looked twice as old as he had the last time I had seen him. His thin, kinky hair was completely gray and his eyes looked like somebody had pushed them halfway into his head. His tacky gold tooth was gone but in its place was a rotted out shell.

Mama had on a stained flimsy brown dress and a pair of shoes that kept sliding off her feet. Carl looked like the rest of those ghetto thugs terrorizing people everywhere they went. He had on baggy pants hanging below his butt. A greasy, plaid bandana was on his head.

"Uh, I've been meaning to call. But I've been so busy with the kids and Joe's got that new filling station in Daly City and all."

"Three kids all you got?" Mama asked, wiping her nose and eyes with a stiff handkerchief

"Uh-huh," I said, moving in the opposite direction. I had planned to take the kids for Chinese food, but I'd suddenly lost my appetite.

"Where you live, sister-girl?" Carl asked, cocking his head. It was then that I noticed a tattoo of a dagger on his cheek and a ring in his nose.

"We have a house on Joost Street." It gave me a lot of pleasure to add, "Four bedrooms." That didn't seem to impress anybody but me. "A retired dentist lives next door. His daughter, Helen, babysits for me."

"Well, do you need anything?" It seemed like a stupid question for Mama to be asking.

"No. We're fine." I didn't say it, but I knew there was nothing Mama had that I needed. Her dress was all but falling off her lumpy body. I assumed she had given up on her hair because a lopsided black wig was on her head, held in place by a faded scarf.

"Sid's got him a good job workin' as a security guard for Bank of America. Daddy got on SSI and gets him a nice little check every month. We got us a nice little house now. You and the kids and Joe are welcome to visit anytime you want to. It's a real nice house on Carson Street next to that dollar store I used to take you to." Mama paused, and then she offered a pleading smile. "We doin' a whole lot better than we used to." I was surprised to see that her dull teeth didn't look any worse than they'd looked the last time I had seen her.

I shook my head. "We have everything we need. Uh, you all take care of yourself now. I got to get these kids home. Joe said he'd take them to the movies." I heard Juliet gasp, because that was a bald-faced lie. Joe had less time for his kids than he did me. I had to get away from my family because I was afraid that I would fall apart and admit how wrong I'd been about the man I'd married. It would have been the perfect time for me to humble myself and resume a relationship with my family. As much as I loved them and wanted to be with them, I still couldn't bring myself to do it. And I think they knew that. They didn't try to follow us, or continue the conversation.

"Rockelle, take care of yourself," Daddy yelled. The farther we got away, the louder he yelled. "If you ever need us, just let us know." His voice faded out like the last scene in a movie.

"Who were those people?" Juliet asked, rubbing her nose as we reached the nearest exit.

"Your grandparents and your uncle. Walk fast," I mumbled, looking over my shoulder. Mama, Daddy, and Carl were standing in the same spot, still looking like dazed sheep. Juliet pulled away from me when I tried to put my arm around her shoulder. This rude gesture from my daughter was nothing new, and I was used to it. But this time it hurt.

"Yuck," Barry said, giggling. I wiped candy smudges from his cheeks and chin with the tail of my dress.

"Mama, that old lady looks just like you," Michael, said, wiggling his nose. My heart felt like it wanted to drop right out of my chest.

I didn't have time to sit around thinking about Mama and the rest of my family, no matter how much I loved them. Besides, I had my disastrous marriage to work on. But instead of getting better, things got worse between Joe and me. His brazen whore started calling the house asking for him. Every time I confronted Joe, he responded with a fist upside my face.

The beatings didn't last long and didn't happen that often. Not because Joe came to his senses, but because he and his little slut eventually packed up and left town while the kids and I were at Marine World.

I got so depressed, I didn't comb my hair or bathe for three days. I didn't have any close female friends to invite to my pity party. It was just as well, because I didn't want anybody to know my business. But the word got out anyway. The only way I could avoid people was to not answer my door. Before long, I didn't have a friend in the world.

My kids became even more important to me, because at

least I had somebody who cared about me. But even that was not what I thought it was. A week after Joe's disappearance, I picked up the extension in the kitchen and accidentally overheard part of a conversation between Juliet who was on the bedroom telephone, and one of her little friends.

"Is that your mama I seen with you at the store?" the child on the other end asked.

*"No!* She . . . she's a maid and she comes over to help my mama take care of us until my daddy comes back from visiting his sick uncle in Canada," Juliet replied.

"She's a creep," the other child said, giggling.

"Yeah, she is a creep," Juliet agreed.

As much as I loved my child, I never looked at her the same way again.


My situation went from bad to worse. I had to break down and go to the county building and apply for welfare and food stamps. I would have enjoyed sitting in a funeral parlor more.

There was a bright side to the mess I was in. My elderly neighbors, the retired dentist and his wife, let their daughter babysit the kids for free when I had to go out on job interviews.

Each day, after an interview, I went to whatever bar I could get to without having to spend money on public transportation or gas and parking for my car. Since I didn't have much money to spend on alcohol either, I went to the places that had the cheapest drinks. I got to like the phrase *buy one, get one free.* I spent hours at a time sitting at a wobbly table in a dark corner, humped over a bottle of warm beer at a tacky place in the run-down Tenderloin District. Next door was a strip joint that offered "wall to wall" sex acts. On the other side of the bar was a flophouse. Streetwalkers strolled into the same bar between romps with their tricks. I was surprised when one finally approached me one gray afternoon last March.

She was a slim, light-skinned Black woman. Her breasts were so full and firm, they looked like they were about to leap out of her blouse. "Girl, you better put a smile on your face. Ain't nobody goin' to pay you nothin' with you lookin' like that," she said, sitting down at the gummy table across from me. She had on a sleeveless white blouse and black leather pants. A white windbreaker was draped across her arm. There was a flushed look on her face. The weather was too dreary and cool for her to be sweating from the heat, so I figured she'd just finished turning a trick.

"I'm not what you think—I'm not *working*," I said fast. I was flattered that she thought a plump, depressed-looking woman like me was a streetwalker. But when I looked at some of the other girls, I realized I looked better than most of them, including the one sitting across from me. She had to be at least thirty-five. Her face, even though it was pretty, was hard, tired, and dry. The heavy makeup that looked like she'd applied it in the dark, didn't hide the circles around her puffy eyes.

"Well, excuse me," the woman said, lifting her neatly trimmed eyebrows. "Since you're a sister, I'll warn you anyway. Girl, you better find you another place to wet your beak. The girls on this block can get real territorial. They don't tolerate no new outlaws. Last week I seen this bitch go after another girl with a box cutter."

"But I'm not a-a," I couldn't even finish my sentence.

She gave me a dismissive wave. "It don't matter. Them bitches will jump you first and ask questions later."

I sighed and started to rise, but the bold woman waved me back to my seat and offered a broad smile.

"You ain't got nothin' to worry about as long as I'm here.

This homie don't play," she said proudly, shaking her fist. "I'm Carlene."

"I'm Rockelle."

"Like the movie star? That's a sharp name."

I nodded, spelling my name. "My mama was into Raquel Welch movies when she was pregnant with me. She thought it would be cute to name me after her, but with a different spelling."

"What do you do?"

"Nothing right now. I'm looking for a job."

"What do you do?" Carlene repeated in a stronger voice, looking at me with her eyes narrowed like slits.

I shrugged. "I'm willing to do whatever I have to do. My husband took off and left me with three kids to support."

"Oh? You ain't got no mama to help you out? No daddy? Nobody?"

"They're all dead."

"Oh." Carlene snatched a napkin out of my hand and wiped some of the sweat off her face. "I ain't got no more family neither. At least none that would claim me after I got . . . busy gettin' paid." She snorted. "And some of them same folks doin' more dirty business in a week than I do in a month. My brother killed his wife, but my family still treats him like some brass-ass king. It's a bitch bein' a bitch. Don't nobody wanna show you no love, unless there's somethin' in it for them."

I nodded. "Girl, I know what you mean." I chose my words carefully. I'd never had a conversation with a street-walker before, so I didn't know what to say to one. The little I knew about the proper etiquette among these women was what I'd learned from novels and movies. I smiled and complimented the woman on how pretty she was. I didn't see how I could go wrong by going in that direction. That made her smile. "Uh, have you been doing what you do long?" I asked.

"Girl, sometimes it feels like I been on my back all my life. At least since I was seventeen. I wouldn't know what else to do with myself. I started off in Cleveland. Sugar Man—that was my man's name—he didn't treat me good, so I ended up in a little town called Richland not far from Cleveland. It's in Ohio, too. I was workin' for this old sister who really knew how to treat her girls. She didn't even try to stop me when I told her I wanted to leave her and move to California. We called her Scary Mary." Carlene yawned and stretched her arms so high above her head I could see the bushy hair under her arms. Then she gave me a critical look before a broad smile appeared on her face. "You thick and pretty. Scary Mary would have liked you."

"I bet she would have." I laughed, sucking in my gut. It was good to hear that somebody appreciated the way I looked.

"Listen, I know you don't know me and ain't got no reason to believe me, but I can help you. I ain't got no man of my own to hook you up with—I been a outlaw ever since I came out here. But I'm in good standin' with the right folks. Judge Messic is one of my regular tricks, so don't nobody mess with me." Carlene leaned across the table and lowered her voice. "Listen, I know a real good brother who ain't goin' to do you nothin' but good. He won't beat your ass, and he won't make you do nothin' that you don't want to do."

"Is he looking for more girls?"

"All the time. He takes calls personally from his best clients. And he got another place where me and some more girls take the overflow calls. Business is boomin', girl. You better get you some of that money."

"What's this brother like?" I asked with interest.

"Oh, he's just as sweet as he can be. Me and him like brother and sister. And he's a family man, see. All his girls he got now, they just love him to death. He calls them his red light wives. Ain't that cute?"

I nodded. "Well, I'll do whatever I have to do, as long as nobody gets hurt," I said firmly. "Give me that man's telephone number."

I didn't even wait to get home to contact Clyde Brooks. I called him from a pay phone in the bar. And he must have had his telephone in his lap. He picked up on the first ring.

Carlene had told me that all I had to say was, "Clyde, Carlene told me to call you. My name is Rockelle."

He grunted and took it from there.

"Rock-elle." He said my name like it was two words. "Meet me tomorrow at Alfredo's at noon. Not one minute after noon, not one minute before noon."

"How will I know you?" I asked. Carlene was standing right next to me with her ear close to the telephone. There was an anxious look on her face. She was breathing so hard, her dangerous titties had popped a button off her blouse.

Before Carlene gave me Clyde's telephone number, she'd confessed that he paid her a hefty finder's fee for each girl she sent his way. She'd also told me that she had scoped me out the minute she walked through the door.

"I'll be the best-lookin' man up in there," he said with enough confidence for him and me both.

"Okay. But what do you look like?"

He laughed. "I'll be the only Black man up in there, sister." He hung up before I could say another word.

I turned to Carlene and gasped. "He didn't even ask what I looked like."

"So? Clyde knows I wouldn't send him no baboon!" Carlene hollered.

"But how will he know it's me when I get there," I asked, feeling light-headed and apprehensive already.

"I'll be hookin' up with the brother later on tonight to cook him dinner. Brother loves him some down-home cookin'. He's been laid up," Carlene said with her eyes watering. "Poor Clyde."

"What's wrong with him?"

"He just got circumcised, so he's been a little testy," Carlene explained.

"Huh?"

"He was born at home in some little hick town in big-foot country. Them dumb-ass midwives in Mississippi; they don't do nothin' but catch babies once they slide out."

"Oh," I mumbled, wondering what I was getting myself into, but not caring enough to run as fast as I could away from Carlene.

"Clyde knows he'll get a more honest description of you from me, than he would from you." Carlene brushed my hair back off my face. "Now you go home and pick out a classy, clean outfit to wear when you go to meet Clyde tomorrow. Don't go there lookin' like you wanna sell pussy. The only time you goin' to act and look like a tramp is after you get with a trick. Come on, sister. Let's get a cab down to the financial district where I can buy you a real drink in a clean glass. And . . . so you can see the kinds of men you'll be dealin' with."

I left the bar with Carlene's arm around my shoulder.

I met Clyde Brooks the next day, and was with him ever since. My bills were all paid up and I even had money in the bank, in a safe deposit box. Clyde had been good to me and for me.

The other girls were good to me, too, because they could feel me and I could feel them. I felt this Lula woman sitting on the couch next to me at Rosalee's place, and I didn't like what I felt. I told Clyde so as soon as I got him alone.

"She's going to bring trouble, Clyde. I just know it."

"Well, you let me worry about Lula, and you worry about Rockelle. Do you hear me?" Clyde said, giving me one of his mean looks. "I can take care of Lula. Real good."

# Chapter 13

# ESTER SANCHEZ

"Shuck it! You know I don't like workin' no double dates with a girl I just met! You said it was goin' to be me and Rocky doin' that thing with them guys from that army base. Or me and Rosalee. *Shit!*"

Since the day I was born, me and Clyde had a real deep understanding between us. He was my homeboy, my man, and sometimes, my best friend. I could talk much trash to him any way I wanted, and I didn't have to worry none about him jacking me up. You show me another girl who can talk trash to her man the way I talk trash to Clyde, and I will show you a girl who's got a miserable relationship with her man. "What's the matter with you, *papi?*"

Clyde could turn his face to stone and stare at me like he could see clean through me. He could be sweet-talking me one minute and cussing at me the next. "Ester, please do me this one favor, baby. See the best—dammit! I ain't playin' with you, girl! Shit."

"Clyde . . . go masturbate!"

Clyde held up his hands, bucked out his eyes the way he did when I took his gun from him and pointed it to his face.

That Glock he carried was still in the waistband of his pants where it always was. He was just fucking with me.

He laughed a little and waved his hand at me. Clyde was not the kind of man I could get mad at and stay mad too long, no matter how much he pushed the wrong buttons on me.

"One day you gonna wake up and I will be gone, man," I threatened. But he didn't even listen to that because he already knew better. Clyde always got his way with women, and I couldn't figure out how. Me, I had my own reasons for being in his corner, but other women had a hard time letting him down, too. He ain't no Denzel in the looks department, and he sure ain't no Romeo in the bedroom. That didn't stop him from always getting his way when it came to women. He just got it like that.

"Ester, baby, everything you do, you doin' for *us,* remember?" Clyde said, looking at me like I was the one with the problem. "I want you to go with Lula to pay Mr. Bob a visit." Clyde stopped talking and sucked in a loud breath, slapping his hands on his hips. "My man's been askin' for two girls all week, and you know how tame he is once he gets drunk. Everybody in the business knows that Mr. Bob is the easiest trick in the world after he done had a few drinks. Even I could go out there to his pad and tickle his dick and he wouldn't know the difference." Clyde covered his mouth, but a laugh squeezed out anyway. "He ain't goin' to give Lula no trouble, and that's the kind of trick she needs to get herself broke in! She ain't never done this kind of shit before . . . or so she says."

"Clyde—"

"Baby, I need you to make sure Lula don't go up in that White man's house and get loose, act ignorant, clumsy, and countrified. I can't let nobody fuck up my reputation with my clients," Clyde whined. "She ain't as sharp as you. And, she ain't as pretty."

Clyde got a real strange look on his face after his comments about Lula, and I know why. I'm smarter than I look, see. He had probably been thinking the same thing about Lula that I been thinking. Was she for real? I mean, I know some dude killed her husband the other night when I was at the motel. I seen the whole damn thing go down through the window of that store, see. I even knew the shooter's name and where he lived, on account of me and him used to live with the same foster family at the same time. Whatever, whatever. Five-O got the goods on the dude anyway because he blabbed to his homies and then they blabbed. I didn't need to say nothing no way, not that I ever would have. Dude knew where I lived, too.

Oh well. I had to get my mind back on Lula. I believed everything else she had told me about her baby daddy playing her and then the baby dying. Now, I did believe that story Lula told me about her mother dying when she was a little girl and her mean stepmother she had to live with, too. But this Lula woman didn't just get out of diapers. She had been around this crazy world for a while. She had more years than my twenty-five. Shit. What seemed crazy was her saying she never done no tricks before and then, at her age, she slide right into the game like her booty been greased with butter.

"You think Lula smart enough to play me . . . us?"

"Heeeelllll no!" I hollered.

I almost choked on the toothpick I held between my teeth. I still had on the trick clothes that got me the most attention: jeans ripped at the knee, a plain tight T-shirt, and sandals. My hair was parted down the middle of my head and in two braids with ribbons tied to the ends. Everybody said this kind of shit made me look like a teenager. A real young teenager at that, like around thirteen or fourteen. I never knew much, but one thing I'd known all my life was every straight man wanted to poke a real young girl at least once. I handled my business with men and it was a full-time job. I had to stay on top of shit if I wanted to get paid. I didn't need Clyde dumping more shit on me.

Clyde stood there looking at me. He was still holding the Benjamins I had greased his hand with as soon as he came through my door a few minutes earlier.

He shrugged and looked at the bills and frowned, like he was wishing the wad was thicker. He didn't say that, but I knew Clyde as good as Clyde knew Clyde. So I always knew what he was thinking. He knew me real good, too. So he knew how to respect and treat me to keep me happy.

"I know Mr. Bob is a easy trick, baby. That's why I'm sendin' Lula to him. I told her it would be like takin' candy from a baby." Clyde followed me to my little kitchen, his arm around my shoulder. "Whether she done turned tricks before or not, she new to us. I can't turn no new girl loose on one of my best clients by herself. She fuck up and I'm fucked up."

Without him asking me to, I poured Clyde a tall glass of orange juice into one of my best glasses. I drank my juice straight from the carton, batting my eyes at Clyde because the juice was so cold it made me shiver. It felt good going down my throat, though. Much better than some trick's slimy pecker. Since AIDS took the fun out of fucking, a lot of tricks didn't want straight intercourse. Not even with a condom. For some reason people thought they couldn't get AIDS from oral sex. Well, I got news for them. We got a homegirl, a White girl name Sherrie Armstrong, over at this clinic where AIDS people go to get attention. She caught AIDS from giving bareback blow jobs. The odd thing about that was, she caught it way before she started selling her stuff. She was from some rich-ass family over in Berkeley and studying at U.C. Berkeley. She was a real smart girl, but she done some dumb shit.

Anyway, our girl, Sherrie, she was the prettiest White girl you ever gonna see outside of the movies. Blond hair that didn't need no help from no dye bottle, big clear blue eyes, lips that should have been on a Black girl's mouth, and legs so long she used to straddle two tricks at the same time. Girlfriend used to be hella hot. Almost as hot as me. Once upon a time, you could stand her up next to that Michelle Pfeiffer, that movie star I seen in *Scarface,* and you couldn't tell one from the other.

Thinking about Sherrie made it easier for me to deal with Clyde. Just knowing how much luckier I was than her eased my anger.

Right after I swallowed my orange juice, I closed my mouth real tight and looked at Clyde. He was standing there looking at me like I just swallowed a rock. I didn't want to say nothing I would regret. Not with Clyde standing so close to me. I wiped my lips with the back of my hand and just nodded. I shook my head real hard so I could get my mind off Sherrie and back on Clyde, because thinking about Sherrie always made me sad.

Clyde put his hands on my shoulders and looked down at me, his eyes in mine, talking to me in his sweetest voice. "Baby, we can't take a chance on Lula goin' up in that White man's house alone and gettin' loose. For all we know that sister might go out there and knock Mr. Bob upside his head and steal everything he got. Then where would that leave us? Didn't I tell you that Mr. Bob told me you was his favorite girl?" Clyde blinked real hard, one eyebrow lifted and stayed up until he blinked some more. When he did that, I knew he was trying to play me.

"Look, Clyde," I had to stop talking long enough to

laugh, but just a little. Clyde was quick to tell anybody he wasn't no Eddie Murphy and didn't appreciate nobody laughing at him when he was trying to be serious. "Look, you know you can't pull that shit with me. Me and you go back to the beginnin'. You told Rosalee that Mr. Bob said the same thing about her last month."

Clyde scratched the side of his head and rolled his eyes back in his head like he was trying to remember something. Then, still scratching his head, he looked at me. "Oh," he mumbled. He let out a deep breath, looked at me real hard, and then put his hands in his pockets. When he did that, his jacket flew open and I seen the handle of his Glock sticking out of the waistband of his pants.

As long as I been knowing Clyde, he never had to use that gun. Well, just one time. One night we was walking down Army Street from a Salsa nightclub. Out of nowhere, a big rat—not some thug—but a real rat, came charging at us like a bull. Clyde let him have it. I seen people get killed before, but it was something I never got used to. Not even when it was a rat.

Rockelle told me that Clyde kept that gun in his pants near his crotch, the way some men put balled-up socks down there, so that when women in bars sit on his lap, they'll feel it and they'll think he's packing a big dick. Of course I told Clyde, and the next time he seen Rocky, he showed her his dick. She didn't say nothing else about what Clyde was packing in his pants. That's the kind of man Clyde was. He didn't have no shame, except when it came to his daughter or business.

Clyde seen me looking at his piece, so he looked down. He pushed that bad boy off to the side and buttoned himself up. Then he blinked at me and swiped his lips with his hand.

"You wanna finish tellin' me that lie?" I asked, glad I didn't have to look at that Glock no more.

"Well, I wasn't lyin'." He pouted, looking straight-up guilty. "Mr. Bob did tell me that same thing about Rosalee, and I believe he meant it. See, last month, Rosie was Mr. Bob's favorite girl. This month, it's you."

I let out some hot air and sucked on my teeth. "Shit, man. I was lookin' forward to trickin' with Rosalee or Rockelle tonight."

"Baby, you'll be trickin' with Rosie and Rocky tomorrow or the next night. Tonight, Lula needs you."

"All right. But after tonight, you owe me a big favor." I shook my finger in Clyde's face, but that didn't stop him from smiling. "I want that cruise you been promisin' me."

Clyde clapped his hands around mine, squeezing first, then kissing them. "Baby, I already got the tickets. This time next Saturday, me and you will be floatin' on the ocean outside of Mexico, smokin' some of the best dope they got down there. Remember them *hombres* from Cabo who we hooked up with in Mexico City last year? They got some good shit, and they know how to party. Who knows, we might even stumble across some of your kinfolks this time."

Clyde knew where my buttons was and he knew when and how hard to push them. He would have kept at me for as long as he had to until he got his way.

Clyde wasn't just my man, he was family. Well, not by blood or even by marriage, but by other things. We go all the way back to the beginning of my life.

I didn't find out about myself and how I got where I am today until I was eleven. I had heard bits and pieces of my story, but it didn't all come out until I got with Clyde. I should say, got *back* with Clyde, on account of he was there for me from birth.

From what I'd heard, from what people told me, and from

some old newspaper clips I seen, I found out all about the things in my sad past. Things that happened when I was too young to remember. See, Clyde was hella older than me, but I knew his story, too. He told me.

When Clyde was a teenager, he was always in trouble. It was the usual "boys will be boys" type of shit. He fucked up in school, beat up on kids, and broke into cars. He spent some time locked up in juvie and was always on some kind of probation. They made him go back to school and work part-time jobs after school and on weekends, so he wouldn't have too much time on his hands to be getting into trouble.

Clyde was being a real good boy. He came all the way from Oakland to San Francisco on the bus every Saturday morning to work at this Mexican restaurant in the Mission District. To break up the boredom, and to make a little extra spending money, him and one of his boys who worked at the same restaurant came up with a scheme.

Before they started working, they would shake down drunk men for just enough money to buy a good lunch and a bag of weed. To show he had a good heart for a thug, Clyde would only take what him and his boy needed, and they never, ever hurt these men. One time he told me that after they robbed one man, they walked him home so he wouldn't get jacked up by nobody else that morning. If one drunk man didn't have no money, they moved on to the next one. They did it while it was still too early for too many folks to be out walking around to witness something they shouldn't be seeing in the first place.

One morning Clyde and his homie followed a drunk old man to the alley behind the restaurant where they worked. They was only going to take him for enough money so they could go to the movies after work. Just before they caught up to the man, they heard some noise coming from the Dumpster behind the restaurant. Thinking it was the puppy he always wanted, Clyde peeped in that Dumpster and got the surprise of his life. He come to find out somebody had dumped a baby! Well, that baby was me.

Clyde fished me out and took off his shirt and wrapped me in it. I was almost dead, and the doctor that examined me said that maybe one more hour in that trash would have done me in. My grave would have been a Dumpster full of every kind of shit you can name if Clyde hadn't been out there to rob that drunk man.

Nobody came forward to claim me. Like what woman crazy enough to dump a baby in the trash would be crazy enough to admit it? Shit like that happened only in the Bible. So, I never knew nothing for sure about myself. Like my race. San Francisco being the kind of place it is, I could be just about anything. My skin is beige, almost the exact same shade as that fat Rockelle (except she calls the color high yellow . . .), my hair is shiny black and wavy. With my face looking the way it looks, I could tell people I was Black, Filipino, Latino, even Indian, and nobody would doubt me because I could be any one. Maybe even all of them at the same time. Whatever.

But because I was found in the Mission District, which is almost all Latino people, and because the social worker who took me over was Mexican, and she'd named me after herself, I went with being Mexican. I spent a lot of years in foster homes run by people who spoke Spanish. And me speaking Spanish, much better than I speak English, helped me choose to claim a Latin background over the others.

I was a lot of trouble to my foster families. I regret that now. I got in trouble at school, I lined the streets with the gangs, and we done all kinds of crazy shit. Even snatching purses from little old ladies. I even seen people get killed on the street by people I knew. That was a lot to see before I even got to my teens. But when you trying to "find" yourself, like I was, you gonna see things you don't need or want to see. Living a crazy life meant a lot of bad surprises.

Most of the foster homes I got sent to was in the Mission District. I didn't go too far away from that part of town unless I had to. Until I was fourteen, the only other place I'd ever been outside San Francisco was that freak-ass Berkeley, across the Bay, right next door to Oakland. I had never been to Oakland, and that was where Clyde Brooks was all that time since he found my little body in that Dumpster.

I can only believe that it was God who brought me back to Clyde after all that time. I was staying with the Rios family on Cesar Chavez Street. I felt like I was living in a zoo because they had hella chickens in the backyard, strutting in and out of the house, waiting to end up in a Crock-Pot. Them chickens and the man of the house, an old mule from Mexico City, his whale of a wife, and five pig-faced foster kids, was what I had to deal with.

The old man had an even older brother who lived in Oakland with his *morena* lady friend. A Black lady. Her grandson lived with her. The first few times that lady and her grandson came to our house didn't mean nothing to me. Now remember, I still didn't know who I was, where I came from, or what race I was at the time. And, for the record, to this day I don't know. All of that was unknown to everybody but God.

Since I didn't even know for sure what my race was, I figured it wouldn't do me no good to dog people out from a race that I could be part of. Señor Rios having him a Black American lady friend wasn't no big deal. Anyway, me and that lady friend's grandson got along real good right off the bat. But most of the time, Clyde went his way, and I went mine.

I'd been told by several people about how I'd been thrown to the garbage right after I got born but it wasn't something to be conversating about with nobody. I never brought it up anyway. I was fourteen and Clyde was like thirty-something. We didn't have a lot of things to talk about. He didn't waste much time with me when he came around. Besides, he had a teenage daughter, and she took up a lot of his time.

One day out of the clear blue sky, when Clyde was at the Rios house, he started talking to me about his teenage years. I'd had some trouble with some girls down the street, and there had been some bloodshed. Not my blood, so I wasn't feeling too bad myself. But I cooled off long enough to hear what Clyde had to say. Being older and trying to do better hisself, he shifted into that position that OGs go into when they trying to get a younger person to do the right thing before it's too late.

When he got to the part about going to rob that man in the alley that morning, but finding a baby in a Dumpster first, I got real stiff and started crying. Clyde had to scoop me up off the floor like the pile of dog poop that I felt like. That's when it all came out. I still had some of the newspaper clips the lady from Social Services (the one they named me for) saved for me, and I showed them to Clyde that day. He got tears in his eyes. There it was in headlines in black and white: OAKLAND YOUTH FINDS NEWBORN IN TRASH. Right up under the headlines was a picture of Clyde standing between two cops. He was grinning like he had won the lottery. Clyde didn't have on no shirt in that picture because he had used it to wrap me in it. The person I owed my life to had come back, and this time I wasn't going to let him get away. It was the spookiest thing in the world. Nobody could tell me that this wasn't God working in His mysterious way.

From that day on, I didn't want Clyde out of my sight. I followed him around like the puppy he never got. But he didn't feel me. He was a grown-up man with girlfriends up the ying yang, and that daughter I mentioned. He was also working at this place selling used cars in Oakland, and he had a lot of friends his age who he wanted to hang out with.

I dropped out of school because it interfered with my social life. I led a real busy life with my homies, and it drove the foster folks crazy. Then I moved into this place with three of my girls when I was seventeen. We took turns letting the landlord feel us up so we wouldn't have to pay the rent when we didn't want to. I was going nowhere real fast.

When we needed money for weed and other necessities like makeup, beer, and hot clothes, we went up to old men on the street and took them in the alleys to give them blow jobs or hand jobs. I couldn't believe how easy it was to make the money. But it was scary. Especially when the man wanted something other than a blow job or a hand job. I sold my virginity for forty dollars and three fresh-baked bear claws to the man who delivered stuff before daylight to a bakery on Mission Street.

A lot of times I got jumped by other girls, or their men, and they took my money. Oh, my life was so cold and lonely and dangerous. I never knew if I would see the next day. I had nightmares about somebody jacking me up and throwing my dead body back in the same trash can I came from. That made me cry a lot.

The only times I was really happy and warm was when I went with Señor Rios's brother to visit his lady friend in Oakland. Because that's how I got to see Clyde. When Señor Rios died, Clyde's grandmother took it real hard. She encouraged me to keep coming to her house anyway. She said me being around kept her from forgetting about Señor Rios. I was a "woman" by now and a hot-looking one, too, I am proud to say. Clyde, loving the ladies the way he did, really started feeling me then.

When I tell people I was Clyde's first "wife," they think he turned me out, wooed me into the sex business. Especially some of his ex-wives. Them ungrateful bitches, they thought that shit because they couldn't get along with Clyde. They made up their minds that he was the one calling the shots. Nuh-uh. *I turned Clyde out.* I was the one to get us both in business.

Clyde needed money more than I did with that daughter of his to take care of. She got run over by a fast car when she was a little baby. To see that poor girl with so many things wrong with her broke my heart. Jesus would weep if He seen her. Now, I never knew nothing about medicine and doctors and stuff like that. Them things remind me of sickness and dying, which I came so close to, so I don't like to think about that shit if I don't have to. That's why I never asked Clyde a lot of questions about his daughter. But he talked about her like she was a gift from God, like people say every baby is. Even though God didn't stop her from getting run over.

Anyway, from what I was told, the girl was normal up until she was around two or three. Clyde's relatives was supposed to be looking after her but obviously, they wasn't if she got run over right in a church parking lot. Clyde didn't have much money in them days, so there wasn't much he could do to get her put back together again.

One of the reasons I get so pissed off with the world is, if you ain't got money, you ain't got no chance if somebody run you over and break your legs and smash your face like they done Clyde's daughter. Poor Clyde. He told me how he started doing some of everything to get paid—washing cars, driving rich and famous people around in limos, waiting tables, and skycapping at the airport. He was even low-down enough to rob folks, like he was on his way to do the morning he found me.

Clyde said that he needed so much money to take his daughter from one specialist to another. The girl went through hella surgeries and still ended up looking like a nightmare. Words cannot describe that girl. When I tried to tell people who never seen Keisha how she looked in the face, I told them to go rent that old movie *The Elephant Man.* They thought I said that to make a joke, but it was the honest-to-God truth.

It broke my heart in two when Clyde told me how them doctors told him that Keisha would probably not live past age twelve and that he should prepare hisself for it, and her. Because of the injuries to her head, Keisha had to deal with fluid always moving around and settling in part of her brain. Something about the vessels getting messed up. The blood, and whatever else we human beings got up in our heads, it couldn't circulate the way it was supposed to. If Keisha wasn't lucky and too much fluid settled in one place for too long, infection would kill her. Clyde said that doctors told him that the older Keisha got, the more the fluid would fuck with her brain. All Clyde could do was make Keisha as happy as he could while she was alive. And let me tell you, that man would have shot the president if it would have made Keisha happy.

But there was a bright side to Keisha's mess, if you wanted to call it that. Keisha's mind was sharp as a tack, so she was a very smart girl. Me, I called it part of God's plan, which to me, had got even more mysterious by now.

As Lula said when she talked about her baby dying right after being born, God was the biggest pig in a poke the world would ever see. He had hella surprises. The good ones was nice, but with so many bad things happening to good and innocent people, I didn't know what the world was coming to.

Clyde and his grandmother, they really was off into church, and the Bible, and all that other holy stuff. They couldn't make no sense out of what happened to Keisha. But they never gave up on God.

Keisha was such a smart and holy girl. She knew she was probably going to be with God a lot sooner than the rest of us, but that didn't even faze her.

I seen a lot of myself in that girl, and I think Clyde did, too. It got easy for me to see why he liked me so much. Me and Keisha kept that "daddy love" thing in Clyde going.

Even with all of the bad habits I had, I had some good in me. And I hoped I always would. I made up my mind a long time ago that if me and Clyde break up our friendship one day, I would always be there for Keisha.


Instead of Keisha dying as a young kid like the doctors said she probably would, she reached her teens and kept on ticking. But Clyde said it was hard on him because for every year Keisha lived, he felt like it was "borrowed" time, so he made the best of it. He got more and more attached to her. He knew it was going to be hard to let her go when her time ran out.

Keisha's legs was so weak, she had to start walking with *two* canes. By the time I met her, she couldn't even lay down for more than a couple of hours at a time because that fluid was settling faster. She had to sleep propped up in a chair because if she laid her head down, she would wake up with a granddaddy of a headache. It made me cry when Clyde told me how him and his grandmother had to get up umpteen times during the night to turn the girl over and make sure she hadn't slid off the chair she slept in. When Clyde moved into an apartment by hisself, he hired a nurse woman to go help his grandmother with Keisha a few days a week. That meant Clyde needed even more money . . .

Clyde told everybody he would do whatever it took to make his daughter's life as enjoyable as possible. That was probably Clyde's biggest challenge. See, Keisha being the smart girl she was, she liked the same things other young people liked—nice clothes, all the latest CDs, her own big-screen TV, eating out. Even though some ignorant people pointed at and ran from Keisha in public, that didn't bother Clyde or Keisha. He still took her out all the time. When he was around ignorant ghetto people, he made sure them motherfuckers all seen that Glock in his waistband. You wouldn't believe how fast they stopped pointing and laughing at Keisha then.

Being treated like a freak didn't never bother Keisha. "Daddy says I'm just as good as anybody," she bragged, grinning out that hole on the side of her face that used to be a mouth. "And even better than some people."

"And he's right," I agreed. I prayed that one day I would have a child as happy and well-adjusted as Keisha.

Even with that face of hers, Clyde took the girl to an expensive beauty parlor and the women kept Keisha's hair looking fly. One month it was cornrows. Another month the girl wanted a weave like Diana Ross.

For her sweet sixteen birthday party, Clyde invited a bunch of kids from the 'hood to come, and every single one of them little devils said no! So Clyde paid them to come, and of course they all came then. I was there, for free, and I was glad to be there. I never seen Keisha so happy than I did that day. Tears came to my eyes when a boy asked her to dance. Even though Clyde had paid him, the boy looked like he was having a good time. And so did Keisha.

"Look at me, Ester! I can dance, too," she yelled, her feet going every which way as that poor boy dragged her across the floor.

Once that girl got the hang of it, she almost danced everybody off the floor. Them useless legs of hers didn't slow her down. And let me tell you, you ain't seen nothing 'til you seen that girl dance the salsa the way I taught her—dragging one leg one way, dragging the other leg the other way, hips bouncing like jumping beans. When Keisha danced, her head looked like a big dented rock, and her eyes rolled back in her head like somebody having good sex. It was such a sight, I didn't know whether to laugh or cry.

Even before me and Clyde got real close, other women, mostly rich White women he met on one of his many jobs, had already spoiled him by giving him money. Besides, it made his life with Keisha easier. So it wasn't no big deal when I started spoiling him by giving him my money, too. I even told him how I got paid. He didn't like the tacky way I made money, but he never turned none down, though.

"Ester, hustlin' them streets the way you doin' will get you killed or messed up for life real quick. Baby, them street tricks'll end up hustlin' you," Clyde told me. "A pretty young girl like you could play with a much better class of tricks. You ought to be gettin' paid in nice hotels with clean dudes from out of town or nice married men in the suburbs. Like the ones I know . . ."

"I don't know how to hook up with men like that. I been in the ghetto all my life," I reminded him. "Where they at?"

"They everywhere. I been dealin' with upscale men like that for beaucoup years," Clyde bragged.

Clyde wasn't lying about that. Even though he was friends with a lot of thugs, and other people who worshipped the low-down side of the law, he really did have "friends" in high places. All of them horny as hell. In addition to all the other jobs he had already done, he worked in some nice restaurants, and he worked in some of the biggest, most expensive hotels in San Francisco. Big stars and other every-day rich people went to them places all the time. Clyde had even parked cars and worked as a cabana boy in L.A. There was nothing like the beaches in a lusty place like L.A. to make weak rich people want to get loose. And Clyde was there to tighten them up.

Clyde was the kind of person rich people liked to take aside and spill their guts to when they got drunk. Some of them same drunk people wanted Clyde to do more than listen to them. You would be surprised at how many fat rich ladies, White ones especially, wanted to go to bed with a husky Black dude like Clyde, at least once. Some of them women wanted to do it real bad so they could get back at their husbands for some shit they done. And some did it just to see what all the fuss was about Black men in the bedroom. Them women wanted Clyde bad enough to pay him some money or give him expensive gifts.

Clyde's own words was, "If they fool enough to give me money to do what I'd probably do to 'em for free anyway, the least I can do is be fool enough to take it." He laughed when he said that.

When it was men sharing their life stories with Clyde, the subject *always* got around to women like me.

"Well, since you know so much, you be my man and hook me up with some of them tricks who come from out of town and who live in the suburbs."

And that's just what Clyde did.

"I make the phone calls, y'all make the house calls," he sometimes joked.

I never really liked sleeping with men for money. To me, it was always just a job.

Clyde's newest "bride" (I guess that's the best description) Lula already said she didn't plan to do but enough tricks to get herself situated. But that's what Rockelle said and look at her now! As much as I hated to admit, that shit Clyde fed to me about Lula being new and maybe cooking up a scam on Mr. Bob made a lot of sense. I *had* to go with her to make sure that didn't happen because I couldn't have no new girl interfering with my money. Mr. Bob was special to me.

I would have been cooking my own goose by not having Mr. Bob's back. He asked for me more than any of the other girls. When he traveled, I was the only one he usually took with him for emergencies. So far, all I'd had to do on those trips was sit around and drink and go shopping with Mr. Bob's credit cards. What more could I ask for?

Mr. Bob was real entertaining, too. He'd play the piano for me, do magic tricks, and teach me French words. The real fun happened once, and if, I got him into his bed. Most of the time he couldn't come if I called him. I think he just liked being naked with women for the thrill of it. He'd flop around on his bed for a minute or two, then deflate like a stuck balloon. But every now and then, Mr. Bob managed to stay sober long enough to do the job. And, believe it or not, he done it good!

Clyde was right after all. It would be better for all of us for me to go with Lula on her first date to Mr. Bob's house.

I would make sure she done a good job on Mr. Bob—but not too good. That was my job.

# Chapter 14

# LULA HAWKINS

Clyde didn't want me to be Rosalee's roommate. After only a month, he suggested I move out of her apartment.

"Rosalee needs her space to keep her mind clear. When she get distracted, I got a mess on my hands. She can be as mean as a old settin' hen. That husband she left back there in Motown let her go around unsupervised. That was why she ran amok to the point where she threw him aside to come out here with her mama. Sister-girl got some seriously spooky, down-home, southern-fried shit goin' on in her head, and you ain't too much better. But you a lot easier to keep in line than Rosalee, and I like that," Clyde told me. I was in his bed with my head on his chest. He had a strong heart. With every beat, my head rose like a cloud.

Clyde was the first man I'd made love to since Bo. Well, there had been quite a few trick sessions since Bo, but they didn't count. To me, screwing a trick was just another bodily function. But it was still on the same page as lovemaking— but at the bottom of the page, even below masturbation.

While a lot of people just shared a cigarette after sex, or a joint in a lot of cases, Clyde and I curled up in each other's arms and had some deep conversations.

I'd only been with Clyde a week before he decided to see for himself why so many of his clients were already calling him up and asking for another date with me. One, the popular Mr. Bob, had already put in his bid to be one of my regulars. That really got Clyde's attention. It got to the point that every time he saw me, he looked at me with a sparkle in his eyes and a sly grin on his face. I knew that the other girls noticed it, Rockelle especially.

"Don't let Clyde's long-eyed looks go to your head, girl. He used to do the same thing to me when I was fresh," she told me with a sly smirk. I noticed right away how Rockelle seemed to keep some distance between herself and the other girls, even when we were all together. She was quick to disagree about something and quick to point out a flaw in one of us. Like the time Rosalee told us how a new trick had admired her long legs. "Too bad you got such knobby knees. And didn't I see a varicose vein the other day?" Rocky said to Rosalee.

Anyway, I ignored Rockelle's comments when it came to the attention Clyde paid to me. Ester was the opposite. "Get ready to spread your legs, girl. Clyde's got that same look in his eyes he had just before the first time he jumped on me."

I guess I could say that when Clyde was ready for me, I was ready for him. I had experienced such an intense sex life with Larry that I had perfected almost every trick in the book and then some. If I didn't know anything else, I knew how to please a man in bed.

Tonight was my second time in Clyde's bed. It had been a long day. Clyde had taken me to see some of the magnificent sights in San Francisco that people came from all over the world to see. We'd had breakfast in a sidewalk café in Haight Ashbury, walked and shopped all over Chinatown, rode the cable cars, and had drinks on a party boat on the Bay facing Alcatraz. Since I had never been outside of the south until now, seeing things that I had only seen in movies and magazines was a real experience for me. I behaved like the country girl I really was.

In the Castro District, home of most of the city's gay population, I played a guessing game with Clyde, trying to determine which people were men and which ones were women.

After a heavy dinner and several glasses of wine in an Italian restaurant near Fisherman's Wharf, and an hour of salsa dancing at a Latin nightclub south of Market Street, Clyde took me to his apartment in the expensive Marina District. We drank more wine and listened to Miles Davis before we wobbled into his bedroom.

I would curse Larry Holmes until the day he died for spoiling me. I knew that for the rest of my life, I would compare every other man I slept with—real lovers and tricks—with Larry. Poor Clyde. Fucking him the second time was just as dull and unsatisfying as the first.

As cool and sexy as Clyde acted and looked, his lovemaking style was on the level of a schoolboy. At least to me. He would have had a fit if I'd told him how Ester and I discussed his bedroom techniques. He was clumsy and loud. And kissing him was like kissing a fish. He pursed his thick lips, kept his eyes open, and made barnlike noises that would have made me laugh out loud if I hadn't been so drunk.

Lying to Clyde about how great a lover he was, was something I knew I was going to have to get used to. So much for the myth about all Black men being such great lovers. As a matter of fact, he didn't even excite me as much as my dead husband, Bo. Poor Bo. He had approached lovemaking in the most unromantic way, spreading my legs and probing and staring at my most sensitive areas like a gyne-cologist.

I was glad when Clyde leaned over and lit up a joint. I just didn't like the conversation he'd started about me living with Rosalee.

"I don't want to live by myself," I told him. "Payin' that high-ass rent, not havin' anybody to talk to would depress me." My head was back on his firm, smooth chest. His heart was beating even harder. I could even hear it thumping like a drum. I liked the way Clyde smelled and tasted tonight. There was butterscotch residue on his lips from a mysterious drink he'd had earlier. I didn't like to think about it often, but if things had been different, I would have wanted Clyde to be more to me than what he was. I felt safe when I was with him.

Clyde waved his hand. The room was dark, except for a dim lamp on the nightstand and the moonlight coming in through the window. "Hold on now. Let me finish what I started." Clyde cleared his throat and started talking in a loud, anxious voice that could have also been described as angry. "Shit, girl. You ain't got to live by yourself. I done fixed it up with Ester. She would love to have you share her place with her."

I didn't like where this conversation was going, but I knew it was useless to try to change the subject. "I don't know about livin' with Ester. That girl's got too much en-ergy. I get tired just listenin' to her talk. It'd be like livin' with a talkin' head. Anyway, I don't think she likes me that much. She makes these pig faces every time I tell her about somethin' you did for me." My breath caught in my throat, my chest got tight. The rest of my body got stiff. I felt like a slab of stone. My head felt so heavy, I couldn't lift it to look at Clyde's face to see his reaction.

"Well, like I said, I done fixed it with her. She'll be expectin' you to move your shit in this weekend. You'll be doin' me a favor, anyway. I want you to keep an eye on her. I don't trust her."

I was finally able to lift my head, even though it still felt as heavy as a brick. I turned to face Clyde. In the glow of what little light was available, all I could see was the outline of his head, the whites of his eyes, and his teeth. For a moment, it looked like his head was floating in midair.

"Ester? You don't trust Ester? I thought she was your main wife."

"Main my ass," he said, laughing. "I don't trust that woman."

"But you trust me?" I asked, my mouth struggling to get the words out. "Why me?"

He laughed again, but then his voice took on a serious tone. "Me and you, we come from the same tribe, same part of the country. If I can't trust you, I can't trust no woman. Besides, if a brother can't trust a sister, he can't trust nobody."

After Larry, a *brother,* I wasn't so sure of much anymore. Especially when it came to trust. But I was learning a lot about the games men played. Clyde had his own agenda. He wanted to keep his women on guard with one another, hoping it would benefit him in some way. I felt it would benefit me if I kept Clyde happy. I hauled off and kissed him.

"I appreciate you feelin' the way you do about me, Clyde. But I'm curious. Rosalee's a sister, and she's from the south, too. You don't trust her?"

Clyde groaned. "Like I said, Rosalee got too many issues. She don't trust nobody, includin' herself. A woman like that is dangerous and leanin' toward bein' downright evil. She superstitious, too. She goes to fortune-tellers, burns candles, and she calls them psychic hot lines."

I wondered what Clyde would say if I told him I went to fortune-tellers, burned candles, and called the psychic hot line, too. But I didn't admit it because I didn't want to know how Clyde would react. Especially since I had him where I wanted him for now.

That weekend, I moved in with Ester. I didn't spend too much time thinking about it because I didn't plan to associate with her, Clyde, or any of the others for too long anyway. Just long enough to get myself straightened out financially. Just like Rosalee and Rockelle were always saying.

Sleeping with strange men for money was something of which I was not proud. But other than for money, I had every excuse in the world. My own mama and how she'd supported us was one of my reasons. And I could not ignore the fact that my own grandmother had predicted my future. Besides, trick money was the easiest money I'd ever made. The way we operated was a lot healthier, safer, and respectable than the girls working the streets. Some nights Ester, Rockelle, and I cruised up and down San Francisco's red-light streets in Ester's Jetta commenting on the pathetic women strolling the streets. A lot of them had serious drug problems so they looked like hell. That's why the easiest, richest tricks came to clean, healthy-looking women like us.

"Holy moly, some of these girls make these blocks look like Jurassic Park," Ester said, a pitying tone in her voice. We all stared as an Asian woman in her *sixties* strutted her stuff in a pair of white hot pants. She was too pitiful for words.

Most people thought that all tricks were just as slimy and crude as some of the women who worked the streets. That was not true. Not only had I been with some of the classiest men in the country, I'd even had fun a few times. And so far, every trick I'd been with had been nice to me.

I was learning a lot about men and sex. That tired belief
that all Black men were great in bed was not the only myth
I'd found to be untrue. Latin men were not the lovers they
were made out to be, either. That was a lie Ester said Latin
men had probably started themselves, which was probably
true of Black men, too.

I had a regular Mexican trick who lived in a big pink
mansion in Pacific Heights. Ramon Suarez was divorced and
owned a popular restaurant near Union Square. Judging
from his size, he must have sampled everything on the
menu. The tight undershirts he wore kept his titties in place,
but when he got naked, he scared me. My biggest fear was
that he would have a stroke or a heart attack while he was in
bed with me. There was more sweaty hair on his chest and
arms than on his head. He weighed too much for me to allow
him to get on top of me. There was so much fat around his
crotch, it wasn't easy finding his short, thick, foul-smelling
dick. I had to straddle him and squat like I did when I went
to the toilet.

And that was exactly what it felt like.

Ramon never stopped talking. Not even when we were
having sex. He bragged about his money, his good family
back in Argentina, his five sons in private schools, his way
with women. "My little *puta* this, my little *puta* that." I didn't
mind Ramon calling me a *puta,* until Ester told me that it
was Spanish for slut or something just as filthy. Just knowing
that he thought of me that way was bad enough. But the fact
that it was true made it seem even worse. I knew that Bo was
probably rolling over in his grave.

I felt even worse about dating Ramon when he made me
promise I wouldn't speak to him if I ever ran into him in
public when he was with his friends.

Ramon's insensitive request made me even more determined to get my shit together and get up out of the business

before it was too late. I didn't want to end up like Rockelle. That uppity, high-yellow battle-ax was so dependent on the fast easy money, she was going behind Clyde's back and freelancing on the streets, too.

Ester and Rosalee also occasionally worked the streets behind Clyde's back. They took overflow tricks to the motel where I'd met Ester, and they kept all the money for themselves. However, they didn't make it a habit the way Rockelle did.

For Rockelle to be on such a high horse, she associated with people I wouldn't want to know where I lived. Ester and I had rescued her twice when two Latina girls got in her face for working their territory.

I smelled trouble. I just hoped that I was long gone by the time it happened, so that I wouldn't get caught up in that, too.

# Chapter 15

# ROCKELLE HARPER

I didn't like it when my wives-in-law made me angry. It made me have feelings toward them that I later regretted. But I couldn't help myself tonight. I wanted to kill Ester and Lula. It was just like those nosy bitches to follow me over to Capp Street in the Mission District. That's where a lot of the street girls worked. They took care of business behind or between parked cars, doing two tricks for the price of one, or for free if the motherfucker was packing a weapon.

I didn't make half the amount of money on the streets that I made working for Clyde, but in my case, every dollar counted. Besides, what I made on the streets was all mine.

Ester and Lula knew more about my business than they needed to know, and I didn't like that one bit. So what if I needed a little extra money every now and then. Let those heifers try to raise three kids on the few dates that Clyde set up for me.

Tonight was a bad one for me. Mainly because I was still pissed off with Ester and Lula for spying on me. I couldn't get rid of the scowl on my face. And it probably had something to do with my trick canceling a date after he saw me.

Clyde had set me up with this Jewish doctor from San Jose, in San Francisco to attend a medical convention.

"Mr. Goldstein is a good time, baby. He's into spankin' so he needs a big, strong, strappin' honey like you. But don't worry, you'll get to spank the shit out of him, too. Don't you hurt him now. He's one of the biggest cash cows I know."

"I've never spanked a man before." I sighed, picturing some freak in a mask greeting me at the door with a paddle in his hand. "I've only spanked my kids," I admitted.

"Just close your eyes and pretend you spankin' one of your kids," Clyde said impatiently. "Anyway, he's a cool dude. I used to play cards with him when he lived in 'Frisco. You'll love him to death," Clyde assured me.

I hadn't met a single one of Clyde's customers whom I "loved to death," even though he said that every time he sent one of us on a date for the first time with a regular customer. It was just a job and there was no love in it for me. Except for the money.

Mr. Goldstein had a suite at the Hyatt Regency, the same hotel Liz Taylor stayed at when she came to San Francisco. As soon as that motherfucker saw me, he decided he wasn't so horny after all and practically chased me back out the door! I called Clyde from my cell phone as soon as I got in the elevator and told him what happened. But that goddamn Jew had already called Clyde and told him God knows what about me! All Clyde told me was, "Dude asked for a stout Black woman. He said he didn't like your attitude, girl. What's your problem?"

"Nothing. I just had some things on my mind," I said, whimpering.

"Well, you better get them things off your mind if you want to get paid," Clyde snapped.

"What about Mr. Bob? He hasn't asked for me in a long time," I whined, so mad and offended I was trembling. I could tell that Clyde was getting impatient by the way he kept letting out his loud breath and snorting.

"Listen, baby, Mr. Bob ain't never called for you on his own. I only set you up with him when there wasn't nobody else to send. Now you sit tight. This is the Christmas week and things is slow. You ought to be at home with your babies anyway."

"That's just it, Clyde. It's Christmas and I want it to be a nice one for my kids. You know how greedy my oldest daughter is. Please, hook me up." I didn't like to beg, but then I did a lot of things I didn't like to do. Like put up with my daughter, Juliet's smart mouth. Juliet was only ten, but she was grown enough to criticize everything about me, from my weight to the way I dressed. I had to do everything I could to please that child. I couldn't stand the thought of her feeling about me the way I had felt about my mother. Well, it had already come to that, but there was still time for me to keep it from getting any worse. My kids were all I had left in the world. I _had_ to keep them happy.

"Oh, I got beaucoup goodies for your three babies. Keisha's at my place wrappin' gifts for 'em now. But I can't help you with no other date tonight, sister. Now you have a Merry Christmas. I'll call you Sunday after I get home from church."

Clyde hung up before I could say another word. I was so angry, I was gritting my teeth like a mad dog. It was still early and I had just enough money on me for a cab to take me over to Capp Street.

It was just my luck to get a cabdriver who was too paranoid to take me all the way there. Cabdrivers got robbed there all the time. A few had even been killed. He dropped me off on Market Street, in the middle of downtown where he felt "safe." I had to take two buses to get to my destination.

Things started to look up once I got to Capp Street. None of the regular girls were on the corner. Just a scowling, homeless old White woman pushing a stolen grocery store cart filled to the top with her grungy possessions. She didn't waste any time getting on my case.

"Hey!" she yelled, waving a gnarled hand at me. She had on enough dusty, ill-fitting clothes for three people—dirty rags she had no doubt fished out of a trash can. A knitted cap covered her head and the top half of her face. I could barely see her bloodshot, beady eyes. But there was no mistaking the extreme look of contempt on her face. "I'm talkin' to you, you low-down piece of shit. The mayor's goin' to run all of you sleazy tramps off these streets. You fat horny pig!"

It had come to this. Even a filthy, garbage-eating old homeless woman had no respect for me.

I surprised her when I said, "Merry Christmas to you, too."

The woman grumbled and moved on. A few minutes later, a few anxious men slowed down their cars and waved dollar bills at me. After four hours and a lot of fumbling around in the backseats of cars that looked like low-riding boats, with men so gross I almost threw up in their laps, I called it a night.

Even though I was depressed, I was glad my kids would have a nice Christmas after all.

# Chapter 16

# HELEN DANIELS

I always kept the door to my room locked when I was in it, and even when I wasn't in it. I didn't want my mama to sneak up on me while I was playing around on the computer Daddy gave me for my birthday this year.

"Maybe this computer'll keep you occupied enough so we won't have to worry about you all the time," Daddy had told me, his gray mustache looking like a fuzzy worm wiggling up over his lip. He looked like a schoolteacher sitting at the desk in my room, showing me how to use my new Dell computer.

"I won't get in no more trouble, Daddy," I chirped. My mind was spinning in so many different directions, I couldn't even remember the last stupid thing I'd done to upset my mama and daddy. I smiled at Daddy before I asked him what else I was getting for my birthday. Like he did most of the time when I got on his nerves, he just waved his hand in the air and rolled his eyes back in his head. Then he trotted out of my room back to the den to do whatever it was he did in there. I didn't care. I had me a Dell computer!

It seemed like every time I turned my Dell on, naked people popped up on my monitor, whether I wanted them to or not. I couldn't figure out how all of those people out there found out about me to be sending me so much stuff! There were titties, butts, and peckers all over my screen!

And I liked it.

I had been looking at naked people and playing around in chat rooms for a week that day when Mama came knocking at my door. She was beating on it like the police.

"Helen, open this door!" For an old woman, my mama had a young voice, and she knew how to use it. I hit a button on my keyboard to make the pictures on my screen shrink to a little bitty space down at the bottom before I ran and opened my door. I cracked it just enough for Mama to see my face.

"Yes, Mommy?"

Before some more words even got out of Mama's mouth, she let out a deep breath and looked at me like she was seeing me for the first time. I could tell she was tired. Her eyes were puffy and red, her arm was up against the wall outside my room to help prop her up. She was a wreck.

"Helen, would you please not lock the door to your room? There is no reason for you to lock your door." Mama's voice did not match her face. She was sixty-six and looked and acted it. Ever since she retired from her job at a bank last year, she stopped dressing up and making up her face. Lines and wrinkles had taken over, making it look like she had on a mask made out of brown crepe paper. But she used to be a pretty woman. I knew that because of all the old pictures she had laying around of her when she was real young. She used to have thick black hair that touched her shoulders, big light brown eyes that slanted up, and because my daddy used to be a dentist, she still had perfect white teeth. I got my mama's looks. Not the way she was now, but the way she looked when she was young. Back then, hella men whistled at her. Uh-huh. Now I was the one the men whistled at. Every time I walked down a street. People would be surprised if I told them how many construction workers rubbed on my butt when I stopped to talk to them on the days that Mama let me go walking by myself.

And I liked that, too. I had been thinking about that just before Mama came banging on my door.

"What do you want?" I asked.

"Rockelle Harper wants you to come to her house in an hour to babysit. She said to bring your sleeping clothes on account of she'll be out for the night. That old man she nurses has gotten sicker, and he will need her more. I hope you don't mind helping her with those children." Mama rubbed her nose and stared at me. She had a face that looked more like a mask. Her expression was always the same. It was hard to tell when she was mad, sad, or glad. The only way I ever knew how she was feeling was when she told me. "I'm so glad Rockelle has so much trust in you." Mama patted her jaw and parted her lips like she wanted to smile, but I knew she couldn't anymore.

I grinned and shifted most of my weight to one side. "Me, too," I said, holding on to my grin.

"It's done wonders for your disposition." Mama stood back and put her hands on her hips. "And that fool Reverend Mays said that there wasn't no hope for you . . ."

I nodded because our preacher was a fool and always had been. The only hope he had was trying to pinch my titties in the church basement. I had refused to go back to that church when Daddy and Mama tried to make me. They gave up real quick when I told them why I didn't want to go back. We even started going to a different church, but I didn't want to go to that one, either. I told them that if God was everywhere, all the time, like Reverend Mays said He was, then I could talk to God without even leaving my room.

"Uh-huh." I stood up straight and opened my door all the way. "Tell Miss Rocky I'll be right on over." Girls like me had a hard time hiding our excitement, but I tried. I started grinning and blinking. There was nothing I liked better than going to Miss Rocky's house. That's where I had the most fun. When she didn't ask me to babysit, and I had no other reason to be there, I'd watch her house from my bedroom window.

After her husband, Joe, left her to run away with another woman, Miss Rocky started having all kinds of strange folks in and out of her house. Every now and then, a man named Clyde with a cute face for a man came by Miss Rocky's house when I was there. He would look at me with a long eye until Miss Rocky would shoo me out of the room.

Clyde never stayed that long at Miss Rocky's house and sometimes when he left, Miss Rocky would be so fidgety she would have to drink a beer or something else. A Mexican woman and two other Black ladies came and went at Miss Rocky's house all the time, too. They would drink and grin and whisper in one room while I looked after the kids in another part of the house. Right after the ladies left, Miss Rocky would start cussing. Then she would tell me that they were greedy heifers because they always slurped up all her alcohol.

Miss Rocky had a computer, too. One night while I was online in a chat room, a man in Australia sent me an instant message, then an e-mail with a picture of his dick attached! At first, I thought it was a long, fat mushroom. So I laughed out loud, LOL in computer talk. But the real fun was all that other stuff that Miss Rocky tried to hide in her house.

Now, I didn't like to snoop through other people's things, but what happened with Miss Rocky wasn't my fault. While I was going through the closet in her bedroom, I stumbled across a box under a pile of clothes. In it, I found a copy of

*The Spectator* with a picture of her in a skimpy little outfit, with her tongue sticking out like a snake.

*The Spectator* was this newspaper small enough to fold under your arm like *The Enquirer,* and just as scandalous. The people in this newspaper liked to get naked or squeeze into some black leather, hide their faces with masks, and show off. Our paperboy didn't bring this kind of newspaper to our house. I didn't know where they sold this nasty stinking thing. I knew about it on account of I found a copy in my big brother's house smashed between some books on a case in his living room.

So, anyway I cracked open *The Spectator,* and there was Miss Rocky in a nightgown, stretched out on a black rug, looking right into the camera! Honest to God, my eyes almost rolled out of my head. I wondered what nasty so-and-so took this picture. Anyway, her just laying there half naked must not have been enough for her. There were words next to her picture: *Let Baby Love cum ROCK your world.* You would think that these people running a newspaper, even a nasty newspaper, would at least learn how to spell *come.* And Baby Love? Uh-huh. She could call herself whatever she wanted to. Miss Rocky's real name was Rockelle Harper.

Right below Miss Rocky's picture was a telephone number. Now I knew Miss Rocky's number by heart, but this was a different one. Then I remembered Miss Rocky had had the phone company come to the house and hook up another phone in her bedroom with a different number two weeks earlier. As soon as the telephone man left, she'd hooked up an answering machine to it and told me not to never answer that particular telephone when she left me in her house to look after her kids.

"Why?" I'd asked her.

"Because I said so, that's why." She waved her thick, lemon-colored hand at me, her long curved nails looking like a hawk's. She was being a real bitch. Well, two could play that game. I decided right then and there to act like I hadn't heard her tell me never to answer that new telephone.

And it's a good thing I did answer Miss Rocky's other telephone, first chance I got. How else would I have found out what I did? Just last night, right after Miss Rocky left her house with that snooty Mexican woman named Ester who wore a red dress and drove a red car, that mysterious telephone started ringing. I just happened to be in Miss Rocky's bedroom looking for the key to her liquor cabinet. Miss Rocky had turned the ringer off, so I couldn't really hear the telephone when it rang. But the answering machine made a clicking noise when it came on, so that's how I knew somebody was calling. Miss Rocky and that Mexican woman pulled off in that red car just in time. I turned up the volume on the answering machine. Come to find out, it was a man, and he had a real nice voice.

I cleared my throat and took a real deep breath. Then I sat down on Miss Rocky's bed with that blue velvet bedspread she just got. I crossed my legs and cocked my head to the side, making myself real comfortable. I pretended I was in my bedroom.

"Hullo?" I said, so nervous I almost choked on some air.

"Uh, is Baby Love in?" He sounded White.

"You mean Rockelle?"

"I'm sorry."

"That's her real name. Sometimes we call her Rocky."

A long time passed. The man was being real quiet, but I could tell he was still there because I could hear him breathing and I could hear music in the background. I cleared my throat to get his attention.

"Is this 555-1986?" he asked, finally.

I looked at the number that was printed on the front of the phone. "Yup," I told the man.

He coughed first, then he started talking again, but this time he sounded different. Like he was nervous. "I'm responding to the ad in, uh, *The Spectator.* I liked the photograph they featured."

I figured that. The telephone number under the picture of Miss Rocky in that nasty piece of a newspaper was the same number on the telephone. "I figured that," I told the man, trying to sound like a smart-ass, the way Miss Rocky did when I got on her nerves.

"Baby Love, Rocky, whatever. Is that you? That's a beautiful woman in that photograph."

"No, but I'm a beautiful woman, too. You ought to see me in my blue dress."

I couldn't figure out why this man was laughing. I didn't think there was anything funny about what I'd just said. "Well," he was still chuckling a little, "is Rocky available?"

"No, sir. She had to go to work."

"I see. Well, uh, when do you expect her back?"

"Oh, she comes and goes." I held the telephone real hard and close to my ear. I looked at the door because I heard a noise. It would be just like that wild child of Miss Rocky's, Juliet, to have her ear propped up against the door like me when I was being nosy. I felt the smart thing to do was whisper. "She's got a lot of friends since her husband left her for another woman. That's why she's always on the go these days, if you know what I mean . . ."

The man took a long time to say something else.

"She sounds like a really interesting gal."

"Oh, she sure is. Especially when she's naked." I covered my mouth. I didn't want this man to hear me giggling.

He gasped and started breathing real hard. "I'm sure you are as hot as she is." His voice was husky, like he knew something on Miss Rocky. "Are you her roommate?"

"Something like that," I said, sounding husky myself.

Uh-oh, this was getting good. It sounded like I was about to get all kinds of good stuff on Miss Rocky. What I would do with it, I didn't know. Maybe if she knew that I knew all of her business, she would treat me more like a friend than a babysitter. Shoot. I really liked Miss Rocky. And other than babysitting for her, I tried to do other things I thought might impress her, too. Now, she liked to read her some books. I thought that if I started reading books like her, she'd see that we had that in common and she would mellow out some.

Well, reading a bunch of books didn't do much good for me. One time I wrestled with this granddaddy of a book that Miss Rocky had read called *Clan of the Cave Bear* and all it did for me was make my head hurt. I couldn't tell what that book was about because I couldn't get past page five. It couldn't have been harder for me to read if it had been in Chinese. Anyway, I never was that good when it came to reading.

I started wrapping the telephone cord around my fingers. Then I slid into the red velvet chair that Miss Rocky kept next to her bed. One thing I could say about the woman was she sure knew what to spend her money on. As soon as my butt hit that fancy chair, I snatched up a cute little bottle of perfume with a foreign-looking name I couldn't read, and I sprayed my face, my crotch, my neck, and my wrists.

"Do you . . . uh, date?"

"Yep! I date all the time," I said, sniffing my wrists.

"What's your name? Uh, or do I already know you?"

Now that was a strange question for him to be asking me. I held the telephone away from my face and looked at it before I put it back against my ear.

"Uh-uh. You don't know me," I said, wondering what made this man think we'd met when he was talking to me for the first time just now.

"I see. Well, tell me more about yourself. If Rockelle is

already too busy these days, maybe you and I could work something out. Would you be interested?"

"Uh-huh."

"I'm Arthur."

"Uh-huh."

"Well, do you want to tell me your name?"

"Helen."

"I like that. And what do you look like?"

"Uh, not too bad. I know how to fix myself up real good."

"How old are you?"

"Nineteen."

"Hmmm. You sound younger."

"I got a California ID to prove I'm nineteen."

"But you have . . . *dated.*" He said the word *dated* in a whisper.

"Didn't I tell you yeah!" I snapped at him because he was trying my patience, the same way Miss Rocky's kids did when they got cranky.

He laughed. "You sound like a real spitfire."

"I am," I told him, clueless because I didn't know what a spitfire was. Him being a man and laughing when he called me that word, it had to be something good. "My dates tell me all the time that I am a real spitfire . . ."

My neck was beginning to hurt from me sitting with my head cocked to the side. I turned my ear toward the door so that Miss Rocky's kids wouldn't come in and catch me. It would be just like that little grown-ass Juliet, Miss Rocky's oldest kid. It seemed like no matter what Miss Rocky did for that child, it was never enough. That girl went out of her way to upset her mama.

"So, Helen. Are you available tonight?"

"Uh-uh."

"I guess you already have another date lined up for tonight, huh?"

"Something like that."

"What about tomorrow night?"

"What about it?"

"Could we get together tomorrow? We can meet somewhere in public. If we hit it off, we can go from there."

I rolled my eyes and shook my head. "Can't I just call you back when I want to go on a date with you?"

"I suppose so." He said that real slow. "You sound like a really nice girl. But for tonight, I guess I could call another number. I might get lucky after all."

"Well, you might and you might not."

The man gave me a telephone number and told me the best time to call him. I wrote the number on the back of a Juicy Fruit chewing gum wrapper and slid it down inside my brassiere. Then I hung up.

I was out of breath and so warm, I had to sit there and fan my face for a while before I felt like myself again. I couldn't understand how a married woman could survive being around the same man all the time. Just talking to a man over the telephone for a few minutes had just about wore me out. It had been a really long time since I'd been with a boyfriend. I couldn't remember all I was supposed to do and say.

I deserved a few of Miss Rocky's beers after all I'd just been through. My face was itching and my throat was dry. And I found out I was wet between my legs when on my way to the kitchen to get them beers. I went to the bathroom to pee.

Looking in the mirror over the bathroom sink, I saw what everybody else saw when they looked at me: a pretty girl any man would want to date. When I wore my long, shiny black hair down, people told me that I looked like a younger Janet Jackson. And that was another pretty woman Miss Rocky liked to talk about like a dog. Just yesterday when I was watching Janet's new video on BET, Miss Rocky waltzed by the television and said, "Janet Jackson is nothing but a glorified cheerleader!"

I never argued with Miss Rocky. She was the last person I wanted mad at me. Where else could I kick back so deep and not have anybody bother me? Where else could I drink beers, snoop, and maybe even meet my future husband over the telephone?

Miss Rocky was my girl. I didn't care how bad she talked about her other friends, or Janet Jackson. I didn't even care about how she tried to hide things from me.

People like me are a lot smarter than some people think. I got away with doing some things because people thought I didn't know what I was doing. And, maybe I didn't know what I was doing. But I did it anyway because it felt good.

See, just by looking at me, or by talking to me over the telephone, a lot of people didn't even know I was retarded.

# Chapter 17

# ROSALEE PITTMAN

I could fill a book with all the stupid shit I did in California. For instance, I didn't believe in ghosts, voodoo, and other things that went "bump in the night." But I still had the nerve to spend money on a psychic. Why? Because I couldn't think of any other way for me to get the insight or guidance I felt I needed to get my life in order. Maybe my only hope was a psychic. What else did I have to work with?

There was one thing I could not ignore. Every time I thought about all of the ghoulish things that I didn't believe in, I had to think about the times that the ghost of my dead playmate had visited me and pulled my hair.

No matter what I did or didn't believe in, the psychic I'd been going to had not done me too much good so far. She'd given me some lucky numbers once, and I'd won a couple hundred dollars playing the lottery, but that could have been a coincidence. However, I figured I had nothing else to lose but something to gain, if I was lucky.

I'd made several trips to the Mission District to see Conchita Diaz, a card reader in her seventies from Cuba. Lula had once visited this particular psychic, a bug-eyed, mole-faced old crone, with a cat named Paco, who Ester had hooked her up with. And even though Lula and Ester had admitted that they didn't have a whole lot of confidence in this woman, that still didn't stop me from making an appointment.

On one of my visits to Conchita, I had to dodge bullets from a drive-by shooting in progress. Another time I had to step over a drunk man covered in piss, lying on the cracked sidewalk in front of Conchita's tagged building. I'd even been chased by a pit bull.

Common sense should have told me that Conchita's psychic powers weren't that potent if she hadn't foreseen all of the mess I had to dodge to get to and from her apartment each time. She lived on Valencia, a street littered with sleazy bars and restaurants that should have been closed down a long time ago.

I'd entered Conchita's jungle three times in the last six months. I kept going because she needed the money, and I liked her. And, she made me laugh. That was something I hadn't done much of since moving to California. "The spirits told me you was comin' today and that you'd be bringin' me a bottle of Wild Turkey and a burrito," Conchita told me on my last visit. Before she even brought out her cards, she suggested I trot across the street to a liquor store to pick her up the bottle and some lunch, just to get her in the mood. I ended up getting drunker than she did that day, so I forgot half of everything she told me. It wouldn't have made any difference if I had remembered everything anyway. Her predictions were either not very accurate or a long way down the road.

So far, none of Conchita's predictions had come true: I had not moved into a big beautiful house with a man who "smooched" my feet, my mama had not gotten any better, and I had not stopped sleeping with strange men for money.

The one prediction that stood out in my mind, the same one that Conchita and a faceless woman on a psychic hot line had revealed to me was that I would return to my husband. It was probably the most far-fetched of all the predictions. I had not spoken to my husband, Sammy, since Mama and I took off. However, I had written him a few letters during my first few weeks in California. When that got to be too painful I stopped. But if I did return to Sammy, then all of the other predictions that Conchita had made would become true by default. Because when I was with him, he didn't exactly smooch my feet, but he did worship the ground I walked on. In my book that was close enough.

Sammy was going to inherit and move into a big house in Detroit that his grandmother had promised to leave to him when she passed on. So if Sammy eventually took me back, I'd be living with him in a big beautiful house.

The thing that I wanted the most was for Mama to "get better" so that I could make plans for my future. No matter how much Mama coughed and moaned when she was around me, I knew that she was not as physically sick as she claimed to be. She would often be on her couch moaning when I went to visit her. But she would leap up like a frog as soon as one of her friends invited her to go play bingo or something—while I was still present. Her most serious ailments were all in her mind. The worst being her belief in Miss Pearl's curse.

I'd asked Conchita on my second visit, "What can you tell me about the curse on my mama?" Conchita had lit a candle for me during my first visit. It was supposed to strengthen her ability to conjure up an effective way for me to make Mama get over her fear of Miss Pearl's curse. Conchita gave me a clueless look, so I asked again. "Remember that curse I told you my mama was so scared of? You lit a candle about it. What can you tell me about that now?"

Conchita's big bosom heaved, and she blinked real hard. "Nothin'," she told me, munching on a burrito. "A evil spirit blew out your candle."

I paid Conchita extra to light a stronger candle, but she still couldn't tell me anything about Mama and the so-called curse that had practically ruined my life. She explained, with tears streaming down her face, that the power and interference of the opposing spirits were too strong for an unsophisticated peasant like her.

I didn't want to think about the fact that Mama was taking advantage of me. I loved my mother more than I loved life itself, and I was willing to do just about anything to keep her happy. She'd lost her husband and all but one of her children. She was in a very desperate position. But then, so was I.


I was not proud of the fact that I'd allowed Mama to make me choose between her and my husband. However, one of the few things that kept me going was the fact that Sammy and I were still very young compared to Mama. We had more of a chance for a long, happy life than she did.

It was hard paying rent on two apartments. Especially Mama's. Her rent was almost twice as much as mine, and her expenses cost a lot more to cover. I couldn't really make any plans about my future because my life was more like a merry-go-round that I couldn't get off.

I hated visiting Mama at the senior citizen's apartment complex where she lived. Being around a lot of sick, fussy old people made me sick myself. Sometimes before I could even make it up to Mama's apartment on the third floor, several people stopped me along the way to update me on their health and to complain about every other thing of which they could think. But Mama could outwhine all of her sad friends. She was convinced that she was dying from some unidentified ailment. I just went along with her, telling her that she was going to "get better."

Even as depressing as it was, I still went to visit Mama at least once a week—unless I was out of town on a date or humping local tricks back to back, like I did when Ester, Lula, and Rockelle weren't available. Sometimes I couldn't decide who was profiting off me the most: Mama or Clyde.

I didn't like the level of my position in Clyde's life. Even though Rockelle complained all the time to me that she felt like the lowest one on the totem pole, I didn't agree. And I didn't feel any sympathy for her. I knew that Clyde would always put Ester above me, but I'd known him before Lula and she already outranked me. Clyde wasn't one to give out explanations or answer too many questions. And all he would say about the way he sometimes isolated me from the other girls—like when he made Lula move from my apartment to Ester's—was something like: "I think it'll be better for everybody."

Being the gullible fool that Clyde was, in my opinion, he was too stupid to realize that women like us did kick back together and share information. By "trusting" the wrong women, Clyde was cooking his own goose. He had Lula handle our finances when he wasn't able to, and I knew for a fact that she was robbing him blind. She doled out money to Ester and Rockelle every time they asked her to. And even me, when I needed extra money because of Mama, so I didn't really care about her being in so good with Clyde. I was glad that she was playing him because if it had been me, I would have done the same thing.

Sometimes when an out-of-town regular couldn't get to San Francisco, Clyde sent us to him. The trick had to pay all of our travel expenses in addition to the usual fee. That's how desperate some of them were.

There was a forty-year-old Chinese man in San Diego

who would walk through a firestorm to get to a woman. But when he couldn't, he had her come to him. He was a jewelry salesman, and he came up to San Francisco a couple of times a month. And he was one of the nastiest things on two legs. Of all the outlandish things for a man to ask a woman to do, this one wanted his butt hole licked! I figured Daniel Wong had a hard time finding a woman in San Diego crazy enough to do that shit. Every time he got a hard-on, he called up Clyde. And when he didn't have business in the Bay Area, he sent for one of us, usually me, to hop on a plane and come to him. Somehow, with plastic covering Mr. Wong's dried, ashy crack, I managed to get him off. And I deserved every dime of the five hundred bucks he paid. Especially the times that sucker farted in my face when he came. Shit!

Every time I had to fly to San Diego to do Mr. Wong, I'd laugh off and on all the way down there and back, wondering what my friends in Georgia would think if they knew how far I'd slid into hell. Especially a snob like Shirley Reese, a law student now, who'd looked down her nose at me all through high school, all the while claiming to be my best friend.

I could imagine how Shirley would stop me on the street, tilt her head back and say, "So, Rosalee, what kind of work do you do out there in earthquake country?" And I'd tell her the truth, leaving no stone unturned. She'd stare at me for a long time, shaking her head. Then she'd probably say something like, "Well, we can't all be lawyers." That bitch was on my mind more than any other person from my past. Including Miss Pearl and her spells and threats, and my husband. Poor Sammy. As much as I still loved him, I tried to think about him as little as possible.

Well, I had to go down to San Diego yesterday to pay Mr. Wong a visit. It didn't take me long to get him off, so I was in and out of his house within an hour and on my way back to San Francisco. But I got delayed because of a security incident at the San Diego airport. Because of the September 11 mess, every time a man with an accent and a swarthy complexion started acting suspicious, people working the airports got crazy. This time it was a well-dressed man screaming in a foreign language about lost luggage, then making threats in broken English to "blow up all." The airport was evacuated, and it was three hours later before I could board my plane back to San Francisco.

I had promised Mama that I would come by and take her and one of her friends to lunch. But when I showed up after dinner, she was sitting in her front window, already in her bedclothes, dabbing tears off her face with a napkin.

When I strolled in, bracing myself for her verbal attack, her eyes got wide, and she started blinking real hard.

"Rosie, where you been? I been waitin' on you all day." Mama sniffled like a scolded two-year-old. Her nose looked like a red ball. "I'm all out of my pills. My plants ain't been watered, my carpets ain't been vacuumed. This place is a wreck," Mama complained, waving her arm around the room. No matter how often I stopped by to clean up for Mama, it was never enough. Empty plates and cups were on the coffee table, old newspapers and magazines littered the plaid couch and love seat, and something red had spilled on the carpet, leaving a sticky trail all the way across the floor. The huge TV that I had bought for Mama had clothes draped across the top, held in place by one of her orthopedic shoes.

"I'm sorry, Mama," I said contritely, kicking trash aside. "I, uh, had to work this mornin' and there was a lot of unnecessary confusion that slowed things down," I lied. Well, it wasn't really a complete lie.

Mama stopped sniffling and gave me a guarded look. That soon shifted to a look of suspicion, and it made me nervous. I was as close to being a real model as Mama was. I never told anybody, but I had attempted to get work as a model a few weeks ago. But according to the agent I'd approached who'd looked me up and down with a critical eye and a frown, I wasn't the type they were looking for. Being tall and thin, and looking like a combination of Tyra Banks and Naomi Campbell didn't do me much good unless a trick was looking for that type. "Oh? Modelin' bathin' suits for Macy's again? I hope you remembered to put some lotion all over on your ashy self, girl. I can't have you up there modelin' with your skin lookin' like a gator's." Mama smiled broadly as she gave my hands a quick inspection. I was pleased to see that Mama had perked up. "See how blessed it is to be so pretty. Us dainty women got to stay on top of nature, ain't we?"

"Yes, ma'am." When I leaned over Mama to give her a hug, she lifted her head and attempted to kiss me on the lips. She gasped when I turned my head. The last thing I wanted was for mama's lips to touch mine so soon after I'd licked Mr. Wong's butt. "Uh, I have a slight cold, Mama," I explained, kissing her sweaty forehead.

"It ain't never stopped you before," she reminded, giving me a hard look. "What's that on your neck?"

"Just a rash. I brushed against some, uh, poison ivy the other day when I was out bein' photographed in Golden Gate Park." Damn that Mr. Wong! I had meant to button my jacket all the way up to hide the sucker bite he had caused below my chin.

Mama's face froze and she gasped. "It sure don't look like no rash to me. It look like somethin' else," Mama accused. "You got a boyfriend, ain't you?" Mama could curl her lips into the most extreme frowns I'd even seen. When she did that, her eyes looked like the target dot on a bull's-eye.

"Now, Mama, you know I don't date. That's the one thing

I promised Sammy I wouldn't do, until . . . until me and him decide whether or not we're goin' to stay married." My voice cracked. "Do you still want to go out to eat? I got Ester's car outside."

"I done already ate. Lunch and dinner. If I was to sit around waitin' on you, I'm liable to starve to death. Come on. Clara's in the kitchen." Mama groaned as she struggled to get out of her seat. I grabbed her arm, helped her up, and led her to the kitchen just a few feet down the hall.

Before we even got into the neat, sweet-smelling kitchen, Mama started bragging to Clara, her White friend from across the hall. Clara was hunched over the stove fishing string beans out of a pot with a fork.

"Clara, this is my girl, the model," Mama said proudly. "Ain't she pretty?"

The woman, her eyes half closed, her blue wig on backward, snatched a pair of glasses out of her housecoat pocket, held them up to her eyes, and looked me up and down. A sour look formed on her plain face, making her look even plainer.

"She's not that pretty," the woman said, chewing and shaking her head.

Mama motioned me to lean closer. "That Clara. She just jealous 'cause you look better than that flat-ass girl of hers. It'd kill her to admit a Black girl is pretty," Mama whispered with a conspiratorial sneer. "Now, Rosie, when you goin' to move me out of this place?"

"Move you? I just moved you in here a few months ago. I can't afford to move you again. And what's wrong with this place?" I hollered, almost choking on the air I sucked in.

Mama ignored her friend and led me back to the living room. "I'm the only Black woman up in here, that's what's wrong with this place." Mama snorted, rolling her eyes at me, as I eased her down on the couch. "Me and you can get us a real nice place together. I can help you get ready to go out on your model jobs. I can iron your clothes, carry your things to and from your jobs, and help you beat off them randy photographers. I read in the *People* magazine—or was it the *National Enquirer*—that when Brooke Shields was modelin', her mama went with her everywhere she went."

I let out a painful breath, cursing myself for weaving such a web of lies and deceit. "Mama, my work is too hectic for a woman in your condition. You know you need round-the-clock care. The doctor said so. I can't take care of you and work, too. You have to stay in here until . . . until you get better." I sat down next to Mama. "How would you like to go shoppin' tomorrow?"

Mama's face lit up like a flamethrower. "That'll work. I told that lady at the Neiman Marcus that I would come back down there soon. She the same one who used to wait on the Pointer Sisters. She used to workin' with celebrities like you. Strange thing though, she keep tellin' me she don't know you. I guess all models look alike to her, huh?"

"Uh-huh," I groaned. I could not understand why a woman like my mother, who had spent her whole life shopping in stores like Wal-Mart, Goodwill, and the dollar stores, now only wanted to shop at the most expensive stores in town. But I guess I was to blame for that. It was my lie about how I'd once modeled swimsuits for Neiman Marcus. "I'll take you to the mall."

Mama gasped so hard she had to cough. "The mall? What mall? Why would I wanna go to a mall? Girl, you got a image to keep up. Respectable models don't be shoppin' at no Payless or Kmart!"

"It's a lot cheaper."

"Cheaper?" Mama roared. "I bet Cindy Crawford wouldn't never fix her lips to pronounce such a word—"

"Mama, we can't keep spendin' money the way we've been doin'," I insisted. "I don't make the kind of money Cindy Crawford makes yet."

"All right then," Mama snapped. "Don't worry about takin' me nowhere. Clara's girl said she'd take me to Neiman Marcus herself if she had to." Mama turned her head toward the kitchen and yelled, "Clara, tell your girl I wanna go with y'all tomorrow. My girl done got too busy to be bothered."

"I didn't say that, Mama. Look, I spend a lot of money on you. You got everything you need and then some," I hissed, looking around the room. Clara was in the doorway, a smug look on her face. "Mama, I can't afford to do no more than I'm already doin'. Be patient. Be happy you are in a nice safe place. Enjoy what you already have and be happy. I promise you, you only have to stay here until you get better."

Mama's teeth clicked and clacked like castanets. She started fanning her face with a rolled-up *Ebony* magazine. The loose skin under her arm flapped like a sleeve on an oversized shirt. "Girl, you know I ain't never gwine to get no better than I am now. That Pearl made sure of that."

It had been a while since Miss Pearl's name had come up, but she was always on my mind. Like I said, I had convinced myself that Miss Pearl didn't really have anything to do with all the tragedies my family had suffered, but I knew that Mama still thought so.

"Mama, if Miss Pearl had really done somethin' to our family, we wouldn't be livin' as good as we are now. We'd probably both be dead by now."

Mama gave me an exasperated look and shook her head.

"Well, I ain't far from death. It's gettin' closer and closer. Every time I look up, they haulin' somebody out of here to the morgue." Mama shifted her eyes, like she was trying to think up more things to say that would strengthen her position. "Just last night I had a real sharp pain cut through my belly like a sword. I hope it ain't cancer. That's what killed Mr. Lang next door."

"Mama, this is an old folks' complex, not a youth camp. Most of the people in here were already half dead when they checked in. They know they won't be leavin' this place alive." I immediately wished that I could take my words back.

Mama's face looked like it wanted to slide into her lap.

"Oh, you really know how to make a dyin' woman feel good. I bet you can't wait to bury me," Mama said, rotating her neck.

"I didn't come over here to argue with you, Mama." I draped my arm around her rounded shoulder.

Mama sniffed, leaned her head back, and shot me an anxious look that was almost childlike. Without warning, she changed the course of our tense conversation. "Rosie, honey, I need me a new color television!"

I moaned and snatched my arm away from Mama's shoulder like I'd been burned. "What's wrong with the one you got now? The warranty hasn't even worn off."

Mama waved her hands high above her head and sucked in her breath, making a face that made it seem like she really was in pain. "Horse feathers. The color ain't no good. I can't be sittin' up in here lookin' at no little green men. And even with my glasses on, I can't tell the Black folks from the White folks on that thing sittin' there," Mama hollered, shaking her finger at the huge television facing us in the living room.

"Yes, ma'am." I sighed. "I'll bring you one the next time I come to visit."

I spent two more hours listening to Mama's list of complaints: her neighbors were racists, her hip hurt, her neck hurt, her back hurt, the quack nurse who came to look in on her had touched her inappropriately and had to be a lesbian, and nightmares kept her from sleeping at night. By the time I left, all I wanted to do was go home and crawl into my own bed.

And that's where I was, hugging a bottle of wine and sucking on a joint, when Clyde called me up around nine.

"Rosalee, if you there, pick up the telephone," he ordered. He was silent a few moments, but I could hear him breathing hard and cussing under his breath. "I ain't playin' with you, girl! Pick up that phone if you there!" I ignored Clyde and turned down the volume on my answering machine, but not low enough. His voice was ringing in my ears. "Mr. Bob's got a hard-on for you, girl. Tonight. Eleven P.M. sharp. Be there. And, I got you, Rocky, and Lula lined up for a foursome with Fat Freddie over in Sausalito tomorrow night. Rocky'll pick you up at nine so y'all can have time to go have a drink first. You better have your juicy, priceless butt on the ball, and you better not be late, girl. Do you hear me? Shit."

I turned off the machine and the telephone and slid down under my covers.

# Chapter 18

# ROCKELLE HARPER

As much as Lula and Rosalee got on my nerves, I didn't mind having to go on dates with them. I didn't like it at first, but the more I got to know them, the easier it got. Especially when the date was that fat-ass Freddie McFarland. Poor Freddie. It took three women at the same time for us to get him off anyway. Compared to Mr. Bob, the trick I always thought of as a dead man walking because he would often fall asleep while he was on top of me, Fat Freddie was one step away from the morgue. But the way he told it, in his gravelly British accent, he was a "ball of fire" who knew how to make women scream. He sure did. When Clyde told me I had to join Rosalee and Lula for a foursome with Fat Freddie, I screamed all right.

Freddie lived in a huge condo, across the Golden Gate Bridge, in Sausalito. He had a live-in cook/housekeeper and a driver, but he sent them off somewhere whenever he entertained women. Like so many men, including that goat I'd married, Freddie thought that all it took to make a woman feel good in bed was a big dick. Well, I had news for him. While the men with the most meat between their legs were running around thinking that they were God's gift to women, the men with the ladyfingers peeping from between their thighs were the ones really keeping us happy. Believing that they were at a disadvantage because of their size, they tried much harder to please.

Freddie was an easy trick once we got him drunk. However, he was a major pain in the ass. He had a face like a mole and weighed more than five hundred pounds, but he still tried to move like a man half his size. And as disgusting as he was, I liked that fat-ass Freddie. He was more than just a trick to me. He was a really nice, fun guy, despite his miserable appearance. He was one of the few tricks I knew who made me feel petite. He was the one who nicknamed me Baby Love, the name I used with my ad in *The Spectator*.

Tonight was no different than any other night with Freddie. The four of us on his king-size bed was a sight. Our four naked bodies—Lula and Rosalee perfect and dark brown; me, light brown and crisscrossed with purple stretch marks; and Freddie, ghostly white and covered in knotty red splotches, like an obscene patchwork quilt. We looked like something that belonged in a Stephen King movie.

Fat Freddie liked to kiss. Since he paid extra for that, I always volunteered to perform that ghoulish task. He didn't mind me keeping my lips closed and my teeth clamped together. I refused to kiss a trick who wanted to stick his tongue in my mouth.

Rosalee and Lula did most of the other work on his vile body. They massaged him all over, commenting on his soft white flesh, and how magnificent his long, fat dick was. Fat Freddie shuddered, squeezed his eyes shut, and squealed like a pig. It took every ounce of my strength to keep from laughing.

After the deed was done, the three of us helped haul Freddie away from his king-size bed. Puffing like we'd been pulling a mule, we escorted him to his living room. We had drinks, slid a dirty movie into the DVD player, and listened to him yip yap about everything from his health problems to all the money he had inherited from his deceased parents.

"You birds sure know how to earn your way. I'll have Clyde set up another little party later in the month for me and the lot of you," Freddie told us, tickling the thick flesh under my arm as I hugged his huge neck. To my everlasting horror, he hauled off and kissed me again. I had to close my eyes and hold my breath. His breath was as foul as horse shit, and his lips felt like rubber. I found it so hard to believe that this man had been married three times, to his first wife for twenty years. It was one thing to get paid to make love with a man as wretched as Freddie McFarland. But I could not imagine getting busy with him for free. I wondered how his wives had managed to do it.

But then again, what did I know? It hurt to know that my own husband had often said some of the same things about me that I thought about Freddie. "Girl, I have to get drunk to get into your stuff anymore. All that lard-smellin' blubber on your ass makes my nature weak," Joe had told me right after the last time we made love. His words had burned like acid. If I'd known his true feelings about my appearance, I would not have seduced him that night. He left me the very next day.

Lula and Rosalee did most of the talking to Freddie, hardly letting me get a word in edgewise. And those two bitches thought they knew everything, telling lame jokes that kept Freddie guffawing. They were too stupid to realize that Freddie was laughing at them, not with them. With their southern accents, half of the time I couldn't understand them. The word *man* came out sounding like *main*. And only countrified women like them would call a man's dick a pecker. Or was it poker they said? I didn't know, and I didn't care, as long as I got paid.

I glanced at my watch. "Let's watch the movie," I suggested, hoping they would all take the hint and just shut up.

"You girls want another drink?" Freddie asked in his hoarse voice. His stiff reddish-blond hair made his head look like a porcupine. My cherry-red lipstick was all over his lips, neck, chest, and face.

I answered for us all. "I'll go make them," I chirped, rushing to the kitchen off to the side of the huge living room.

I took my time mixing a pitcher of strong margaritas. Being alone gave me time to do some thinking. I had had a lot on my mind lately and most of it involved my daughter, Juliet. The girl was driving me crazy. She was not doing well in school, she couldn't get along with her brothers, and she went out of her way to torture me. "Mama, you are getting so fat. You got gray hairs. Mama, you smell like lard." Every one of her complaints stabbed at me like a knife. I actually felt the pain. It was all in my mind, but pain was pain.

The only adult Juliet seemed to respect was Helen, my retarded babysitter. They got along like best friends. The only times that Juliet was tolerable was when Helen was present.

But Helen had been acting strange lately. A few times I'd caught her eavesdropping on my telephone conversations. And just yesterday, I'd come home to find my house smelling like cigars.

"Helen, was somebody in this house?" I'd asked, sniffing and rubbing my nose. It was past midnight. Helen was curled up on my living room sofa under one of my best goose-down comforters. This was where she usually slept when she spent the night. I loomed over the couch, still in my trick clothes and the long trench coat that I often wore on my dates.

"Huh? Huh?" Helen blinked stupidly, her lips moving like one of those talking dummies. She shrugged and gave me a blank stare.

I had only known a few retarded people in my life, so I didn't know that much about their habits and behavior. But Helen was docile and pleasant, and my kids were crazy about her. Especially my daughter, Juliet, who was the most difficult child I had ever known since . . . since myself.

"Who was smoking in here?" I asked, trying to hold back my anger. The last thing I wanted to do was scare this girl off. I needed her more than she needed me.

Helen sat up, rubbing her eyes, yawning, and stretching. "I was, Miss Rocky."

"Cigars?" I asked, watching her carefully. I was too concerned about the cigar odor to ask her about the empty beer cans lined up on the floor in front of the couch. I already knew that Helen often helped herself to my alcohol. "You smoke cigars?"

Helen stretched and yawned some more and gave me another blank stare. "Uh-huh." She looked around the room with a sheepish grin on her face.

"Girl, you know I don't allow smoking in my house!" I boomed.

Helen stood up from the couch so fast, the comforter slid to the floor. The cigar smoke was one thing, and that was bad enough. But I was surprised as hell to see that the girl was naked, too. Looking at her for about half a minute, I realized I was jealous. It was hard to believe that I'd once been as lean and firm as Helen. Without giving it much thought, I sucked in my gut, but the flab around my middle had a life of its own. I shook my head to compose myself.

Like me, Helen was a rough sleeper. Her eyes were puffy. Her arms had scratches from her clawing herself in her sleep. Joe used to tell me that when I got up in the morning I looked like I'd been in a fight. Helen looked like she'd been in a fight. This was the first time I'd seen her look like this and she had slept at my house dozens of times.

Helen shot me a sharp, stunned look. "But what about the times your friends smoke weed in here?" she asked, blinking hard. It was then that I noticed that her eyes were also slightly bloodshot. The same way mine looked after a rough date, something that my daughter had mentioned on more than one occasion.

"Now, look. What I do in my own house is my business. You don't live here. What would your mama say if she found out you were over here smoking?"

"My mama smokes," Helen answered. "My daddy smokes, too. My big brother David smokes."

"Well, just don't do it again. At least not in my house. If you bring cigarettes over here, or cigars, you go out on that porch to smoke. Do you hear me, girl?"

"Uh-huh," she said, nodding hard.

"And another thing—when did you start sleeping naked?"

Helen had a difficult time responding. Her eyes rolled back in her head, she bit her bottom lip, then she looked me in the eye. "Tonight," she said in a meek voice. She then stared at the floor.

I dismissed Helen with a wave of my hand. She returned to the couch and pulled the comforter up over her head. I let her sleep until almost noon the next day, wondering what all my kids could have done for her to be so tired.

After Helen left my house later that Saturday afternoon, I noticed a man's comb in my bathroom on the sink. It had blond hair in it.

But Helen explained that later in the evening when she galloped back across my lawn, running in the front door without knocking. There was a major grin on her eager face. As soon as she got inside, I asked her about the comb.

"It's one of my daddy's old combs. I was using it to practice combing Juliet's new Barbie doll's hair," Helen said in a
steely voice.

"And what about all those beer cans I found on the floor
last night?"

"What about 'em?"

"Didn't I tell you not to drink when you come over here?"

Helen shook her head. "That ain't what you said. You told
me to stay out of your liquor cabinet. Well, I couldn't find the
key nohow, so I got the beers from the refrigerator. The liquor
cabinet and the refrigerator are two different things." She
sniffed so hard her eyes watered.

My exasperation level was as high as it could get. "Your
mama and daddy don't want you drinking *any* alcohol over
here."

Helen shrugged. "Who is going to tell them I been drinking? You? I sure ain't."

I sighed and threw up my hands. "Look, from now on,
when you babysit, I expect you to leave my house looking
just the way you found it. Do I make myself clear? Don't be
leaving combs full of doll hair on my sink and do not drink
any of my alcohol. Do not drink any alcohol, period. That
means, don't bring any over here from home or anywhere
else. Is that clear?"

"Yes, ma'am, Miss Rocky." Helen had a look on her face
that could have meant anything. Her eyes were blank, and
her mouth was hanging open. It was the same way my
daughter, Juliet, looked when she was lying or just trying to
be a smart-ass. I could never tell when Helen (or Juliet) was
lying or just messing with me.

I had to keep reminding myself that Helen was more on
Juliet's level than she was on mine. But Helen's childlike
mind was trapped in the body of a woman.

And that was a dangerous combination.

* * *

"Girl, what's takin' you so long with them drinks?" Rosalee hollered from Freddie's living room.

I cleared Helen out of my thoughts. "I'll be right out," I yelled. I had to take a big swallow of tequila before prancing out of Freddie's kitchen with a tray of drinks to rejoin the activities on his couch.

Once Freddie was asleep, we dragged him to his bed, which was a difficult thing for us to do, considering his weight. We were all panting like dogs. It was such a chore, Rosalee and Lula had to rush back to the living room to have another drink. I stayed in the bedroom a little longer to go through Freddie's wallet. I had decided that I deserved an extra hundred dollars. And I didn't feel bad about "robbing" a trick. Especially one as rich as Freddie. It added a little fun to an otherwise unbearable game. And without some amusement and additional benefits, my job would have been just that much harder.

After I dropped Rosalee and Lula off, I rushed home, driving at breakneck speed because I'd been out longer than I had anticipated. Like I'd hoped, Helen and the kids were all watching music videos on BET.

They hardly paid any attention to me when I sprinted across my living room floor to my bathroom. I rinsed out my mouth and took a long bath with water so hot it felt like my skin was melting.

Other than the money, a bath was the best part of a date.

# Chapter 19

# HELEN DANIELS

I didn't like it when Miss Rocky tripped out on me. She'd been doing that a lot lately. It made me nervous when she gave me strange looks and asked me a lot of nosy questions. It looked like I was going to have to keep both of my eyes on her—with her great big, fat self!

That woman was too nosy for her own good. Now I see why her husband left her for another woman. I couldn't believe that she'd had the nerve to get in my face over a little cigar smoke and a few beers the other night. If I hadn't been so groggy and buzzed from drinking that beer, I would have reminded her that she told me to my face that when I was in her house, I was welcome to make myself at home. And that's just what I'd done. Shoot.

Now I'd have to tell that man Arthur he couldn't smoke his cigars in Miss Rocky's house no more on account of Miss Rocky didn't like surprises.

I felt so much better after I had some time to think about stuff. In a way, I could understand why Miss Rocky didn't like coming home and being surprised. Surprises could cause all kinds of problems.

My mama hated surprises, too. I overheard her talking to somebody on the telephone one day about what a shock I'd been to her, when she found out she was pregnant with me. "I can't believe that God was mean enough to give me another child at this time in my life; I wanted to die," Mama had said. *My mama wanted to die because of me . . .*

After I heard what Mama said, I guess I wanted to die, too. That was one time I wished I'd never snooped around to listen in on somebody else's conversation. I felt like that blind kitten my uncle Billy held down in a bucket of water and drowned. Because of what my mama said, I knew I should never have been born in the first place. Or, I should have been born a whole lot sooner, so I wouldn't have been such a big, bad surprise. I knew one thing for sure, life would have been a whole lot better for everybody if stuff had happened that way.

Mama was in her late forties when I was born. Other than my brother, David, who was even older than Miss Rocky, my mama didn't have any other kids. I don't know why, but being born retarded meant that there were a lot of things I didn't know or understand, no matter how hard I tried. For me, the hardest part of being retarded was being smart enough to know I was slow. People didn't think I had feelings, but I did. Like normal people, all I wanted in life was to be happy.

Mama and Daddy were too old to spend much time fussing with me when I was a little girl. And with me being a "retard" like the kids in my neighborhood said I was, I was always getting myself into something that would upset the normal people in my life. Like getting pregnant when I was just twelve.

It wasn't my fault, though. It was that boy from that big green house across the street from us. Donnie Reese was fourteen and always taking me to his bedroom so we could get naked and lay on his bed. That creep joined the army and got his butt shot up. Because of his injuries, according to Mama, Donnie's brain was as "raggedy as a bowl of sauerkraut." Maybe now he feels some of the same pain he caused me. As mean as he was to me, I still thought about him and me from time to time. Just the good times we'd had, though. He was my first boyfriend, and to every girl—even girls like me—the first boyfriend is the one you never forgot.

"Helen, don't you want a real boyfriend?" Donnie asked me one of the days we were naked. We only did that when his mama and daddy and his sister and brother were out of the house. Donnie's bedroom was nowhere near as cute as mine. I had dolls and white furniture and posters of movie stars. I even had a daybed by the window that I slept on some nights. Donnie's room was a mess. He had baseballs, dirty clothes, apple cores, magazines, and other junk all over the place. And his bed was never made up.

"I thought you were already my boyfriend," I told him, lying next to him on his bed. His long leg was rubbing on mine, and he was patting my titties.

"Well, boyfriends and girlfriends have to do a lot more than just get naked," he explained. His long orange tongue slid across his lip as he climbed on top of me, spreading my legs with his. I just couldn't get over how hard Donnie's body was compared to mine. "Now this is goin' to hurt a little bit . . ."

It did hurt and I tried to holler, but Donnie's hand was covering my mouth. It was still hurting when he rolled off me a few minutes later.

"Is that it?" I asked, my face screwed up, and the insides of my thighs on fire.

"What?" Donnie was putting his pants back on and giving me a mean look. Then he ripped a page out of one of his magazines and wiped blood off the insides of my thighs.

Cussing under his breath, he balled up that piece of paper and tossed it into a wastepaper basket on the floor next to his bed. But that wasn't enough for him. He ripped out some more pages and covered the bloody one with them. Now you tell me that wasn't crazy. "What did you say?" he asked, talking in a real gruff voice. He stood there with his hands in his pockets, looking at me like he didn't like me no more.

"Did you cut me?" I asked, sliding my fingers along my thigh, frowning because he'd left a few drops of blood.

"You wanna know somethin', Helen, you done gone from dumb to dumber," he said, letting out a laugh.

"Are we boyfriend and girlfriend now? For real?"

Donnie nodded real hard, biting his bottom lip at the same time. "Uh-huh. Whatever!" He laughed, but I couldn't figure out why. The hardest part of being retarded was not being able to make any sense out of normal people. It made my head spin when I tried. Some days I went to bed so dizzy, I couldn't stand up straight. All from trying to be normal. After a while I just let myself be what I was: retarded. It was so much easier, and to tell you the truth it was a lot more fun than trying to be normal.

"You going to kiss me?" I asked with a smile on my face so wide my ears could feel it.

Donnie's face got even meaner. "Heeell no! Girl, you get your funky ass up off my bed and get the hell up out of here before my mama comes home!" he screamed, shaking his finger in my face. He put some spit on the palms of his hands and slicked back his hair, giving me hot looks all the while.

I was so confused I couldn't think straight. It seemed like the room was going round and round. I closed my eyes for a moment and sucked in some air. When I opened my eyes again, Donnie was standing there looking at me like he wanted to kill me.

"Didn't-I-tell-you-to-get-out-of-here?" he said. I don't

know how he was able to talk with his teeth clenched, but he did.

"All right." I stumbled off the bed and put my clothes back on. "What about that candy and pop you said you'd give me?"

Donnie stomped up to me and poked me in my chest with his finger. "Look at my bed! You left your pussy jizm on it!" He pushed me aside and started to smooth over the spot on the bed where we had just been. He let out a loud breath and looked at me, shaking his head. "It's a damn shame all the shit boys have to put up with just to get a piece of tail. I knew I should have just jacked off. Look at that bloody mess on my bed!" Donnie shook a mean finger at the wet spot on his bed. "Get on out of here before I fuck you again!"

"All right," I mumbled, mad with myself for bleeding on Donnie's bedspread. Somewhere in my mind was some wild story Mama had told me about girls and women bleeding once a month. Something about a period. Well, I'd just finished one three days ago! Why I had bled with Donnie on the bed was a mystery to me. And it probably would stay that way because I wasn't about to ask Mama or anybody else what was up with that. I had enough mess to try and unravel.

As soon as I finished dressing, Donnie shooed me out of his room. He marched me through his mama's living room, then out of that big green house. Before he slammed the door in my face, he told me that if I ever told anybody what we'd just done, he'd beat me up.

As soon as I got back across the street to my front porch, I sat on the steps watching Donnie's house. I didn't leave my spot until he came out, whistling and bouncing a ball. He looked across the street at me and didn't even wave or say another word. But the mean look was still on his face, so I knew he meant business about beating me up if I told anybody what we had done in his bed.

I didn't tell anybody what Donnie and I had done because I wanted to do it again. And I did do it again. And again and again. I don't know how many more times I did it. Not just with Donnie, but with some of his friends. Every time Donnie's family left him alone, he called me to come over to his house.

On one of those days, I got back in Donnie's bed with him and four of his friends, all in the same day. Not all at the same time, though. Donnie was first, and then he went to be on the lookout for his mama and daddy or any other nosy person, while I was with one boy after another in Donnie's bed.

After a little while with all of these boyfriends, sex didn't hurt. It felt good. And, you know what, I liked it. Finally, somebody was treating me like I was a normal girl. I think . . .

By the end of the summer, I had more boyfriends than I knew what to do with. Some of them only came around once, but there were a few who came for me two, three times a week. When we couldn't go to Donnie's bedroom, we laid on the ground behind my daddy's garage. Sometimes we hid in the bushes.

Then I started getting sick and real fat. Mama and Daddy being so old, they didn't notice any of that. But my nosy brother, David, and his witch of a wife, Annabel, did. I didn't call my sister-in-law a witch just because she had long bushy hair and a crooked nose like a real witch, but because she was real mean to me most of the time.

It was Annabel who took me in the bathroom and pulled up my dress that day. Her high yellow face got all red and mean when she looked at my stomach. "Mother Daniels, get in here!" Annabel yelled, her mouth hanging open, her eyes stretched as wide as they could stretch.

"What's wrong now?" Mama asked in her tired voice as

she barged into the bathroom, fanning her face with the tail of her apron.

"This girl is pregnant!" Annabel told Mama, closing the bathroom door with her foot, her hand still holding up my dress.

"Oh, my God. Helen, who did this to you?" Mama asked, her hands on the sides of her face.

"Did what?" I wanted to know.

"Who has been messing with you, girl?" Mama grabbed my shoulders and shook me so hard, my stomach moved to one side.

"Nobody's been messing with me," I hollered, sucking in my breath, trying to make my stomach flat again.

"Tell me the boy's name who did this to you! Was it Donnie?" I had never seen my mama so excited. Her hands were shaking; she was crying. "Tell me who did this to you, Helen!" Mama was talking so loud, my brother snatched open the bathroom door. As soon as he saw my stomach, he started in on me.

"I knew this was going to happen sooner or later," David yelled, his brown face turning black. He gave me a hot look. His eyes looked tired and old at first. Then all of a sudden, his eyes looked like balls of fire. His lips trembled, and I could see spit oozing out from both corners of his mouth. "Who is the bastard who did this?" I didn't know why he was shaking his fist or who he was shaking it at.

Annabel pulled my dress down and looked me in the face. She started talking to me real soft, with her hands clamped on my shoulders to hold me in place. Like I was a baby or a puppy or something. "Helen, somebody has taken advantage of you, and you need to tell us who it was. This boy, whoever he is, has done a terrible thing to you, and he has to be held responsible. His parents need to know," Annabel told me, her eyes full of water. I didn't know why she was all balled up ready to cry. It seemed like I was the only one in trouble. "Now you take your time and try to remember the boy's name." Annabel turned her head a little and looked at me sideways. All of a sudden, she turned to my brother, her eyes looking wild and angry. "You don't suppose she's been raped?"

Mama let out a sharp gasp. Then she fell against the bathroom wall so hard, the medicine cabinet shook and the top button on her dress popped off. "Oh, God," Mama said, one hand holding up her head. "Helen, who did this to you. When? Where? Did he force himself on you?" Mama started swaying like a willow tree, her head rocking from side to side.

I looked at David, standing in the doorway with his hands in his pockets, his eyes scrunched up so hard it looked like he had just one eyebrow. Annabel stood next to him with her arms folded, a mean look on her face, which was as red as a rose. She didn't like me, and I didn't like her. Mama started swaying from side to side, still holding her head.

I let out my breath and shrugged. "I . . . we . . . I . . . I had some boyfriends, but they don't come around me no more," I admitted.

"Who?" David screamed, his hands on his hips. "I'll beat the dog shit out of the bastards."

In a way, I still liked Donnie, and all the rest of the boys who had made me feel so good. I didn't want my big mean brother to beat them up. "Um, it was this boy named Dennis." Being retarded didn't stop me from being a liar and making up a boy.

"Dennis who?" Annabel asked, her voice getting loud again.

A surprised look slid across Mama's face. I knew she didn't like that. Because, like I said, my mama hated surprises. Every time I remembered that I'd been Mama's biggest surprise, it made me feel sad. Then all I wanted to do was find somebody, anybody, who would like being with me. Donnie and his friends had done just that. "The Cooper boy?" Mama asked, her eyes blinking hard.

"Huh? No, not Reverend Cooper's son." There was a real boy named Dennis Cooper, but he had never been one of my boyfriends. "No, a new boy. He was just here for his vacation. He was from L.A., I think he said. His name is Dennis Cooper, too, but his friends call him Denny."

"Well, who is this Denny's people?" Mama asked, shaking a finger that she said was crooked from arthritis.

"I don't know. I met him at the park," I insisted, almost believing my own lie! My brain felt like it was going to explode, ticktocking like a time bomb. I could even hear bells ringing. Then something real crazy happened. While I was standing there, something inside me popped and water ran down my legs. My stomach started hurting so bad, I had to lean against the bathroom sink. Then everything went black.

I woke up in the hospital. My head had stopped ringing and my stomach had stopped hurting. And, my stomach was flat again. Mama, Daddy, David, and Annabel were all hovering over my bed like balloons with faces.

"What happened?" I wanted to know, trying to sit up.

"Baby, everything's going to be all right now," Daddy told me. Him and Mama, and even my brother and his wife, all looked so much older than I remembered. I wondered if I'd slept as long as Rip Van Winkle, twenty years, I think. I got real scared. Because that meant that I had got real old, too!

"Where's the bathroom?" I hollered. I didn't even wait for anybody to answer. I must have scared them all when I jumped up out of that bed and ran to the bathroom just to look in the mirror. I looked real tired, but I didn't look like an old woman. I padded back into the room and climbed back into the bed.

"Dr. Mason took real good care of you," Mama told me. Something that looked like a smile was on her face. Her lips were so dry they had cracks in them.

They didn't tell me much and what they did tell me, didn't make much sense. I'd had a baby! I couldn't take it home with me to play with, or even see it. I didn't know if I'd had a baby boy or a baby girl. That made me cry. It would go to a nice home where somebody normal could raise it. And, Mama told me again, "Dr. Mason took real good care of you. You won't ever get pregnant again." That made me kind of sad. Because I always thought that someday I'd have a child of my own to raise. But, like everybody kept telling me, girls like me had too many limitations to live normal lives. I guess I did. Because half of the stuff that was said to me that day didn't make no sense.

It wasn't long before things got back to normal again. If you could call it that. Mama and Daddy started acting like old people again, sitting around reading books, watching television, and running back and forth to the doctor.

The only thing that was different was my brother, David, started coming to the house more often. He was some kind of businessman. I don't know what he did, but he carried a briefcase. When he wore his glasses and a hat, he looked like a Black Clark Kent, who was really Superman up under his clothes. I'd seen my brother without his clothes; he wasn't no Superman. He had an office downtown where he bossed people around.

My brother's wife started taking me shopping and to their house out by the beach. "I'll keep an eye on Helen," she told Mama.

Well, after a while, Annabel got tired of keeping an eye on me. When I was allowed to go out by myself, I ran into a few of the boys who had been my boyfriends. But I never let another boy touch me again, *unless* he gave me money or something nice. And some of them did.

Before I could get bored with those boys, my brother started inviting me to go places with him. Being the witch that she was, my sister-in-law didn't like to let my brother out of her sight for too long. But she didn't care where he went as long as he had me tagging along. It was always a movie and the mall. He treated me to pizza and stuff. Then, one day we went to visit some lady on Noriego Street. A real pretty Chinese lady. Mai Ling.

David and his Chinese lady friend would leave me in her living room watching television or playing with her poodle while they went off to another part of her house. Each time on the way home, David stopped and bought me a pizza or something else good. Sometimes he gave me money, too.

"Our little adventure is a secret between you and me." David said that, or something like it, every time he took me with him to the Chinese lady's house.

I wasn't as dumb as they all thought I was. I knew what David and that lady were up to. I peeped in the lady's bedroom and saw them naked on the bed. But I never told nobody. I was just glad to have something to do. And, I was always glad to get them pizzas and that money.

It was bad enough being limited, but I was unhappy, too. I went to parks, dances, and other places for kids like me, with other girls like me from the special school I'd attended. But they were just as retarded as I was, if not more. And there was nothing more boring to me than hanging out with a bunch of retarded kids. We'd go places and get picked on by normal kids. And a few times when I got lost and confused, the police had to bring me home. Then, Miss Rocky next door became my friend. Finally, I had something else to do with my time.

Miss Rocky was my only normal friend, so I really liked her. I did everything I could to keep her happy. As soon as she had her kids, right off the bat she started asking me to come next door to babysit. The good news was Mama and Daddy didn't have to worry about me coming home in a police car when I went places with Miss Rocky. So in a way, Miss Rocky was also babysitting me.

It had been a long time since I'd had a boyfriend. I was glad when that man called Miss Rocky's house and asked me for a date. I didn't want to go to his house, like he had asked me to. And I didn't want to meet him somewhere downtown. It was my idea for him to come to Miss Rocky's house the other night.

He was White, just like he sounded on the telephone. His first name was Arthur, but he wouldn't tell me his last name. Or where he lived or worked, or anything else. He wasn't as cute as I had hoped he would be. Me, I was more into Brad Pitt and Tom Cruise when it came to White men. Arthur was more like a Homer Simpson, and just as old, if you could imagine a real man looking like one from a cartoon. Well, even if you couldn't, that's what Arthur looked like. But the man really knew how to dress up in a way that made him look better. He had on a San Francisco Giants cap with a matching T-shirt, Nikes, and some blue jeans. I don't know what kind of car he had because he'd parked it down the street and walked the rest of the way in the dark to Miss Rocky's house. Except for his looks, he was the perfect man.

"You have to be real quiet so you won't wake up the kids," I told him when I let him in the front door.

"Kids? You have kids?" he asked, stopping in the middle of Miss Rocky's living room floor, looking around. The way he started scratching his head and chin, and frowning, I thought he was going to change his mind. But then he stared at me real hard, bobbing his head as his eyes looked me up and down. He looked at my chest longer than any other part on me. When he finally looked in my face, he smiled and smoothed back hair that looked like yellow wires. The sparkling beads of sweat on his forehead reminded me of diamonds.

"Oh no. I had me a baby a long time ago, but somebody else took it home to raise. You want some beer?" I led him across the floor, pulling him by his arm as he waved his hand like a lobster. But instead of sitting down, he just stood in the middle of the floor looking around at all the nice stuff Miss Rocky had. "Miss Rocky likes to shop," I explained, shrugging. He seemed to like Miss Rocky's nice furniture and thick carpets as much as I did, because that smile was still on his face. And so were the beads of sweat. I was glad when he reached in his pocket and pulled out a handkerchief to wipe off that sweat. "Don't you want to sit down?" I asked, waving him to a seat. I sat down on one end of the brocade couch Miss Rocky was so proud of, wondering if the White man was going to spend the rest of our date standing in the middle of the floor smiling. White people were so strange. I guess I would have been strange, too, if I'd been born White. As if I didn't have enough problems just being retarded.

Arthur glanced around real quick and started scratching the side of his neck. "Uh, you don't look the way I expected," he told me, finally sitting down next to me.

"You don't either," I said, lying, because he looked a lot like other White men I had seen. He was older than he sounded on the telephone, and only had them few strands of blond hair on a head shaped like a peanut. He had on glasses, reminding me of Dr. Mason, the one who had fixed me so I wouldn't have no more babies.

"Uh, when we talked on the telephone, you said you'd

make this date worth my while," he grinned, showing gums as pink as bubblegum.

I nodded. "Well, I'll do whatever you tell me to do," I told him. That must have been what he wanted to hear because he pulled out his wallet and fished out some bills and handed them to me. "Three hundred dollars?" I looked at him with my mouth froze open like a dipper. "You giving me three hundred dollars?" The words almost scorched the inside of my mouth. I would not have been surprised if smoke had floated across my lips.

Arthur's face got stiff, like his hair. "Hey, that's what I've always paid you girls," he said real quick, holding up a hand, shaking his head. "If you got something else in mind, maybe I should wait for the other girl."

"Don't you like me? I thought you wanted a date with *me*," I said, pouting.

"Sure—"

"This is a lot of money! More money than anybody ever gave me! Except that time my aunt Irene gave me five hundred dollars for Christmas!" I said, losing my breath from talking so fast. I unfolded the three one hundred dollar bills and looked at them real close and long, running my fingers back and forth.

Arthur laughed and patted my arm. "Calm down, there's plenty more where that came from. If you be a good girl, you'll get a lot more." He cleared his throat, sniffed, and smiled. "And don't worry, it's all real." Arthur looked at me for a long time. "You know, you really are a beautiful girl," he said, rubbing my thigh. He reached up behind me and put his arm around my neck. Then he pulled me close enough for him to kiss me on the jaw. He leaned back and started grinning. "I would never try to stiff one of you girls," he told me, crossing his legs, which was hard for him to do because he had a big stomach. He rubbed along the side of my thigh, making moaning noises under his breath. The same way that Donnie Reese and his friends used to do when they were with me. Then he started to poke me between my legs with his finger.

"You rich?" I asked, squeezing my thighs because his hands were making me tingle. My eyes were still on the money in my hands.

Arthur gave me a strange look and didn't answer my question. "Have you done this before?" he asked, rubbing the hair on the back of my neck. I was glad I had a perm. My hair could get pretty mean if I let it.

"Oh, yeah. Lots of times." I looked at his face. He seemed nervous, because he kept looking toward the door. And, he was sweating so much it was dripping off his face onto his shirt. "Don't you like the way I look?" I asked, getting nervous myself.

"Sure. Sure, you're beautiful. Nineteen, huh?"

I nodded so hard my neck hurt. "Yep."

"You seem, I don't know, innocent, I guess." Now he was kissing me up and down my neck. "Do you have a room we can use?"

"For what?"

He gave me an even stranger look this time, blinking at me like he had something caught in his eye.

"Listen, you seem a little out of it. Maybe I should wait until Rockelle is available," Arthur said in a serious voice.

"Miss Rocky had something else to do," I said. "She won't be back until late. Real late." Miss Rocky had left the house with that Mexican woman named Ester. God knows where they went. I had asked Miss Rocky if she was going off to take care of the bedridden old man she had told everybody she took care of. She must not have heard me because she didn't answer. But that Mexican woman had laughed. Who could figure out normal people? I know I couldn't.

"Where is your bedroom?"

"Uh, this way," I answered, leading him to Miss Rocky's room. As soon as I shut the door, he got naked and grabbed me around the waist. He ripped my blouse trying to get it off me so fast. I didn't like what he did to me, ramming two fingers inside my pussy for a long time. He let me go, and then he ran over to where he'd left his pants on the floor and took out something. Before I knew what was happening, he ran back to me, stopping close to my face. I didn't know a man his age could move so fast.

"What is that?" I asked while he played around with his dick and that thing he'd removed from his pants pocket.

He moved back a few steps, his eyebrows shot up. "It's a condom." His face froze and he stared at me for a minute. "Honey, don't you use protection?"

"Huh?"

"You don't use condoms to protect yourself and your partner?"

"Oh yeah. I do."

Arthur finished putting that rubber thing on and pushed me down real hard and fast on the bed. He let out a grunt and climbed on top of me, but he didn't stay long.

I was glad when it was over. Happy now, Arthur started rubbing my titties and butt, and kissing me. His spit leaked all over my face.

After he got tired of doing all that, we got up off Miss Rocky's bed, got back in our clothes, and went back into the living room. That's when he lit up that nasty cigar and stunk up the whole house.

Before Arthur left, he kissed me some more and he told me to call him in a few days. But I made him promise not to tell Miss Rocky, explaining that she was the jealous type. He frowned when I told him that Miss Rocky would probably want more money, and that it would take him a lot longer to get her out of her clothes because she was so fat. He thanked me and kissed me again before he left.

I didn't know it that night, but it wouldn't be long before another man called up looking for a good time. Two nights later I had another date in Miss Rocky's house. Others had called, and I promised to see them when I could find the time. I didn't know that there were so many more men in this world just like Arthur. I was lucky they all brought the condom things with them, but they seemed upset because I never had any.

I never dreamed that I would get so busy. It got even better after I got on my computer. It was not easy, because not knowing how to read a lot of strange words slowed me down. But somehow, I managed to surf around on my Dell until I had all the information I needed about condoms.

I didn't waste no time getting over to the Walgreen's drugstore. But at the first one I went to, a nosy woman who used to visit my mama worked there. I just bought some gum. I went back home to get my bus pass, and I rode all over the place until I seen another Walgreen's. I went in and used some of the money I'd got from my last date, and I bought up a whole bunch of condoms.

# Chapter 20

# LULA HAWKINS

Clyde had asked me if I wanted to go on the cruise to Mexico that he finally took Ester on yesterday. I told him that I didn't want to go. From the looks that Ester had given me as she leered at me over Clyde's shoulder, I knew she didn't want me to go with them anyway.

"Lula, you turnin' down a free cruise?" Clyde asked, a surprised look on his face. "You didn't go out with us for Christmas or New Year's Eve. I want you to be happy, girl."

"I am happy, Clyde. I don't need to go on no cruise," I said.

"She gets seasick," Ester threw in. It was a lie, but a good one. Clyde stopped asking me to go on that cruise.

I was glad to have the apartment to myself. It gave me time to think. Lord knows I had a lot of things to think about.

Even though Clyde's main function was to arrange the dates, some of the regulars called us on their own when Clyde was not in town or if he didn't get back to them soon enough, or if they couldn't cut a deal with one of Clyde's competitors. I had turned down six dates in the last two days.

Like I said, I needed some time to think. Time to myself was the only thing I needed more than money.

I couldn't do much thinking without including Larry Holmes and how he had deceived me. And as much as it still hurt, I thought about him all the time. I thought about Bo, too, and how nice he had been to me. I believed in my heart that if he hadn't been killed, I would have had a good life with him. After all, Bo had been the kind of man any woman in her right mind would have been proud to have. I was glad that I had had him, even for what seemed like only fifteen minutes. Even dead, he still brought a smile to my face.

Verna and Odessa had called and left me a lot of messages and sent me Christmas cards. I took my time getting back to them.

"Girl, we was beginnin' to think you was dead," my stepsister yelled when I finally did call her back after she'd left her last message five days ago.

"Verna, I'm fine," I told her. "How is Odessa?"

"That horny bitch is layin' right here next to me, her pussy itchin' like she got fleas." Verna laughed. "What about you?"

"What about me?"

Verna clicked her teeth and snorted. She never did have much patience. "You gettin' any?"

"Uh, I haven't met anybody yet."

"Girl, you better get out there and meet you somebody. I'm sure you know by now that life is too short. You here today, but you could be gone tomorrow, just like poor Bo. You can't spend the rest of your life pinin' over Larry and Bo."

"I won't." Just hearing the names of the two men who had meant so much to me caused a tight feeling in my chest. It was so severe I could hardly breathe. Before I could rub it away, a huge lump rose up inside my throat. I had a hard time swallowing, too. As much as I loved talking to Verna and Odessa, I couldn't wait to get off the phone.

"Where's your roommate?"

"She's on a cruise in Mexico with . . . her boyfriend," I replied, rubbing my chest so hard that the rubbing was hurting me more than the tight feeling I'd been trying to rub away.

"Well, the next time I call you, I hope she tells me the same thing about you."

I chatted with Verna for a few minutes more, getting an update on Daddy, my stepmother, and the twins. Daddy's latest girlfriend, a twenty-year-old, had attacked him with a frying pan when she caught him with her sister. Now he was walking around with a bandage cap on his head. Etta, my long-suffering stepmother, was threatening to divorce Daddy. But that was not news. She'd been threatening to divorce Daddy as far back as I could remember. I was glad to hear that the twins were behaving themselves.

I rarely called Daddy and he rarely called me. When I tried to reach him, he was out almost every time. I didn't like talking to Etta, so when she answered the telephone, I was as brief as I could be with her. But not brief enough. She made it her business to tell me every time she saw Larry and his little family and how happy they looked. That old wench wondered out loud what a handsome man like Larry had seen in me, and then she softened that blow by telling me that at least I was better looking than Verna, her own daughter.

"When you comin' for a visit?" Odessa was on the phone now.

"Maybe in a few months," I said, knowing I had no plans or desires to see Mississippi again any time soon.

"How's your job at the police department?" Odessa asked.

"Huh?"

"Ain't you workin' as a receptionist for the police?"

"Uh, no, that didn't work out, Odessa." I had forgotten all about that black-ass lie I'd told. I prayed that neither Odessa or Verna had tried to call me there. "Uh, I got on at this engineerin' firm downtown. Typin', filin', makin' photocopies. It's a real strict place so I can't take no personal calls. I got a mean boss, too."

"Sounds like that hellhole I work for. Well, you keep your eye on them California dudes. All that sun and sand done gone to their heads, but don't let them go to yours."

"I won't, Odessa."

To this day, I don't know where my mind was when I met Richard Rice. Other than Clyde and my tricks, I had not paid much attention to any other men since I'd moved to California eight months before. For the rest of my life, I would remember in detail how Richard happened to me.

Right after my conversation with Odessa and Verna that day, a Saturday afternoon in January, I got dressed and took a cab downtown. My original plan was to catch some of the after-Christmas sales.

As usual, there was a ruckus on Powell Street where I'd had the cab drop me off. For a country girl like me, a trip to downtown San Francisco was like a trip to a circus. In addition to the mob of tourists, most of them foreigners with cameras slung around their necks, there was a strange collection of individuals crowding the street. Dozens were in line waiting for a ride on the famous cable cars.

But some of the things I saw that day almost made me forget why I had come downtown in the first place. There was a man who had been spray-painted all over with gold paint, even his clothes and hair. He was standing in one spot, like a statue, holding a tin can and a sign requesting donations. A blind man wearing dark glasses was sitting on the ground with a German shepherd squatting next to him. The dog had on dark glasses, too. There was a cigar box on the ground between the man and his dog for the donations. An Asian midget impersonating Elvis was gyrating his hips and singing "Jailhouse Rock." An elderly Black man was preaching and handing out religious flyers. A group of rough-looking Hispanic boys stood glaring at another group of rough-looking Hispanic boys, shouting angrily at one another in Spanish. I decided to move on when a transvestite tapped me on the shoulder and asked me if I was Paul, the bartender from the Cock Pit bar.

I lost interest in shopping and ended up walking a block up Powell Street to Tad's Steakhouse to eat lunch instead. As usual, the loud cafeteria-style restaurant was crowded, so I had to search for a seat after I got and paid for my lunch. I almost didn't notice the handsome man with skin the color of pecans and just as smooth, waving and grinning at me from a corner in the back of the room. My heart started racing because at first I thought he was one of my tricks.

Most of the men I slept with were from out of town, and White, but I had an occasional local trick. Unlike Rosalee, Rockelle, and Ester, I didn't have a problem turning tricks with Black and Hispanic men. Rockelle flat out refused to deal with either race, claiming she didn't trust them, and that the few she had slept with had treated her like shit. Rosalee and Ester avoided them, too. They felt that they were too judgmental, rough, and sometimes mean. White men were often just as much trouble, but we all agreed that the best tricks were the Japanese. Especially the super rich ones from

Tokyo. With them, it was all about business. They bowed and grinned more than they talked. After they got off, they handed over the money and sent us on our way.

If the man in Tad's Steakhouse beckoning me had been Asian, trick or no trick, I would have joined him without hesitation. With the exception of that nasty-ass Daniel Wong in San Diego—a trick I had to do when Rosalee wasn't available—my experiences with Asian men had always been pleasant.

There was another thing that was bothering me about the man looking at me. He had on a dark brown uniform, similar to the ones the UPS men wore. Just like Larry. And it was the same color of the vehicle that Larry's wife had climbed out of that day she attacked me in that parking lot.

It didn't take long for me to decide that the Black man looking at me wasn't somebody I knew. And being that my complexion was dark brown, I realized just how silly it was to let a uniform the same color disturb me. There were no other empty seats, so I moved toward the table with the handsome Black man in the dark brown uniform.

"Go on and sit down, sister. I ain't goin' to bite you . . . unless you want me to," he said, grinning. He was even better looking up close. His black eyes sparkled as he looked me up and down. He had a neat, thin goatee, which was nice because with it, his face didn't look as round as it really was. He had on a uniform, but that didn't hide his muscular build. His head was full of wavy, dark brown hair, parted on the side. It made him look like a choirboy.

"Thank you." I sat down, hoping he was not the chatty type. I hated when strangers struck up conversations with me. It seemed like everybody I'd met in California wanted to tell me their business and wanted to know mine. This brother was no different.

"I'm Richard," he said, wiping salad dressing off his lips with a wad of napkins.

"I'm Lula," I told him, talking with my head down. I felt like a frumpy old maid. I didn't have on any makeup and a red scarf covered my hair. I figured if I started reading the paperback copy of *The Coldest Winter Ever,* which Rockelle had left at the house, he would take the hint. I was wrong.

"Now that's a book you don't wanna put down 'til you finish," he said.

"So I've heard," I said, flipping to the page where I'd left off.

He was chewing and talking at the same time. "I've seen you around."

My head snapped up. "Where at?"

"You ride on my bus every now and then."

"Oh." A bus driver.

"I always remember the pretty ladies."

I was reading but I was not retaining a single word. But every word coming out of the man's mouth across from me was going straight to my head.

He ignored the annoyed look I gave him and kept right on talking. "Uh, you married, sister?"

I dog-eared a page and slid the book back into my purse, giving him a look that I hoped would let him know he was annoying me. "Yeah, I mean no. My husband died." The steak, with swirls of steam still floating from it, almost slid off my plate every time I cut off a piece. I felt uneasy, and I suddenly lost my appetite.

"Sorry to hear that. My wife died in the big quake we had in '89."

A wave of sadness swept over me like a warm blanket. I bit my bottom lip and cleared my throat. "Did y'all have any kids?"

He nodded, chewing so hard his whole face moved. As soon as he swallowed, he coughed to clear his throat. I noticed tears in his eyes. "My two-month-old son died with her. They were drivin' back from Oakland when the Cypress Freeway collapsed."

I felt a wave of sympathy. Just being in the company of another person who'd also lost a child did that to me. My son would have been crawling by now, if he had lived. And as spooky as it was, Richard was what Larry and I had agreed to name our child. Oh, I was good and ready to conclude this conversation and hightail my ass on back home. But I didn't. "I'm sorry to hear that. I read about the freeway and part of the Bay Bridge goin' down." Blinking hard, I gave him a thoughtful look. "And I was still crazy enough to move to this doomed state anyway." I sighed and speared a huge piece of meat.

"Well, you ain't the only one crazy. I never thought I'd leave my hometown to move out here. But once you set foot in this pretty place, you don't wanna leave. It grabs ahold of you and won't let you go. Sometime I be walkin' around some of these streets, so dazzled by the beauty, I feel like I done landed in the Land of Oz."

I nodded. "Tell me about it," I murmured, knowing just what he meant. I didn't know if it was the beauty of San Francisco that had me so whipped, or if it was all the misery I'd known in Mississippi made me want to stay here.

Richard sipped from a tall class of Coke. Like a child staring at a monkey in a cage, I watched his Adam's apple bounce up and down. He noticed me staring at him. "I hope you like what you see," he teased.

"I've seen better," I shot back.

"I bet you have. A lot better."

I gave him an exasperated look. "Were you here when that earthquake happened . . . Richard?" It hurt for me to say the name out loud, or to even think it. But it also kept my deceased child's memory at the front of my brain. *Richard.*

"I was in New Orleans for a family reunion. My wife, she wouldn't go with me on account of she and my mama never got along."

"You from Louisiana?"

"Uh-huh. Bigfoot country." Richard sniffed and laughed. "And I'm a country boy to the bone."

"I'm from Mississippi," I chirped. I don't know why I suddenly felt the way I did that day, but the stranger across from me didn't seem like a stranger anymore. He had a gentle way about him, and a way of looking at me that made me feel warm all over. I found myself wondering why men like him always found women like me too late.

"See, we got somethin' in common. So, is there any way I could get in touch with you sometime, Lula?"

"I don't think so." I shook my head so hard my scarf slid down across the top of my face. Even though my hair was a knotty mess, I slid the scarf into my purse.

Richard offered a casual shrug, but he didn't give up (praise the Lord). "Well, why don't I give you my telephone number? If you change your mind, you can call me."

"Look, Richard, you seem like a nice man. You don't need a woman like me in your life."

"Why don't you let me make that decision? Richard Rice is a big boy." He tapped my hand, sending a chill down my spine. "You work around here?"

"I work everywhere," I snapped, waving my hand. "See, I sell pussy. Happy?" I must have said it too loud because people at the table next to us looked over at me with amused expressions. My face burned, and my stomach got tight.

To my surprise, Richard didn't even seem shocked or surprised. "Well, you in the right place. There's a whole lot of money in San Francisco. A lot of the workin' girls ride my bus home when they get off the stroll," he said.

I couldn't believe that this man was talking to me in such a calm way about something as serious and *nasty* as what I'd just confessed.

"I don't stroll the streets," I said real fast, speaking almost in a whisper. What I did with my body was bad enough. The last thing I wanted was for anybody to think that I was as trifling as the women working the streets.

Richard grunted as he gnawed on the last piece of his steak. "My grandpa always said, if you goin' to be a bear be a grizzly. Sound like you one of them *high*-priced call girls," he remarked, a leering smirk on his face. The way he pronounced his words, I couldn't even tell he was from the south. But he did have the quiet, mannerly ways of a country boy. He stared at me so hard that the back of my neck felt like ants were crawling on it.

"Somethin' like that." I swallowed hard and sat up straight. "You don't seem like the kind of man who would want to associate with . . ."

"Let me tell you somethin', girl. I grew up in one of the sleaziest neighborhoods in New Orleans. There was this old bootlegger livin' next door to us. That brother sold some of everything: watered-down whiskey, stolen property, fried chicken dinners, fresh fish, women. My sister used to babysit for the women, nice women. On a busy day you couldn't tell if it was the women you was smellin' or the fish." He laughed. I laughed. "Nobody called them women hoes, sluts, or nothin' like that. We called 'em sportin' ladies, and the bootlegger wasn't runnin' no whorehouse. It was a sportin' house. Just like in Storyville. You know about Storyville?"

"Everybody knows about Storyville. It's that place in that red-light 'hood in New Orleans where they have whore-houses," I snapped.

Richard shook his head and waved a scolding finger in my face. "Sportin' houses," he corrected sternly.

"Whatever," I mumbled, trying to hide the fact that I was enjoying his company. To anybody who didn't know us, we looked like any other young couple having lunch. Even though Richard had my attention, I could still see other men looking at me, smiling and nodding. One of the few things about myself of which I was proud was I didn't encourage men to come on to me. With Clyde being the busy body he was, I didn't have to.

Richard noticed two young brothers across from us steal-ing glances at me. "I hope I ain't keepin' you from gettin' paid," he said, his voice cracking.

"Look, you ain't stoppin' me from doin' a damn thing. Why don't you stay on the subject?" If he'd been anybody else, I probably would have cussed him out and left. But he was not a man any woman in her right mind could walk away from that easy. That gave me something to worry about. Falling in love at this point in my uncertain life was the last thing on my mind.

Richard grinned. "Anyway, like I was sayin', our neighbor-hood was always crawlin' with tricks. One night, when I was around ten, this nervous old White dude knocked on our door. Not no dirty, barefoot redneck in overalls, but a clean-cut businessman in a suit and tie. My mama's cousin Lottie Mae who lived with us, she answered the door. Sister-girl was forty, had a face like a sow, and weighed as much as me and you put together. When dude asked her how much she charged, she bounced a fryin' pan off his head. Funny thing was, she went around for years braggin' about that honky in a suit who tried to buy some of her stuff. What was even funnier was Cousin Lottie Mae startin' sneakin' in and out of that bootlegger's house at night herself when she thought we was all sleep." Richard paused and looked at me like he was trying to read my mind. Lucky for me, he couldn't. Because, I liked him. "I bet there ain't a woman alive who ain't done some level of sportin' when she needed a little somethin'."

I had to cover my mouth to keep from laughing. Then, I pushed my plate away and stood to leave. I was so shocked when Richard grabbed my wrist and motioned for me to sit back down. I gave him a mean look, at least that's what I tried to do. He just tilted his head to the side and smiled at me. The he laughed.

"Let me give you my telephone number anyway."

My eyes wouldn't stop blinking, and I had to force my lips to stay pressed together so I wouldn't laugh. I lifted my chin and managed to give him a stiff look.

"I don't think you can afford me on a bus driver's salary," I said abruptly.

"I *know* I can't afford you on my salary, girl," he guffawed. "But, take my phone number anyway. If you ever need to talk and want somebody to listen, you can call me. I'm a good listener." He whipped out a pen and scribbled on a napkin. "I work the afternoon shift right now, but my shift changes from time to time. Sunday is my only day off, but I'm in church most of the day."

"Oh?" Church? He was in the church. I didn't know if that was good or bad. Clyde was in the church, too.

"If you call and don't catch me at home, you can leave me a message, and I'll call you back as soon as I can," he said, rising. "Lula, you take care of yourself." He squeezed my hand when he handed me the napkin with his telephone number. His flesh was so hot, I flinched.

Then he was gone.

I crumbled up the napkin and dropped it on the table, but before I left, I picked it up and slid it into my purse.

# Chapter 21

# MEGAN O'ROURKE

To me, San Francisco and Oakland seemed to be on two different planets. Truth is, the San Francisco Bay, which takes about eight minutes to drive across on the Bay Bridge, is all that separates the two cities. As beautiful as San Francisco is, it is no paradise when it comes to crime, but the world had come to know Oakland as an absolute hellhole. It was the last place on Earth I wanted to be on a Saturday afternoon.

"You are going to Oakland *alone?* Have you lost your mind?" Mom's horrified voice rang in my ear like a siren. The telephone suddenly felt like a piece of hot coal in my hand. "What does your husband have to say about this?"

"It was Robert's idea, Mom," I mumbled, shifting the receiver to my other hand, hoping to find something else to distract me. The cleaning woman who came in twice a week kept everything looking showroom organized and clean. Even the telephone in my hand smelled like Lysol.

My mother had a hearing problem and refused to wear a hearing aid. She spoke in a voice that was so loud it almost pierced my ear. I didn't look forward to my daily conversations with her. And it wasn't just the volume of her voice that irritated me. Her special talent was making me feel like an idiot. "I don't know about you, Meg. All that money you spent on that therapist was a waste. Can't you find a suitable car in San Francisco? Do you really have to go to Oakland to buy one? And a *used* car at that." My mother's voice rose even higher. "And that's another thing, what's the point of buying a used car? You'll just end up paying for the previous owner's negligence. By the time it's over and done with, you'll have spent the same amount of money that you would have spent on a new car. Maybe even more. And why are you going to look for a car? That's a man's job." There was a triumphant tone in the way Mom sniffed.

I held the telephone away from my face for a moment, rubbing my ear as Mom's words continued to ring.

"Robert's boss recommended this place, Mom. I've already visited six dealers in San Francisco. And, I am sure that women are intelligent enough to pick out a car."

"Don't you dare talk to me about intelligence. Do I have to remind you that you flunked out of college?" I could hear Mom sucking her teeth and mumbling novenas under her breath. "Do you still have that can of Mace I gave you?" My mother's gruff voice was more irritating than fingernails scraping a blackboard.

"Yes, Mom. It's in my purse."

"Do you know how to use it?"

"I'm sure I could figure that out if and when I ever have to use it."

"Make sure your cellular phone is working. If I don't hear from you by four, I'm calling the police. What's the name of that used car place you're going to?"

"C and L Used Cars, Mom. On International Boulevard."

"All of those savages shooting, stabbing, and taking drugs. And the police can't seem to do much about it. It's a miracle that all of the Whites haven't moved away from Oakland. It's a good thing your father had enough insight to get us out of that town before it was too late. As if this family hasn't had enough heartache already."

I didn't even try to hide my exasperation. But the harsh tone of my voice never fazed my mother before, and it didn't now. "Now you sound like Robert," I scoffed.

With a steely voice she continued, "I am not a racist, dear. But you know as well as I do that those Blacks, Hispanics, and Asians are the ones giving Oakland such a bad name. When you get to that car place, make sure you find a White salesman, if they have one . . ."

"Mom, I'll call you as soon as I get back."

*"If* you get back—"

"Bye, Mom."

It took longer for me to drive from my house on Steiner to a Bay Bridge entrance, but the ride across the Bay was smooth and quick. Eight minutes. Twenty minutes later, I was in the heart of East Oakland, driving into the parking lot at C and L Used Cars.

Before I could park in the customer parking section, a plump, middle-aged salesman in a gray suit greeted me with a toothy grin and a bandaged nose. Mom would be pleased when I told her he was White.

"Are you Lou Cummings?" I asked, climbing out of my two-year-old Lexus.

"At your service, ma'am." He nodded and extended a wide, soft hand with nails that looked just as well-cared for as mine.

"I'm Mrs. O'Rourke. We spoke yesterday." A confused look appeared on his round face. He squinted his beady green eyes and smoothed back his long, but thin gray and black hair.

"Oh yes." Lou snapped his thick fingers. Then he did a brief shufflelike jig and made a face that would have put Jim Carrey to shame. Lou was unusually spry for his age—early to mid forties. His cartoonish behavior put me more at ease. "You're my first female customer today and where I come from, that means good luck for somebody."

"Well, I hope that somebody is me," I replied with a broad smile. "I've been to several lots. San Francisco, San Bruno, Brisbane. I've looked at more than a dozen cars, and I haven't seen anything to my liking. And frankly, most of the salesmen I've encountered so far didn't seem as friendly as you." I felt even more at ease, but I was anxious to conduct and conclude my business.

Lou nodded and caressed his chin, which was surprisingly pointed for a face as round as his. "Well, if you're looking for a good deal on a good car and friendly service, you've come to the right place."

"Thank you, Lou." I looked around the lot. It was a small business, with no more than a dozen cars occupying about a corner of the block next door to a Vietnamese restaurant. A huge American flag was displayed in the front window.

"Now let's get down to business. You wanted a little something for your daughter. Well, I am sure that we can get you fixed up real nice. Now what did you have in mind? Girls are a lot harder to buy cars for than boys. The main thing a girl wants is something cute. My niece insisted on something in a color that would show off her tan in the summertime. Go figure young people." Lou gave me an exasperated look and waved his hand. "Now how much do you want to spend, dear lady?"

"I don't care about the price. As long as it's something dependable."

"And cute?"

"And cute."

"Let's see now. How about a Tercel? We have a couple of those in stock, and the young girls seem to love them."

Just then another car pulled up and parked next to mine. There were already two other cars in the customer parking lot.

"Why don't you just let me look around, please? I'm not in a hurry, so you can go take care of someone else first," I told Lou.

As Lou trotted toward another customer, I clutched my purse as two young scowling Black men strutted past me, looking at me as if I'd just arrived from the moon. Suddenly, Black men seemed to be everywhere. Two more drove into the lot, rap music blasting. Another one was strutting in my direction. But this one was different. Only the Devil himself could have startled me more than Clyde Brooks.

"Megan, is that you?"

I looked into the face of the last Black man in the universe that I ever wanted to see again.

"Clyde? Oh my God!" I exclaimed. First, my body swayed, and then I felt like I was levitating. "It's been years," I said, wailing.

"Twenty-eight and a half," Clyde said, sneering. "That's a whole lotta years. Some folks don't even live that long." The expression on his face was grim and determined.

"Uh, yes, I know," I stammered.

Clyde was wearing a black denim jumpsuit. I had planned to go to the gym later, so I had on a gray sweatshirt, a plain cotton skirt, and running shoes. My hair, longer than I usually wore it, was in a ponytail. Except for the silver Lexus, I didn't look like the wife of a wealthy architect.

"I thought it was you. After all these years, I'd know them legs anywhere. Even from behind."

"Jesus Christ!"

"Not quite, but if I had more hair, and if it was wooly, I'd look like Him. Now don't be standin' there lookin' like you ain't glad to see me. I used to be your favorite nigger—oops, excuse me, African-American."

I looked around before responding. For the first time in my life, I prayed for an earthquake. One that would open up a hole under my feet and swallow me whole. "How are you, Clyde Brooks?"

"I'm fine, Megan Carmody."

I shook my head. "It's O'Rourke now."

"Oh, that's right. My grandmother told me that your mama called her up back when, and told her all about you marryin' some rich architect. I was sorry to hear that it was to one of them highfalutin peckerwoods that would love to give me a one-way ticket to Africa," Clyde said with a smirk as he scratched his chin.

"Uh, I haven't seen you since . . . since . . ."

"Since our daughter was born. That pretty little girl you didn't want nothin' to do with," he said, growling.

I glanced at the ground. I had to compose myself before I could respond. After a few deep breaths, I looked in Clyde's eyes. His glare made me feel transparent and frightened. "I-I was just looking for a little something for my daughter. She's in Europe spending some time with her grandparents."

He nodded and folded his arms. "Uh-huh. So you got married and got you *another* daughter?" he asked with his brows furrowed.

"Heather is eighteen. My son, Josh, is twenty." I sucked in some air and forced a smile. "You look well," I offered, looking him up and down.

"Oh, it's all good. I could complain, but I won't. I just got back from Mexico, and it did me a lot of good. I got me a lot of rest, did a lot of dancin' and drinkin', and burned every candle at both ends." He paused, grimaced, and rubbed the side of his head. "I done got too old for all that high livin', but that ain't never stopped me. I'm fin to go to Hawaii next."

"Have a nice trip," I said, attempting to leave.

"Hold on now," Clyde said, stepping in front of me. "I ain't seen you in years. Don't be rushin' off like that." He crossed his arms and gave me a look that made me even more uncomfortable. "Now, if you don't mind me sayin', you still lookin' mighty good. I guess married life agrees with you."

"Yes, I have a good life. Uh, how is your grandmother?"

"She's as good as can be expected for a woman her age. But to hear her tell it, she got one foot in the grave, and the other one on a slippery rock. She 'bout to drive me crazy talkin' about the kind of funeral she want and shit. She'll probably outlive me and you both."

I stepped around Clyde, and started to move toward my car again. "Well, it was good seeing you again, Clyde. Tell Effie I said hello, please." I froze when Clyde grabbed my arm, squeezing so hard it throbbed.

"Don't let me scare you off. Again. We still friends, ain't we?"

"It's not that," I told him, prying away his grip. Even after he'd removed his hand, my arm continued to throb. "But I am in a hurry, and I don't see anything to my liking. My daughter is so picky."

"Look, you ain't got to be scared of me. I'm just tryin' to be friendly. That's all I ever tried to be with you. I ain't just another nigger off the street, or did you forget? I guess that rich architect done clouded your memory. Where is that racist son of bitch at now? At home nailin' up a cross to light up in somebody's front yard or washin' out his sheet? Or both."

"That was unnecessary, Clyde," I hissed. I could imagine the ugly picture Mom had painted of Robert for Clyde's grandmother. Yes, my husband was a bigot. But he was not as bad as Clyde made him sound.

"I bet. But the truth hurts, don't it?"

I was exasperated beyond belief. "Clyde, it was nice seeing you again, and I'm glad to hear that you and your grandmother are doing well. But things are different now," I said as firmly as I could. A sour taste was spreading throughout my mouth.

"Tell me about it. Are things too different for you to even *ask* about your daughter?"

My flesh crawled at the mention of my daughter. "How is she?"

"She?"

I shrugged. "I don't know her name," I said hotly.

"Her name is Keisha, and she's fine. You want to meet her?"

"What?" My legs buckled. I stumbled and fell against Clyde. His arm went around my shoulder.

"Come on. She ain't got to know who you are. She's asleep anyway and ain't even got to know you was here."

Clyde led me into the office where Lou was yelling at someone on the telephone. He looked up and glanced from me to Clyde, but said nothing as Clyde led me into another room toward the back of the small, cluttered office.

There was an old file cabinet, a water cooler, a CD player blasting Toni Braxton on a desk, and a small refrigerator humming noisily in a corner. Next to the refrigerator was what appeared to be a cot or a daybed. On it, lying on her side facing the wall, was a woman with long blond hair in neat corn rows. A thin blue blanket covered her up to her shoulders.

"This is your daughter," Clyde announced.

I stood back by the door with my trembling arms folded.

"Come look at her," he urged, beckoning me with both hands.

I couldn't feel my legs as I moved toward the lump on the cot. As soon as I got close enough, Clyde gently pulled back the cover. I almost fainted. One side of my daughter's face was twisted and so severely swollen I could barely see her eye.

I gasped. "What happened to her? Was she attacked? You promised my family and me you'd have your relatives in Mississippi raise her. I—"

"I promised I would do just that, and I did."

"Then why is she here in California?" I asked, waving my arms. "Is she . . . is she here for a visit?"

A blank look appeared on Clyde's face. I couldn't believe how soft his voice sounded. "When she was three, somebody ran her over with a car. In a church parkin' lot at that. Me and Grandma Effie, we went to see about her as soon as we heard. It was a hit-and-run so we never found out who the low-life bastard was who done it. If I ever do find out, I'll be goin' to prison. My baby was in a coma for months, and wasn't expected to live. But she did." Clyde paused and leaned over to stroke the girl's face. I moved away a step when she stirred and moaned softly. "Don't worry; this girl could sleep through Armageddon." Letting out a deep breath, Clyde turned back to me. "When she came out of the coma, she had to learn how to walk and talk again. My folks down south told me right off that they couldn't deal with no child like her no more. But they didn't even have to go there. I knew from the get-go that my baby was comin' back to California with me, and that I was goin' to do whatever it took to take care of her."

"I didn't know. I had no way of knowing. I never saw her."

"I know all of that shit."

"Well, is she normal? I mean, does she get by all right?"

"Hell no." With that, Clyde snatched back the blanket and revealed legs that were not only crooked, but unusually thin. "Because of that damn accident, her blood couldn't keep circulatin' the way it was supposed to. With her still a growin' child when it happened, her legs didn't grow straight and strong like other girls.' "

"Can she walk? Can she get around all right?"

The more Clyde talked about Keisha, the softer his voice got. "She gets around all right, one way or another. Sometimes she gotta use two canes. Sometimes, I carry her."

I covered my mouth and stumbled to a metal chair in front of the desk. Clyde handed me a Styrofoam cup of water and sat down on the corner of the desk.

"Do you keep her at home?" I asked in a voice that was low enough to be considered a whisper. Clyde cupped his ear and leaned toward me. "Do you keep her at home?" I repeated, much louder.

He gave me an incredulous look. "What's wrong with you, woman? Of course we keep her at home. This is my child. Where else am I gonna keep her? See, that's the problem with you White folks. First thing y'all wanna do is hide somebody like Keisha in one of them asylums. Well, my girl ain't crazy, she ain't retarded, and she ain't got no other problems that me and Grandma Effie can't handle."

"That's not what I meant. It's just that, well, trying to take care of someone with physical limitations must be difficult."

"Look, lady, just livin' is difficult. Even for folks like you and me. Yeah, it's hard takin' care of Keisha, but I been doin' it all this time. Me and Granny Effie. And as long as I'm alive, I goin' to take care of my child." Clyde lowered his voice and added, "Which is more than I can say for some folks."

"I have to go now." I set the cup on the edge of the desk and rose. "I'm happy to see that you, your grandmother, and Keisha are all doing well, Clyde." I sighed and nodded. "I really mean that."

"Where you live?" he asked abruptly, looking at me with contempt. "We don't get too many customers like you," he added with a sneer.

"I presume you work here, too?" I asked, looking around the congested office.

He nodded. "C and L Used Cars. I'm the C, my buddy Lou out there, he's the L. Now, answer the question I just asked you. Where you live at?"

"Uh, we live in the city."

"You been in the Bay Area all this time and I ain't seen you? I got me a place in 'Frisco, too. How come I ain't seen you until now? You know me, I get around. I done run into everybody I knew from when I first moved to California. Everybody but you, until now."

"We lived in Sacramento for a while after we were married. We don't get out much. The house and the kids keep me busy. And, we travel a lot. We just got back from visiting Robert's family in Ireland. My daughter might remain there until she starts college this fall. My son's in the navy."

Clyde nodded. "Uh-huh. Well, I doubt if I'll go to Ireland any time soon. Too much mess is goin' on at them airports these days. Mexico is about as far as I go." Clyde sniffed and scratched his neck. "Y'all got a phone?"

"Why?" I gasped. My eyes felt like they were going to pop out and roll across the floor.

"Just askin'," Clyde said, holding up his hand. He returned to the cot and sat on the side, crossing his legs. He pulled the blanket back up to Keisha's shoulders and looked at his watch. "I'll have to get her up in a little while. She can't lay on her side for too long. Fluids might drain and settle on the side of her head where she got the most injured. That's the way it's goin' to be for her 'til the day she die." Turning to me with a look I could not interpret, Clyde folded his arms and cocked his head. Words slid out of his mouth like venom. "I hope I see you again real soon, Mrs. O'Rourke."

Just as I was about to attempt to leave again, Keisha sat up, yawning and rubbing her eyes.

"Hello, Sleepin' Beauty," Clyde cooed. Nodding in my direction he blurted, "This is your mama."

I gasped and stumbled against the wall.

Keisha looked from me to Clyde and back to me with a warm smile. "Daddy said I got my good looks from you," she said.

"Hello, Keisha," I managed, furious that Clyde had put me in such an impossible position. "You . . . you are lucky to have a daddy who loves you so much," I stuttered.

"Did you come to see me?" Keisha asked, struggling to swing her legs to the side of the cot. She groaned, shuddered, and rubbed the side of her head.

"You all right, baby?" Clyde asked.

"Daddy, I'm fine," Keisha insisted, keeping her eyes on me. "So why did you come?"

"Uh, I came to buy a car." I had almost forgotten the real reason I had come to Oakland. "I didn't expect to see you," I mumbled.

"I'm glad you came. I always wanted to meet you, but I didn't think I ever would. Daddy said it was better for you."

"There's a lot more to it than that, Keisha. I was very young when you were born. I was scared and unmarried."

"So was Daddy," Keisha reminded me, rising. With a great deal of effort, she stumbled over to me. "You can hug me if you want to."

I hugged my precious daughter for the first time. It was too late for tears, but that didn't stop them from coming. Clyde handed me a paper towel.

"Mama . . ." Keisha stopped, moved away from me, and looked at Clyde. "Daddy, what do I call her?"

"Her name is Meg, girl. You know that."

Turning back to me, Keisha said, "You can come see me whenever you want to, Meg. If you want to."

For the first time in my life, I couldn't talk. I dropped the soaked paper towel to the floor. Then I snatched open the door and ran all the way back to my car.

I didn't look back, but through my rearview mirror I could see Clyde and Keisha in the window watching me as I sped out into the street.

# Chapter 22

# ESTER SANCHEZ

It had taken Clyde long enough to take me on that damn cruise to Mexico that he had been promising me, but I'm sorry I went. We had a lot of good margaritas, smoked some good dope with some locals in Puerto Vallarta, but I didn't really have the good time I thought I would.

It was nice to be around all them Mexicans. So what if I'm probably Mexican, and California is crawling with people who look and talk like me, but being in that country made me sad. It *could* be the place where my family really came from. Somewhere in Mexico, there was probably an old woman I should be calling my *abuela,* my grandmother. Maybe she had a daughter she helped sneak across the border so she could have a better life. The lady got herself in with the wrong man and he left her when she got pregnant with me. And that's how I ended up in that Dumpster.

Even though I never liked to talk about it with Clyde, or anybody else, what happened to me when I was a baby was always on my mind. Day and night, seven days a week. It didn't make me feel no better when I read in the newspaper or seen on television how somebody else found another thrown-away baby. And it seemed to be happening more and more every day. I wondered what kind of world I lived in where people were making babies and throwing them out with the trash, or in a toilet. I was one of the lucky ones. The last one I read about somebody had tossed into a furnace to burn up. A cleaning man had found what was left of that poor little baby.

The same morning that Clyde and I got back from Mexico was my birthday. I had cheated death out of twenty-six years.

"Ester, are you all right? You been actin' real strange all day. You sure you don't wanna do nothin' special for your birthday?"

I shook my head. "Lula, I got some things on my mind. Close the door and leave me to myself." I was in my lonely bed, with sticky shit in the corners of my eyes and dribble on my lips. Lula gave me a mean look and acted like she wanted to get in my face. But she didn't. She left me to myself.

Clyde, acting like he was still high from all that shit we smoked in Mexico, was out in my living room with Lula. It was her job, which she decided on herself, to tell Clyde everything that went on while he was out of town. Just like she was somebody mama! And, as much as I hated to admit it, she was. It didn't take me long to realize that.

Lula got mad when I crawled in her bed when I had cramps, or when I just didn't want to be in my own bed alone. But she let me stay with her, cradling me like she probably would have cradled the baby she lost. I wasn't the only one who went to Lula to be babied. Rosalee was always calling up on the telephone or coming to the apartment to talk to Lula about one problem or another. Lula was a good listener, and she sometimes doled out good advice. Whether we took her advice or not was another thing.

It was just good to have a woman like Lula around to go

to with a problem. Dr. Lula. She hated to be called that. "It makes me feel old and like I should be shoulderin' everybody else's problems," Lula complained. But it didn't make no difference.

Clyde was nobody's fool. He knew when he was not around, his wives did whatever they wanted, no matter what he'd told us to do. Me included. We'd run off to Vegas and lose a few thousand dollars, pick up a stray trick to get more money to fly to L.A. to go shopping on Rodeo Drive, and eat at the same restaurants where the stars ate. Sometimes we would do all of that and Clyde would never know about it. Sometimes we would sneak out on dates with our regular tricks. That meant more money for us to do shit with other than grease Clyde's palm. We would only admit it when the tricks blabbed to him.

Clyde was the coolest, most kicked-back man I knew. Other than his child and his grandmother, sometimes it seemed like he didn't give a damn about nothing else. He never got into the kind of violence his rivals got into, beating their girls with coat hangers and stuff like that. And taking all of their money. But Clyde wasn't no wuss, and he did get tough with us when he felt like he had to. He used to slap me around a little when I got on his nerves. He stopped when he got tired of me fighting him back. He still had scars from where I bit and scratched him. The last time we ended up on the floor, bleeding and laughing about how stupid we looked. Violence was not really part of my relationship with Clyde anymore. When Clyde got mad at one of us, he would pull out his Glock and point it at us. But it was always a joke. Because we'd take it from him, cuss him out, threaten to leave him, and things would go back to normal. Why he even bothered to carry that damn gun was a mystery to me. He didn't even need it.

The last time Clyde got violent was with that Rockelle.

She got so desperate for more money, she tried to take some from his wallet when she thought he was drunk. Anyway, Rockelle was always bad news, and we all knew it. That's the real reason Clyde didn't hook her up on as many dates as he did the rest of us but he still cared enough about her to let her stay on his agenda. Besides, he loved them kids of hers. And couldn't nothing tame Clyde like kids. Nobody on this planet could say that man wasn't a good man when it came to kids. Clyde, Lula, Rosalee, and even Rockelle and her kids, they meant a lot to me. They were the closest I could come to having a real family. But that didn't stop me from feeling lonely.

I waited in my room until I heard Clyde and Lula leave my apartment. Then I got dressed and left myself. I didn't always travel in my shiny red Jetta, especially when I went over to the Mission District. I stopped doing that shit when I got tired of coming back to my car and finding some motherfucker had broken in, or stole my goddamn tires.

I took a cab downtown. From there I rode the bus to Valencia Street. For some reason, every year on my birthday, I had to go back to that place where Clyde found me: the alley that was meant to be my grave. The same place that so many drunk people go to pee, throw up, or to rob somebody. If somebody was to find out about me going back there and ask me why, I couldn't tell them.

Anyway, there was something about the alley that drew me like a magnet every year. That was the only time I went near that place. The building the alley was behind used to be a restaurant, but they turned it into a bar. Some pretty rough characters hung out there, but I never let it stop me. I just *had* to go there and feel it. Just like those people who go to that Wailing Wall I read about.

When I got to *my* alley (it was hard for me not to think of that place as mine), there was a drunk man on the ground in a puddle of his own piss and vomit. There was still a Dumpster there, but for years it looked too new to be the one I'd been left in.

For one whole hour, I sat on the ground on the side of that Dumpster with my eyes closed, making up shit in my mind. It was not a pretty story. I seen a lady, very young and pretty. She was scared. She couldn't take care of herself or the baby she just had. I was feeling that place I came from, wondering what my mama was thinking just before she dumped me. Before I could get to the worst part of my thoughts, the drunk woke up. Right away he gave me the "lady can you spare some change" look. I gave him a five dollar bill and he went on his way.

Birds was flying all up above my head, dropping their shit on the ground around me. The sky was gray, like I felt. My head was aching and my stomach was turning upside down. When I had felt enough, I got up, brushed off my jeans, and walked down to Army Street on shaky legs. I'd stayed longer than I usually did, and the drunk had come back with some of his friends looking too hard at my expensive leather jacket. The first few times I visited my spot, I'd cried when I left. I didn't cry no more. The years had made me too tough for that.


A lot of the people I used to know when I lived in the Mission District was still hanging around on the street, doing nothing, going nowhere, but to the street. I guess you could say they got as far as they was going.

It turned out to be a better birthday this time. I seen somebody I hadn't seen in years, and it was somebody I was glad to see.

"Ester Sanchez, is that you all grown up?" Coming up to me was Manuel Vasquez. He used to run these streets. He had fought with every weapon you could name, with everybody who got in his way, so that he could keep his control. He used to sell all kinds of shit out of the trunk of his lowrider. Mostly stuff that him and his homeboys got from breaking into houses in rich neighborhoods. But he'd sold weapons and dope, too. I was fifteen the last time I seen Manny. I was one of the faces in the crowd that stood around watching some racist cops stomp the crap out of him.

"Manny!" I hugged him like he was a paying trick. "You look good for an old man." Manny was only about ten years older than me, but he had the eyes of a much older man. He was still one of the best-looking Latinos I ever seen.

*"Aye yi yi! Mamacita,* you lookin' like a little Jennifer Lopez these days." He tried to widen his hooded eyes, and that made him look even older. Poor Manny.

My face got hot, and I blushed. "I only wish I had J.Lo's money and her butt." Finally, I felt really glad to be alive. My heart started beating like crazy. I couldn't remember the last time seeing an old friend had made me feel so happy. Especially one who I thought was either dead or on death row.

"Where you been, girl?" Manny lifted my chin with a shaky hand and looked at me real close with his mouth hanging open. "I thought you was dead!"

I laughed and slapped his hand. "No, not yet. Maybe closer than I wanna be, though." After my little pilgrimage, it was hard for me not to have such a grim thought.

"What you doin' here? Everything is okay?" Manny leaned back on his long legs and looked me over, rubbing my sweaty hand. "You look hungry. You want somethin' to eat? I can cook somethin' for you. I got a place over the way on Penn Street."

"I don't need no food. I-I'm just a little tired, that's all. Today is my birthday."

"Well, in that case, let me help you celebrate. You old enough now to have one of my margaritas." Manny wrapped his arm around my shoulder and kept it there all the way to his apartment four blocks away.

Manny's apartment didn't look no different or better than any of the other places I'd been inside in the Mission. It was kind of dark in his teeny-weeney living room, like the inside of a bar, even with the lights on. And like every other Latino home I'd ever been in, one wall had dollar-store pictures of this saint, that saint, the baby Jesus, and the Virgin Mother. I couldn't take my eyes off the picture of St. Jude, the saint who the most hopeless people prayed to. I never left home without a picture of St. Jude in my wallet, and I prayed to him every day of my crazy life. I believed that my prayers had kept me from getting into too much trouble. And I think it had a lot to do with me wanting to do something better with myself someday, besides selling my body.

"You got a wife now, Manny?" I asked that question because Manny's place looked too neat for a man. Even though the carpet had holes and was faded in some spots, it was clean. His lumpy couch had a nice plastic cover on it, and everything else was in place. His plants even looked nice.

"Not no more. Remember that girl from Tijuana that I used to go around with?"

"The one with the mustache?" I asked, sitting on the couch. The plastic squeaked and made a crackling noise.

"And the bow legs. Well, she married me."

"Oh." I started standing back up. The last thing I wanted to do on my birthday was fight off a jealous wife. "Lucia's a big-ass woman," I said, making a face.

"Sit back down." Manny laughed. "She left me last year. I think she's back in Mexico now." He rolled his eyes, with a sad look about them, to the side, like he couldn't face me when he said what he said next. "Back to the mama I took her from when she was fifteen." Manny looked at me now with his chest pushed out. That sad look was still in his eyes.

"Oh." I sat back down. "I guess she got tired of the gangster life, huh?"

"Oh yeah." He sighed and let out a low whistle. "And so did I. Ain't no old gangsters, just dead ones."

It was only then that I noticed the long ugly scar on the side of Manny's face, but I didn't mention it.

"What do you do with yourself these days, girl? You married?" he asked with anxious eyes. No matter how much he smiled or how he tried to express his face, his eyes never changed. It was too late and even though he was not really an old man, the eyes were. And I had a feeling they had been that way for a long time. Lately, I'd been seeing that same tortured look in my own eyes. I was lucky because I could hide mine with makeup.

"Not yet," I told him, tapping my foot on his puckered, faded carpet.

"Don't worry. A pretty girl like you, when you get ready to marry, you can choose any man you want." Manny snapped his fingers and winked at me.

All of a sudden, I didn't feel like I belonged in the same place with Manny. I stood again.

"Listen, I have to go now," I said real quick.

Manny seemed disappointed, but he didn't try to stop me. "Now that you know where I live, maybe you will come visit me sometime and let me cook you some dinner and make you a margarita."

"I don't know about that, Manny." I was moving to the door.

"You work around here? Live around here?" he asked, following me.

I shook my head.

"Well, don't hide yourself for another umpteen years, girl.

Come and visit with me sometime. I got a job cookin' at El Sol restaurant, so I know how to fix anything you want."

"So, you don't do your hustle no more?"

Manny looked at his saints and made the sign of the cross.

"Like I said, ain't no old gangsters," he told me. "But I didn't turn into Holy Moses now," he admitted with a grin. "I still smoke a little weed with my homies, I still buy shit that fell off a truck, but nothin' like before."

I was glad that I had run into my old friend, and I was glad that now when I felt bad, I had somewhere else to go.

Manny didn't need to know my business, but I knew if I told him, it would not have surprised him. Some of the girls I used to kick it with back in the day was the same ones I seen selling themselves on the Mission District streets. Like I said before, some of these people got as far as they was going to go. There was no life for them beyond the streets.

I felt like a new woman when I left Manny's apartment. Just before I'd run into Manny, my feet had felt as heavy as bricks as I'd dragged myself down the street. Now I was prancing like a colt.

# Chapter 23

# MEGAN O'ROURKE

I returned to San Francisco from Oakland in less than an hour. But I drove right past my house on Steiner.

I glanced in my rearview mirror and saw a woman I didn't want to know anymore: the woman I had been trying to hide from for almost thirty years. Because of my unexpected encounter with Clyde and our daughter, fear had attacked me like a cancer, and it was spreading fast.

I couldn't remember driving back down Oakland's International Boulevard after leaving Clyde. I couldn't even remember getting back onto the Bay Bridge. One minute I was talking to Clyde and the next thing I knew I was back across the bay, meandering down one street after another. I remembered the sounds of the road rage I'd caused, though. Horns had blared at me, gruff voices had cursed me, and some irate motorist had hurled a beer can, clanking it against the side of my passenger door.

How long I drove around, I couldn't say. My body was in one place, my mind was in another. But even my confused state of mind didn't prevent me from finding my way to a bar, with a name I couldn't remember, off the freeway.

I had hit something—a dog, a cat? If I'd hit a human I'd find out soon enough. I vaguely remembered something thumping against the front of my car as I wandered off the Bay Bridge at the first exit, my Lexus creeping along like a snail. I glimpsed blood on the left side of my front fender when I parked my car in the lot at the tacky bar next to a dusty truck with the "T" missing from Toyota. I staggered into the bar, ignoring the unholy stench of burned grease and the gum on the floor that stuck to the bottom of my shoe. Like a falling tree, I fell sideways onto the hard plastic seat in the first empty booth I found.

Big, hairy, beefy-faced, foul-smelling truck drivers and bikers sat and stood on either side of me. During my delirium I must have ordered a drink because I blinked and a double shot of rum appeared on the table in front of me. I snatched it and drank with the eagerness and desperation of a junkie getting an overdue fix. With my sudden potent buzz, I placed my head on the table like it was a guillotine.

I had not been confronted by any drug addicts, muggers, or carjackers in Oakland, but I was lucky I made it back to San Francisco alive. After seeing Clyde Brooks and the daughter that he and I had produced, my life was about to flash before me anyway. The same way I heard it did when a person was dying.

Clyde had entered my life at a very early age. It was the summer of 1968 when we were both eight years old.

According to Mom, '68 was the year that "evil spirits" courted every young person in America, especially the San Francisco Bay Area, which included such hotbeds as Oakland and Berkeley. Mom blamed some of America's uproar on Vietnam, the Democrats, Jimi Hendrix, all males with

long hair, all females who associated with males with long
hair, and drugs. Even though we lived in a huge stucco house
on a palm tree–lined street in Oakland Hills, the turmoil of
the sixties was as much a part of our home as it was the
streets of Berkeley.

Trying to prove that our family was liberal, my parents
didn't protest when Clyde's grandmother, Effie Brooks, our
maid for the past twenty years, brought Clyde to work with
her the morning that altered my future. So far, other than our
Black maid and our Panamanian handyman, my association
with people of color had been very limited.

My curiosity overwhelmed me. I tried to find out as much
as I could about the mysterious dark people making such a
fuss over everything. Unlike the other kids my age on my
street, who still enjoyed Bugs Bunny and Fred Flintstone
cartoons, I preferred news programs that featured stories
about the protestors in the southern states, updates on Dr.
Martin Luther King's assassination, and the angry news-
makers right in my backyard: the Black Panthers.

Clyde Brooks had been my first best friend. Well, at least
my first Black friend. And my first "boy" friend. In my fan-
tasies, he was a Black Panther waiting to happen. The first
time I saw him, he was standing on our front porch with his
grandmother. There was a scowl on his face so extreme, he
looked like he was ready to blow up the world. I was vividly
impressed.

Clyde was standing in front of his grandmother, with his
thin arms folded across his narrow chest. His smooth dark
skin and neat, well-oiled Afro glistened in the early morning
sunlight. I peeked from behind my mother when she opened
the door.

"Mornin', Miss Carmody. Uh, this my grandson, Clyde,
what I brought back from Mississippi on the train last

night." Effie paused and sniffed, her gnarled hand rubbing Clyde's shoulder. "My cousin Bobby Lee, he changed his mind about takin' the boy in. I couldn't leave this boy back there in Mississippi by hisself." Effie paused again and looked from Mom's face to mine, then back to Mom's, her hand still rubbing Clyde's shoulder. Effie grunted and let out a deep breath that had become familiar. That was the way she expressed her impatience. Like a lot of the Black and Hispanic women who worked as domestics in our neighborhood, Effie had a lot of power. She practically ran our house, making up rules for us to follow. And as long as Effie's demands were not too outrageous, we usually did as we were told. Effie took off work when she wanted to, with pay. She had even talked Daddy into paying for her medical coverage. When it came time for our carpets to be cleaned, Effie had Mom call in a carpet cleaning service. And, as if it were a running joke, which in our case it wasn't, Effie didn't do windows. Before Mom could respond to Effie's comments about her grandson, I already knew Mom's response. But, Effie asked anyway. "Can Clyde play with Miss Meg while I do my business? This is the only child of my only child, may she rest in peace," Effie rattled on. She had just returned from burying her daughter, a woman she herself described as, "A wart on Satan's butt."

"Where's the boy's daddy?" Mom asked, her voice sounding more like a kitten's meow. My mother and Effie had little in common, but each had recently buried a child. Effie's daughter, Bonnie Jean, had been killed in a barroom brawl in Pearl, Mississippi. My older, and only brother, Paul, had lost his life in Vietnam three months ago.

Effie shrugged. "That's somethin' I ain't never knowed. He took off before this boy was even born. Come to think of it, I never even knowed who that scallywag was in the first place. Bonnie Jean had a army of 'em paradin' in and out of her house. That gal of mine, fast as she was, ain't slowed down long enough to tell me who planted this boy in her. With all her drinkin' and God knows what else, it's a wonder the boy turned out as good as he did. He got teef that would snap a nail in two." Clyde grinned for the first time, revealing the whitest, strongest-looking teeth I'd ever seen. "And look at his hand. Look like a shovel, don't it?" With a broad smile, Effie lifted Clyde's right hand and handed it to Mom who blinked, turned the small ashy hand over, inspecting it like she would a piece of fruit at the farmer's market.

I covered my mouth to keep from laughing. The way Effie was talking, she made Clyde sound like something you'd find in a cabbage patch.

A slight noise in the background made Mom and me turn around. Dad was standing in the doorway leading to the kitchen. My brother had been Dad's favorite and he was still overwhelmed with grief. He spent most of his time in his study or roaming through the house like a ghost. Dad blinked at the commotion at the front door, and then fixed his eyes on the floor. Without a word, he returned to the private gloom of his study.

Clyde's eyes were like none I'd ever seen before. His gaze was cold, flat, and hard. It was the first time I had ever seen a tiny image of myself reflected in another person's eyes. But when he blinked, my reflection disappeared, even though I was still standing in the same spot.

"Has he had all of his shots?" Mom asked. This time it was Clyde who covered his mouth with his hand to keep from laughing.

"Oh, y'all ain't got to worry about catchin' nothin' from this boy. He clean as a whistle. That's the one thing his mama done right. She kept the boy clean. Shame she didn't get him circumcised." Effie lowered her voice and leaned closer to Mom. "A midwife delivered the boy at home," Effie whispered. I didn't know what *circumcised* meant at the time, so I didn't react with an embarrassed giggle the way Clyde did.

"Granny, hush!" Clyde ordered, jabbing his grandmother's side with his elbow.

"Well, I guess it's all right. For now, at least," Mom said, her voice weak and hollow.

"It'll just be until I can work somethin' out with Sister Price next door to my house. As soon as she heal from her hip surgery, she'll be keepin' a eye on the boy. But that won't be for a spell. In the meantime, him and Miss Meg can keep each other occupied," Effie declared.

*Occupied* was a mild word for my relationship with Clyde. The first time I got him alone, I felt his hair and his skin.

"What's wrong with you, girl?" he asked, slapping my hand away. "You don't know me. Don't be puttin' your hands on my hair." Clyde moved a few steps away and patted his Afro, looking at me with contempt. "It took me all mornin' to get my 'fro lookin' this good. Shoot."

We were alone in the bedroom I'd once shared with my older sister, Fiona. Fiona was "living" somewhere in the southern part of the state. According to Mom, Fiona shared a "snake pit," and her drugs, with a bunch of other barefoot hippies. We hadn't seen or heard from her in weeks. She had come home for our Memorial Day barbecue with a long-haired, scruffy, wild-eyed man she'd introduced as Charlie. The world would later know that murderous creep as Charles Manson.

"I just wanted to see what your hair felt like. I like it," I replied with admiration and pleasure.

"You can tell that just by lookin'. Y'all White folks ain't got enough to do, you gotta always be messin' with Black folks. Well, don't nobody mess with me!" Clyde exclaimed.

"I am just tryin' to be friends." I pouted, adding a sniff.

"Well, I don't need no White girl for no friend," Clyde insisted, clicking on the portable television set on the dresser facing my bed. "Y'all got any pop?"

I nodded. "Uh-huh. But I—"

"Go get me one," Clyde ordered. He had the same authority in his voice as his grandmother. I sprinted from my room and returned within minutes with a can of Pepsi and a glass of ice on a tray. I handed it to Clyde with a grin. "Go shut that door," he told me.

I did that, too.

By the end of summer, Clyde had me and most of my friends at his beck and call. We eagerly lent him everything from money to expensive clothes. We marched behind him like he was leading us to the Promised Land. He was usually the only Black boy in the parks where I played with my friends, but that didn't seem to bother him. He was in control, and that intrigued me.

I was sorry when September rolled around that year. Clyde would have no excuse to be in our neighborhood. Living in the guts of East Oakland, Effie enrolled Clyde in one of the roughest elementary schools in Oakland. The year before, a twelve-year-old boy raped a teacher and beat her up so badly she was in a coma for a month. And girls as young as eleven were dropping out of school to have babies.

As the years crawled by, Effie's health declined and she had to reduce her hours at our house. I only got to see her two days a week. I missed her companionship and guidance, but the part of her that I missed the most was Clyde. It was almost eight years from the summer we became friends before I saw Clyde again.

To help out at home, and hopefully keep him out of trouble, Effie made Clyde work after school and between his visits to the juvenile detention center. He had become the kind of boy my mother had warned me about.

That was reason enough for me to keep a safe distance between myself and Clyde Brooks. But I didn't realize that until it was too late.

# Chapter 24

# LULA HAWKINS

I knew Clyde well enough to know that something was bothering him big time. He hadn't been to the apartment in a week for a quick romp in the bed with either me, Ester, or both of us at the same time. And that was something he rarely failed to do at least twice a week. Especially since we had him thinking he was so good in bed, which still was not the case. But it made our lives easier for him to think he was.

Clyde not coming by to flop around in bed with us was one thing, but him not coming around to collect his trick money was another. When he was out of town, it was my responsibility to collect from the girls. And even then, he would call several times a day to make sure I was on my job.

Rockelle claimed that she had spoken to Clyde a day earlier, so we knew he wasn't out of town, in jail, in the hospital, or dead. "He was acting and sounding strange. Even for him," Rockelle reported, sounding more than a little concerned.

It was a sad subject to bring up, but my guess was that Clyde was having more trouble with his daughter. He never complained about how hard it was to take care of her. But he was always dropping hints about how much he depended on the extra money he got from us, and how he wouldn't know what to do with Keisha if he didn't have us "helping him out." Since I had lost my only child, and it didn't look like I would have another one anytime soon, parenthood was a depressing subject for me.

As much as I adored Clyde's daughter, I avoided being around her. Mainly because it broke my heart to see a man like Clyde having to deal with such a heavy load as taking care of a severely handicapped adult child. But if my son had lived, it wouldn't have mattered to me if he had horns and hoofed feet. I would have moved mountains if I had to, to make his life worth living. Clyde was not perfect, but his devotion to his daughter was almost saintly. But as it turned out, Clyde's odd behavior had nothing to do with his daughter.

"I called up his grandmother and asked her if everything was all right with Keisha," Rosalee said. "She handed the telephone to Keisha and she told me herself that she was fine. I asked if she knew what was botherin' her daddy and she said she didn't notice anything different about him."

Then another week went by. Clyde still hadn't called or come by the apartment or communicated with me or any of the other girls. One of the things that Clyde hated was for us to cancel or turn down a date with a regular. That Friday night, Ester and I both turned down dates with regulars. For the first time, Clyde didn't cuss us out like he usually did when we did that. Then the situation got even more mysterious. Not only was Clyde acting odd, but Ester was looking and acting downright crazy, too. I didn't want to say it to her face, or share my thoughts with Rosalee or Rockelle, but I began to think that Ester and Clyde were in some kind of cahoots. Like maybe she and Clyde were planning a major scam that would involve the rest of us, but not benefit us.

Lately, Ester had a glassy-eyed look on her face. She wasn't running her mouth like a motor the way she usually did. And, she wasn't even eating or drinking as much. That little woman gnawed on tortilla chips and guzzled tequila like it was water. When I finally got up enough nerve to talk to Ester about her strange attitude, she surprised me with a bombshell of a response.

I'd entered her bedroom and found her standing in front of the window, hands on her hips, staring out, looking at the sky. Her long dark hair was in a single braid, hanging across her shoulder like a rope.

"So what if I been acting and looking crazy. I can say the same thing about you," Ester told me as I shuffled across her bedroom floor, careful not to disturb the expensive, thick throw rugs covering most of her shaggy beige carpet. I never could figure out why Ester covered a carpeted floor with throw rugs. Especially when there were no little kids around to make a mess on it by spilling Kool-Aid and other kid-friendly shit. "You got me worried as much as Clyde," she added. "You ain't been eatin', you been lookin' weird, and you ain't been talkin' much. Wassup with you, girlfriend?"

Ester was right. I had been acting unlike myself, too. I sighed and plopped down on Ester's bed, which reminded me of her floor. Short thick blankets and about half a dozen pillows hid her beautiful blue goose-down comforter.

"There's this man I met. A bus driver, would you believe," I laughed, looking upside the wall on the opposite side of the room. "I can't believe I'm sittin' here tellin' you this," I admitted. Out of the corner of my eye, I saw Ester's head snap around to face me.

"That's why you acting so strange? Because you met a man? Me, too!" she gasped.

I marched over to Ester with my arms dangling. "You,

you met somebody, too?" Then my heart almost stopped. "I hope you ain't gettin' all excited over a trick," I hollered.

Ester didn't waste any time shaking her head. "What you take me for? I ain't desperate like that Carlene. I would never get serious with a trick." Carlene Thompson, the woman who had steered Rockelle and Rosalee in Clyde's direction, had recently run off to Las Vegas with one of her regular tricks and married him. They had moved to Richland, Ohio, so that Carlene could help take care of her former madam, Scary Mary, who was in her nineties and raising all kinds of hell.

"Then he's a civilian like my bus driver?"

"Somethin' like that. But I didn't just meet him. I been knowin' him since I was a kid. His name is Manuel Vasquez. Manny. I seen him on my birthday when I was hangin' out in the Mission." Ester paused. A look appeared on her face that I had never seen before. She smiled, but just a little, and her eyes started blinking real fast, like she was trying to hold back some tears.

"Was he your boyfriend? Or just your man?" I wanted to know.

"My man? What you mean by that?" she snapped, a stunned look on her face.

"Is he, uh, like Clyde?"

"Look, Clyde is the only man in this crazy world that I ever sold my little pussy for. I ain't like them other girls out there, you know that. Shit. Manny would never let me do somethin' like that for him."

"I didn't mean anything. It's just that . . ."

Ester held up her hands and gave me a sharp look. Her lips were quivering. "I can't change what I already done in the past, just the future." Ester moved to the bed and plopped down, her palms flat against her knees. "Manny's a good man, a strong man. He would be good for me."

"What does he do for a livin' then?" I asked, my heart beating a mile a minute.

As much as I liked Ester, she was one of the crudest women I'd ever known. From what I knew about her, in my opinion, Clyde was probably the best she could do as far as getting a man who wasn't just a trick. I felt bad about feeling the way I did, but I couldn't help it. Unlike Rockelle, who still thought her shit didn't stink, I usually kept certain thoughts to myself. I knew I was not going to be sleeping with men for money until I got so worn out they wouldn't want me. But since Ester had been in the business so much longer than me and never really talked about retiring any time soon, I assumed she'd end up staying in it as long as Carlene did.

I liked Ester and hoped that she was stashing away enough tax-free money in a safe-deposit box like the rest of us, so that she could live comfortably in her old age. "Ester, is Manny dealin' drugs?" My breath caught in my throat when I saw the hurt look on Ester's face. "Uh . . . or does he have some other hustle goin' on?" The more I talked, the more it seemed like I was putting both my feet deeper and deeper into my mouth.

"He cooks in a restaurant. Happy?" she snapped abruptly, giving me one of the dirtiest looks she could come up with.

"Oh, so he's a chef." I smiled, hoping it would soften her.

"I ain't said nothin' about no chef. Chefs is what they have in them fancy places downtown. Manny cooks greasy burritos, oxtails, tongue sandwiches, you know all that shit we crazy Mexicans eat." Ester gave me a dry look. "You think all I can get is a thug, don't you? You think I can't get me a *bus driver* like you?"

"Don't be gettin' all crazy on me. What else could I think? Whatever he is, I'm happy for you. There ain't nothin' wrong with bein' a cook," I said.

Ester shook her head, and an embarrassed look appeared on her face. "That's what he does now, but he used to do all kinds of other shit, he shouldn't have been doin'. Stealin' shit, sellin' that shit out of his car. Dealin' drugs when he couldn't find nothin' to steal. But he's hella straight-up now. I would be very proud to call him my boo. It's just that, bein' with another man, like that, while I'm still with Clyde . . . well, I don't want to think about tryin' to please them both." Ester paused and let out a weak laugh. "You know how deep my people get caught up in that passion shit. When we love somebody, they stay loved." She let out a loud sigh and shrugged. "But . . . I don't think I can be with Manny as long as I'm workin' for Clyde. It wouldn't be fair to Clyde, or to Manny, or me."

Ester's words made the insides of my stomach shift. I joined her on the bed and put my arm around her shoulder. Unless we were in bed, at the same time, with the same man, I rarely got this close to Ester or any of the other women I dealt with.

I nodded and gave her a thoughtful look. Ester's comment about developing a relationship with another man while she was still part of Clyde's crew was ringing in my ears. It was sad but true, but at the moment, I needed Clyde more than I needed a bus driver in my bed. I suddenly found myself wishing that I'd never laid eyes on Richard Rice, or that he had at least been an obnoxious asshole. Then I could have cussed him out that day in Tad's Steakhouse and gone about my business. Love had to be the most painful emotion in the world. It was love that had caused me to make a fool of myself with Larry.

"So, what about the man you met?" Ester asked, turning to face me.

"You know, I must be losin' my mind," I said with a heavy voice. "Now that I think about him, I realize a broke-ass bus driver ain't nobody I'd want to get involved with. Especially a man with a cheesy name like Richard Rice."

Telling such a bald-faced lie was so painful the inside of my mouth felt like I'd slid a burning match into it.

# Chapter 25

# MEGAN O'ROURKE

It had been three weeks since my encounter with Clyde that Saturday. I'd appeased Mom that day by telling her that I had not made it to Oakland and had gone to have lunch with a woman from my exercise class instead. And, Robert, well he had not even asked if I'd found a car for our daughter. He'd been in Baja on a fishing trip for the past ten days. With him and my mother out of my hair, I had more space and time to think. But even with all of the space in my house, it felt too claustrophobic, and there were too many things in it to remind me of the life I had with Robert.

I was nursing my fourth drink in the same dingy bar I'd ended up in after seeing Clyde that grim day the month before. But I had to relive it all before I could figure out how I was going to handle my future.

My mind traveled back in time again. I replayed some of the things I'd already filtered through during the previous weeks.

A month before my sixteenth birthday, my sister, Fiona, died from an overdose of heroin. My parents were still mourning the death of my brother at the time. Losing another child almost destroyed us all so I promised my parents that I would not cause them any further grief. And I probably would have kept that promise if Clyde had not reentered my life. This time, he had accompanied his grandmother to work so that he could earn a few dollars doing odd jobs around our house. He cut our grass, washed the three cars we maintained, and groomed our three collies.

Clyde was more handsome than ever. However, I couldn't take advantage of his good looks the way I wanted to. I had too many other distractions to keep me occupied at the time. Like my upcoming birthday party and my cool friends who always seemed to know where to get the best dope. I never got that heavy into drugs, not after what happened to my sister. But everybody I knew smoked pot. To me it was no worse than smoking cigarettes. I was usually too stoned out of my skull to pay too much attention to Clyde until the night of my party.

Effie had made all of the snacks, and agreed to work late that night to serve and clean up afterward. Of course, Clyde had not been invited, but he wandered into the recreation room in back of our house facing our kidney-shaped pool, just as my party was winding down.

"Granny said for me to bring y'all the last of them sandwiches," Clyde yelled, strutting past Dennis Russo on the floor, the only boy I knew personally who came close to being a drug dealer. Dennis had just come in from our back patio where he had puked for fifteen minutes. His face was red, his eyes dilated, and his legs so weak he couldn't stand. Clyde hopped around Dennis's prostrate body, then looked from Dennis to me, handing me the platter of sandwiches. "I guess dude done did enough partyin' for one night, huh?" Clyde glanced around the room with an amused look on his face. There were only four other kids left. I was the only one still able to stand.

"Oh, he's fine. He had a little too much to, uh, eat," I lied.

"I bet he did," Clyde said, smirking, then added in a low voice, "and another thing, I bet he had too much of the bad shit."

I set the platter of sandwiches on the pool table. "And what do you mean by that?"

"Girl, you know damn well what I'm talkin' about. You people wouldn't know good dope from a bale of hay." *You people?* Clyde glanced toward the door, then leaned closer to me. "If you ever want to feel real good, just let me know."

Effie's sweaty Black face floated into the room on a body that had spread in the most peculiar way over the years. From the neck down, she looked like a lumpy pyramid. "Clyde, get your narrow butt movin'. Lickety-split!" she yelled, clapping her hands and stomping her foot. Still facing Clyde, she spoke in a sharp voice. "And, Miss Meg, Miss Carmody said I can clean up tomorrow. On account of I don't want to be out too late waitin' on no bus with all them rapists on the loose." Effie paused and gave me a sly glance over her shoulder. A huge crooked black vein bulged out on the side of her neck like a snake. She casually cleared her throat and continued, speaking with her hands on hips that looked like they had a mind of their own. "She says if we go now, she'll give us a ride home and we won't have to take that bus."

"Can I ride along, too?" I asked quickly, intrigued by Clyde's remarks about making me feel "real good."

"What about your friends?" Effie wiggled her nose and made a sweeping gesture with her hand. Dennis was moaning and twisting around on the floor. One thing I had to say about my parents, they never disrupted my parties unless some busybody neighbor called the cops when the music got too loud. Tonight's party had been tame compared to the last one I had when Lynette Sweetser attacked Deborah Retner with a punch bowl for dancing with her boyfriend.

"Oh, they all live around here. They can find their way home," I insisted, already rushing from the rec room to get my purse. "I'd like to see where you live."

When I had opened the back door on the passenger side of Mom's Buick for Effie to crawl in, Effie ignored me and snatched open the front passenger door and sat down, looking at me with a smirk. "I don't sit in the back of nobody's vehicle no more. In the state of California or in Mississippi. Ain't got to no more," she purred with defiance. A glare from her deep-set, shiny black eyes alone was enough to make any normal person tremble. Mom trembled and turned beet red. Like I said, Effie always did what she wanted, and she would have, whether the civil rights law said she could or not.

One of the many things that puzzled me was, if there were other Black people as proud and fierce-looking as Effie and could control a situation as well as she could, why was the Black race in such a mess? I didn't even think that Effie could answer that question, so I never even thought about asking.

"Clyde, where is your manners, boy? Don't you see Miss Meg standin' here waitin' on you to help her into her mama's car?" Effie said smugly.

With a look that displayed both surprise and annoyance, Clyde stepped aside and held the back passenger door open for me. The cool breeze from the night air on my face helped clear my head. But I became even more alert when Clyde's knee touched mine. It stayed there all the way to Effie's dreary street.

We were in an area in Oakland that I had never been in before in my life. It was a foreign-looking neighborhood with old houses in desperate need of paint and repairs and boatlike cars that looked older than I was. Garishly dressed dark-skinned people with outlandish hairdos occupied the corners, staring hungrily at every moving car. Surprisingly, I was not the least bit afraid. For some reason, I felt safe with Effie and especially Clyde. If anything, I was curious about these mysterious people. I felt like I was on an African safari.

I got so curious during the next few days, that I decided to pay Effie and Clyde a visit on my own. I had recently acquired my driver's license, but I was only allowed to drive Mom's car. I knew enough about East Oakland to know that it was not a safe place for an expensively dressed White girl to be alone and driving a nice car. Short of putting on an Afro wig and a dashiki, I made myself look as inconspicuous as possible. Even though it was night, I had on dark glasses, a scarf, and dark clothing.

As soon as I reached Clyde's street, I slowed down so that I could see the houses better. When I stopped, a scowling, bearded man leaped out of nowhere. He tapped on my window and held up two fingers. I stepped on the gas and didn't stop until I was back on the freeway.

I didn't know why then, and I don't know why now, but I stopped at the first pay phone I saw and dialed Effie's number. I prayed that Effie would answer so I could just hang up, but it was Clyde who answered. I was surprised to hear soft, easy listening music in the background. If anything, I had expected either some of Effie's wailing gospel music, something Motown, or one of the many disco tunes that Clyde and every other teenager I knew liked.

"Clyde, this is Meg."

"Meg who?" he said, sounding more annoyed than curious.

"Carmody."

"Oh. What the hell do you want?"

"Uh, I drove by your house a few minutes ago." I don't know what I was feeling at that moment, but I had come too far to turn back now.

Clyde took his time responding, clicking his teeth in a way that made me think he was doing it on purpose to annoy me. "For what?" He didn't even try to hide his impatience.

His arrogant attitude did annoy me, but I didn't want him to know that. "I thought maybe I'd see you."

"You drove by my house thinkin' you'd see *me?* What would I be doin' roamin' around outside the house this time of night? That's what cats and puppy dogs do when they got to do their business." He laughed.

"I just wanted to talk. I've known you for so many years, and I really don't know you."

"Well, what you want to know, Miss Meg?"

"Clyde, you don't have to call me 'Miss' if you don't want to. You're just as good as I am. We're equals."

Clyde was silent for a long time before he responded to my patronizing comment.

"I can call your White ass anything I wanna call you. And fuck that 'we equal' bullshit. You ain't nowhere near my equal." He laughed. "I don't believe your sorry White ass. Now what the fuck you want with me, bitch? I got more important things to do with my time than stand here on this phone listenin' to your whinin' ass."

I was so horrified, I could barely speak. I surprised myself when I did. "Clyde, I didn't mean to offend you. I just want you to think of me as just another one of your friends. Do you call the Black girls you know 'Miss?' "

"Fuck no! Is that what you called me up to talk about?"

"No, I—"

"Then quit pussy-footin around the damn bush, and say what you got to say. Shoot."

I took a deep breath and glanced around to make sure I was still alone. I gripped the telephone so hard, my palm ached. "You got any good pot?" I whispered.

"Everything I got is good. And I do mean *everything*. When you want it?" he asked eagerly, in a more pleasant tone.

"Uh, can you meet me somewhere?"

"Yeah, I can do that. Where you wanna meet at?"

"How about one of those motels off 880, just before the airport turnoff?"

"I ain't got no car, so wherever we go, I got to take a bus to get there. Unless you wanna come out here and pick me up," Clyde told me. The harshness had returned to his voice.

"Can't you get to one of those motels off the freeway by bus?"

Clyde cursed under his breath. "Look, girl, I know you don't know nothin' about the way folks in the *real* world live. You been livin' the Ozzie and Harriet lifestyle all your life. Now if you want to hook up with me, that's fine. But I ain't about to drag myself around, transferrin' to two different buses, and then havin' to walk part of the way, just to get to one of them motels off the freeway. Not for you or anybody else. Goddammit. There is one bus I can walk to from here, one block, get on it, and it'll bring me all the way downtown. There's motels, hotels down there. I . . . wait a minute. What's wrong with me? I ain't got to go through all them damn changes. You want some good weed, *you come to me*. Plain and simple. Like everybody else. Shit."

I swallowed hard. "All right. Be standing in front of your house. I will pick you up in fifteen minutes."

"That'll work."

"Uh, what do you have?"

"What you want?"

"You said you had something, uh, real good."

Clyde was taking too long to answer.

"Clyde?"

"I'm still here, baby." He sighed. "And like I said, everything I got is good." He laughed.

"Clyde, are you coming on to me?" I teased.

"You would think that. Let's get one thing straight right now, not every brother want to get down with you just 'cause you White. Sure, if you was to let me, hell yeah, I'd hit it. But I'd do that even if you was purple. With my eyes closed, I can't tell one pussy from another. I'm all for equal opportunity. Get it?"

I let out a noisy sigh. "Let's just concentrate on getting high."

"That'll work for me. You the one brought up all that other shit. Shit."

"I'm on my way, Clyde."

"That's cool. But if you ain't here in fifteen minutes, I'm gone."


I picked Clyde up ten minutes later. There was never any doubt in my mind that it would be up to me to cover the motel expenses, but I brought it up anyway.

With a sharp gasp, Clyde leaned against the side of the passenger door of Mom's car and looked at me out of the corner of his eye. "Fuck no, I ain't payin' half, a third, or no other part of no motel bill." He laughed and shook his head. "For you people to be so smart, y'all sure can come up with some dumb-ass shit. What do you be thinkin', girl?"

"And what's that supposed to mean?"

"It means a lot of things, Megan. Like, why would a girl like you be out here by yourself with somebody like me?"

I shrugged. "Don't you like being out here alone with a girl like me?"

"Don't flatter yourself. Rich White girls come at me everywhere I go. You ain't nothin' special. Look at you," Clyde said, tilting his head to look at me out of the corner of his eye. "You ain't even cute."

I decided to keep my thoughts and comments to myself until we reached the motel.

Less than an hour in that first motel, we fucked. When we needed money for more pot and motels, I was always the one responsible for that, which was usually no problem. But when it did get to be a problem, like my folks demanding to know what it was I suddenly needed so much money for, I got real creative.

I knew of several girls at my school who worked for escort services. And as hard as it was for me to believe, there were men out there willing to pay good money just to have a cute young girl like me do the same things with them that I did with Clyde for free. I signed up with two services, using a fake ID with a fake name.

"Look, Meg, you ain't got to be layin' up with none of them dudes if you don't want to. We can always get money from somewhere else," Clyde told me when I was forced to tell him what I was into, after I'd broken so many dates with him. "I got all kinds of ways to make money."

"Knocking drunk old men in the back of the head, ripping off drug dealers, breaking into cars—is that any better than what I do?" I wanted to know. I didn't enjoy working as an escort. But it was the only way I could get the money I needed to be with Clyde as often as I wanted.

"That ain't the point. They got some maniacs out there

doin' all kinds of shit to girls when they get 'em alone. You ain't scared of hoppin' in a car with a stranger? You ain't like them girls from my neighborhood and the barrios. Sisters and Latinas, they know how to get down when some motherfucker try to disrespect them and get ugly."

I shrugged. "I can take care of myself, too," I insisted, waving the ten crisp twenty dollar bills I had just made an hour earlier. Clyde's anxious eyes lit up as he looked at the money. "The service checks the men out first. Old businessmen, regular customers. These men are not only real harmless, some of them are quite nice. That guy from United Airlines that I went out with tonight, all he wanted was a simple hand job. It only took ten minutes," I said proudly.

An anxious look appeared on Clyde's face. "And?" In a flash, he snatched the money from me and was looking at it like it was something rare and precious. To a boy like him, I assumed it was.

"And what?"

"And what else did you do for a trick?" With his tongue sliding across his bottom lip, Clyde counted the money with a flourish, tapping it with the tips of his fingers before folding it in half. Then, like it was money that he had earned, he stuffed it all into his pocket. "It was that easy, you say?"

I nodded. "It was that easy."

Clyde gave me a brief blank look, and then a naughty smile eased onto his face. "Shit," he mouthed, patting his pocket with the money in it.

"Most of the guys do want hand jobs, tittie fucks, blow jobs. I haven't even had to fuck any of them yet," I revealed, cringing at the thought of my next date with a stranger.

"Hmmm," Clyde said. "Like I said, you ain't got to be layin' up with them dudes to make money. But, if you ain't got no problem with it, I ain't got no problem with it neither. You just keep bein' cool, and I'll do the same thing."

"That's cool," I said, proud that I had become so street smart.

Clyde still came around to do maintenance work at our house, and, on me, on a regular basis. I had lost my virginity the year before to the visiting cousin of a casual friend. And I'd also slept with a few other boys before Clyde, but making love with Clyde was an experience within itself. I had never enjoyed sex as much as I did with him, and I never would, not even with the man I married. *Especially* with the man I married. With Clyde, I would get excited just by the sight of his dark brown skin being close enough to mine to make us both sweat. I had no trouble sneaking out to meet him in motels and drive-in movies, paying for it with money I'd collected from the many eager men, young and old, who had made my life more exciting and so much more fun.

During the seventies, having unprotected sex was not that big of a deal. Almost everybody I knew had had a curable sexually transmitted disease at least once. Abortions were legal in California, so getting rid of a baby before it could be born only meant a side trip to a clinic and a few hours to recuperate. It was nothing more than a minor inconvenience. I had girlfriends who had already had more than one abortion, but the notion frightened me.

I don't know where or when I got pregnant, and I don't know why I was surprised when it happened. The first and only time we discussed condoms, Clyde laughed and said, "Usin' a rubber is like takin' a bath in a raincoat—what's the point?" Him pulling out of me before ejaculating made him laugh just as hard. "That's like chewin' up a piece of fried chicken, then spittin' it out instead of swallowin' it. Shit. What's the point?"

I was not prepared for Clyde's reaction when I told him I

was pregnant. We were sharing the well-used backseat of Mom's new Buick in the last row at a drive-in movie theater. I don't even remember what movie was playing that night. Clyde's body stiffened, and he pushed me away as soon as I'd revealed my condition.

"You been mighty busy at that escort agency. How I know it's my baby?"

"I have not had full sex with anybody but you in the last three months," I told him, and it was the truth. "And you are the only person I've ever fucked without a condom."

"Well, whether it's mine or not, what you plannin' on doin'? What you goin' to tell your mama and daddy? This kind of news could kill 'em."

"Oh, I doubt that. Not after all they've been through, losing my brother and my sister and all."

"Well, I ain't got much to offer, jobwise, but I'll marry you, if you want me to." Clyde scratched the back of his head, which no longer sported a bushy Afro. He was one step from being bald. And on him, even that looked sexy.

*Married?*

I was the one laughing this time. "You have got to be kidding. *I* can't marry *you*." I could not believe my ears. My friends and family would never accept my marriage to Clyde. Not because he was Black, but, like he said, he didn't have much to offer me.

I had heard too many horror stories about abortions, so that was out. But even before I told Clyde, or anyone else, that I was pregnant, I had made up my mind to have the baby and give it up for adoption.

"Well, if you think you too good to marry a brother, I got news for you, *Miss Meg,* I'd be too embarrassed to bring you around my family, too. With your flat ass, stringy hair, and your my-shit-don't-stink-'cause-I'm-White attitude. But I'd be willin' to put up with whatever shit I had to put up with to be there for my child. I plan to do what my daddy should have done for me. Put your clothes back on so we can get the hell up out of here."

Clyde and I left the drive-in movie in silence. We were halfway to his house, where I would drop him off, before we spoke again.

"So, how far along are you?" he asked in a distant voice.

"A couple of months, I think."

"Let me know when you wanna go to the place to get took care of. We ain't got to tell 'em our real names or nothin'. The county'll pay for it, too."

"I'm not having an abortion, if that's what you're talking about!" I yelled. I didn't tell him that two of my closest friends could no longer have kids because of botched abortions.

"Well, what else the hell do you plan to do? If you plannin' on havin' it, you and your precious family can expect to see me at your house *every* day anyway 'cause I'll wanna see my kid."

"You care enough about this baby you want to be a part of its life, but you'd be willing to let me abort it?" I hissed.

Clyde slammed his fist against the side of the car door so hard the windows rattled. "What's your plan then?"

"Adoption," I said calmly.

"Bullshit! Oh—heeeell no! Ain't no child of mine goin' to be out there in the world bein' raised by some stranger as long as I'm alive. If you have this baby, you give it to me. I will see that he or she get taken care of real good."

After losing my brother, Paul, to Vietnam, and my sister, Fiona, to the unknown, Mom and Dad had experienced enough pain where their children were concerned to last them a lifetime. My little "problem" didn't raise as much of a ruckus as I'd expected. I was my parents' only hope if they wanted to have grandchildren. However, my first child was considered more of an inconvenience.

"My cousin in Mississippi, Bobby Lee, he'll keep the child with him and his wife down there in Mississippi. That way, y'all ain't got to worry about nothin' embarrassin'," Effie insisted. "White folks is too frail-minded to be tryin' to raise a half-Black child. Especially y'all."

Effie, Clyde, my parents, and I had gathered in my parents' living room, for the last time, I might add, to discuss the situation.

"We will take care of all financial obligations until the child is of legal age," Dad said, clearing his throat. My poor father looked twice his age. In the last ten years, he'd lost all of his hair. And the handsome face that I'd bragged about all through elementary school looked ragged and beaten. Mom didn't look too much better. There was sadness in her eyes that no amount of makeup could hide.

"We don't want your money," Clyde barked, holding his hand up defensively. "All I want from y'all is my child." He leaped up from his seat and started pacing the floor like a caged tiger.

"Clyde, raisin' a child is expensive. We gwine to need all the help we can get. These folks are the child's grandparents, and they have some say-so," Effie insisted, looking older by the minute. She was already in her late sixties, and sometimes needed as much care as a baby herself.

"I want to be with my child," Clyde insisted. "I don't want no countrified relatives in no hick town in Mississippi raisin' a child of mine. They couldn't even deal with me!"

I could not believe my eyes. Clyde was crying!

"Then you can take it to Mississippi when it comes and stay there to help raise it," Effie snapped.

"I don't want to go back to Mississippi," Clyde whined, wiping his eyes with the back of his trembling hand.

"Then shet up!" Effie roared with such emotion, everyone in the room jumped.

"I'm goin' down there to see my child every chance I get," Clyde stated, a determined look on his face.

"Son, whenever you want to visit with the child, we will cover all your travel expenses," Mom offered.

"That won't be necessary, y'all," Effie said, looking from Mom to Dad. "We want that baby; we'll be responsible for that baby. Y'all can go on about your business like nothin' ever happened." Effie rose with her hands on her hips. "Now if y'all will give me and this boy a ride home, we'll be on our way." Turning to me, she added, "Miss Meg, you take care of yourself. I don't want you givin' us no puny baby."

Effie retired shortly after I gave birth to a child I chose not to see, not even once, and I never saw or heard from Clyde Brooks again.

Until now.

# Chapter 26

# ROSALEE PITTMAN

Everything started to unravel right after Clyde and Ester got back from that cruise to Mexico. Clyde would leave messages on our answering machines with date instructions. But other than that, he was avoiding everybody. It was by accident that I ran into him at the bar in Alfredo's, the Fisherman's Wharf restaurant where Clyde spent a lot of his time drinking and socializing with friends like that creepy Lou Cummings from the used car lot. I happened to be there with my favorite out-of-town trick, a software specialist from New York. A lot of the out-of-towners liked to go out to dinner first, before hemming one of us in a hotel room.

I wouldn't have noticed Clyde sitting at the bar, hunched over his drink, if I hadn't gone to the ladies' room before leaving.

My trick, Dylan was his name, had changed his mind at the last minute about which restaurant to go to for dinner. I would have ignored Clyde and he would have ignored me, like we'd been instructed. Clyde didn't like to be around us when we were with a trick. He said that his presence at such a crucial time might make the trick nervous. But the place was crowded, and I had to do a lot of maneuvering to get to the restroom. For about a minute, I was within a few feet of Clyde.

Clyde was a heavy drinker, but he was pretty good at holding his liquor. I had never seen him staggering and slobbering around the way some people did when they had one too many. This time was different. He glanced at me with the strangest expression. Looking over my shoulder to make sure my trick wasn't watching, I leaned toward Clyde. I didn't know how many drinks he'd had, but he smelled like a distillery.

"Clyde, you want me to call you a cab? You look awful, and you smell even worse. You really need to start takin' better care of yourself, brother," I whispered, touching his arm. Despite how I felt about what I did for Clyde, I cared about him. I guess when you've lost as many loved ones as I had, it was hard not to transfer the leftover love in your heart to someone else.

Clyde looked at me like he was seeing me for the first time in his life. He rubbed his nose and grunted, blinking eyes so red, it scared me. He looked sick.

"It's me, Clyde. Rosalee," I whispered.

"Oh." He shook his head and waved me away. "Don't you worry about me. You just go make that money, honey."

"You don't have to worry about that. That's a done deal. It's you I'm concerned about. All of us are worried about you, Clyde. You haven't been yourself lately."

Clyde lifted his glass and drank, then he waved me away again, muttering something about some "crazy White bitch . . . she don't know all what I been through . . ."

I didn't want to know what that was all about. And I didn't want to stir up any mess so I didn't mention the incident with Clyde in Alfredo's to Lula, Ester, or Rockelle that night. We all had enough problems already. We didn't need to start worrying about Clyde bringing a White woman into our lives, too.

Lula and Ester were already walking around looking like pallbearers. And Rockelle was one step from grabbing tricks by their dicks off the streets. And me, well, I was sick and tired of lying to my mama about how I was making my money. But I felt even worse about the way she was controlling me.

After each of my trips to the senior citizen's complex to visit Mama, I got so depressed I had to get good and drunk just to make it to the next day. If Clyde had lined up a date for me for that same day, I had to get doubly drunk to go.

It seemed like we were all already in some kind of mysterious grieving period, all for different reasons. So when Sherrie Armstrong died, we were already in mourning.

Sherrie already had full-blown AIDS by the time I met her. From what I'd heard from Ester, Sherrie got infected with HIV when she was seventeen, twelve years ago. I was happy to know that she had not caught the virus from a trick. She'd caught it from the first guy with whom she had a sexual relationship. But the most ironic thing was, she'd caught it just from having oral sex with the guy.

Ester said that Sherrie had told her that during the time of her relationship with the guy who'd infected her, she'd had an open sore in her mouth—some kind of an ulcer that a mild gum disease had caused. Sherrie didn't go to a doctor when weird things started to happen to her body after she'd sucked that guy's pecker a few times: flulike symptoms, mysterious sores that took too long to heal, extreme night sweats, and the list went on. Since I wasn't a doctor, I didn't know that much about medical situations except my own. And so far, all I'd ever had to deal with were menstrual cramps and other mild ailments that most healthy people experience.

From what Ester had told me, Sherrie knew she was sick even before she started turning tricks. But that didn't stop her. She made her tricks use two condoms at a time, and she refused to kiss any of them on the mouth. Not even with her teeth clenched and her lips pressed together.

However, as soon as Clyde found out, he "divorced" her, so to speak. I remembered some comments he'd made when I first started working for him. The subject was condoms and Sherrie, and why he'd let her go.

"I can't have one of y'all killin' off none of my regular tricks. If one of y'all fuck one of 'em to death, that's one thing. Some of them older tricks ain't nothin' but heart attacks waitin' to happen anyway. A good piece of pussy is all it'll take to push some of 'em into the grave. But that AIDS shit—uh-uh. I can't hang with that shit," he said.

Anyway, Sherrie had lived on her own and still turned tricks for as long as she could. But when she got to where she couldn't take care of herself, she went home to her family in Berkeley to die.

By the time I met Sherrie, which was about three months ago, she was experiencing some kind of dementia. On some days her mind was as clear and sharp as mine. On others, she would see big green elephants in her room, and long black snakes crawling up the walls.

I liked Sherrie. She was the first White woman with whom I'd ever really associated. But I could not bring myself to go to her funeral. After going to the funerals for my daddy and all four of my siblings, all in less than five years, I had developed a phobia.

I was surprised that I had not gone stark raving mad, or at least as nutty as my mama was. I had not told Mama or anybody else, but the only other funeral I planned to attend was my own. I didn't even think I could go to Mama's, if she went before me. With the business I was in, my chances of going before her were about fifty-fifty. I didn't think that I'd catch AIDS from my relationships with my tricks, but other things concerned me.

Every now and then, we heard about tricks going off on other working girls. And not just the foul, buffoonish tricks you see picking up street girls, but the so-called upscale gentlemen in thousand dollar suits. The police had found one of the most expensive call girls in town, in one of the most expensive hotels in town, strangled to death. The out-of-town trick who had killed her, a Chicago-based computer company CEO, had confessed, but offered no explanation as to why he'd killed the woman. Tricks didn't need any good reasons to do whatever they did to us. Other than getting paid, we had no other civil rights. Rockelle told me that she'd read in one of her books that back in the old days when they were still burning women at the stake for being witches—the equivalent of our ugly stepsisters—women like us were either stoned to death or run out of town. If a woman was unlucky enough to be considered a slut and a witch, her goose wasn't even worth cooking. When it came to respect, as far as mainstream society was concerned, we were one step above child molesters.

One of the first dates that Clyde set up for me was with a fallen priest. A regular trick had called Clyde up and told him that his ex-wife's brother had just left the church, and at forty-eight, he couldn't wait to get his hands on a woman for the first time. And after spending several years, doing whatever missionaries do in some village in Africa, and having to face the healthy butts of the tribeswomen, he couldn't wait to get his hands on a Black woman. And, he'd requested one of the blackest. As soon as I got my orders from Clyde, telling me "get your Black ass out there and act as Black as you can, girl," I headed for the South San Francisco address I'd been given. A tall, dark-haired man with an Irish accent opened the door and invited me into a living room that was even more disorganized than mine. I felt right at home. There were so many old magazines, newspapers, fast food containers, wine bottles, and empty glasses on the couch, the only place for me to sit was on the frisky ex-priest's lap in a corner on a flowered love seat.

It didn't take much or long to please this man. He paid me three hundred dollars just to let him fondle me, massage my ass, and play with my titties. He said he didn't think that he was ready for intercourse yet. Explaining that procedure was a little extreme for a forty-eight-year-old virgin. He wanted to take a few weeks to get more familiar with women's bodies. That was his excuse, but I'd accidentally glimpsed a pecker that couldn't have been too much bigger than my thumb.

While I was in the bathroom scrubbing off as much of his sweat as I could, that sucker went into my purse and stole back the money he had paid me! I didn't know what he'd done until I got all the way back to my apartment. When I called his house to cuss him out, he had a surprise for me. "Hark! You're nothing but a wench, a she-devil!" he roared. "A demon will erupt from your loins! You will burn in a lake of fire!" Before I could get a word in edgewise, he hung up on me. Clyde retaliated by not sending us on any more dates with the trick who had referred the backsliding priest.

Anyway, we never knew what to expect from a trick. Sherrie's death was just a reminder of what could happen to us if we got too close to the wrong man. You would think that with my history and my devotion to my superstitious mama, I'd be working in a convent or a children's hospital. I thought about what could happen to me all the time and each time, I told myself that I was one day closer to quitting the business.

With me having to pay Clyde's "commission," in addition to my expenses and Mama's expenses, it was next to impossible for me to save much money. I had a few thousand dollars in a brown padded envelope that I kept behind my refrigerator, but that wouldn't get me too far.

The bottom line was, I didn't have a plan. I didn't know where I was going to go. I didn't know what I was going to do with Mama. I didn't know what I was going to do with myself.

All I did know was I had to get out of the business I was in before it was too late.

# Chapter 27

# HELEN DANIELS

I was so glad that Miss Rocky didn't take her kids to that lady's funeral that she had to go to. I was real sad about that lady dying, but in a way I was glad. With me having to babysit for Miss Rocky while she was at the funeral, I had a reason to get away from Mama and Daddy.

As soon as Miss Rocky called me up that morning and asked me to come over, I dropped the telephone while she was still talking. I took off running out the door, wearing mismatched shoes and a blouse with all of the buttons undone. But there was nothing strange about the way I was looking. I left my house looking like a slob to go to Miss Rocky's all the time.

I was just that happy about having a reason to get out of the house. And I know Mama and Daddy was just as happy about me having to babysit as I was. Old people like them had a real hard time dealing with me. It was one thing for me to be "limited," as they said I was. I'd never been anything but that. But Mama and Daddy both sometimes acted just as limited as me! They were so forgetful that they would go out somewhere and come home in a cab because they couldn't remember where they'd parked our car. They'd hide money somewhere in the house and couldn't remember where until weeks later. My daddy left our house one time without his false teeth. He didn't realize that until he got all the way to his doctor's office. When I watched television with Mama and Daddy, I was the only one who could keep up with who was who on the screen. Now who couldn't tell Bernie Mac from Chris Rock?

Now, my parents' limits were not always bad. At least not to me. Mama would give me my allowance in the morning and by noon, she would have forgotten. She'd give me another allowance. Sometimes more than she gave me the first time. Sometimes she misplaced clothes I never wanted to wear in the first place. Daddy was even worse. Two days after he gave me my new computer, he came home with another one for me. I loved my parents, and I felt sorry for them, but in a way, I was glad that they got to see what it had always been like for me. They were glad we had Miss Rocky right next door. I knew that because I heard them say so a lot.

Just the other day I overheard my daddy say to somebody he was talking to on the telephone, "Rockelle Harper moving next door was just what we needed to help us cope with Helen. Maybe Helen can learn more about life in general from Rockelle. And those children of Rockelle's are a double blessing. The more Helen spends time at Rockelle's house, the more contented she seems." Boy did Daddy get it right for a change. This particular day, I was babysitting for Miss Rocky for free.

Things had become so bad for Miss Rocky that she had been paying me to babysit on credit anyway. And lots of times, she just plain forgot to pay me at all. So, I told her before she even asked that I'd look after the kids for her today for free. If a funeral wasn't reason enough to do somebody a favor, I didn't know what was.

Before I told Miss Rocky not to pay me the night before last when she had to go out, she was like, "Helen, I had some unexpected expenses this week. Can I pay you later on in the month?" I wanted to laugh, but I didn't think Miss Rocky was trying to be funny. She didn't crack a smile. When she was serious, her face got so straight and spooky it looked like she'd strapped on a mask. And it was something you wouldn't want to see if you went walking all by yourself down a dark alley. But "unexpected expenses" was the same excuse she used every single time. The reason I wanted to laugh was because her latest unexpected expenses included a new DVD player and a three hundred dollar hair weave (on top of being fat, Miss Rocky's real hair was so scandalous, you could almost see her skull). I had almost forgot about that time Miss Rocky told me she couldn't pay me because she'd had a out-of-town emergency that she had to take care of right away. It must have been a doozy of an emergency because all three of her kids came over to my house to brag about how they were all getting ready to go to Disneyland that weekend.

Well, for one thing, my family was not poor. I didn't even need money from Miss Rocky. I didn't think she needed to know, but I never needed any of the money that I made from babysitting. My mama, my daddy, and even my pain-in-the-jaw big brother, David, and his pig-faced wife—they all gave me money, and all kinds of other good stuff.

I told Miss Rocky, "You really don't have to pay me at all today." That's when I pulled this big ole handful of money out of the red brassiere I had bought. The one my men friends liked so much. If I didn't do nothing else right, I always made sure I was looking good when I had to deal with men. Yeah, I sometimes left my house wearing mismatched shoes, and my blouse unbuttoned or buttoned up wrong, but that was only when I went to Miss Rocky's or to the corner store. When Mama let me go shopping at the mall on the bus by myself, I never went there without my makeup looking perfect and my clothes looking like I'd just removed them off a rack.

I had a good reason not to give myself too good of a makeover when I went to Miss Rocky's house. I didn't want to make her feel bad standing next to a pretty girl like me. I figured that out after something Mama told me: "That Rock-elle would be so much more attractive if she'd lose about forty pounds and get rid of that fake hair. I wonder what goes through her head when she's with those other beautiful women she hangs out with. I bet Rockelle feels like Moms Mabley standing next to slim women like Ester, Lula, and Rosalee. And she wonders why her husband ran off. Hmmph!"

Miss Rocky had enough problems. I didn't want her to feel bad about her weight or anything else on account of me. Sometimes I went to her house looking like a bag lady on purpose, just so she could say something like, "Helen, you would be a real pretty girl if you'd fix yourself up better. Comb your hair, put on a little lipstick. And don't walk around wearing mismatched shoes."

Miss Rocky's words had hurt my feelings, but to make myself feel better, all I had to do was remind myself what Mama had said about Miss Rocky looking like Moms Mabley. That would always make me feel sorry for Miss Rocky. One thing my limitations didn't screw with was my feelings. I could care as much about another person as a normal girl.

Miss Rocky's eyes got real real big, and she gave me this

look that made me tremble. Like I said, this woman could screw her face up like a mask. My face got real hot as Miss Rocky stared at me and all that money in my hand. I got nervous because I didn't know what she was thinking. Not only did I have on makeup that day and a tight blouse covering up my red brassiere, but I had on a pair of brand-new pumps. I couldn't have Miss Rocky thinking I couldn't look like nothing but a frump all the time. This particular day I looked like I was going out on a date, and I was hoping I was. All I had to do was wait for Miss Rocky to leave the house so I could send her kids to their rooms to watch television.

"Helen, where did you get all that money?" Miss Rocky snatched it out of my hand and looked at it some more. I bet she was thinking it was fake. She flipped through it, counting it out loud, her eyes getting even bigger. "Girl, there's more than two thousand dollars here!"

"And it's all mine," I said, real proud of myself. As I should have been. Sarah Freeman, a girl my age who lived two houses down from me, worked at Burger King. Every time I saw her, she complained about the measly paycheck she got. I didn't have to complain about nothing. And that heifer was always making fun of me, calling *me* a retard. I wish her friends could have seen the look on her face the other day when I told her to kiss my rich retarded ass.

"But where did you get it?" Miss Rocky's voice was lower. She started glancing around, like to make sure nobody was listening. "You didn't do something you shouldn't be doing to get all this money, did you?" Miss Rocky's eyes looked me up and down, but she still didn't say nothing about how good I was looking today.

"Like . . . what?"

Miss Rocky cocked her head to the side. She looked at me real hard some more out of the corner of her eye, which by the way, had too much mascara and eyeliner. "Like, stealing? You haven't been in your mama's . . . or anybody else's purse, have you?" Right after Miss Rocky said that last part, she looked at her purse on the couch.

I shook my head so hard my ponytail slapped my face. "I would never steal from nobody." I nodded toward her purse and added, "Especially you. I heard my mama say what a low-down, funky, deadbeat your husband was. I know it takes a lot of money for you to keep this house and pay for your three kids. And to go to that beauty parlor you go to on Ocean Street so they can sew up some hair on your head." My eyes rolled up to look at Miss Rocky's fresh new hairdo. She said all the time she didn't like bangs, but she had them. She'd been wearing bangs ever since I told her they would hide the lines on her forehead. "I like them bangs, Miss Rocky," I said, knowing a compliment would make her feel good and maybe forget about trying to get up in my business.

"Thanks, Helen," Miss Rocky said, patting her hair, like she wanted to make sure all of it was still on her head. She let out a deep breath and rubbed the side of her face, closing her eyes so tight they almost disappeared into all the meat on her face. When she opened her eyes, she leaned closer to me and looked me in the eyes, like she was trying to see what I was thinking.

"What's wrong, Miss Rocky?"

"Helen, where did you get all this money?"

My stomach started doing weird stuff, like moving and hurting like somebody had hit me in it. I rubbed my stomach and turned my back to Miss Rocky. But that didn't do me no good. She grabbed me by my shoulders and spun me back around so we were eyeball to eyeball. "Uh, I made it doing stuff," I managed, my chest getting so tight I couldn't hardly breathe no more. I was hoping I wouldn't pass out or die in front of Miss Rocky. That would have made me look real bad. She already had one funeral to go to.

"Your folks know you got all this money on you?" Miss Rocky shook me but I pulled away from her, shaking my head. "You sure you didn't steal this money? Tell me the truth now."

"I didn't steal it, Miss Rocky. Honest to God. I got it from doing stuff."

"Stuff like what?" Miss Rocky's mouth stayed opened, and I could see red stuff on her teeth. I hoped it was lipstick, not blood.

"Miss Rocky, remember that time you told me to mind my own business when I asked you about that pile of money I seen in your refrigerator locked up tight in that Tupperware bowl?" Miss Rocky's eyes got real narrow, like a snake's. She half turned her head and looked at me. I didn't even give her a chance to say nothing else about my money. "Well, I'm telling you the same thing you told me. 'My money is my business.' "

"All right now. I just don't want you to be getting yourself into any kind of trouble." Miss Rocky turned around and walked like a penguin out of the living room where we'd been standing and talking, next to the sixty-inch screen television she had bought for her kids. That big boxy thing was one of last month's unexpected expenses. The back of Miss Rocky's tight black blouse was still half unzipped. She looked like a great big sausage to me.

Miss Rocky was always trying to lose weight, but it never worked. She had Slim-Fast in her refrigerator, diet books on her bookshelf, a thing she was supposed to run in place on, and even some tapes that she was suppose to dance to. Every time she tried to exercise when I was around, she ended up falling out on the floor and I'd have to help her up.

"Miss Rocky, you are just like Oprah. She's still a great big fat woman, and she's been trying to lose weight ever since she got on television. Maybe you and her were meant to be great big fat women. That's what my daddy says about you and her both."

"If you insult me again, I'm sending your smart ass home, girl," Miss Rocky told me, tossing some chips into her mouth. "I'd be fine if I could lose some of this meat off my bottom."

"But you got just as much meat at the top," I reminded.

I didn't get sent home, but I got a dirty look from Miss Rocky that day.


Most of Miss Rocky's clothes were too small for her, but that didn't stop her from squeezing into them and then prancing out of her house to go take care of that sick old man. His name was Mr. Roy and he lived in Oakland, but that's all Miss Rocky ever told anybody about him. Oh, she said that he paid her real good money.

And another thing, I never could figure out why Miss Rocky always dressed up real nice just to go take care of a sick old man. I didn't have enough nerve to ask her, but I figured my mama would know.

"Mama, why do Miss Rocky dress up to go nurse an old man?" Miss Rocky had been going to nurse this mysterious old man since right after her husband took off. I couldn't figure out how she did that, and run around with that Clyde and those other three women, too.

"If he's straight, it doesn't matter how old and sick he is, he'll appreciate looking at a well-groomed woman. Even one as stout as Rockelle. Men are like dogs. Their eyes never stop roving," Mama told me, looking me up and down as she talked, brushing my hair back off my face. She wiped a smudge off my jaw. I never knew what my mama thought about me being the way I was. All I had to go on was what I could eavesdrop. I did know from hearing bits and pieces of conversations she had with folks over the telephone, that she still worried about me getting in trouble with men again. "Well, at least there won't be any more babies for Helen for us to worry about no matter how many more men take advantage of her. But a baby would be a picnic compared to her catching something that could kill her," Mama said into the telephone. I didn't like the fact that I was such a popular subject with my mama and her friends, but there was nothing I could do about it.

I wasn't sure what it was I could catch from a man that could kill me. I had a feeling it had something to do with Mama taking me to doctors all the time for them to draw blood out of my arm. Sometimes it seemed like my biggest worry was my mama. Daddy was too busy watching ball games and sleeping, so he wasn't too much of a problem to me. I don't know what would have become of me if it wasn't for Miss Rocky and her kids living next door.

Miss Rocky's phone that the nasty men called up on was always ringing off the hook. Every time she left me alone with the kids, I'd put the kids in the living room, and I'd go to Miss Rocky's bedroom where the fun phone was. I'd sit on the side of her bed and wait for the answering machine to click when those men called. They would leave messages left and right.

One night last week a woman called! And let me tell you, she was hella mad. As soon as I heard her going on and on about finding the telephone number in her husband's pocket, I snapped off the answering machine and picked up the telephone. "Uh, hello," I said in a real soft voice.

"Who am I speaking with?" It must have been a White woman because she had the same voice that the mother on *The Brady Bunch* reruns had.

"Me," I told her.

I couldn't picture the Brady mother's husband calling for a date with a Black woman. I couldn't even remember ever seeing a Black person on their show.

"Me who?"

"Just me, lady."

"Shit! Don't fucking play games with me! I just want to know one thing! Are you a working girl, bitch?" the woman asked, sounding real, real mean.

It was a real letdown to find out that a woman who sounded like Mrs. Brady knew cuss words and used them.

"Huh?"

"Is my husband paying you for your services?"

"Not if he's the one who lost his wallet? See, I—"

"You little tramp! I don't have time for games. I want to know if Joel McKlanski is one of your clients!"

"Hmmm," I said, scratching the top of my head like a monkey. "I don't know nobody named Joel. What he look like?"

"Look, you trash, I told you not to play games with me!" the woman screamed. "I'll find you, and I'll kick your fucking ass!"

I gasped and held the telephone away from my face and stared at it. I knew right then and there that I would never look at *The Brady Bunch* the same way again.

"Uh, lady, I have to go now." I hung up before the madwoman could get any madder and throw a real hissy fit.

At least I didn't lie to her. None of the men I'd talked to, or been with was named Joel. He was probably one of the ones I'd missed because Miss Rocky had got to him first.

* * *

Like I said, Miss Rocky's date phone rang left and right. She had more than enough men to keep her busy. I didn't feel bad about stealing a few. The strange thing was, some of the ones that I'd let into Miss Rocky's house changed their minds once they got inside. One man flat out asked me if I was "mentally challenged."

"Hell no!" I told him, reminding myself that if the Brady Bunch–sounding woman could cuss, so could I. "I'm just retarded," I told that sucker. He all but ran out the door, and I didn't really care. He had shown me right off the bat that he wasn't a nice man. To the nice men, me being retarded was no big deal. Some even said it was cute. Besides, as one told me, I had the same parts a normal woman had, and I knew how to work them just as good.

The good news was, I didn't have to worry about none of the men I got with telling Miss Rocky anything about me. Once I told them how fat she was, and about the gray hair shooting up out of her skull, they were glad it was me who picked up the telephone and not Miss Rocky.

The best man I ever stole from Miss Rocky was that White man named Arthur. I guess he was special because he was the first one I took a call from and made a date with. Poor Mr. Arthur. Sometimes he had to pay me on credit, too. Like that time he got robbed by some Black dudes on his way over to Miss Rocky's house. I couldn't figure out why some Black folks couldn't behave themselves! Instead of robbing folks and breaking into houses to steal other folks' stuff, them creeps should have been doing something nice to get money. Like I did.

Mr. Arthur said he really liked me because I'd sneak him into Miss Rocky's house all the time, and I liked having dates with him in the house. I felt like a wife. Since I would never be one, I decided to pretend that I was a wife as many times as I could. Mr. Arthur didn't know that I didn't live there, too. He honest to God believed that me and Miss Rocky were roommates. He was the one who gave me most of the money I had stuffed inside my brassiere. Besides him, there were only five other men I fooled around with in Miss Rocky's house. I didn't like them, though. The men who didn't want to come to the house had me take cabs to wherever it was they happened to be. Hotels mostly. One man had me take a cab to his house in Daly City, way out there toward the airport. Only bad thing about me having to go to the men was I couldn't sneak out until Miss Rocky's kids were asleep. Once I put them to bed, they always slept all the way through the night. So it didn't matter that I would be gone for a few hours. One night I went to visit a man at his hotel right when *America's Most Wanted* was coming on. The same show was still on when I got back, so sometimes I didn't even have to be gone for a whole hour.

It made my head hurt when I thought about some of the mean things some of the men said to me. Like this snaggle-toothed, bug-eyed, flat-headed, shiny Black ballplayer from Miami. "Girl, you know you ain't mentally fit to be doin' this kind of shit. You get your tail up out of this hotel." That was just like a Black man. Talking about me like I was a dog. My own brother behaved the same way that ball playing nigger did, so it didn't surprise me. I expected this kind of foolishness from him.

Mama was always telling me that boys and men were nothing but naked apes. She started telling me that right after that little accident I had when I was younger—getting pregnant, I mean. She'd been telling me that ever since, hoping it would help keep me out of trouble with men. Every time I went out on a date now, I wondered what my mama and my daddy would say if they knew. I didn't spend much time wondering about that, though. Trying to keep my dates straight and thinking about a hiding place—other than my brassiere—for the money they gave me, was enough for me to worry about.

The Black ballplayer had been one of the fussy ones I couldn't get to come to Miss Rocky's house. He'd called from some hotel room. I could tell there was something strange about him by the way he talked. He had come to town to go to somebody's wedding, or so he said. And that tale he told me about owning a nightclub, I bet that was a lie. Who would have time to play ball and run a nightclub? He didn't look much older than me and if you ask me, he wasn't much smarter than me. But, even after he told me to get out of his hotel room, before I left, he did stretch out on the bed with me and we fooled around a little bit.

Why men liked to get their things licked was beyond me, but they all seemed to like it. I figured they didn't get weaned when they were babies or something. The two hundred dollars that the ballplayer was supposed to pay me, well like I said, he wasn't much smarter than me. He had lost his wallet. I had to pay for a cab back home, with my own money. But that still didn't make me feel bad enough to get mad at Miss Rocky for not paying me to babysit while she went to that funeral. Me not getting paid wasn't no big deal. I had plenty of money, and I knew how to get plenty more when I needed it.

Anyway, Miss Rocky had finally left to go to that funeral with those other women she ran around with. Looking after Miss Rocky's kids at night was better than looking after them in the daytime. At night, they watched television then I put them to bed. I couldn't have no fun until I got them out of my way. But it was a whole different story during the day. Them kids were worse than mice. They ran all over the place, squealing, and acting wild.

The two little boys were not that bad, but that girl Juliet could be a real pit bull. She didn't want to do this, she didn't want to do that. She was going to tell her mama I was mean to her, she told me.

"I don't have to listen to no retarded girl like you," she'd tell me when she didn't want to go to bed.

She knew how to get at me real good and that was by calling me retarded. I didn't ask to turn out the way I did, but I tried to live like a normal girl. One thing I didn't need was people reminding me what I was. That was the one thing that made me cry the quickest. Especially coming from a child almost half my age. One of the good things about being slow like me was I could bounce back from being sad to being glad real fast.

One thing I learned from Miss Rocky was you had to treat Juliet the way she wanted to be treated if you wanted her to behave herself. Which meant, letting the girl do whatever she wanted to do. Since that little sister thought she was grown, I let her act grown. It was my idea for her to keep an eye on the two little boys while I went to visit this man who called right after Miss Rocky left the house to go that funeral. It sounded like the same punk-ass man who said he was a ballplayer! And a nightclub owner. I guess he changed his mind about me. I had started to tell Mr. Ball-Playing Nightclub Owner that I was not available to come to his hotel room no more. But then I got to thinking: why not prove to him he that was wrong about me that other time that he had me come to his hotel?

"Now, Juliet, you know how to use the telephone. So if anything hap-pens before I get back, you call nine . . . uh nine . . . uh . . . nine . . . one . . . one." I was only really good with numbers when it had to do with money. "And you can always run next door to get my mama or daddy if the house catches on fire or if some maniac breaks in," I told the girl, coating my lips with some of Miss Rocky's lipstick in her bedroom mirror. The house had a smoke detector, and maniacs didn't know where we lived, so I wasn't worried about nothing bad happening while I was gone.

Juliet stood next to me, looking me up and down. Her eyes, which were already too big for her face, were bulging out of the top of her head like a frog's. With her pretzel-thin arms folded across her flat chest, she started talking, fast and loud.

"Where you going?" Juliet's voice sounded more like a woman's than mine.

Now, the girl was pretty, but I guess she had trouble believing it. She was always in the mirror, worried about her baby fat and sucking in her stomach and jaws trying to make herself look real trim like me and Janet Jackson. She was scared to death she was going to grow up and be a great big fat woman like her mama. Her turning into Miss Rocky scared poor Juliet more than the threat of a whupping. I felt the girl. That was why I spent so much of my free time at Miss Rocky's house trying to help out. But I still had my own self to help out first.

I didn't know much, but I knew enough about my situation to know I'd never have me a husband and some kids. I didn't know what was going to happen to me once my mama and my daddy died. And the way they were looking and acting lately, one of them might be the next funeral. Knowing that busybody big brother of mine and his pissy-poo wife, they'd make me come live with them. And guess what, I just found out last week that the pissy-poo wife had a baby on the way. Which meant, they'd use me as a built-in babysitter when I had to go live with them. I wouldn't have no choice. So I had to have as much fun as I could while I could. Once

I had to go live with my brother and his wife, my fun would be over. Because when they came around, they watched me a like a mama hawk.

"Uh, I'm just going out for a little while to see somebody. Now, now, uh, be a big girl and keep the boys out of trouble." I didn't even have to tell Juliet that. Keeping the boys out of trouble was the easiest part of babysitting for Miss Rocky. Them little dudes were the easiest kids I'd ever seen. They didn't clown in public like other spoiled brats I seen kicking and screaming in stores. And them little dudes of Miss Rocky's did everything I told them to do. But that Juliet was another story. The girl had everything she wanted and then some. The only thing she didn't have, but needed more than anything, was a whupping! I swear to God, Miss Rocky had to be scared to death of that little bitch. I don't like to use cuss words, so I only did it when I had to. But most of the time, that Juliet was nothing but a bold-faced bitch! If I didn't know no better, and if I was bat-blind and could hear Juliet and Miss Rocky conversing, I'd swear that Juliet was the mama instead of Miss Rocky. Because, like I said, the girl sounded like a grown woman when she talked.

"Helen, how come you talk to me like that? I'm not no baby," Juliet said, her face screwed up like she was sucking lemons.

That's what I meant. That was the kind of smart-mouth crap I was talking about.

"Juliet, I know you are a big little girl. I didn't mean it like it sounded. Now, you go on in the living room with the boys. I have to finish my makeover," I said, waving her away.

Juliet just looked upside my head.

"Did you hear what I just said, Miss Girl?" I hollered, shaking my finger at her.

"Why you fixing yourself up like that? You look like those nasty girls in those rap videos. And, I can see them

Raisenettes you got for nipples," Juliet said in a real low voice. "Men are going to jump all over you if you go outside wearing all that makeup and that tight, low-cut blouse." Juliet laughed, cackling like a witch.

I couldn't hold back the smile that slid across my face.

"You think so?"

Juliet nodded. "When Mama takes me to the mall with her face made up and her clothes real tight, men stare at her and some of them even whistle."

"Mmmm huh." A real warm feeling covered my face, hot tears filled up my eyes. It took a lot of hard work for me to get attention and keep it long enough for it to matter, but it was worth it.

As soon as Juliet sashayed her grown, busy body out the bedroom, I sprayed myself between my thighs and up and down my crack with some of Miss Rocky's butt spray. Then I sprayed some of her Red Door perfume between my titties like I seen Miss Rocky do before she went out. After Juliet's comments about my makeup and clothes and how things like that got guys' attention, I couldn't wait to get to my date.

If men stared and whistled at Miss Rocky when they seen her in makeup and sexy clothes, fat as she was, there was just no telling what my date was going to do when he seen me this time.

# Chapter 28

# MEGAN O'ROURKE

"**W**ould you like *another* drink, ma'am?"

I could hardly lift my head to see who was talking to me. And when I did, my eyes burned when I blinked. It took me a moment to realize where I was and even then I was not sure. Looking around, rubbing my head, it all came back to me. I was in hell. I'd been sitting in the same bar for hours, reliving my life.

"Ma'am, are you all right?" The waitress was about what you'd expect. She had long, stiff orange hair with black roots, pasty complexion, too much dime-store makeup, bad teeth, and a dingy white uniform with a button missing.

"Uh, just some coffee please. Black." I let out a long, painful sigh, raking my shaking fingers through my hair. "Are there any more bars in this neighborhood?" I asked hoarsely, the inside of my throat feeling like it had been scraped with a dull knife. I couldn't take a chance and visit a bar where I might run into someone I knew. And from the looks I received in this place, I didn't want to become too familiar with this crowd. I recognized some of the same brooding faces I'd seen on my first visit.

"I'm not sure, ma'am. I only work here. I live in Oakland." Despite her grim appearance, she had a pleasant voice. Just the mention of Oakland made my head throb.

"Then how far am I from Market Street?"

The waitress gave me an impatient look and shrugged. "Like I said, I live in Oakland."

"Just some coffee please," I managed again.

Four cups later of what was supposed to be coffee, I felt sober enough to rise. But my legs felt like Jell-O. If I hadn't held on to the table, I would have landed on my face. All eyes were on me as I staggered to the restroom with the red door, a door that wouldn't shut all the way. I ignored the single unflushed toilet and peed in a trash can. There was no toilet paper. I splashed water on my hands anyway, dried them on the tail of my dress, and stumbled out. I clutched my purse with both hands as I eased toward the exit. A bearded man with a ponytail winked at me on my way out.

I don't know why I was surprised to find the Lexus intact. It had been broken into two times in the last year, both times on the street in front of my own house in broad daylight.

"Who would think that those thugs would even know how to get to Steiner from the ghetto," Mom had scoffed.

I didn't comment when the perpetrator, the son of the judge next door, was caught trying to sell the CD player he'd ripped out of my dashboard.

I ignored the faces peeking out of the window from inside the bar, watching as I staggered and stumbled across the parking lot. By the time I reached my car, the same bearded goon who'd winked at me coming out of the restroom, exited the bar and stood blocking the door, watching until I fell into my seat and strapped on my seat belt.

Everything seemed normal when I got home. Almost every light in the house was on. Mom had left two messages.

Heather had called from Europe and left a message that she'd changed her mind about the car. She decided to use the money to return to Europe, and backpack through France and Italy next Christmas with some new friends she'd made in Dublin. Robert had left a message saying he would be home in a couple of days.

My buzz had been downgraded to a light headache, but my mind was still a ball of confusion and fear.

A long hot bath, with a highball in my hand, made it easier for me to continue revisiting my past.

I'd never told any of my friends about my teenage pregnancy. In my fourth month, when I could no longer hide it, I was sent to Sacramento to stay with Dad's older sister, Rita, a bitter, divorced woman who reminded me on an hourly basis of the shame I'd brought on the family. "If you are lucky enough to find a decent White man who'll marry you, I advise you to kiss the ground he walks on," Aunt Rita, her pale, sharp-featured face close to mine, told me. Her finger poked my protruding belly. "It'll take you the rest of your born days to live down this curse."

Aunt Rita rarely mentioned the fact that my deceased sister had associated with Charles Manson. But I heard about my disgrace with a Black boy every day that I lived with my aunt.

I spent as much time as I could holed up in the miserable bedroom my aunt had prepared for me. And it was a dark, musty, congested little space. I was so depressed that I was in labor for six hours and didn't even know it. By the time my aunt got me to the hospital, I was delirious.

I chose not to hold or even look at my child. I returned to Oakland a week after giving birth, assuming Clyde and his grandmother had turned my child over to their relatives in Mississippi and that my shame would never be mentioned again.

For the next few years, I maintained a low profile and stayed close to home and out of trouble. That seemed to appease my parents. But they were disappointed when I flunked out of college and started wandering from one boring job to another. It was three years after Clyde before I was with another man.

Robert O'Rourke was the thirty-year-old nephew of one of the partners at Dad's law firm. Conservative, aggressive, ambitious was the best way to describe his personality. I overlooked his plain features and receding hairline and went out with him anyway because my parents adored him. And even though I didn't love him, I married him, hoping it would make up for the disgrace I'd brought to my family.

The sex was about what I'd expected: dull and perfunctory. Each of my two pregnancies—Josh first, and Heather two years later—constantly reminded me of the first one and the child I would never see. I couldn't stand to look at children who appeared to be biracial. And not a day went by that I didn't wonder what had happened to mine.

Keeping busy was more than an option, it was the distraction I needed to make my marriage work. Robert was a very successful architect so we traveled extensively. We lived in Dublin near his parents for a while before we returned to the States and settled in San Francisco, two blocks from my parents on the same street.

By the time Heather and Josh entered school my life had become routine. Carpools, PTA meetings, women's clubs, parties. The sordid shenanigans of my youth had become a blur.

With a maid to oversee the house and kids, Robert and I spent a lot of time socializing. But it wasn't long before that came to a standstill, at least for me. Robert spent most of his time entertaining his business associates and when he was around, he spent most of that time pointing out my faults. Like my out-of-control spending and my fading looks. I spent more time at the gym and the beauty parlor than I did with Robert. But my twenty-pound weight loss and face-lift didn't make much of a difference to him. Despite my improvements, I saw even less of Robert.

A divorce was out of the question and having an affair was not an option. I had too much to lose. Besides, it had devastated the marriage of my best friend, Joan Richmond.

"So, Joan's run off with some greasy Mexican," Robert informed me during one of his rare appearances at dinner.

"She won't be the first and she won't be the last," I scoffed. I was the one who had encouraged Joan to flee, and I was glad I did. She called me from Long Beach sounding happier than ever. However, I didn't have the courage to take my own advice.

"Well, the way she's consorted with *those people,* that's about all she deserves now."

Robert's vision didn't include much diversity. He socialized with minority business associates, but he generally disliked Blacks, Latinos, Asians, and anything in between. And he viewed them all as lazy, useless criminals who had no right to the privileges we took for granted.

With the exception of my Jamaican maid, Robert made sure I had no relationships with people of color, and he wanted to keep it that way.

There was no way in hell I could let him know about Clyde and Keisha.

# Chapter 29

# ESTER SANCHEZ

I don't know why Sherrie's funeral made me so sad. We all knew she was going to die soon anyway. It was a bad day for me. I didn't want to go, but it was like I really didn't have no choice.

I knew Sherrie longer than Lula and Rockelle. She and I went all the way back to the old days. For a long time, she and I were the only girls working with Clyde. She used to make jokes about us being "wives-in-laws." Sherrie joked all the way up the end.

Last Saturday when me and Lula went to see her, laid out in her bed like she was already dead, she managed to lift her head and move her swollen lips long enough to croak, "I got a huge bone to pick with God as soon as I get to Heaven for allowing me to live such a miserable life."

Heaven. Yeah, right. Like women doing what we do gonna end up in a place like that. I ain't that stupid. You get to Heaven all you gonna see is a few billion babies and maybe a few thousand nuns.

We didn't stay long at that funeral. It was too depressing.

Our turns would come soon enough. Me, Clyde, Lula, Rocky, we just stayed around that church long enough to satisfy our conscience and to pay our respect. Sherrie's family didn't know who we was, or what we was, and we didn't want to hang around long enough for them to find out.

What I did know was what Sherrie told me. Her family knew she had been turning tricks. Why she was doing it was something they probably wondered about as much as I did. The girl didn't need the money. But who could figure White girls from rich families? When you come from a family like Sherrie's—she used to have her daddy's chauffeur drive her to her dates with her tricks—you turned tricks because you wanted to. Sherrie couldn't even put the blame on a man. No man had turned her out and no man had hooked up with her to take her money. Yeah, she had done that shit because she wanted to. And she could have stopped any time. Well, she had stopped for good now.

Getting into a straight life was something I thought about a lot. Especially after I seen my old friend Manny and the way he'd turned his life around.

"I'm gettin' sick of lookin' at y'all with them long faces." I was surprised to hear Clyde say such a stupid thing when we got back to my apartment after we left the funeral. "Y'all ain't gonna make no money walkin' around lookin' like you been suckin' on lemons."

"Man, we just came from a funeral, Clyde," Lula said, talkin' loud and mean. She talked to Clyde like that a lot, but even more so lately. The mean looks he gave her didn't faze her one bit. Like me, Lula had other things on her mind that didn't include Clyde. After he'd acted weird for a while, Clyde seemed almost like his old self again. Whatever had been bothering him, he had kept to hisself. I was shocked when he wouldn't even tell me his problem. The closest we got to finding out anything was a few bits and pieces that Rosalee got out of him while he was drunk at the same bar Rosalee and her trick happened to be in. Something about a White woman Rosalee said he'd told her. And that was all.

"Well, I want all of y'all to get your moneymakers in gear. That computer geeks' convention starts in a few days and we gonna be busy as hell. We got a real important new client who wants to see you tomorrow night, Lula. This trick is from Hollywood and he parties with Tom Cruise, Denzel, and Sean Penn, so you know he's got some serious money. And we need to get our hands on some of it." A glazed look swept across Clyde's face. He always got that look when we discussed really impressive tricks. "And, our good old faithful horny friend Mr. Bob done left three voice mail messages. He horny as hell. Ester, he asked for you." Clyde sniffed and took a long drink from a bottle of beer he had snatched out of my refrigerator. Sitting down on the arm of the sofa next to Lula, he looked at me and rolled his eyes. "Ester, you hear me talkin' to you?"

"I'm on my period, Clyde. And, I got some bitch-ass cramps," I said, talking soft on account of I wasn't as bold as I usually was. I was sitting next to Lula, hoping she'd keep her eye on my back.

Looking out for folks was something Lula not only was good at, but she seemed to like doing it. I guess when you lose your only baby, you'll use your mother-love on anybody that'll let you. She was real mammy-fied sometimes. When she noticed me drinking more than I was eating, she got in my face. "Ester, you lay off that tequila and get in the kitchen and feed yourself before I do it for you," Lula told me once. We lived in my apartment, but to anybody who didn't know that, it seemed like Lula's place. I sometimes felt and acted like I was just a visitor. Now that's a damn shame to feel like that in your own place. But one thing I could say was, it made me feel good knowing somebody cared about me for something other than what I had between my legs.

I knew that Clyde cared about me as much as he could. But when it got down to the facts, he was still a man, and I was still a woman. He seen me first as something to be enjoyed.

"Your period ain't never stopped you before. Girl, if you don't get out to Marin and fuck that man, I will," Clyde said, burping beer. He was the only one who thought he was funny, because nobody but him was laughing.

"I'll go," Rocky said, standing in the window with her back to us. "I need the money." Why she had wore a tight outfit to Sherrie's funeral was a mystery to me. Like, what man was going to make a date at a funeral? But at least the clothes she had on was black, so I couldn't get too upset about Rockelle's appearance. If I wanted to be real mean, I could have mentioned the fact that she'd gained a few more pounds.

Clyde waved his hand at Rocky like he was shooing a fly. "You ain't goin' no place, woman. The man asked for Ester, and if Ester don't go, ain't nary one of y'all goin'. Shit." Clyde yawned and stretched his arms up over his head, waving that beer bottle at me. "Ester, Mr. Bob is still the easiest trick in the world. All he'll probably wanna do is lick your pussy, anyway. You know that."

"I told you I'm on my period, Clyde," I said.

"I'll check in with you." He stopped and looked at his watch and buttoned up the jacket to the black suit he'd wore to Sherrie's funeral. "I'll check in with you at six o'clock. Tell Mr. Bob I said hi. Come on, Lula. Let's take Rocky home."

I drove to Mr. Bob's house in Marin, bloody pussy and all.

As it turned out, Mr. Bob didn't care what he put his mouth on. He had turned into a pig. He even told me some story about how the Hell's Angels initiated new members by making them eat a woman's pussy while she was on her period.

Now, because of AIDS, and because Sherrie caught that shit from doing blow jobs without a condom, I wasn't stupid enough to let a man even lick me without protection. Mr. Bob wasn't no exception. It didn't bother him to have to cover my crack with Saran Wrap long enough for him to do his business. Like I said, Mr. Bob had turned into a real pig.

My period ended the next day. Damned if that Mr. Bob didn't call for another date with me. Clyde sent me back to Mr. Bob the very next night.

I knew that Lula was with Clyde, but that wasn't the reason why I didn't want to go home after I left Mr. Bob's house. Something was happening to me. I was wondering if it was because I was getting older. I wasn't having the fun I used to have no more. It seemed like I was feeling sadder than ever before. The tricks that were nice to me and fun to be with, the money, kicking it with Clyde and the girls, it all felt different. Sometimes I wondered if I was losing my mind, or finally coming to my senses.

Some of the things that Manny had said to me at his apartment kept coming back to my mind. Especially that thing he'd said about there not being no old gangsters. I seen women old enough to be my grandmother working the streets, looking so pitiful they could only get ten dollar dates and sometimes not even that. I knew that old age was a long

way off for me. But I had to ask myself if I was going to wait
until old age before I stopped dating, or now while I still had
some time to do regular things. Like get married and have
some kids. I didn't plan on it, but I just kept driving, and I
didn't stop until I reached Manny's place.

Manny lived in a neighborhood with a lot of creeps. Even
bigger creeps than Manny used to be. I didn't like leaving
my car parked on the street in front of his building with all of
them tacky lowriders lined up like pieces of junk. But I didn't
have no choice. He didn't answer his door when I knocked,
but that didn't bother me. He'd left his television on, so I
knew he couldn't have gone too far for too long. Instead of
waiting in my car, I walked the two blocks to Padre's, a run-
down Mexican restaurant. I drank two shots of tequila and
slid a lopsided burrito around on a cracked plate. I ignored
the burrito after I seen a bug crawling out of it.

Like I expected, all kinds of thugs tried to play me, but I
don't play that shit. Boys way younger than me, decked out
in their gang colors and tattoos, was the ones trying the
hardest. Latinas, some of them fat, ugly, and hairy, was
working the street in front of Padre's when I got there and
when I left. By now it was real late and I didn't have no
weapons on me, but I wasn't scared. Not even when these
boys, eight or nine of them, started following me.

Now, I come from the streets, so nothing that happened
on the streets surprised me. I always expected some shit. But
I was not prepared when somebody grabbed me from behind.

Being the little woman that I am, I had a lot of advantages,
but just as many disadvantages. It seemed like a hundred giant
hands had ahold of me. Before I knew it, my feet wasn't even
touching the ground no more. Something hit the back of my

head so hard I saw stars that wasn't even there. And then I didn't see or feel nothing.

I don't know how long I was in that condition, but when I woke up, I was on the ground in the alley behind Padre's, on my back and naked.

The pretty blue silk blouse with matching skirt that I had wore to Mr. Bob's house was ripped to pieces and covered with dirt and blood. My shoes and panties was on the ground next to me. I tied my clothes around my top and bottom. Just to show you what kind of neighborhood I was in, the girls working the street in front of Padre's didn't even say or do nothing when I stumbled out of that alley carrying my shoes and covered in ripped, bloody clothes. If anything, they gave me mean looks for stepping on their turf.

I was hurting all over. I don't know how many of them motherfuckers fucked me, but my little pussy felt like a Mack truck had drove up it. My head was throbbing and so was every bone in my body.

Of all the shitty things I thought would happen to me sooner or later, I never in my life expected nobody to rape me! Tough girls like me never got all emotional about things like rape. I'd seen it happen to other girls when I was running the streets during my teenage years. Them same girls would get up off the ground, dust off their clothes, and then go on about their way until it happened the next time. And it usually did. I didn't like getting raped, but what bothered me more was getting fucked and not getting paid! My neck was hurting real bad because one of those motherfuckers had tried to strangle me. Nothing hurt me more than knowing that somebody hated me enough to leave me for dead in an alley. Twice!

I made it back to my car without getting jumped again. I don't know how long I sat there, but it was a long time. I prayed out loud to God that them assholes didn't give me AIDS. I wanted to see Manny more than ever. He woke me up by banging on the window of my car.

He was as glad to see me as I was to see him.

# Chapter 30

# ROCKELLE HARPER

Nothing could have prepared me for what happened next. It was the Saturday after Sherrie Armstrong's funeral. I didn't have any plans for the day, so I was glad when Clyde and Lula dropped in.

Clyde took Lula and me out to lunch at the same restaurant where I'd first met him. The man spent almost as much time in Alfredo's as he did in his own apartment. But him extending an invitation that included me was rare, so I went. As soon as we got back to my house and stepped on my front porch, the telephone in my living room started ringing.

It was Helen.

"Miss Rocky, can . . . can you come get me?" she mumbled in a voice so low I could barely understand her.

"Speak up, girl," I ordered, my hand cupping the telephone receiver. I first assumed that Helen had taken the kids to her house. She often did that when I left them alone. I didn't have a problem with that as long as her parents didn't mind.

"Hi, Miss Rocky, can you come get me?" Helen said, sounding like she had a mouth full of food, making me almost drop the telephone. My sons peeped around the corner, but they disappeared as soon as they realized I'd seen them.

"What the hell—girl, where the hell are you? What the hell do you mean going off leaving my kids in this house alone?" I couldn't contain myself. I was glad Clyde and Lula had come in for a drink. They rushed over and stood next to me with anxious looks on their faces. Lula leaned her head toward the telephone to try to hear. "It's Helen!" I said, looking from Clyde to Lula.

"I'm at the Hyatt Regency hotel honeymoon suite. I had some whiskey and I . . . I think I'm drunk," she slurred. Then she let out a loud hiccup. "I been with a man. He's in the bathroom, so I can't talk long."

"You're what? Drunk? You stupid bitch! What the hell have you done?" I looked from Clyde to Lula again. "This damn girl is off somewhere drinking with a man!" I roared.

"Holy shit," Clyde mouthed, his hands on his hips. Lula wrapped her arm around my shoulders to keep me from falling, I was wobbling so hard.

"See, this is what happened, Miss Rocky. I had a date with this man, but he got crazy and started talking real mean to me and then he took all my money and called me names and a skanky whore. He's . . . he's a creep! I tried to get him to come to your house for our date, like the other ones that called up on your telephone in your bedroom did. I didn't want to leave the kids alone because I knew you might get back before me and be mad. And that's just what happened. Miss Rocky, I won't do this no more," Helen yelled.

I thought my head was going to split in two. I could not believe my ears. My mouth was hanging open as wide as it could without dropping off my face.

Clyde and Lula stood there like mutes with stunned expressions. By the time I got the whole story from Helen, I was horrified.

"Clyde, that damn girl's been turning tricks!" I wailed, slamming the telephone down. "She's tricking with some asshole who just went off on her damn ass. Can you go get her?"

Clyde had a look on his face that I'd never seen before. His lips moved for several moments before any words came out. "Son of a bitch!" he yelled, with a look of absolute rage on his face. He turned a shade darker, right before my eyes. "That retarded girl that babysits for you?" he asked in a hoarse whisper.

I nodded. "That little slut!"

"Helen?" Lula hollered. "Helen's been turnin' tricks?"

"What the fuck—how she get caught up in this shit?" Clyde wanted to know.

I started wringing my hands and pacing the floor. "Clyde, I don't know. I guess . . . she's not as retarded as we thought she was."

"I guess not! What you been tellin' that girl?" Clyde waved his arms, giving me looks that would have made my flesh crawl under any other circumstances.

"I haven't told her anything about . . . my business, and I didn't have a damn thing to do with this shit she got herself into!" I shrieked.

Lula's eyes were stretched open so wide, I thought her eyeballs would pop out.

"Where she at?" Clyde shouted, already heading for the door with his keys in his hands.

"She's at the Hyatt in the honeymoon suite. That dumb ass got drunk *and* robbed," I told him.

Clyde practically ran out the door with Lula behind him. They were not gone five minutes before Helen's mother was at the door, wild-eyed and frantic. I kept as far away from her as I could because she looked like she wanted to rip my head off.

"Rockelle, what is going on? Helen just called and said she's in a hotel room," Mrs. Daniels screamed. She had on a plaid housecoat and some gray house shoes. Her hair was in rollers. "She said a man got her drunk and took a couple of thousand dollars from her. Where did Helen get that kind of money? What you got my baby doing?" Mrs. Daniels continued, moving toward me with both her hands balled into fists. "Talk to me!"

With my hands held up, I stumbled until my back hit the wall. I stood there like a statue, with nothing moving but my mouth. "Mrs. Daniels, calm down. I don't know what that girl's been up to," I lied, still trying to sort out the mess Helen had just told me.

The truth hit me like a ton of bricks. That sly little wench had been answering my trick calls, fucking in my house, and leaving my kids alone to go hook up with her tricks. "I thought she was responsible. She's never done anything like this before," I managed. I got so light-headed I thought I was going to faint.

"Well, she won't be coming over here anymore. What you do is your business, but you won't be involving my child. You lucky I don't call the cops on your yella ass—"

"You can't blame me for this shit. I tried to help Helen feel more like a normal girl. If you cared so much about her, maybe you should have been paying more attention to her," I shot back.

"Don't tell me how to raise my child, you sleazy bitch. You can trash your life, but you won't trash my child's. As long as you live, you better not ever ask Helen to babysit your brats again."

I would have said more to Helen's mother, but she ran out the door. Before I could go check on my kids, Juliet stumbled into the room.

"Mama, what's wrong out here? I heard loud voices," she said, rubbing her eyes.

"Baby, are you all right?" I asked, putting my arms around her. It hurt when she pulled away from me.

"Yeah, I'm all right. Why?" she asked, shrugging.

"Uh, Helen won't be babysitting for us anymore."

"Why?"

"Uh, she left you guys in the house alone. That's way too dangerous," I explained.

Juliet shrugged. "That mean you won't be goin' to work no more?"

"Well, no. I'll still have to go out to work, but I'll get Mrs. Johnson from across the street to watch you and your brothers." Helen had always been my primary babysitter. But Rolene Johnson, a lonely old widow with no children of her own, had always made it clear that when Helen couldn't babysit for me, she would. "But I probably won't be able to work as much."

"Oh." Juliet seemed wide awake now. Nothing got that girl's attention faster than the subject of money. "That mean we won't go shopping and buy a lot of cool stuff no more?"

I loved my daughter, but she was one of the coldest individuals I'd ever come across. If she was this trying already, I couldn't imagine what she was going to be like when she got older. I had a hard time believing how much control she had over me. As much as I did for her, it never seemed to be enough. What hurt the most was admitting that she was just like me. Or at least, the way I used to be. It never ceased to amaze me how much my life had turned out like my mother's. Even the fact that we both had a daughter first, then two sons. And like Mama, my daughter was to me what I had been to Mama. *What goes around, comes around.*

"Uh, no it doesn't. I don't care what I have to do, I'll see to it. We'll have just as much money to spend as we always did."

"We better," Juliet said with a cold, hard look on her face.

# Chapter 31

# ROSALEE PITTMAN

I knew that things couldn't get any worse when I still had to get drunk before I could talk to Mama. It didn't matter if it was over the telephone or face-to-face.

I'd gulped down a few sips of rum before I left my apartment, but I had to whip out the bottle I carried in my purse and do a few more shots during the difficult ride in the cab to Mama's.

My head was swimming, and I was dizzy, but I noticed the cabdriver glancing at me through his rearview mirror. He had seen my bottle, staring at it like he wanted a dose, too. He must have thought I was really smashed because he drove several blocks out of the way, humming as he shifted his glance from me to the meter. Normally, I would have said something and held back the tip, but this time it didn't matter. I was glad that the ride was taking almost twice as long as it should have. Even after the cab stopped in front of Mama's building, I had to take a couple more sips from my bottle, spilling more on my lap than I did in my mouth.

"Ma'am, do you need help?" the Middle Eastern cabdriver asked in perfect English, tapping his fingers on the steering wheel.

"Huh? No, I'm all right." I paid the huge fare and the huge tip and staggered out onto the sidewalk, almost falling on my face.

I stood in the same spot for several minutes, swaying like a lone tree in a strong wind as I looked around the neat, quiet neighborhood. My heart felt like it was beating a mile a minute. I glared at the beige stucco high-rise building Mama lived in, with its sliding glass doors and a lawn that looked like a bright green tablecloth. It was a long way from the red-shingled house we'd lived in back in Georgia. And much nicer and more modern than the dump we'd lived in back in Detroit. I reminded myself, with a groan that I felt all the way down to my feet, it was more expensive than Georgia and Detroit put together.

The stout, middle-aged Hispanic man operating the elevator looked at me like I'd stolen something as I staggered in. He frowned at the wet spot on the lap of my jeans where I'd spilled rum on myself in the cab. The way he was rubbing his nose, my guess was that he probably thought I was so drunk I'd pissed on myself.

The elevator stopped on the second floor. Mama's nosy, chatty friend Clara wobbled in, holding a covered Tupperware bowl. "Rosalee, is that you?"

"Yes, Miss Clara," I managed, leaning against the wall to keep from falling.

"You look like you've been run over by a bus," Clara noticed. "*Star* is always printing stories about all the drugs models use."

"I don't use drugs, Miss Clara," I snapped.

"I hope not. You've already started to lose your looks."

"We can't all be as fortunate as you," I responded dryly, praying that this rude busybody had a different destination than mine. Clara seemed to spend more time in Mama's apartment than she did her own, which was one of the reasons I didn't like to visit. "Uh, where you off to this mornin'?"

"Oh, Mr. Baker in the penthouse had a slight stroke the other week," she told me, blinking hard. "The hospital released him this morning. I'm surprised that those greedy quacks at the hospital didn't keep him longer so they could squeeze more money out of him."

"I know what you mean, Miss Clara," I mumbled. "And that's a cryin' shame."

Clara nodded so hard her stiff blue wig slid to the side. "Uh-huh. And it's an even bigger shame that his children are too busy to come and see about him." Clara paused and adjusted her wig. Then she tied the frayed belt to the pink-and-blue plaid bathrobe she practically lived in. "I hope I live long enough to see just how busy they'll all be when they find out *I* convinced Mr. Baker to change his will. All five of those useless brats will get a dollar apiece," Clara said, cackling. She sniffed and gave me a narrow gaze with eyes that looked like they belonged on a snake. "They are not half as thoughtful as you. You're a good daughter."

"Thank you, Miss Clara."

I trotted out of the elevator as soon as it opened, surprised to find the door to Mama's apartment unlocked.

"Mama, you should keep this place locked at all times," I scolded, marching across the living room floor.

Mama was stretched out on the couch, her eyes glued to a show she had recorded a few days before. Without looking up, she roared, "Rosalee, don't slam the door so hard. I can't hear my program as it is." Mama was as all decked out in a neatly pressed blue cotton dress with a fake rose pinned to the lapel. Her hair was neat, but her face was covered with too much powder and rouge. Shiny red lipstick was smeared across her lips and on her false teeth. She clutched a huge glass of lemonade in one hand and a wad of napkins in the other. She looked like one of the serene old sisters they featured on the covers of hymnbooks and church fans.

I marched over and clicked off the television. "Mama, we need to talk," I said, standing in the middle of the floor with my arms folded, my shoulder bag dangling. I hadn't tightened the cap on my bottle so more rum spilled out, soiling Mama's thick beige carpet.

She gasped in horror and sat bolt upright on the couch. "Girl, what's wrong with you? Look at how you messin' up that floor!"

"Mama, we gotta get out of this place," I said quickly, bracing myself for her outburst.

"What in the world are you babblin' about this time? Get out of what place? Go where?" she asked, setting her glass on the coffee table.

I took a deep breath and continued. "We can't stay out here in California any longer. I'm goin' crazy. We're goin' back home."

From the look of pain on Mama's face, I thought she was having a stroke, too, like poor old Mr. Baker in the penthouse. "What you mean, we leavin' California?" she asked in a weak voice, swinging her legs off the couch, smoothing the tail of her dress. "This is home now, and I ain't gwine no place," she protested, her eyes on my face. "You—you brung your long tail up in here, interruptin' my Bernie Mac Show tape to talk some crazy mess like that? Girl, have you lost what's left of your mind? Turn that television back on and get out my way, gal!" she said, motioning with her hand for me to move.

"Mama, I don't want to stay out here anymore. We've been out here long enough. Too long, if you ask me. I want to go back to Detroit. Now if you want to stay out here, you can stay, but I'm goin' back to Detroit," I told her, refusing to leave my spot.

"And do what? You want to give up modelin' to go back to workin' in that dollar store?"

"I don't care what I have to do when I get back there. I am leavin' this place." I didn't realize my hands were trembling until my purse started to slap against my side.

"I don't understand you no more, girl." Mama paused and stretched her eyes open as wide as she could. "You done got fired, ain't you? I knowed it! Clara said you was puttin' on too much weight to keep modelin'—"

"No, I didn't get fired. Uh, but I can't keep modelin' too much longer anyway. I'm not gettin' any younger, and the modeling agencies are always lookin' to hire younger girls. You tell me that yourself all the time." I had weaved so many elaborate lies about my bogus career, that I almost believed the shit myself. "And, Clara's right. I have put on weight," I said, letting out my breath so my stomach would stick out more. "I can't get jobs as easy as I used to . . ."

"And because you losin' your shape, you wanna uproot me and drag me back to all that mess we left behind?" Now Mama was dabbing at her eyes and nose with the napkins. Her tears made her lips shine even more.

"It's not just that, Mama. I'm sick of this place, and the sooner we get out of here, the better."

"I see. Well," Mama paused and coughed, rubbing her chest to make it look good. "Well, I guess it don't matter 'cause I ain't gwine to be around much longer nohow. I'd just as soon die in Detroit as anywhere else." Mama coughed some more and started rubbing her chest even harder.

"Would you rather go back to Georgia? I can get in touch with Cousin Anna in Fayette. You can stay with her if you want to," I offered meekly.

Mama gasped again. Her cheeks, usually round and

firm, looked like they had suddenly deflated. "And what would I do back there? Sit around on Anna's front porch and swat flies and drink pot liquor outta mason jars? And what about you? What would you do back there? Get a job on the railroad? Pick peaches? Ain't no decent work back there. Especially for a highfalutin supermodel like you."

"Mama, this city is too expensive, and it's gettin' harder and harder for me to pay rent on two apartments." I looked around at all of the expensive items I'd bought for Mama. A new DVD player was in a corner, still in the box. My stomach churned when I thought about how many thousands of dollars I'd spent trying to keep her happy. But I felt good knowing that I'd done more for my mother than most of the children of the other elderly residents in the complex had done for their parents. I darted around the room, clicking off lights. "And your utility bill out here is three times what it was back in Georgia," I reminded.

"Well, you was the one who wanted to have a separate place of your own. I don't know why you thought you couldn't live with me and model them clothes, too."

"Look, Mama. I'm tired and I need to get myself together so I can start makin' plans. I've said what I came over here to say and that's that. I'm goin' back to Detroit."

Mama sniffed and wiped her tear-stained face again. "I never thought you'd do me like this, Rosalee. After all I've been through. I done lost everything I loved, but you. First your daddy, then both your sisters and your brothers. *Aaar-rrgggh!*"

"Mama, stop all that bawlin'! Don't start that shit about Miss Pearl's curse bein' responsible," I hollered, waving my arms, wishing I had another way out of this mess. I cursed myself for getting us in it in the first place. "What happened to our family was goin' to happen anyway. I knew it then, I know it now."

Mama stopped crying and gave me a stern, surprised look. "Well, Miss Supermodel, if you thought Miss Pearl's curse was nothin' but a bunch of hogwash, why you bring me out here in the first place?"

"Because I love you, Mama. I felt I had to do all I could to make you happy. I promised you I would." It took all of my strength for me to keep from screaming my lungs out. For some strange reason, I could barely feel the buzz that had been so potent when I walked in the door. Without giving it much thought, I rooted through my purse, fished out my bottle and drained it, letting out a loud burp.

Mama shook her head, waving her napkin at my bottle. "Is that what's this is all about?"

"What?" I slurred, swaying so hard, I had to sit down on the arm of the couch.

"You drunk, that's what." Mama stood, her hands on her hips, rubbing her face with her napkins. "I'm gwine to brew a strong pot of coffee, and then I want you to stretch out on this couch and pull yourself together."

I grabbed Mama's arm. "I don't need no coffee, and I am not drunk. My mind is made up."

Mama stared at me with her mouth hanging open. "What you bring me way out here to California for, Rosalee?"

"I wanted you to be happy," I said meekly, sliding my empty bottle back into my purse. "I've told you that a dozen times. Well, now it's time for me to think about my own happiness for a change."

"But you don't want to see me happy now?"

"Don't twist my words. Look, I'm tired and I'm goin' back to my apartment to start packin'. If you don't want to go with me, fine. You stay here. But my mind is made up." My neck ached as I looked around the room. "What we can't sell, we can give to Clara and anybody else who wants it." I sucked in my breath and gave Mama a hard look. "I've already had the Goodwill truck pick up some of my stuff."

"Girl, you just like your daddy's side of the family. Selfish and foolish. If your uncle hadn't took up with a jezebel like Pearl in the first place, we wouldn't be in this mess."

"Mama, Miss Pearl had no more supernatural powers than I do."

Mama's mouth dropped open again. "Is that right? Well, I noticed you didn't say that when you had that problem with Annie Mae's ghost and needed Pearl to straighten that out."

"I was a child, Mama. I didn't know any better. Maybe it was just my imagination. I don't believe in ghosts," I said, recalling the many times that the ghost I didn't believe in visited me and tugged on my hair. "Now like I said, you can come with me, or you can stay out here. My mind is made up."

Mama was crying like a baby by the time I left her apartment, but I didn't care. I mean I did care, but it had gone beyond that. I was losing my grip on reality. If I couldn't save myself, I couldn't save Mama. I felt like I was sliding deeper and deeper into a bottomless pit, and I didn't want to drag Mama along with me. Selling my body had taken its toll on me. The easy money didn't cut it anymore. I was so sick of looking at naked bodies, I could barely stand to look at my own anymore. Now when men looked at me in public, it almost made me throw up. I had even started to have dreams where naked White men were chasing me across the Golden Gate Bridge, their dicks flapping like wings. Hovering above the naked men was a black angel: Clyde.

I cried all the way back to my apartment, trying to sort out my thoughts and sober up. No, I never really believed in Miss Pearl's curse on my family. But Mama did. I kept telling myself that, because I felt that I had to keep it fresh on my mind. I'd left my husband to run away with Mama because I felt I had to. I had wanted to make my mother's last years happy ones. I'd done that until tonight. But I was tired now.

I had been avoiding Clyde, Lula, Rockelle, and Ester for days. But when the telephone rang a few hours after I got home, I was glad to hear from Lula.

"Rosalee, where have you been, girl?" Lula's voice sounded like an echo.

I took my time answering. My chest and jaw muscles were still tight from my run-in with Mama. "Lula, I had some things I had to sort out," I said, the telephone in one hand, a straight shot of tequila in the other. My head was aching, my eyes were burning, and my stomach felt like it had been turned inside out. "It's a family thing with my mama. The woman's out of control," I explained, hoping Lula wouldn't press me for the details. There were certain things I liked to keep to myself. "You know how it is."

Lula let out a heavy sigh. "No, I don't, but I wish I did. My mama didn't live long enough for us to lock horns the way you and your mama do."

I forced myself to ignore the sad tone in Lula's voice. "Well, old people can get on the last nerve, girl. And, with Clyde and the tricks, I got enough to deal with."

"Well, I'm feelin' you there, sister. I got things I need to sort out myself."

"So, has Clyde been keepin' you busy?" I could have answered that question myself, but I just threw it out there because I couldn't think of anything else to say. And the last thing I wanted to do was let too much information slip out about what I was planning to do. I was still just drunk enough to do that, if I wasn't careful.

"Uh-huh. Like a goddamn plantation overseer. With you

doin' whatever it is you've been doin', me and Ester have been coverin' your tricks." I didn't like the smug tone in Lula's voice. I could tolerate Ester and Rockelle talking trash to me, but not Lula. She was as close as I could get to having a homegirl. Or another sister to replace the two I'd buried.

There was a long moment of silence before I said anything else. "How's Rocky?"

"Oh, girl, you don't want to know." Lula sniffed then told me about Rockelle's retarded babysitter turning a few tricks of her own. "Clyde's mad as hell about Rocky runnin' her own game, advertisin' for tricks in *The Spectator.* Helen spilled the beans as soon as Clyde rescued her from that hotel."

"Well, we both know what's on Clyde's agenda. It's all about us gettin' laid and him gettin' paid," I grumbled.

"Yeah, but the brother surprised the shit out of me when he busted into that hotel room and dragged that retarded girl out of there and took her home to her folks. But not before he beat the shit out of that trick. I wanted to get violent myself. What kind of man would take advantage of a retarded child? It pissed Clyde off real bad. With him havin' a daughter just as helpless as Helen, naturally he took the shit real hard." Lula stopped just long enough to take a deep breath. "So, why you been keepin' such a low profile? And don't tell me it's just your mama. I know you better than you think, girl."

For Lula to be just a few years older than me, she had a lot of motherly ways about her. Even though she certainly didn't look like a mammy, she sure acted like one. And she had Clyde's nose opened so wide, it wouldn't have done me any good to challenge her authority.

"I'm just tired, Lula. That's all. I just needed a break." The last thing I wanted to do was tell Lula more than she needed to know so she could blab. She carried a lot more weight with Clyde than I did. And it was no wonder. She and Ester were the only ones he was fucking and the ones with whom he spent the most time. That meant I couldn't trust Lula with information I didn't want Clyde to know. Especially with him acting so strange lately. Clyde had never been violent or that mean to me, but he had come to depend on the money I gave him. "Can I talk to you tomorrow? I want to get some sleep now."

"I feel you. Ester's in her room cryin' so I better go see about her. Sherrie Armstrong's funeral wore her out, and then she had to go do Mr. Bob two nights in a row. I think once we all get some rest, we'll feel better. I'll talk to you to- morrow."

*No you won't,* I said to myself. Not tomorrow or any other day.


I had to have another drink before I did what I had to do before I crawled into bed. I called my husband in Detroit. I wasn't surprised, but I was disappointed when a woman an- swered the telephone.

I cleared my throat and clutched the telephone with both hands to keep from dropping it. "Can I speak to Sammy?"

"Who is this callin' here this time of night?" the woman asked, growling. I knew that my husband didn't tolerate homely, hard women, but this one sounded like a straight- up, juke joint–hopping wench. I pictured an out-of-shape cow with buck eyes, a ratty wig, and a cruel scar on her face.

"His *wife!*" I hollered. "His wife," I repeated, just to make sure that heifer heard me right. I heard some muffled voices in the background, then after what seemed like five minutes, Sammy came on the line.

"This is Sammy," he said, talking loud. "What can I do for you?"

Sammy sounded impatient and annoyed, and that made me even more nervous. I almost hung up.

"Sammy, this is Rosalee," I mumbled.

"I know who it is. Shit."

"Who was that woman?" I asked in a shaky, but firm voice. I'd come too far to back out. "Why is she answerin' your phone?"

"What's it to you?" Sammy barked, sounding even more impatient and annoyed.

"Sammy, can we talk?" I asked, my voice more level. "I need to talk to you, real bad."

"Uh-huh. You been gone almost over two years. After all this time, what we got to talk about, Rosalee? You want to give me a address so I can send you them divorce papers?"

"Sammy, I don't want a divorce. I want to come home." I was surprised at how easy it was for me to get the right words out. I held my breath, waiting for him to respond, hoping he wouldn't cuss me out and hang up on me. That's what I would have done if the shoe had been on the other foot.

He laughed long and loud. "Well, do say. You run off and ain't called me not one time to see how I was doin', now you want to come home. Well, I done heard everything now!" he said in such a sharp tone, his words almost cut into my ear.

"You don't want me to come back home?" I said, pouting. "You don't want things to go back to the way they were?"

"It don't matter what I want no more. You showed me what kind of woman you was by takin' off the way you did. Now you out there in sunny California, I advise you to stay out there with whoever you with."

"I am not with another man, if that's what you mean."

"Yeah, right. And Santa Claus ain't got nothin' to do with

Christmas. You been gone all this time, and I'm supposed to believe you ain't been fuckin' no other man?"

"Well, I haven't," I said, crossing my fingers. "You are the only man I ever loved and I-I want to be with you, Sammy Pittman."

Sammy let out an eerie laugh. It sounded like a screech.

"Sister Pittman, you gonna have to come up with a better reason than that." He cleared his throat. "What kind of fool you think I am?"

We didn't speak for a minute.

"You got somebody else? Is the hussy who answered your phone your woman now?" My voice was getting weaker by the second, and I was about to lose my nerve and hang up after all. But I couldn't. There was too much at stake.

"What do you think? And what do you care? I'm still a man, and I'm gonna do what a man do."

"All right. Don't take me back into your life as your woman. But take me back as a friend. You and I were friends before we were lovers, all through school. We can be just friends again. I'm comin' back to Detroit. Me and Mama."

"Rosalee, you got more nerve than a crooked politician. Hold on, let me get my cigarette."

I breathed through my mouth while I waited for my husband to come back to the telephone. I heard more mumbling in the background. My heart almost broke clean in two when I heard him laugh before he got back on the line.

"Girl, you somethin' else," Sammy said harshly. He paused again to laugh some more. I was getting impatient and annoyed myself, but like I said, I had too much at stake. I sat on the side of my unmade bed, clutching the telephone like it was going to jump out of my hand. "Rosalee, I didn't know if you was dead or alive. Shackin' up with another dude or what. Well, I didn't let that stop me from livin'. Now if you comin' back to Detroit, fine. That's your business. I know damn well you didn't expect me to welcome you back with open arms after the way you took off. Shit."

"We can't even be friends? You won't help us out 'til I get a job when I get back there?" I asked, my voice bleating like a wounded lamb.

"Look, this is a bad time to be talkin'. And anyway, I got company."

"Do you still love me, Sammy?"

"That don't make no difference. And, yes, I do . . . but, you tripped out on me. I wasn't expectin' to hear from you no more."

"Sammy, I'm comin' back to Detroit. If you don't want to be bothered with me, fine. I won't bother you once I get there."

"Bye, Rosalee. Whatever you do, I wish you all the luck in the world. You gonna need it. And, one more thing, I hope you be a better woman to the next man you get." Sammy slammed the telephone down so hard, something popped inside my ear.

I sat staring at my bedroom wall for about ten minutes before I was able to move again.

While I was packing, the telephone rang. Assuming it was Clyde or one of the girls, or worse, Mama, I let the machine pick up. I was surprised, but happy, to hear Sammy's voice again.

"Sammy?" I said, out of breath as I clicked off the machine and picked up the telephone. "Sammy, baby, I'm here!" I yelled, sitting down on my bed so hard my tailbone ached.

"Why you soundin' so surprised? I thought you'd be glad to hear from me."

"I didn't give you my phone number."

"Star sixty-nine."

"Oh."

"Uh, I couldn't talk too easy when you called. Clarice, uh, my lady friend, was here."

"I see. So, uh, y'all seriously involved?"

"Involved, yes. Seriously, no. At least, not yet," he admitted. Sammy's words felt so much like bites, my ears tingled. But I couldn't blame the man for gnashing his teeth. "I ain't too anxious to get off into another relationship. Especially after what you done . . ." Sammy cleared his throat. "Listen, if you serious about comin' back to Detroit, I can find a place for y'all. But, you can't stay at my place. My life is already complicated enough."

"Sammy, I don't want to make things any harder on you. And I can understand if you don't want me back. But I hope we can still be friends. You are the best friend I ever had, male or female." I was begging, but under the circumstances, I wasn't too proud to do it. And, it was a small price to pay if it got me what I wanted. "If you do find me and Mama a place, I'll pay you back when I get a job." I had a few thousand dollars of my trick money, but I wanted to hold on to as much of that for as long as I could.

Sammy sucked his teeth and grunted. "Aw, girl, you ain't got to pay me back nothin'. When, and if, you come back here, you go your way and I'll go mine. I can't be bothered with your drama no more. If I was to let you back up in my life, next thing I know, you'll take off again. I can't deal with no more crazy shit like that, Rosalee. I'm a man, not no Incredible Hunk or some no-brain robot."

"And you won't have to deal with no more drama from me. I just need you to help me and Mama get situated. As a friend."

Sammy blew out his breath, sighing so hard he had to cough. "I swear to God, you somethin' else, girl. I am scared of you. I didn't appreciate what you done to me, and I ain't never gonna let you forget it. Everybody always talkin' that shit about how doggish Black men are, well I'm a good brother and look what it got me. I done my best to make you happy, girl. I left my job, home, and family back in Georgia to run off to Detroit with you. Not many men, Black, White, yellow, or brown would do that for a woman. You didn't have to up and leave like you done. That shit . . . that shit hurt me to my heart. You can't expect to come back to me like you been on a vacation or somethin'. You left me, and I should have got a divorce from your black ass by now anyway."

Sammy had every reason in the world to scold me. And I took it like the woman I thought I was.

"I was wrong, Sammy. I know I was wrong now. I love my mama, but I should have drawn the line when she asked me to leave Detroit and move out here to take care of her."

"Naw, you should have drawn the line way before that."

"I know, I know. Listen, you can still get a divorce, Sammy. I'll be more than happy to sign the papers or do whatever else I have to."

"There ain't never been no divorce in my family. That's the last thing I wanna do," Sammy said gently. The sincerity in his voice surprised me.

"But you brought it up first, not me," I reminded.

Sammy mumbled something I couldn't understand. "What did you say?" I asked, my heart thumping so hard against the inside of my chest, I could hear it.

"When you comin'?" he asked.

"Just as soon as I can. Tomorrow if I can get us a flight."

"Your mama want to do this thing too?"

"Not really. But I told her she can come with me, or she can stay out here."

"My mama didn't want me to marry you, you know. She wanted me to marry one of them sanctified Wheeler girls."

"That's your mama's business. She didn't have to live with me. And you can let her know that you can still marry one of the Wheeler girls. I won't stand in your way."

"Shit. This is a hell of a way for us to get back together. And, by the way, just what you been doin' out there? California is a tough nut to crack if you ain't got no college education."

"Huh? Oh, just workin' hard like everybody else. I had a few jobs . . . secretary, waitress. But it's so expensive to live out here. San Francisco makes Detroit seem like a hick town." I forced myself to laugh. "I guess they want everybody to help with the upkeep on that Golden Gate Bridge."

"Ain't that the one all them folks be jumpin' off of?"

"Uh-huh. A person can get real depressed out here," I said, sadly recalling a newspaper report about a man leaping to his death off that famous bridge a week ago.

"Well, at least I ain't got to worry about you doin' nothin' that desperate. Do I?"

"I would never do somethin' like that," I said stiffly. "I got too much to live for." Mama's face flashed across my mind. I knew that as soon as we got back to Detroit, she would brag all over town about me being a model. So I had to lay the groundwork for that. "Uh, I did some modelin', too."

"No shit? You kiddin'."

"No shit," I said stiffly, wondering how many other women had told the same lie.

"Well, you sure got what it takes. I doubt if you can do much of that back here."

"Oh, I'm through with that. I want to find somethin' more stable. Modelin' is a short-term career."

"They hirin' at Ford Motors," Sammy announced. "It ain't as much fun or glamorous as modelin', but Ford pays a pretty penny, too. I just got on the payroll last month."

My heart was finally beating the way it was supposed to. My lips had even curled into a smile. "That's good to know. I'll put in an application as soon as I get there."

"Rosalee." Sammy stopped and I waited a long time before I said anything else.

"Yes, Sammy. I'm listenin'," I said, using the same seductive voice I used with my tricks.

"You take care of yourself, Rosalee. I-I'll see you when you get here."

After Sammy and I hung up, my telephone started ringing off the hook. Clyde left two frantic messages, Ester left two, Lula left three, Mama left three. Rockelle even called and left one. But I ignored them all.

I turned off my answering machine; turned off the phone; took a long, hot bath; and slid into my nightgown. For the first time in weeks, I slept like a baby.

# Chapter 32

# ROCKELLE HARPER

I knew that my life would really start to unravel after the stunt that dumb-ass Helen pulled. Helen's parents had even stopped speaking to me, and they rolled their eyes at me every time I saw them. I was lucky they had not tried to file some kind of charges against me. Not yet, at least and I prayed they wouldn't. I didn't know much about the law, but I was sure that there was something on the books about contributing to the delinquency of a retarded person.

The kids missed Helen and hated crabby Old Lady Johnson. "How come Helen can't come back?" my son Michael asked with tears in his eyes.

My precocious daughter, Juliet, answered that question for me. "Because she's not responsible! She shouldn't have been leaving us alone!" Juliet exclaimed.

And I hadn't been too responsible myself for leaving my babies with a person like Helen in the first place. I was lucky that nothing worse had come out of this mess.

Two days ago, I ran into Helen's brother, David, at the corner drugstore. I didn't know Helen's older brother and his wife that well, but I did know that they often advised Helen's parents where Helen was concerned. As soon as I saw David, my heart started beating like a drum. With his narrow face, droopy features, and expensive suit, he looked like the vengeful type. What made that even more frightening was the fact that he worked at City Hall.

But he surprised me by being pleasant. It didn't take long for me to realize that he didn't know the truth about what had happened.

"Helen gets into too much trouble for Mama and Daddy to cope with now at their ages, so she's moved in with me. It wasn't so bad years ago for them to deal with her, when some asshole got her pregnant. I have my own problems to deal with, and even if I didn't, I'm no spring chicken myself." An unbearably sad look slid across David's face. "Mama was already in her thirties when she had me. She was almost fifty when she had Helen. That's a dangerous age for a woman to have a baby. I thank God that retardation was Helen's only affliction."

I gasped. "I didn't know about Helen's pregnancy. Who did it?"

David frowned and shrugged his rounded shoulders, already looking like a much older man. "It could have been just about anybody, Rocky. The girl was loose as a goose, and she's always been so attractive. That's a hell of a biological snafu common with girls in her mental state. Men have a hard time not noticing her." David paused and shook his head. His features seemed to droop even more, right before my eyes, making me feel worse than I already felt about my role in Helen's downfall. "That girl would have dropped her drawers for Satan. If Mama hadn't had her fixed, she'd probably have half a dozen babies by now." A painful look appeared on David's face as he raked his fingers through his thin hair.

"Being a parent is not that easy," David said, giving me a grave look. "It's got to be one of the hardest jobs in the world. That Helen. She is so hardheaded. She talks to Mama, Daddy, and me any old way she wants to. But the girl can't help herself."

"Tell me about it," I said strongly, trying not to think about how hard my job was raising three kids alone, especially Juliet.

David sucked in his breath and shifted his weight. It was then that I noticed the contents in his shopping basket: Ex-Lax, a heating pad, a huge bottle of brandy, some Geritol, black hair dye, and some Rogaine. He cleared his throat to either get my attention back or to distract me. I was glad I had not picked up what I'd come for: a jumbo pack of condoms to get me through the weekend.

David grinned and announced, "I just got transferred to Sacramento, and I'll be taking Helen there to live with us. Annabel—you remember my wife?—is expecting in a few months. It'll be good to have Helen there to help with the baby." The sad look returned to his face. "Here I am forty, and about to be a daddy for the first time. Annabel and I will probably have to deal with the same type of shit with our child that my mama and daddy had with Helen. It won't be easy chasing after a toddler, then a few years later, a teenager."

I shook my head. "But you'll have Helen there to help you. She is so good with kids." I let out a huge sigh. "I sure do miss her."

"And I'm sure she misses you and the kids, too." David stood straight, but his shoulders still sagged. "Listen, Rockelle, I never got to know you that well, but I know my sister spent as much time at your home as she did her own. I appreciate all the time you spent entertaining her. As limited as she is, the girl's all right by me. She can't help herself. It's up to the folks that care about her to look out for her. Help keep her out of trouble."

I nodded, and laughed, but only slightly.

"It was nice seeing you, David." I patted his arm and rushed to get my condoms.


Twice as many tricks started calling me on my private line requesting my services. Or maybe it just seemed that way now that Helen had stopped intercepting my calls. Old Lady Johnson, my new babysitter, was a greedy old crow. She charged me by the hour, so every minute I was away from the kids counted.

Then, out of the blue, Rosalee mysteriously disappeared. Clyde had called her number, and a recorded message said that it had been disconnected. At first, we didn't know what to think. Rosalee's absence could have meant anything from her running off to be kept by a sugar daddy, to her sleeping with the fish at the bottom of the San Francisco Bay.

Clyde shared a tragic story with us for the first time about one of his earlier wives, a beautiful young woman from the Philippines. He still carried a picture of her in his wallet. "Maribel didn't come back from a date one night. A week later they found her headless body floatin' in the bay," he stammered. "Some maniac from Fresno was the culprit. The next girl he tried to do, she got away. But she had his wallet. Cops found Maribel's purse and panties in that freak's house."

"Clyde, you know Rosalee's too streetwise and tough to let her guard down long enough for a trick to hurt her. Besides, her telephone has been cut off. I bet she skipped out on her own," I assured him.

Rosalee's landlady confirmed my theory. She told Clyde

that Rosalee had checked out of the apartment two months late with her rent, leaving nothing behind but some tacky old wicker chairs and a few pieces of clothing. Neglecting her rent told me that Rosalee had been planning her getaway for a long time.

"That long-legged heifer," he said, growling. Clyde was furious, but the worst was yet to come.

Lula went to the senior citizens' place where Rosalee had dumped her fussy old mother to see what she could find out. The nosy old White woman who was always up in Rosalee's mama's business told Lula that Rosalee had packed up her mother and they'd both climbed in a cab, suitcases and all. Hearing that upset Clyde even more. We all knew that if Rosalee took off with her mother, she wasn't coming back. Come to find out, Rosalee hadn't paid her mother's rent for two months.

Rosalee's mother had gone behind Rosalee's back and talked Clyde into cosigning for a ten thousand dollar loan. Then she told Rosalee she had won the money playing the slot machines in Reno. The old woman had used the money to buy herself a three thousand dollar brass bed and used the rest to finance a trip to Vegas. Rosalee had a lot of regular tricks who had been dating her exclusively. Her running out on those tricks and her mother's secret loan had cost Clyde a fortune. He was fit to be tied. He got so mad, he had a panic attack. He had to take some pills *and* get drunk.

"That ungrateful bitch! I can't afford to be played like this. Wherever that heifer hidin' at, she better be hid good," Clyde roared, his voice booming throughout his living room. He hurled a glass against the wall and waved that gun of his in the air.

It gave me a lot of pleasure to tell Clyde that I thought he never should have allowed Rosalee into our lives. I didn't like his response.

"Rockelle, you worry about you and let me worry about everything else. I'm still the head nigger in charge," he told me, giving me a look that made me tremble. I decided to watch my step. I wanted to stay on Clyde's good side until it was time for me to defect, too.

Clyde was a peculiar man, but it was impossible to hate him. Every time I tried to do just that, he'd show up at my house unannounced cradling his daughter in his arms. He'd been doing that a lot lately, trying to get over Rosalee. I figured it would be a feather in my cap to accommodate him when I could.

Last Friday night just as I was about to take the kids to Mrs. Johnson's house so that I could get to my date at the Mark Hopkins hotel, I glanced out my front window. I spotted Clyde, grinning and stumbling up on my front porch. He was carrying Keisha in his arms, like she was still a baby. She and I were about the same age and she was almost as tall as Clyde. Keisha liked to walk with her canes, but Clyde liked carrying her more. They saw me peeping out my window, so I didn't have time to close my curtains and pretend I wasn't home.

I opened the door with a fake smile and a lie. "I am so glad to see you two," I squealed, holding my screen door open with my foot as Clyde struggled to get in. Keisha weighed quite a bit, too. Not as much as me, but she was still a big woman. I guess it didn't bother her that Clyde still treated her like a child, because she seemed to enjoy his extreme devotion.

"Hi, Rocky!" Keisha greeted, flashing her crooked but beautiful smile and swinging her legs. I envied her deep, husky voice.

It had been weeks since I'd seen Keisha. Since that time, her appearance was different but not for the better. The eye on the injured side of her face had changed its location and shape. It was now noticeably lower and smaller. It looked like Keisha had a hard time keeping that pitiful eye open. When she blinked, her lid barely moved. It just broke my heart to see such a lovely young woman in her condition. I was so grateful that all three of my kids were okay. The problems I had with Juliet were nothing compared to what Clyde had to deal with. But Clyde didn't seem to mind taking care of his daughter at all. I often wondered just how much more of a fool he'd be without her.

Keisha was wearing a beige sweat suit and a black baseball cap. Her long blond hair was in braids, the style she seemed to wear most of the time.

"I ain't seen you and the kids for a long time, so I made Daddy bring me over here," Keisha said, grinning. Decked out in an outfit identical to Keisha's, Clyde beamed like a searchlight.

"Well, I'm glad he did," I said, closing the door behind them, glancing at my watch. "Where are you two on your way to?"

"Just over here," Clyde replied, looking me up and down as he gently placed Keisha on my couch. "Granny's havin' prayer meetin' at her house tonight and Keisha didn't want to deal with that."

Keisha was not that popular with my kids. Her distorted face frightened my boys, so they usually stayed in their room when she visited. Juliet didn't care one way or the other about Keisha and practically ignored her. I ended up entertaining Clyde and Keisha by myself.

It turned out to be a pleasant evening after all, even though I'd missed my date. About an hour into the visit, Clyde pulled me into the kitchen and started whispering.

"I'm goin' to need you to help Ester and Lula take up the slack that Rosalee left 'til I find us a new girl. Her regular tricks threatening to do business with somebody else's girls—I can't have that," Clyde said nervously. "Now . . . now I need to know if I can count on you."

I nodded. "You know you can. I don't know what I would have done if you hadn't helped me out."

"Things gonna get real busy now."

I nodded again. "Good. I need the money." I felt bad about what I was thinking in the back of my mind. As soon as I stashed away another few thousand, I was going to leave Clyde, too. I hoped that by then he had him another wife.

I hugged Clyde and kissed him. "Let's have a drink."

Clyde was depending on me to help Lula and Ester take up the slack until he replaced Rosalee. I couldn't believe it. In a way I was flattered. Up 'til now, I'd always been the lowest one on the totem pole. Despite what Clyde had told me in the beginning about my weight not being a problem, a lot of upscale White men, like most of our tricks, wanted to roll around on a bed with a slim woman like Rosalee. But when women like Rosalee were not available, and those same men wanted a Black woman, they settled for me. And believe me, when I was with a White trick, I didn't boast about being biracial because when a White trick requested a *Black* woman, that's what they wanted.

It was ironic for my popularity to rise to such a high level just when I'd started to seriously think about quitting the business. Before Rosalee's mysterious disappearance, I had planned to "retire" within a couple of months. Now I didn't know when I'd be able to do so. But it had to be soon. I was losing my grip on reality.

From day one, even before Clyde sent me on that first date, I'd promised myself that I would only stay in the business long enough to get myself in financial shape. Well, now I was in better financial shape than a lot of people. My rent was paid up three months ahead, all three of my kids and I had more new clothes then we needed, my credit cards were in good shape, we had plenty to eat, I had a new Camry for which I'd paid cash, and I took the kids to Disneyland on a regular basis—at two thousand dollars a turn. Greed and loyalty to Clyde were my only justifications now.

I'd recently taken the civil service test, so there was a possibility that I would get hired on at the post office. In between tricks, I'd practiced my typing and learned new software, so I'd also applied at a few offices for secretarial work. I was a high-maintenance woman, and I could continue to be one if I managed my money right.

I was pleased with myself because I had a plan. A real plan. After I stashed away a few more dollars into that safe-deposit box I maintained at Wells Fargo Bank and got a regular job, I'd move into a cheaper place.

Besides, it had become uncomfortable living next door to Helen's parents. I didn't see them that often, but even once a week was one time too many. The last time I saw Old Lady Daniels and her husband outside of that tomblike house they lived in, they were standing on their front porch looking at me with such evil eyes it hurt me just to look at them. It gave real meaning to the phrase "if looks could kill." I'm lucky that I'm not telling my story from beyond the grave.

On my way to a trick from San Diego, staying at a hotel across the Bay in Berkeley, I came across an affordable apartment that was in a nice neighborhood and close to a school. The apartment manager told me that if he could verify my employment, the place was mine. When we needed to list a place of employment on credit applications, or any other documents, we referred people to that used car scheme that Clyde and his buddy, Lou, ran as a front. Not wanting Clyde to know my new address once I left him, I couldn't take advantage of the C and L Used Cars ruse. I *had* to get a real job now, or I'd be stuck forever in a situation that was slowly destroying me. No matter how good and easy the money was, what I was doing was hurting me now as much as it was helping me.

Rosalee's desertion had made Clyde so cranky. Something told me that if I wanted to avoid his complete meltdown, I'd probably have to go AWOL even sooner myself.

Just like Rosalee.

# Chapter 33

# LULA HAWKINS

Clyde had left me several messages since the day before, and so far I had not called him back. His first message had sounded quite casual, but by the time he'd left the last message, I couldn't deny the desperation in his voice. Losing a gold mine like Rosalee had crippled his spirit and his wallet, at least temporarily. Spending so much of his time with his daughter and grandmother, and supervising our movements didn't leave him a whole lot of time to go out headhunting for another wife.

Besides, Clyde complained all the time about how hard it was to find "a good woman" in our profession. I couldn't agree with him more. From conversations with tricks, I had learned a lot about the business. Things had changed from the days when a man could organize a stable of women, tell them what to do with their body parts and their money, beat them and get away with it, and expect to remain in control. Yes, there were still men out there running that kind of show and women who let them, but the new millennium had brought with it a whole new attitude in the sex industry.

Greedy strippers, porn movie heifers, and horny house-

wives—as if they didn't have enough to keep them busy—
were boldly taking away business from the established working girls. It drove Clyde up the wall.

"Them cows! They ain't got no more class than them
quarter peep shows and them life-size blow-up dolls," Clyde
complained when the subject came up. "And, it's them
fuckin' *Pretty Woman* movies and other Hollywood foolishness that's hurtin' this business. New girls that buy into that
shit don't wanna do no real work no more, thinkin' they can
work it like Julia Roberts, and a Richard Gere is just around
the corner!"

I mean it made Clyde so mad, he scared me. And, Clyde
was a scary man when he was in a bad mood. That Glock
that he usually carried in the waistband of his pants didn't
scare me as much as his eyes when he got mad.

Clyde had nice eyes when he was in a pleasant mood.
When he was with his daughter, his eyes were as bright as
new money. But when he got mad, upset, or sad, his eyes
took on a sinister look. The sparkle that was usually there
would disappear and the pupils would get real dark. Like the
flat, lifeless eyes you'd see on a doll or a shark.

I knew that I would have to face Clyde sooner or later, or
haul ass the way Rosalee did, but right now I had other
things I had to address first.

I could always count on my stepsister, Verna, and her
lover Odessa when I needed them. I hadn't called or written
to them back in Mississippi in weeks. Like I'd expected,
Odessa picked up the telephone on the first ring the Saturday
morning that I called, two months after going to Sherrie
Armstrong's depressing funeral.

"Odessa, you must sleep with the thing right next to you
on the pillow," I teased, right after she'd mumbled a sleepy
greeting.

"I sure enough do. When my woman is on the road, I like

to have the phone as close to me as possible," Odessa replied with an affectionate tone in her voice. It didn't take long for her to sound wide awake, which she should have been long before now. It was 9:00 A.M. in her time zone.

"So my big sister's out on her job?" I kept a telephone close to me when I was in bed, too. When Clyde called, he wanted immediate attention. With Ester and I each having a bedroom extension, and a phone in the living room and our kitchen, one of us almost always grabbed the phone on the first ring when we got a call. And, everybody I knew packed a cellular phone. So, if somebody wanted to reach me, they could—if I wanted them to.

"Lula Mae, your big sister is always on one job or another. Lucky for me . . ." Odessa let out a mysterious chuckle. Then she made a slurping noise with her tongue.

"You nasty buzzard!" I hollered.

As low-down, funky, and nasty-minded as men were when it came to sex—and nobody knew that better than I did—lesbians could get pretty loose, too. I couldn't count the number of times I'd walked in on my stepsister and her lover licking all over each other, then describing everything to me that I'd missed.

"Verna's doin' a run to Mobile, Alabama, to drop off a pile of live chickens for this redneck motherfucker your daddy been doin' business with for years." It saddened me to think about some of the other high-risk jobs Black women performed. As dangerous as my "job" was, I didn't have the nerve to drive trucks for a living like Verna.

"I see," I muttered.

"What you been up to, Lula? We ain't heard from you in a cat's age."

"Uh, I've been real busy."

"Too busy to send anybody a postcard or to call us? What about your daddy and your stepmama?"

"I sent a birthday card to Daddy last month, and I called him. He wouldn't even come to the phone," I replied sadly.

"Call him at work if you want to talk to him. If you called the house and he wouldn't come to the phone, it's probably because that witch he married wouldn't let him know he had a call. She do that shit to Verna all the time."

"Oh. Well, I hope she's not interceptin' the notes and cards I send to him."

"Like I said, if you want to talk to your daddy, and he don't answer the telephone himself when you call his house, you best call him at work. Now, what you been up to, girl?"

"Odessa, I met somebody. A bus driver. His name is Richard Rice." No matter how hard I tried to deny my feelings toward Richard, and no matter how I had dogged him out to Ester, that man was constantly on my mind. Some days I'd walk around smiling, recalling the warm feeling I'd had sitting across from him at that table in the steakhouse. "Uh, I think I want to get to know him better. He might be my last chance. He's from Louisiana and . . . and, he's the kind of man every woman wants." I had to pause because I realized I was beginning to sound like a love-struck schoolgirl.

"Not me," Odessa reminded, laughing and sucking her teeth at the same time.

"Oh, you know what I mean. But, sister-girl, if you were straight, he'd be the kind of man you'd want. He's nothin' like any of the other men I've known so far." I caught myself before I said anything too stupid. Odessa's brother Bo, my dead husband, had been one of the sweetest men to walk the Earth. "He reminds me of Bo," I said as fast as I could. "Even looks a little like him."

"Is that right?" Odessa asked, her husky voice sounding more like a woman's instead of a man's, which wasn't too often.

"Uh-huh. I'm goin' to call him up tonight to see if he still wants to see me. I've been thinkin' about him ever since we met a few weeks ago."

I had to keep checking myself to make sure I didn't sound like a fool. Every few seconds I looked toward the door, prayin' Ester wouldn't walk in. I hadn't seen her in three days, but I knew she was all right. She'd left me several messages, telling me not to worry about her and that she was spending some time with one of her Latino friends in the Mission District.

"You be careful out there, girl. I know you don't think so, but your daddy still loves you. So do the twins, and me and Verna will coldcock you if you fuck up out there. We love you, too."

"What about Etta? She ever ask about me and how I'm doin'?"

"Fuck that bitch. You don't need her. Verna's her own daughter and livin' right around the corner, and she don't have nothin' to do with her."

"I figured as much. Well, when you see the twins, you can give them my phone number and tell them I said hi. Same for Daddy."

I hung up and started searching for Richard Rice's telephone number. When I hadn't found it after ten minutes, I took that as a bad sign. I picked up the book I'd been reading when I met him even though I'd finished it. Wedged between two pages was the napkin that he'd written his telephone number on.

With my hand shaking, I dialed his number. He answered on the fifth ring. "You probably don't remember me, but my name's Lula . . . we met at Tad's Steakhouse a few weeks ago." I held my breath.

"The sportin' lady I met at Tad's Steakhouse near the cable car turnaround?" he asked in a tone so dry and distant it made me uncomfortable. I wasn't sure if he was trying to be funny or sarcastic. I didn't like either one.

"Uh, yeah." It felt like something was burning inside my chest, and I had to rub myself. I wondered if I'd made a mistake calling up Richard.

"I sure enough do remember you. How you been?" Now he sounded more than a little pleased to be hearing from me. "I'm so glad you called."

"I've been fine." For the first time in my life, I felt shy. Even though he couldn't see me, I lowered my head and kept my eyes on the floor.

"How's business? You workin' hard or hardly workin'?"

My face burned. "Business is good." I cleared my throat. "You told me to call you if I wanted to hook up or somethin'."

"I did and I do. Girl, I am so glad you called! I been thinkin' about you day and night."

"Oh? You do remember *everything* I told you about myself, right?"

"Uh-huh. I just asked if you was the sportin' lady, didn't I? You said yeah. Hold on, baby. Let me get my beer." He returned within seconds, breathing hard. "That's better," he said, slurping. "Now, what do you like to do to have a good time?"

I felt more relaxed. "Oh, I like movies, goin' out to dinner, walkin' on the beach."

"I see. I tell you what, if you ain't busy tonight, let me take you out to a movie, then dinner, and a walk on the beach."

I had never felt like a teenager, even when I was one. I felt like a teenager at that moment.

"Where you live at?" Richard asked.

"Give me your address. It would be better if I came to you," I said, sucking in my breath so hard, my chest hurt.

"Whatever." Richard got quiet for a long minute and then he said in a rush, "You sure I won't get my black country ass kicked by one of your jealous gentlemen friends?"

"No, you won't. But it would be easier if I came to your place. I got this moody roommate, and I don't want to upset her."

Richard gave me his address, but I didn't even have to write it down. I memorized it on the spot. Then he told me to take a cab and that he would pay for it, which I declined.

He was one man whose money I didn't want.

# Chapter 34

# ESTER SANCHEZ

I was hoping that Lula was out on a date or something. She'd been depressed lately, and I didn't like leaving her alone in the apartment when I was at Manny's for a few days.

When I'd called him to come get me the other day, I told him to park his car at the corner so he wouldn't upset my neighbors. The people on my street was not used to seeing cars like Manny's cruising around. I really don't even know exactly what kind of car it was. Something long, low to the ground, white all over except for a design that's suppose to be a flame of fire on the hood. He had a ornament perched on the front end of his hood. The same typical Latin foolishness I seen every day. It was one of them big-tittie women with a misshaped head and flaps that I couldn't tell if they was wings or a cape. A huge pair of foam dice was dangling from a string off the hook on his rearview mirror. The same place where normal people hung baby shoes.

Speaking of babies, I had to deal with one of my own. Don't ask me why, 'cause I couldn't say why God let some things happen. Up to now, my life had been more than a little crazy. But what happened to me in that alley in Manny's neighborhood put the icing on the cake. I didn't know none of them guys who jumped me and ripped off my panties and fucked the hell out of me. I didn't care then, I don't care now. It's too late to care about anything. Since I was in a fucking coma or something while I was getting fucked inside out on that ground, I couldn't say if any of them bastards used condoms. I should laugh at myself for even thinking something so crazy. Since when did rapists care about safe sex? And anyway, guys desperate enough to rape somebody, they probably already got every disease in the book.

I didn't tell nobody at first about me getting raped. Not even Lula. I had to tell Manny. And that was only because he was the one who found me sitting in my car that night with blood all over me and my clothes ripped to shreds. Calling the cops was a joke. They barely came to this neighborhood when somebody got murdered. I had left my car unlocked, but I'd lost my keys back at the scene of the crime. After Manny took me into his place, wiped me off, and put me in one of his big shirts, he went out with a baseball bat looking for them thugs. He didn't find them, but he did find my purse. My car keys was still in it, but my money was gone. My credit card was gone, too. But that worthless piece of plastic had been canceled by the bank anyway because I kept going over my credit limit and forgetting to pay the bill.

I was glad to be back in Manny's place. It felt more like my home than my own home.

Compared to my sharp apartment, the dark, musty (but clean), postage stamp–size place Manny lived in looked like part of a flophouse. The wallpaper was so cheap I couldn't tell if the faded designs was roses, balloons, or what. Why he even bothered to cover his windows with the drapes he had, I don't know. You could see straight through them things. But since Manny lived on the third floor he didn't have to worry about nobody peeping in on his business.

The couch in Manny's living room was so hard and lumpy, my butt and back was aching like I had been with ten tricks in the same day, back-to-back—as I had been just a week ago! But I wasn't sure then that I was with this baby. When I went to see a doctor he gave me some good news: I was pregnant and I wasn't HIV positive so I didn't have to worry about AIDS. But even before my visit to the clinic, I had promised myself that if I was pregnant and HIV, I still wasn't having no abortion. I was going to have my baby and do the best I could for as long as I could. I would give my child a better chance than my mother gave me. I wanted to do at least one thing in my crazy life that I could be proud of.

Anyway, Manny had this lopsided chair across from the couch that was even worse. The last time I sat on it, I fell clean through the seat. He covered the seat with cardboard and a flat, musty pillow and that's where he was sitting, looking very handsome. Picture that movie star Andy Garcia, a little younger, looking a little rougher. That's the kind of handsome I seen when I looked at Manny. Now like I said before, I been knowing Manny since I was a real young kid.

During my teenage years when I rode shotgun with them outlaw gangbangers, Manny was already in OG territory. He was a veteran, and I had just started doing things like fucking and bleeding every month.

I had heard about Manny before I even knew who he was. The street reporters told everybody how Manny handled his business. Nobody got in his way, and if they did, they only done it one time. One weak-minded asshole who had to be crazy or new in town and didn't know Manny's rep tried to jack Manny and take his new Nikes right off his feet. He was the only man Manny killed and got caught for. But he only had to spend like five years in San Quentin.

I heard while he was in that place, he had some more trouble. Some White dudes into that White supremacy shit called a challenge to Manny, and that was a big mistake. Now from what I heard, Manny didn't even have to kill that sucker hisself. There was tons of the Mexican mafia in lockdown with Manny, and they had a lot of love and respect for him. He had them take care of that White punk. Before the deed was done, Manny got cut up in a few places and came so close to taking his last walk of shame, they had even called in a prison priest. But guys like Manny never die easy.

Anyway, once Manny got out of the joint, battle scars running up and down his back and belly, he had put all that shit behind him. Hell, he was even talking to young kids, trying to get in their heads what a precious thing life could be! And if that wasn't saintly enough of him, he sent money back to Mexico to help support some of his relatives. Now here he was: ex-con, ex-killer, ex-thug. Yeah, Manny was a changed man. He was somebody I could tell anything to.

"Manny, I'm goin' to have a baby," I said during a commercial break for *Friends*. He was sitting next to me on that lumpy couch of his.

He didn't say nothing at first. He just looked at me and blinked, and then he started laughing. "So that's why you keep refusin' my margaritas." He took my hand in his and forced me to look in his eyes. "Ester, you are a very lucky woman. You been blessed with a gift from God."

I trembled. "What do you mean by that? Ain't you goin' to ask me who is the daddy?" I knew it was too soon for my baby to be moving, so it had to be my own heart slamming against the inside of my chest.

Manny shrugged. "It don't matter who helped you make

that baby. You still need to give thanks." Manny smiled, showing me teeth that was no longer sparkling with them cheap gold caps I sometimes seen grinning between the lips of too many people thinking they looking fly. He was still smiling when he scratched his neck and looked off to the side. "I hope it's mine."

A pain shot through the side of my belly, straight up to my head, forcing tears into my eyes. Manny's words made my head spin and my eyes burn.

I was two months pregnant. I had just been with Manny, for sex I mean, for the first time just three weeks ago. No way was he the father of my baby. He got me to his bed after I'd finished with a really handsome and sexy trick that night—a very famous star from television! Every now and then I got a little pleasure from screwing a trick, but never the kind I wanted. Not even when it was a sexy famous person. The trick that night had almost done me some good. He would have if he'd done the job a little bit longer. One thing I never did was to try to get a trick to keep fucking once he had cum—unless he wanted to. A trick was all about business for me, not pleasure. So after I left the trick's hotel room, I drove to Manny's apartment, anxious for some sexual healing for myself for a change. I had been making my own orgasms for years. That was a sad confession for a woman my age, but it was true.

Manny did a good job in the bed, at least for me, he did. Nothing like that lazy, clumsy Clyde. Manny had a real nice body—most of it at least; six-pack across his chest, toned arms, nice butt, something nice between his legs. I overlooked his battle scars and skinny legs.

"Manny, look, I been in all kinds of shit these last few years." The commercial was over, but we didn't look at *Friends* no more. Manny was still looking in my eyes.

"I know that," he told me, sipping his second shot of tequila. I wanted some myself so bad, my mouth was itching. But I had my baby's health to think about.

"And how do you know that?"

"Because I know you," he said, pointing from his head to me. "Maybe you been mulin' shit inside every hole in your body from Mexico for the cartels like my three sisters. Or, maybe you been robbin' everybody in San Francisco but the mayor. Maybe you got some games I ain't never even heard of up your sleeve." He shrugged, blinked. "I used to do all that shit and then some, but not no more. And you know what," Manny paused and took a real deep breath, beatin' his chest with both fists, "it feels good. I didn't know what it was like to walk down the street and not have to watch my back until last year. I'm thirty-six fuckin' years old now, and I feel like I just was born. I feel . . . real good." Manny had a beautiful smile, and it was aimed in my direction. I giggled like a little girl when he pulled me onto his lap. "Let me tell you somethin', *mamicita*. Even when you was a little kid tryin' to hang with the gangs, I had my eyes on you. You been comin' to me now," he nodded and winked and motioned toward his cracker box of a bedroom, "sharin' with me my bed. I like havin' you here."

"I didn't have nowhere else to go," I admitted. "Nowhere. I ain't got nobody I can call my own. I still got a posse still alive over here, but, well . . ." The homegirls I used to hang with in the old days, the ones who started having babies at twelve and thirteen years old, now their daughters was strolling around them same streets with babies of their own. There was a lot of *grandmothers* in the Mission still in their twenties. I could have been somebody's grandmother by now. "I'd much rather be here with you than with them," I said. I felt myself drifting farther and farther away from Clyde.

Manny squeezed my hand real hard. "Listen, you wanna be with me, I wanna be with you. If you down with me, ain't nobody gonna jack you up and get away with it." He looked down at my stomach and patted it real gentle and quick. "Whatever you want to do about the baby, I'll be with you." He sucked in his breath. "Now, you plan to have it or what?"

"Don't you want to know who gave it to me?"

"Do you want me to know?"

"It happened . . . that night." I wanted to cry, but I couldn't. "I don't know which one is responsible."

"Oh," Manny said, sighing. He tried not to look mad, but I could see anger in his eyes. He bit his lip and rubbed the back of his neck. He slid me off his lap, and he stood up in front of me. "You want me to help you get rid of it?"

It took a lot to shake me up. My face got so hot, I felt like I was on fire. I stood up from that couch so fast, I almost pissed my pants. Manny moved back a few steps.

"I would *never* get rid of my baby. I don't care if a demon came straight out from hell and got me pregnant, I would never in my life turn my back on a child of mine," I said. My voice seemed like it was coming from my heart instead of my mouth. Manny always knew about me, how I was left with the trash in that alley when I was born. It was something I didn't like to talk about, so most of the people who knew me didn't bring it up that much. "I got raped down your street by so many guys I couldn't count them. They didn't hurt me that much, and I got over it real quick. But they left me a baby. *My baby.*" It dawned on me that my mother could have been raped, too. That was all the more reason for me to keep my baby. I couldn't repeat my mother's crime.

Manny's handsome face dropped so fast and far I thought it would hit the floor. "Hey, I'm sorry. I just thought, well, you know, it bein' so hard to raise kids and all, chicks get abortions left and right. My landlady's daughter, cheesy bitch that she is, just had her *seventh* abortion."

I sighed and sat back down. "Now that you know I'm keepin' some rapist's baby, do you still wanna see me? And even after my baby comes, will you? Because, maybe I'm gonna get me a real job." Like Manny just said about hisself, I was feeling real good, too!

Manny's eyes slid to the side, and he looked kind of nervous. But then he looked at me and shrugged. "I went from workin' the streets, makin' bank, gettin' paid." A sad look that I seen on Manny more times than I wanted to, slid across his face now. "At the same time I had so much, but still, I had nothin'. Cops and other hustlers always breathin' down my neck, so many guns bein' aimed at me I felt like I was facin' a firin' squad—even in my own house." Manny then lifted his head high up and showed me a proud face, smile and all. "Now I'm a cook in a restaurant that's so bootsy it ain't even listed in the phone book. I don't make much money, but, I wouldn't go back to the old crazy life if you paid me." And then Manny said something that just made me want to ball up and cry my eyes out. He said, "I want to live."

Then I got serious, because I wanted to live, too. "I . . . If I want to get my shit together, I'm gonna have to move from my place, cut loose, uh, cut loose some people I been kickin' it with for a long time . . ." I couldn't believe the words sliding out of my mouth! Clyde didn't know about the baby yet, and I didn't plan to tell him until I had to. Soon, though. Things had changed so much with him. His daughter and his own expenses was still at the top of his list. He was still pissed off with Rosalee for running out on him, putting a dent in his income. Now he was losing even more money, left and right, because of me and Lula ignoring his messages and hiding out from him. Since Clyde ran his business in such a loosey-goosey way, instead of the way other men like him did, enforcing strict rules and using serious violence, he couldn't expect nothing better from us.

But things had changed with our little family. We were outgrowing Clyde and the business. It wasn't just because of Rosalee running off and them guys jumping me in that alley.

Things was changing because it was time.

# Chapter 35

# ROCKELLE HARPER

I had a feeling Ester was up to something that was going to affect us all, one way or the other. But I was not prepared for the information I was able to pry out of Lula.

"Ester's pregnant," Lula told me when I called her up the morning after Ester had fainted for the third time in three days on my kitchen floor.

"No way? How could she let that happen? Who is the daddy?" I shouted, looking at the yellow kitchen telephone in my hand. I frowned at chocolate smudges on the receiver that had been left by one of my three little pigs. I padded across the floor to dampen a paper towel to wipe the telephone. Clyde was on his way over, and I liked for everything in my place to be spotless when he visited. Even this late in our relationship, I still looked for ways to impress him. And one thing I could say about Clyde Brooks was he liked a clean woman.

"I think I'll let Ester tell you that herself," Lula insisted, talking in a low voice. "She's comin'," she said, gasping. "Gotta go." Lula hung up before I could say another word.

Ester was the last person I expected to get pregnant, especially while she was still in the business. Apparently, she had already started using her condition as a reason to refuse or cancel dates. The night before she developed a sudden mysterious backache on her way to visit a bedridden trick in Oakland. Clyde called me while I was in the middle of a trick myself.

"Rocky, what you doin'?"

"If you really must know, I'm sucking dick," I told him, and I was. The only reason I'd answered my cell phone was because all three of my kids were sick, and I needed to be available if my babysitter had to get in touch with me. My trick, the nervous nineteen-year-old virgin son of another trick, didn't seem to mind the interruption.

"As soon as you finish, call me on my cell. We got an emergency situation with Ester, and I need for you to take over."

The night before that, Ester had claimed a severe stomachache. Clyde had to dispatch Lula to take care of Ester's trick, who had requested any other woman Clyde had available. I expected a lot more problems with Ester because of her pregnancy, but I didn't have much sympathy for her.

I had already had my kids when I started turning tricks, so I couldn't speak from experience. But I had often run into a lot of pregnant women working the streets. Some of them still dated all the way up to the day or night they delivered. Then, as soon as they were able, it was business as usual.

There was a bowlegged sister from Panama working Capp Street. She went into labor while she was in the middle of turning a trick in the backseat of an Oldsmobile. I knew about it because I was in the front seat with her trick's buddy taking care of my business.

"For me, havin' babies is as easy as ridin' a bicycle," the Panamanian sister had told me, with so much pain on her face I flinched every time she had a contraction that night.

Her trick was so stupid and drunk, he thought that he was the one responsible for all that screaming and moaning she was doing.

After the double trick, my girl and I hopped into my car and made it to the hospital just in time. Her son was born twenty minutes later. A week later, sister-girl was back on the street.

Being pregnant didn't stop a woman from turning a trick if she wanted to. Especially a woman as rough and tough as Ester.

"So, Lady Ester said she was through turning tricks?" I asked Clyde, handing him another shot of tequila, the third in less than twenty minutes. He had arrived immediately after my telephone conversation with Lula. Clyde's business was rapidly going down the tubes. Rosalee's disappearance, Lula hiding most of the time, Ester getting herself pregnant and taking up with a reformed *cholo*—it was all about to push Clyde over the edge. "You cool with Ester's condition, Clyde?"

"Hell no, I ain't cool with that shit!" Clyde roared, looking around my living room for the kids. He trotted to the doorway leading from my living room. "Where them kids at? I don't want them to hear me actin' a fool."

"I just got them a new PlayStation. They won't come out of the boys' room until I force them," I said.

He sniffed hard and unzipped the light jacket he had on, revealing the handle of that useless gun he carried all the time.

"She'll regret it," Clyde predicted. "She ain't never goin' to find another man that'll treat her as good as I did," he added with a frosty pout. "I guess I didn't give her enough attention," he complained, sounding more like he was Ester's father.

With the long history that Clyde shared with Ester, and as

hot as he was for Lula, I never thought that I would end up being the only one of his wives he felt he could turn to when he was as distressed as he was. My sudden new position of power and my plan to get out of the business myself soon forced me to use the situation to my advantage. I rubbed Clyde's shoulders as he sat down gap-legged and depressed in one of the new plush wing chairs I'd recently purchased along with the new bookcase facing it. A shopping bag full of new books, hardcovers mostly, still sat on the floor waiting for me to stack them on the bookcase.

"You are way too tense, brother," I told Clyde, kneading his shoulders like he was a pile of biscuit dough. "Let me take care of you."

To my surprise, Clyde had made love to me for the first time earlier while the kids were at the movies with their babysitter. But it was just as lame for me as it was for him. He couldn't even come, blaming it on his nerves. His fly was still open and I could see that he still had a massive hard-on, but I had no plans to do anything about it. One thing I had in common with the runaway Rosalee was I hadn't enjoyed sex since my husband.

"Yeah, I'm tense!" Clyde yelled, an unlit cigarette dangling from his lip, a harsh look on his face. "I got so much shit on my mind these days, it's a damn shame." He gave me a thoughtful look as he crushed the cigarette in an ashtray then clasped his hands. "Rockelle, I saw my daughter's mama the other week. Megan. Blond hair, blue eyes, just as White as she can be. And what kinda name is Megan?"

"Hmmm. I didn't know you still kept in touch with her." I poured more liquor into Clyde's glass and made one for myself, too. I needed it.

"I hadn't seen that heifer since Keisha was born."

I gave Clyde the most sympathetic look I could afford. I knew the whole story about Clyde and Keisha's mother.

From the part about her working the escort services before she got pregnant with Keisha to the part about the hit-and-run accident that had disfigured Keisha for life. Clyde had even told us about the woman's sister hanging out with Charles Manson before his downfall and her death from an overdose of heroin. There was enough to this drama for a movie of the week on the Lifetime channel. Of us all, I had to admit that my history had the least amount of pain. Lula had lost her mother, her son, and her husband; Ester had been abandoned at birth and thrown out with the trash; and Rosalee had buried her daddy and all of her siblings, and left the kind of brother I should have married. I considered myself lucky. I would not have traded places with any one of them.

"Did that Megan woman say something that upset you?"

Clyde grunted as he turned to look at me. "Just seein' her upset me." An angry look suddenly slid across his face. I didn't know if Megan was a subject I wanted to deal with any further. But it was too late to stop him now. "Her smug White ass is livin' like a queen while I'm livin' *la vida loca,* and strugglin' like a galley slave to take care of Keisha."

"Well, what are you going to do about it? Is Megan going to be in Keisha's life now? Is she going to help you with some of Keisha's expenses?"

"She sure is. She just doesn't know it yet. You just watch me."

"I hope everything works out the way you want it to, Clyde. It doesn't sound like it's going to be easy, though. Especially now that Ester's gone and got herself pregnant."

"That Ester," Clyde said, chuckling. He leaned back and moaned. I was still massaging his shoulders, but it didn't seem to be doing any good. He was still as stiff and tense as a plank. "And I always thought that she was my girl. She wouldn't have even told me she was pregnant if I hadn't asked her. I ain't stupid. I knew somethin' was up when she threw up on my new shoes the other night," Clyde snapped. "And, she been lookin' mighty plump around the middle lately."

"She sure is," I agreed, hoping Ester's pregnancy would ruin her shape the way mine did to me. It was a mean thought, but I couldn't help myself. I had just read a book written by Mo'Nique called *Skinny Women Are Evil,* and I agreed with everything she said.

I squatted in front of Clyde, looking in his eyes as he squeezed my hand and guided it to his crotch. There was a rare look on his face. He stared straight into my eyes and slid his tongue across his lip. Then he gave me a crooked smile and ran his finger along the side of my face and winked.

"That was real nice what you done for me," Clyde said in a hoarse voice, motioning with his head toward my bed-room. "You got some pretty good stuff between your legs for a big woman," he said with affection, not malice.

Clyde's frank comment made me uncomfortable, and I didn't like the gleam in his eye. The last thing I wanted this late in my relationship with Clyde was to start sharing a bed with him on a regular basis. Unless money was involved, I had no interest in establishing a physical relationship with another man until I met one for whom I had feelings. I took my hand away from Clyde's crotch.

"Clyde, can you line something up for me this weekend? A few hours with horny old Mr. Bob would be nice, but if he's not interested, whatever you can put together would be fine. Do you think you can do that for me?" I asked, no, I pleaded. Not just with my tone of voice, but with my eyes as well. I blinked at Clyde the way my kids blinked at me when they wanted something. "I'll even do Fat Freddie, with his ugly self," I added with a chuckle.

Clyde's red eyes stared hard. He twirled his shot glass before he took another sip. He shook his head. "No, baby. I can't do that. I can't hook you up with Fat Freddie no more."

"But I thought Freddie liked me," I whined.

"That ain't it, Rocky." Clyde paused and rubbed his forehead. "You know Cisco? Cisco who comes out from San Jose all the time." Clyde didn't give me a chance to answer. "One of Cisco's wives fucked Fat Freddie to death. Literally. Dude had a massive heart attack while they was doin' the do." Clyde shuddered and gave me a pensive look. "Mr. Bob wants to see Lula this weekend, Friday *and* Saturday night. I just hope that lazy-ass heifer don't let me down."

I wobbled up from the floor and peeked around the corner to make sure the kids were still out of sight. "Oh. Well, what else is going on?" I positioned myself in front of Clyde with my hands on my hips. He had already seen me naked tonight, so I didn't worry about my bathrobe being open. I still received a lot of independent calls from men who'd seen my ad, which I had upgraded a week ago, in *The Spectator*. My new ad showed me in a more revealing outfit—a black leather thong and a see-through bra—and I was in a more provocative pose: one finger in my mouth, my eyes closed, and my other hand massaging my crotch. Since my days in the business were numbered, I figured I would go out with a bang.

I knew that Helen had found out what I was up to when she stumbled across an issue of *The Spectator* with my first ad in it. She'd shared that information with one of the tricks she'd stolen from me, and he told me. Even if her brother, David, had not seen my ad, I was sure that Helen's angry mother would eventually tell him about me, if she hadn't already blabbed.

Clyde shook his head. "I got a urgent call for a blonde from a dude who knows a dude who pays *three thousand* for an all-night date. Dude plays golf with my partner, Lou. His

regular chick got drunk and rolled down another trick's spi-
ral staircase and broke her leg in three places. I wouldn't
have such a clumsy cow workin' for me," Clyde said, his lips
snapping over his words. "Especially if she gonna cost me a
three thousand dollar date."

"I have a blond wig," I blurted, half joking, seeing huge
dollar signs in front of my hungry eyes. The most I'd ever
been paid to do an all-night date was a thousand dollars. To
me, that was a lot of money, but not to the wealthy tricks.
One particular trick who was in high-level management at a
downtown bank told me that the majority of the businessmen who paid for sex were clever enough to incorporate
their payments into their business expenses. It was funny
knowing that a blow job and a fax machine both fit under
"miscellaneous" on an expense report. I often wondered
about the uptight men who'd interviewed me for office positions before I contacted Clyde. Those smug suits with their
Palm Pilots, e-mails, and conference calls—well, I made
more money than some of them now.

"What you smilin' about? What's wrong with you?"
Clyde asked, giving me a suspicious look.

"Nothing. I just thought of something funny," I told him.

Clyde gave me a serious look, and then his eyes lit up like
fireflies. A strange smile slid across his face.

"Are *you* all right?" I asked, leaning toward him, my
hands back on his shoulders.

"Uh, yeah . . . where is your telephone book?" Clyde was
already moving around my living room, searching. "I need
to look up a number, and I need some privacy. Right now!"

I handed Clyde the telephone book and started walking
out of the room. I was disappointed, but not surprised to find
my daughter, Juliet, hiding outside the doorway.

"What the—girl, what do you call yourself doing?" I
hissed, talking in as low a voice as I could manage. Now that

I was so important to Clyde, I wanted to keep him happy for as long as he needed me, and for as long as I needed him.

Looking over my shoulder, I saw Clyde frantically dialing a telephone number and looking toward the door. I tried to wrap my arm around Juliet as I escorted her back into the hallway. "Juliet, you shouldn't be listening in on grown folks' conversations. Nice little girls don't do things like that." I don't know why I was trying to smile. I could smile until my teeth fell out, and it still wouldn't faze this difficult child of mine.

"I heard you talking to a man on the telephone the other day about a new apartment. We moving?" Juliet stopped outside her bedroom door. She reared back on her young legs, slapped her hands onto her narrow hips, and looked up at me with a pleading look in her eyes.

I held my finger up to my lips. *"Shhhh . . . I don't want you to repeat that to anybody,"* I said, praying that Clyde didn't hear her. "Uh, one of these days you're going to hear something you don't want to hear by eavesdropping. Now, get back into your room and watch that big-screen TV I bought for you," I said, trying to sound firm enough to get through to Juliet. An extreme pout popped up on her face.

I chased Juliet to her room and shut the door. Then I leaned against the living room wall, trying to hear Clyde's conversation. He was speaking in a low voice but I could hear him anyway.

I should have known who it was he had called. It was that Megan he was talking to; the White woman who had caused him so much grief.

# Chapter 36

# MEGAN O'ROURKE

It had been about three months since the day I'd run into Clyde Brooks in Oakland. As far as I was concerned, he was out of my life again. This time for good, I hoped.

Even though I had not seen Clyde for years, every now and then he crossed my mind. But there was no room in my life for him. And, as hard as it was for me to admit, there was no room in my life for the daughter we'd created. My other kids filled that space.

I had received a letter from my son, Josh, complaining about the weather in Australia and the navy's bland food. Heather called me up a few days ago from Robert's grand-parents' home in Dublin, Ireland. Her five-minute voice mail message instructed me to locate and secure her an apartment in Berkeley no later than August. No matter what else, it had to be near campus—and cute. The thought of my being alone on a permanent basis in the house with Robert didn't appeal to me at all.

After twenty-two years of marriage, to say that Robert and I had grown apart would be putting it mildly. We lived together, but we led separate lives. Even in the bedroom. On a typical day, he was up and out of the house before I even opened my eyes. Some nights he didn't return until I was already in bed, usually asleep.

Our sex life had dwindled to once a month, maybe. And even then, it seemed like we were in different locations. There was no passion, no foreplay, and for me, no satisfaction. And it did me no good to complain, which I did until I was literally blue in the face. Sexy lingerie, wine, adult toys, candlelit dinners, and other tools of seduction didn't work either. The man I'd married had become a stranger right before my eyes. And a hostile one at that.

"For Christ sakes, Meg, is sex all you think about?" he'd said one night three years ago when I'd greeted him at the front door wearing nothing but a smile and holding two glasses of wine. We had not made love in more than three weeks. I'd sent the kids to my parents' and turned off the telephones. With a brutal scowl on his face, he pushed past me and went into his office. I was asleep when he joined me in bed.

One night, about a month later (we'd just made love), he turned to me with a rare smile. "You look different. Did you do something to your hair?" he asked. I shook my head. The difference in my appearance was my twenty-pound weight loss. Then I decided I would "do something to my hair." I became a brunette for six months after being a blond all my life, and my husband didn't even notice it.

Hobbies and trips didn't help, and there'd been many over the years. I belonged to a women's club, a book club, and a group that traveled together. It was no wonder I focused almost all of my attention on my children. But then even that had caused problems. I didn't just "mother" them; I "smothered" them with attention. Josh had joined the navy right out of high school. He called home frequently but his conversations were brief. Heather was a little more attentive. She called a lot, but usually only when she wanted something. Like that damn car she'd requested.

It was my daughter Heather I was thinking about, and how much she looked like Clyde's daughter, the night I got the telephone call that increased my distress.

"Hello, Meg." Even before he identified himself, I knew it was Clyde Brooks. "This is Clyde Brooks."

If a vampire bat had flown through the window and landed on my neck, I couldn't have been more startled. I had to strain and press my legs together to keep my bladder under control.

"Where the hell did you get this number?" I demanded, whispering even though I was alone.

"Is that any way to greet a old friend?"

"Why are you calling here, Clyde?" My mouth got dry, and my breath caught in my throat.

He laughed. "If you didn't want to be bothered, you shoulda got a unlisted phone number."

"What do you want?" I wound the telephone cord around my fingers, cutting off my circulation to the point where I felt faint. Lines of perspiration started sliding down my back like snakes.

"I need to see you. I need to chat with you about somethin' real important."

"That is out of the question, Clyde. Now if you will excuse me—"

"Woman, if you hang up on me, you'll regret it for the rest of your life. I need to talk to you."

"We have nothing to talk about, Clyde," I said in a steady, hushed tone.

"Oh, yes we do. Me and you, we got a whole lot to talk about. Now unless you want me to make a little trip to Steiner Street to discuss it in front of that nice husband of yours, you'll do what I tell you."

"What do you want, Clyde?" I asked, whimpering.

"There's a bar on Front Street called O'Grady's. It's a nice little Irish place so you'll feel right at home. Meet me there tomorrow at noon. If you get there before me, get a booth in the back so we can have some privacy. I advise you to be there, and don't be late. If you don't show up, you'll be fryin' fish or scrubbin' toilets by the time I get through with you."

"Clyde, I'm begging you not to do this to me. If I've hurt or offended you in any way, I'm sorry. But I have a new life, you have a new life. What good could come from us associating with each other now?"

"That's what we need to talk about. You just have your ass at that goddamn O'Grady's like I told you. Do you hear me?"

I took my time replying.

"Woman, you listenin' to me?"

"I'll be there," I said, my voice shaking so hard my teeth clicked.

I crawled into bed, but I couldn't sleep. I didn't respond when Robert rolled in after midnight. I was in the same position and hadn't slept at all when he left the house the next morning.


Clyde was already seated and clutching a drink when I arrived at O'Grady's the next day at noon. Wearing dark glasses and a sport jacket, he looked out of place among all the Financial District suits and ties.

"Why are you doing this?" I asked, sitting down across from him, clutching the eel skin purse Robert had brought back from his fishing trip to Baja for my birthday. He had not wrapped it or removed the price tag. I had showered a couple of hours ago, but I still felt hot and sticky. I'd pulled my hair back into a ponytail and wrestled myself into a blouse and skirt. Like Clyde, my eyes were hidden behind a pair of dark glasses.

"What you wanna drink?" he asked. "My treat." He took a sip and shook his glass at me. "This is some good shit."

I shook my head. "What do you want from me, Clyde?" I asked, nervously tapping my fingers on the table.

"I need a little favor. I need a favor real bad, and I need it real quick."

"And what does that have to do with me?"

"I'm havin' some financial difficulties this month." He paused and cleared his throat. "I thought you'd be able to help me out a little."

I started to rise; he grabbed my wrist and pulled me back to my seat.

"You arrogant nig—"

Clyde gasped and held up his hand. "Now I know you ain't goin' *there,* Goldilocks." He frowned and gave me a disgusted look. "I swear to God, you just as White as you can be. But if you," he paused and pointed a finger in my face, "ever spit out that N word at me again, I will show you a nigger. It didn't bother you when you was wallowin' around in all them motel and hotel beds and the backseat of your mama's car with my nigger ass."

I sighed. "I'm sorry. You know I didn't mean that." Clyde gave me a long, brutal stare, as if one apology was not enough. "I said I was sorry." I let out a painful breath and shifted in my seat. My backside was numb. My legs had cramps. "Now would you tell me what it is you want from me, so I can get out of this place," I said firmly.

Clyde tilted his head and started talking out of the side of his mouth. "This is the deal: I love my daughter more than I love life itself. She's got some serious problems, but I wouldn't trade her for five normal kids. I think I love her more because of her condition because I know she'll always need me." He paused, as if to let his words sink in. "Do me a favor and get that frozen look off your face."

"How do you expect me to be, Clyde?" I retorted. "Do you think I want to be here?"

"Shit, I don't want to be here myself. If you had invited me to your house, neither one of us would be up in here."

"Finish what you have to say!" I snapped.

He let out great sigh and looked away before he returned his attention to me. "Now it ain't been easy for me to take care of Keisha by myself all these years," he muttered casually. "She gets help from the disability benefits, but that don't cover none of the things that really keep the girl happy. Every time I look up, she wants somethin' new."

"You . . . you want money? From *me?*" My voice was so sharp, it whistled. "Is that what this is all about?"

Clyde removed his glasses and glared at me, pursing his lips.

"Somethin' like that. Is that a problem?" he asked, one eyebrow lifted.

"Look, I don't know what you think, but you are wrong if you expect me to—"

"No, lady, you wrong. Now you sit still and listen to what I got to say." He leaned across the table, his chin in his hands. "I had some unexpected expenses this month. Keisha got a notion she wants to go on a cruise. See, I went on one recently and me braggin' about it got her wantin' to go. You know how young folks are. Last week I had to come up off two hundred dollars, just to get her a new hairdo. Thing is, I'm a few thousand in the hole. Last month I had to have a new roof put on my grandma's house. I thought you'd be glad to help me out, just this one time. For that cruise for Keisha, I mean." An obscene smile crossed his face.

"Well, you're wrong. I wouldn't help you out this one time or any other time."

"Ahhhh," he said, stretching his mouth open so wide I could see the back of his tongue. The look on his face was so smug, I couldn't have removed it with a Brillo pad. "I think you will. Now, I need three thousand dollars by Monday. And don't tell me you ain't got it. If you ain't got it, you can get it. I know what you worth, girl."

"My husband handles all our finances. I even have to ask him for the household money."

"Then get it from him. Tell him you wanna make a donation to some charity or somethin'—Save the Children, Save the Whales, Save the Niggers, save whatever ain't been saved yet. Tell him you wanna take a cruise to Jamaica. Or, you can tell him the truth, tell him you wanna help out a old friend."

I gave Clyde an incredulous look. "And what would I tell him the next time?"

Clyde shook his head and finished his drink. "Won't be no next time. You do me this one favor, and you won't never hear from me again. I swear to God." I couldn't believe he had the audacity to cross his heart.

I shook my head. "You're crazy."

"Three thousand. That's all I need. Think of it as back child support. Listen, if you scared to ask your husband, get it from that nice mama of yours. She always was a real generous lady. My first Christmas in Oakland, she played Santa Claus and gave me a brand-new bike. She told me you helped pick it out. Remember that?"

"I would never ask my mother for that kind of money to give to you."

"Then get it from Daddy Dearest. And don't sit here and tell me you can't. Old Man Carmody was always so fond of that good Irish scotch, he wouldn't know the difference."

"Never!" I shrieked.

Clyde shrugged. "Of course, you can always sell somethin'. I know you must have all kinds of jewels and shit that your hubby won't miss."

"I have nothing to sell!"

"Oh, but you do. Now listen close." Clyde glanced around then leaned forward some more, his chin almost touching the table. "I know a way." He paused again and sniffed, not taking his eyes off my face. "Remember back in the day when we needed a little financial assistance?"

My body felt like it had been turned to stone. "You're sick."

"Hush now and listen to what I got to say," he ordered, holding up his hand, licking his lips. "With all due respect, you ain't no bad-lookin' woman. The years have been good to you." Clyde leaned to the side and stared at my legs. "But knowin' you, you done helped Mother Nature hold back Father Time with a little help from one of them cosmetic-friendly surgeons, ain't you?"

"You are crazy!" I attempted to rise again, sliding my watch back and forth on my wrist.

"Unless you wanna find out just how crazy I am these days, you'll sit your silk panty–wearin' ass right back down and listen to me. Now you don't want to make me mad. I ain't the same tame little country boy you used to play with."

I sat back down, trembling so hard, I couldn't cross my legs.

"I got this friend, he got a friend, and he needs a little favor this weekend. You'd be surprised what a lonely man will do. All you gotta do is spend a little time with this lonely friend. You ain't got to do nothin' you don't wanna do. You make him happy, you make me happy. I know you still remember how it works."

"That was a long time ago, Clyde. You can't ask me to . . . to sleep with a stranger for money."

"Look, I never did. Must I remind you, you was the one who made that leap. 'Clyde, I'd do *anything* to be with you.' You remember tellin' me that? Huh? You remember them escort services you hooked up with?"

"I can't believe what I'm hearing."

"Every time I looked up they was sendin' you out to do your thing. And you enjoyed every minute of it."

"I-I can't listen to this anymore." I couldn't hold back my tears, and I couldn't ignore the stares we were getting.

Clyde handed me a napkin. "Well, you better. I know where you live now. Now you wipe off them crocodile tears before one of them nosy motherfuckers come over here and make me get real ugly up in here."

"You can't blackmail me. I won't let you." I swiped my face so hard, it ached.

"Who said anything about blackmail? I'm just askin' you for a little help this weekend."

"I can't do it, Clyde. I'll get you the money, but not *that* way. I-I . . . my husband is the only man I've been with since I got married. Twenty-two years. I've never even looked at another man."

"Look, I told you not to make me get ugly up in here. You ought to be flattered that a man would be willin' to pay you that kind of money for a little fun. I know a lot of much younger women who would jump at the opportunity to spend a nice evenin' in a five-star hotel with a nice clean gentleman."

"Why don't you get one of your much younger lady friends to do it?" I hollered, tossing the soaked napkin back on the table.

"I . . . want . . . you." Clyde paused and glanced at his

watch. "I'll call you again tomorrow night after I get everything set up."

"Don't bother. I'm not doing it, Clyde. Can't you get that through your head?"

I could not believe how calm he was. He just blinked his evil eyes and continued. "What's the best time to call? If somebody other than you answers, I'll hang up, but you'll know it was me. I'll keep callin' 'til you answer the phone, like today."

"You are sick," I mumbled. I was almost too weak and overwhelmed to talk any further.

"If I don't talk to you so we can set things up, I'll be talkin' to that husband of yours. I wonder what old Robert will say when I tell him about all the fun I used to have with his pretty blond wife, and that he got a biracial stepdaughter. Now you have a nice day."

Clyde tossed a few dollars on the table and left.

# Chapter 37

# LULA HAWKINS

Richard Rice lived on Webster Street in a shabby neighborhood in a big brick building tagged with gang graffiti. Men of all ages, with desperate looks on their faces, stood on every corner, smoking and drinking from bottles in paper bags. Their colors ranged from the palest white to pitch black.

As soon as I tumbled out of a cab at the corner, unintentionally exposing more thigh than I meant to, the men started aggressively leering at me, making lewd comments in a variety of accents. Equal opportunity sexual harassment; I was used to it by now. Just as a tall, swarthy man with a stringy gray ponytail lunged at me, making smooching noises with his puckered lips, Richard popped out of a doorway, hopping on bare feet. Without saying a word to my admirer, Richard grabbed my arm and led me to the living room of his basement apartment.

The living room was also his bedroom. A dark green couch and a coffee table faced an unmade bed. A small television sat on the only chair in the room. There was something vaguely familiar about Richard's apartment. It was the smell of fried chicken, greens, and corn bread in the air, and a bowl of mean-looking gumbo on a card table by the door. It reminded me of home. Not the hellish place I'd shared with my daddy and my vicious stepmother, but the apartment I'd lived in during my doomed relationship with Larry Holmes. I got misty-eyed, and for a brief moment, homesick. I was proud of the fact that I no longer got angry when I thought about Larry. I felt it was better to use that energy on something more positive, which I was trying to do.

Richard did not let go of my arm until we were safely inside and he had shut and locked his door. In addition to a chain lock, the door also had two dead bolts. Behind the door, propped up in a corner, was a lethal-looking metal baseball bat, with what looked like nails sticking out on both sides. Richard saw me looking at the curious object with my neck tilted back and my face screwed up into an open-mouthed frown.

"Don't let that headbuster bother you. I ain't never had to use it," he said, smiling.

"I hope you never do," I said, shivering even though the room was about ten degrees too warm.

"I was surprised to hear from you, Lula. I been thinkin' about you a lot since that day in Tad's."

"I've been busy." I sat on the side of his bed, looking toward the one window he had. It faced a round-sided refrigerator in a corner that served as a kitchen. I'd had a few three hundred dollar dates with another man who also made his living driving buses, so I knew bus drivers made fairly decent money. But knowing that Richard sent money back home to his relatives in Louisiana, I was not surprised that he lived in such a depressing place himself. His clothes hung from a rack that faced his bed. Half a dozen pairs of shoes, the heels well-worn, were lined up on the floor outside his postage stamp–size bathroom.

"Yeah. This is one busy city . . ." he said, handing me a beer. He had on a plaid flannel shirt and a pair of black jeans, ripped at the knees. His hair was matted, making his head look like somebody had sliced off the back half. Even so, he was still the best-looking man who'd ever paid any attention to me. I hadn't met another man yet as nice as my late husband, Bo. But, I had a feeling that Richard was a strong candidate to fill that spot.

"You . . . know what I do. But you still asked me to call." I gave him a dry look as I took a sip from the bottle of beer. It was so cold it stung the insides of my throat. That was good because it dissolved a lump that had been roosting there for hours.

Richard sat next to me, making the bed tremble and the springs squeak. A minute after he'd sat down, the bed was still moving like somebody was having good sex in it. That thought gave me mixed feelings. I didn't think of sex the way I used to, not since I'd started selling it. Every time a trick or Clyde was on top of me, I concentrated on a red brick wall until it was over—unless I had to do something that involved a lot of theatrics and contortions. The wall facing Richard's bed was made of brick. Not red like in my vision, but off-white. But brick was brick. I didn't know if that was a bad omen or just a coincidence. And at the time I didn't really care. Richard had revived feelings in me that I thought I had buried with my sweet husband.

"I'm glad you did. I really did want to see you again. Now, what's this goin' to cost me?" he asked, rubbing his hands together like he'd just won a car on the *The Price Is Right*.

I gasped. "I didn't come here for that," I said real quick, sliding a few inches away. "You think all I'm about is gettin' paid? Well, if that's what you think I came here for, you wrong. Besides, from what you've told me, I don't think you can afford me," I told him, a sly look on my face.

Richard chuckled and gave me a thoughtful look, holding his bottle of beer with both hands. "You right about that. My money is so funny, even my cash bounces."

"And anyway, I'm about to get out of this business," I said in a whiny, childlike voice.

"I'm glad to hear that. You got too much goin' for you to be makin' a career out of . . . what you do," he said, slidin' his fingers along the side of my arm. "If you don't mind me askin', what's your backup plan? San Francisco is one expensive city." He sighed and looked around his room. "This hole costs me fifteen hundred a month, and that's cheap."

"I'll find somethin'. I can do a lot of other things."

Richard's hand was still rubbing my arm when he hauled off and kissed me, long and hard. There was nothing special about the way he kissed, but it felt good. It felt even better when he did it again. He eased me down on the bed and unbuttoned my blouse.

Richard was out of his clothes so fast it made my head spin. His hard body, healthy and meaty in all the right places, was a sight to behold. All I wanted to do was just lie there and admire it. But when he jumped on me, I pushed him away. "You forgettin' somethin'," I said.

"Oh, I ain't forgot nothin'," he said, panting like a dog in heat, sweat dripping off his smooth skin like raindrops. He gave me a puzzled look and then he sighed. "You ain't got to worry about catchin' nothin' from me. I'm clean. HIV negative."

"So am I. And I want to stay that way," I said seriously. It was a disappointment to know that he was willing to fuck me without protection. Especially knowing how I made my money.

I leaned toward the floor and fished out a package of condoms from my purse. Richard reluctantly reared up far enough for me to slide it on that hungry-looking thing between his legs.

I had not enjoyed sex with a man since that fiasco with Larry Holmes. I hadn't had enough time with my husband to develop a routine, so I would never know if he could have made love to me the way I liked it. With my eyes closed, making love with Richard for the first time was like being with Larry again. I had almost forgotten how much I enjoyed it.

I was not watching the big clock on Richard's wall above the bed, but it seemed like we wrestled around on that weak mattress for hours.

Afterward, I lay in his arms, watching his chest rise and fall, wondering how I was going to keep this man in my life, and how I was going to get rid of Clyde.

"Will I see you again?" he asked, breathing on my face.

"I hope so," I said in a shaky voice. "I just don't know when, though. I still want that dinner, movie, and a walk on the beach you offered." I grinned.

"That and more. I just hope it won't be another few weeks before we can do it. I'd like to see you again, real soon."

"I have a few things I have to settle first. I need to get a job and another place, real fast."

Richard sat up and stared down at me. "I don't want to get all up in your business. I mean, you ain't got to tell me nothin' you don't want to. But if you in trouble, or if you need to hide out 'til you get your situation straightened out, you welcome to crash here with me."

His generous, thoughtful offer almost took my breath away. "You mean that?" I managed.

"I wouldn't say it if I didn't. I care about you, Lula, and I will help you if you let me. Now, you know I ain't no rich man, and I ain't got much to offer, but I want to be with you."

"You don't even know me, Richard. I could be the bitch from hell," I admitted, gently rubbing his back.

He nodded and turned to face me. "You could be, but I could be even worse." I can honestly say that I never felt more loved before in my life. "I know what I need to know about you, Lula. You didn't have to tell me what you told me that day in Tad's. I didn't have to ask you to hook up with me. I don't do nothin' I don't want to do. I know enough about you to know that we could probably have somethin' good together. Besides, I done already told you, I grew up around the same kind of shit you livin' now. I know people can change. There's a whole lotta shit I did that I ought to be ashamed of. You didn't try to hide nothin' from me from the get-go. At least I know now, so I can make up my mind now." He paused and stared off into space.

"I'm still here," I said, tapping his arm.

Richard sat up on the side of the bed, rubbing the side of his head.

"Lula, before I came to San Francisco, I was livin' in L.A. I was one wild and crazy-ass nigger. The Crips was my homeboys. I sold drugs, busted a lot of heads, beat up on my women. You name it, I done it, I had it. I cruised around town with a gangster lean in a low-ridin' pair of wheels, sunroof top, and diamonds in the back. Then, them same folks I thought was my friends set me up over some dumb shit but one of the same women I'd beaten and abused believed in me. She scraped up some money, and we hauled ass that same night. I been walkin' a chalk line ever since. Well, after that angel got me straightened out, I married her."

Richard's past sounded similar to Ester's boyfriend. It was good to know that at least two ex-thugs had straightened out their lives.

"She the one who died in the earthquake with your son?" I asked, rubbing his back some more.

Richard nodded and turned to face me. I can honestly say that I never felt more affection for a man before in my life as I did at that moment. But it was a scary feeling. I had loved Larry Holmes from the bottom of my heart, and I'd lost. I didn't want that to happen to me again. My brain was whirling with confusion, and my emotions were as out of control as a runaway train.

"I still can't move in here with you." I sighed, sitting up, my knee pressed against his. "I wouldn't feel right about it. I want to make it on my own. I got enough money saved up to pay rent somewhere until I get a job. Maybe you could help me find a place and a job." I squeezed his hand. "We'd probably have a better chance if we took things slower, keep our own space."

"Well, there's always a vacant place over here," he said, looking around the room. "If you ain't too particular. This ain't the best neighborhood in the world, but the units in this buildin' come furnished, and it's better than a lot of places. You got a lot of stuff to move?"

"Just my clothes. The furniture belongs to the girl I live with."

"When you plannin' to make your move?"

"I don't know. Like I said, I have a few things to settle first."

"Lula, I wasn't lyin' when I said I cared about you. You got my attention the first time you rode on my bus. You don't know how excited I was when you set down at my table in Tad's that day. All that shit I told you about my years in L.A., I didn't even scratch the surface. I ain't the man I used to be, and I never will be, because I wanted to change. I know you do too, and I know I can be the one to help you do just that."

I looked away because every time I looked in Richard's

eyes, I felt myself getting weaker and it was weakness that had made such a mess of my life. "I better go now," I said, looking at my watch and feeling around on the floor for my clothes. "I'll be in touch."

"I hope you will, Lula. I hope you will."

# Chapter 38

# MEGAN O'ROURKE

If I could live my life over, things would be a lot different for me now. I had made enough stupid choices during my youth to last a lifetime. I could not imagine Robert's reaction if he ever found out about the relationship I'd had with Clyde.

I no longer loved my husband, but compared to most women, I had a good life, and I didn't want to lose it. At least not yet. Robert and I were not happy together, but I wasn't ready to make it without him. And as miserable as our relationship was, I enjoyed the prestige of being married to a successful architect.

My father owned the house we lived in, so if Robert and I ever did split up, I'd always have a place to live. But I still had way too much to lose. I didn't want to think about how a divorce would affect the kids.

I called Clyde at his used car location. "I need to see you," I said stiffly.

"Uh-huh."

"We need to get a few things straight."

"We done already done that. I done told you what you got to do. All you need to know is where and when."

"It's not that simple, Clyde. I don't want to discuss this over the phone. I need to see you tonight before my husband comes home."

"Well, you caught me at a bad time. I got somethin' else I need to take care of tonight. We can discuss anything we need to discuss right now. Like I said, all you need to know is where to go and when. After you done what you supposed to do, you call me at this same number. We hook up somewhere, you give me my money, and that's the end of it. You won't hear from me no more."

"You son of a bitch."

"Tomorrow night, the Hyatt Regency Hotel, room 301, eight o'clock. Don't be late."

"I hope you burn in hell."

"And I probably will. But in the meantime, I got to do what I got to do. Now, we straight?"

I sighed with defeat, convinced that there was no way out of this mess. "I'll be there."

"Well, you better be your White ass there. Oh, and wear somethin' normal. Show some class. Put on a business suit, some low-heeled pumps, make up your face, carry a briefcase, wear your hair in a bun, and splash on some Chanel No 5. Don't go up in that hotel lookin' like no two-dollar streetwalker."

Two hours after my difficult conversation with Clyde, I was still awake when Robert crawled into bed. I flinched when his toenail scratched the side of my leg.

For the first time in a month, he slid his arm around me, patting my crotch and nudging me with his knee.

"Meg?"

I ignored him.

"Meg? Honey, how about it?" he whispered in my ear.

I could feel his erection against my ass, the hardest one I'd felt in years. But I ignored that, too.

I wore a yellow tweed suit that I had not been able to squeeze into since before my weight loss. I crawled into a cab and headed for the Hyatt Regency Hotel, near Union Square, the following night after my conversation with Clyde. I could feel the four shots of vodka I'd drunk in place of a dinner, floating around like acid inside my empty stomach.

Robert had left the house earlier that evening for a business meeting, not that his presence would have made a difference. He never asked what I was doing or where I was going.

I had allowed myself enough time to sit in one of the hotel bars, where I gulped down another shot of vodka.

Finally, I took the elevator to the third floor, but it took five minutes to drag myself to room 301 from the elevator, a few feet away.

I'd been in the same hotel before for the same reason as tonight, many years earlier. More than once, I'd shared my body with men whose faces and names I could not remember. A stockbroker from Sacramento, an Iranian businessman on vacation, a bachelor party with a group of rowdy college boys from U.C. Berkeley. A trick was a trick, but this time the trick was on me.

I held my breath and knocked. My husband opened the door.

# Chapter 39

# LULA HAWKINS

I didn't know how Ester was going to react when I told her I was moving out, and I didn't care. She and I both knew that sooner or later our relationship would either end or change drastically. But Ester had her own agenda, and that was something I'd realized long before now. I'd never met this Manny dude she had told me about. From the way she smiled and the way her eyes lit up when she mentioned his name, I knew that she had already laid the groundwork of her own to break away from Clyde. I was glad she had decided to have her baby.

"And I hope it's a little girl," Ester squealed, sounding more like a little girl herself. I had never seen her look so happy. Her beautiful cameo face was glowing, her eyes sparkling like jewels. I felt her. I had experienced the same jubilance when I was pregnant.

"If so, I hope she turns out a lot better than her mama and gets herself a real job, you worn-out ho, you," I teased, trying to hide how nervous I was. Every time we heard a car outside, we both almost jumped off the couch. "Does Clyde know?" I asked, ignoring the margarita in my hand. I didn't enjoy drinking as much in front of Ester now, since she couldn't join me. I set my drink on the end table, planning to finish it when Ester left the room.

Ester nodded so hard her hair fell across her face. "I had to tell him. He got suspicious anyway when I barfed in front of him. He wasn't happy about it."

"Well, I don't owe Clyde nothin'," I snapped. "It was good while it lasted, but I have to get away from all this shit now, before it's too late. I'm beginnin' to feel like a robot sex machine."

Ester nodded, giving me a thoughtful look. "I hear you. So what you gonna do?"

I hadn't told Ester about my plan to move in with Richard. I didn't want to take a chance on her telling Clyde where to find me. Not after the way Clyde had reacted to Rosalee's disappearance. I had just decided that morning to take Richard up on his offer to move in with him, and I was still not sure I could go through with that. Sure, I had enough money to get a place of my own, but the truth was, I didn't want to be alone. I wanted to be with Richard. I felt that if I didn't do it now, I would probably never have another chance. I knew I was bringing a lot of baggage to this relationship, with him knowing about me fucking for money and all. But that was the thing. He already knew about that, and he'd already gotten beyond it. Besides, if everything he told me was true, he had just as many skeletons in his closet as I had in mine. We could release them together.

Clyde showed up ten minutes later wearing a white suit and a white hat. He looked like the Lone Ranger. The only thing missing was a black mask.

"Evenin' ladies. I ain't seen too much of y'all lately," he greeted in a dry voice, strutting across the floor. "Ester, get me a beer." He plopped down hard on the couch next to me. "Lula Mae, it sure is good to see you again, girl." He put his arm around my shoulder, but I pulled away. Clyde smelled like he had bathed in a tub of alcohol.

"Clyde, there ain't no easy way to tell you this, but I want to get it over with," I said as Ester handed Clyde the beer he'd requested.

I could already feel the tension filling the room like thick black smoke. Ester was standing in the middle of the floor, staring blankly from me to Clyde.

Clyde turned the bottle upside down and took a long drink. His Adam's apple bounced up and down like a rock tumbling down the side of a hill. "I'm listenin'," he said, his eyes on me. He let out a great belch and thumped his chest with his fist.

"Clyde, I'm gettin' out of the business. Me and you, we can still be friends, but I can't hang with you like that no more. I can't do no more tricks," I said evenly, surprised that I was able to get it all out in one breath.

First, Clyde just looked at me and blinked stupidly. Then he rubbed the back of his neck and gave me a sharp look. "So that's why you been duckin' and hidin'?"

Ester cleared her throat and took a tentative step toward Clyde.

"Clyde, you been real good to all of us. But things are different now. I mean, look at us, man. We both tired," Ester said, her voice shaking. This was the first time I'd seen fear in Ester's eyes. "Even if I wasn't pregnant, I'd be quittin', too, *papi*."

"Uh-huh," Clyde said, nodding. "I guess it bees that way sometime."

"Clyde—I'm . . . me and Lula, we really tired now, man."

"Tired of what?" he mumbled, glaring at Ester. Then he whipped his head back around so hard to face me, his hat fell off. He had the desperate look of a wounded beast. "Things was fine 'til I got caught up with your country ass, Lula Mae," he boomed, giving me a mean look so extreme his eyes crossed. Just like Bo's. "I tried to help you out when you ain't had nobody else to turn to," he declared, almost whispering. I thought about that scene in the *Wizard of Oz* where the wicked witch melted. Clyde seemed like he was melting away. I knew it was just my imagination, but everything on him was getting smaller and smaller.

"Clyde, it ain't like that," Ester said, moving toward the couch waving her arms. The glow was gone from her face. She looked as desperate as a trapped mouse. "Lula met somebody, too."

"Oh, so that's it." Clyde was blinking so hard, his eyes looked like balls of black fire. "Y'all done both found you some more suckers to play, like y'all done me. Well, I don't appreciate that shit!" He stood, pulling me up by the arm. "You black-ass bitch." I don't know why he laughed; he looked mad as hell. "You had it good with me, now you think you can just walk out on me? And I bet it was you who talked Ester into gettin' pregnant." Clyde pointed his beer bottle at Ester and waved it. Then he turned back to me. "Ester was in my corner all the way before you got in the picture, Lula."

I didn't like the way he was squeezing my arm. And as hard as I tried to pry him loose, I couldn't. "Clyde, get your hand off me, and if you know what's good for you, you'll get the hell up out of here or—"

"Or what?" With his other hand, he snatched his gun from its clumsy hiding place. He did it so fast and rough, he popped the button on the waistband of his pants.

Ester and I were used to Clyde pulling that Glock out and waving it at us. One night after we'd all been drinking, it went off accidentally and blew a hole the size of a grapefruit in the base of one of Ester's lamps.

"Put that gun away, Clyde," Ester said, stumbling across the floor until she was backed up against the wall. "You put that thing away right now! Go sober up, and let's talk about this tomorrow. You want some coffee?"

"Oh, y'all scared now, ain't you?" He grinned, waving the gun high above his head. "Let me say somethin' right here and now. You bitches ain't gonna have nothin' but bad luck from now on!"

Clyde still had a grip on me. Each time he swayed, I swayed with him, trying as hard as I could to pry his fingers from around my arm. His breath was hot and sour. His eyes looked like they wanted to explode. He would grin one moment, scowl the next. Sweat was pouring off his face and neck. A dark ring had formed around the collar of his white jacket. With the wide black circles around his eyes, he looked like a panda.

All the other times that Clyde had played around with his gun, I hadn't been afraid. I wasn't really afraid now, but I was mad. I didn't like the way he was responding to our announcements.

If I had had time to think about it, I probably would have reacted some other way. Maybe I would have taken back what I'd said about leaving him or offered him all the money I had stashed away. But I was not thinking straight when I grabbed his hand.

Before I knew what was happening, I was wrestling with him, trying to shake that gun out of his hand. I didn't want Clyde to hurt himself, or us. We fell back to the couch, then to the floor in what felt like slow motion. My mind was a complete blank, but I still heard that damn gun go off. Just like it did the night Clyde accidentally blew a hole in Ester's lamp.

But this time the hole was in Clyde's head, and the gun was in my hand.

# Chapter 40

# MEGAN O'ROURKE

It was not easy for me to recall the events that occurred in the order that they happened, because it all seems like a bad dream now.

Robert and Clyde were both out of my life for good. I didn't feel good about it, but in a way I was glad that my nightmare was over. Well, the worst part of it was.

The minute I'd realized that it was my husband standing on the other side of the door at the Hyatt Regency Hotel in a white hotel robe, a drink in his hand, a smile that froze then immediately shifted to an ominous scowl, waiting for the woman he had arranged to sleep with him for money, I knew that my marriage was over.

Robert's words will ring in my ears until the day I die. "Megan! What the hell is this? How did you—"

"How did I find out what you were up to? I didn't!" I screamed. "I am your fucking date! The one you're willing to pay three thousand bucks for!"

"Oh my God!" Robert dropped his glass and moved back a few steps, a look of stunned disbelief now on his face. He grabbed me and snatched me into the room, kicking the door shut with his bare foot so hard a pitcher of water crashed from a nightstand to the floor. "How the hell did this happen?"

"Why don't you tell me," I managed. Random thoughts raced through my mind, which included his lack of interest in sex with me, and his frequent, prolonged, mysterious absences. My teeth accidentally bit into my tongue, drawing warm, salty blood. Words could not describe how I was feeling at that moment, but I can still feel the sting of the slap of his hand across my face. "You bastard." I kicked, bit, and punched him, but it was a fight I knew I could not win.

How long the fracas went on, I couldn't say. It seemed like an eternity. By the time it was over, we both looked like we'd been mauled by an army of pit bulls. I'd literally been beaten out of my shoes. One lay at my throbbing feet, with a heel broken clean in two. Robert had attempted to strangle me, so my throat felt like a noose had been around it. My teeth prints were on both sides of his rapidly reddening face. Both of his lips were busted and bleeding. I'd kneed his crotch so hard, we both crumbled to the floor, Robert landing on top of me. He was already writhing in agony and howling like the beast he was as he clutched his private parts, but I offered a few more punches against the side of his head.

Momentarily, we managed to wobble up off the floor, gasping for breath, stumbling from one side of the room to the other. With my eyes flooded with tears, I watched Robert struggle into his pants. "It's over, it's over," I said, sniffing in between huffs. I didn't care how I looked as I retrieved my purse from the floor, snatched open the door, and fled.

Robert didn't come home that night.

The next day, I found out in a roundabout way that Clyde Brooks's death and my showdown with Robert had occurred around the same time. I normally perused the *San Francisco*

*Chronicle* every morning, focusing mainly on the sales, the entertainment section, and the high-profile stories. Even if it had not been such a tense morning, I still wouldn't have read the six lines in a corner almost at the bottom of page A14. The headline read: USED CAR DEALER SLAIN. I glanced at the lead stories and ignored the rest of the newspaper, before I folded it and left it on the kitchen counter. Surprisingly, I had only two unanswered messages on the machine that Mom had left the night before. I glared at the telephone like it was a snake, wondering which call I feared the most: the one from Robert or the one I expected to receive from Clyde any minute.

After an hour had passed, I couldn't stand the silence any longer. I had no idea where Robert was, but I wondered what he was thinking and planning. He knew that I had been prepared to sleep with a stranger for money. But he was that stranger willing to pay for sex, so I considered us even in that respect. The worst was over. My sudden and desperate need for money had altered my future—money that I'd needed to keep the secrets of my past in the dark. But now that didn't seem so bad anymore.

A strange laugh filled my kitchen, and it took me a moment to realize that the cold, distant cackle was coming from me. The telephone rang, but I ignored it. When the caller hung up without leaving a message, I convinced myself it was Clyde. He had already confessed to a few other hang-ups a few days earlier.

I laughed again, a string of convoluted thoughts swimming through my mind. Surely, Clyde and Robert would have communicated. Then, a grim thought exploded in my brain: *Maybe Clyde had purposely set up my date with Robert.* I dismissed that theory immediately. It didn't make much sense. Clyde had no reason to pull such a stunt as long as he had me under control. And his desperation for money had been too intense. Besides, even though I had everything to lose, Clyde had nothing to gain by dispatching me to Robert's hotel room. If his plans had worked the first time, there was no telling how many more money-making schemes Clyde would have come up with that involved me.

When the suspense got to be too much for me, I dialed my parents' number. My "reunion" with Clyde had brought about a lot of changes in my otherwise regular routines. I didn't go out as much, I saw less of the few friends I had, and I even avoided my mother as much as I could. Mom answered in a tired voice.

"Oh, Meg, it's just awful! It's just awful! Oh, why did Father O'Conner have to be out of town today when I need his comfort so desperately?" Mom began dramatically. My first thought was Robert had shared his version of the events that had occurred the night before. My heart start pounding. Beads of perspiration sprang up like mushrooms on my face. "Poor, poor, Effie. What will she do now? We must go to her. She was there for us when we suffered our losses."

"What are you talking about?" I asked, licking my dried, cracked lips. I had more than a few bruises from my fight with Robert. However, there were none on my face, or any other part of me I couldn't conceal with clothing.

Mom sighed. "Why, Effie Brooks, girl. It's just awful."

Just hearing Clyde's grandmother's name made me see spots. "Effie . . . Brooks? Our former housekeeper? What about Effie?" The perspiration had soaked through my blouse, and a burning sensation had formed in my chest.

"Well, isn't that why you're calling? It was in the newspaper this morning."

"Mom, you are not making much sense. What was in

today's newspaper? What does it have to do with Effie Brooks?" I didn't know where this conversation was going, but I knew it couldn't be anything positive. Not if it involved Clyde's grandmother. "Mom, are you still there?"

Mom sniffed and blew her nose before answering. "Yes, dear."

"Is . . . Effie . . . ?" I couldn't even finish my sentence. Our former housekeeper had to be ninety if she was a day. Even when she worked for us, more than twenty years ago, she had complained about one health problem after another. In fact, it was her poor health that had forced her to retire. But she'd continued to communicate with my mother. I didn't know until I encountered Clyde that day that Effie had been helping him take care of Keisha. My heart, which had been beating like a drum, felt like it was bouncing off the walls of my chest. My relationship with Clyde didn't affect my feelings for his grandmother. She was a wonderful woman. She'd been totally devoted to my family. I would always respect and adore her. Despite my feelings for Effie, I had not attempted to communicate with her since the last time she cleaned our house. I was not surprised when she did not acknowledge the invitation to my wedding.

"She's lost her grandson, her only grandson. Uh, I'm sure *you* remember *that* boy. Clyde . . ."

"What's happened to Clyde?" I asked, the words dancing off my lips. "Where is he?"

"Well, the newspaper didn't say much. But then they never do when it's just a Black person, unless they're rich and famous. That Clyde. What a waste of life." Mom sighed and sucked her teeth. "Lusting after women the way he did was a crime against nature. It's no wonder a woman is what killed him." Mom's voice shrank to an eerie whisper. "You were one of the lucky ones. Thank God, you got away from him before he ruined your life completely."

"Clyde Brooks is dead?" I asked, my voice so raspy I hardly recognized it myself.

"Yes, dear." Mom's voice trembled. "It's just awful!"

# Chapter 41

# ROCKELLE HARPER

The last time Clyde came to my house, five days ago, he poured himself a huge drink and started telling me a story about a hearse following him from his apartment for seven blocks. Even though he'd thought it was funny, I wouldn't allow him to finish his ominous story. Especially so soon after Sherrie Armstrong's funeral.

"Clyde, you should keep that kind of stuff to yourself. Talking about it could bring you bad luck," I'd told him.

Clyde waved his drink in my face. "Sister-girl, luck ain't nothin' but a four-letter word. When it's my time to go, it's my time to go." That was the last time I saw Clyde Brooks alive.

I didn't go to Clyde's funeral. As far as I knew, Ester was the only person I knew who did go. Lula was sitting in jail waiting for her preliminary hearing. But she probably would have attended if she could have. Then again, she might not have.

I spent the day they buried Clyde packing. Even though my rent was paid up two months in advance, I could not stay in the house where I'd gone through so many painful changes any longer than I had to. I could no longer stand to have another man's flesh against mine; not for all the money in the world. I could no longer live the life I'd been living. Ester's rape (she'd shared that traumatic episode with me when she called to tell me that Lula had killed Clyde in self-defense), Clyde's death, and the hole that Lula had dug for herself by killing Clyde, had all pushed me out of the business immediately. And if all of this mess wasn't enough for me to get out now, nothing would be.

I'd passed the civil service test, but my score was so low, I doubted if I'd get a job with the government. I was willing to accept anything they offered. Even standing at a counter all day selling stamps or delivering mail.

The sex hot line that I had installed, listing the number in the personal ads in *The Spectator* was the first thing to go. I didn't even wait for the truck from Goodwill to come. That sucker, along with the answering machine I had attached to it, went in the trash can within minutes after I'd received the news about the shooting at Ester's apartment.

"Listen, Rocky, no matter what you hear from nobody else, it was an accident. I seen the whole thing. Clyde was the one with the gun, drunk as hell, playin' around and shit. Lula was only tryin' to make him stop before . . . before somebody got hurt. I seen the whole thing."

Ester stuck to her story. She told the same story to the cops. I never heard Lula's version, and I didn't want to. Because it would not have made any difference to me.

I didn't have a job yet, but I had several interviews lined up. Cashier, receptionist, waitress; I was willing to accept the one I got offered first. With the money I'd stashed away, and with what I was getting from welfare, the kids and I could get by in a low-rent apartment an apartment manager had called me for yesterday. It was not far from the same run-down neighborhood I grew up in. I'd come full circle, but I was still in better shape than Lula and Ester.

"Mama, can we take our big-screen TV to the new apartment?" Juliet had tiptoed into my room, quiet as a mouse. With her usual smirk missing, I realized for the first time just how beautiful my child was.

Juliet and I had had what I hoped was our last hostile confrontation, moments after I'd told her and her brothers that we were moving.

"You must be crazy!" Juliet had roared, waving her arms so high above her head, the veins in her neck stood out like blue lines. "*I'm* not goin' to live in no ghetto!"

It was at that moment that I realized I was the one in control, not my ten-year-old daughter. With my frightened sons, Barry and Michael, cowering in a corner like they always did when Juliet and I went for each other's throat, I took back my position.

"Juliet, I . . . am . . . tired," I started, surprised at how firm my voice sounded, considering how tired I really was. Juliet was reared back on her young legs, with her hands on her just-beginning-to-fill-out hips. But when she realized how serious I was, she wobbled and backed herself against the wall, with me marching like a soldier inches away from her. "Girl, you listen to me and you listen good, because I'm only going to say this one time."

I paused and pointed a finger in her surprised face. With my nails as long as they were, my finger must have looked like a dagger to her. "If you think you are so grown that you can decide where you want to live, you do just that. You go find you someplace else to live. Your brothers and I are moving into the new apartment whether you come with us or not." I took a deep breath and steadied myself as I continued my declaration. The words seemed to leap out of my mouth on their own. "I have taken all I'm going to take from you. I should have said something long before now. I didn't, but it's not too late." Juliet stood there staring in slack-jawed amazement. "I will no longer put up with your bullshit attitude. You will respect me, or we will find a foster home for you before I do something to you I'll regret."

My words had just as much of an impact on me as they did Juliet. However, I felt a certain level of relief because it was a major step in my taking back the control that I, as a parent, deserved. I wasn't perfect, but I'd done the best I could with my children. I felt that if I continued to let Juliet get away with her surly behavior toward me, I deserved it.

The look on my daughter's face told me that I'd made my point—at least for the time being. I had finally put my child back in a child's place. And, I was sorry that my mother had not done the same with me. It might have made a difference and my adult life would have turned out much better than it did.

"Mama, I-I didn't mean—"

"I don't give a damn what you meant. I meant what I just said." My words had hurt Juliet, but they had hurt me, too.

Standing in front of me now, Juliet seemed so much smaller and thankfully, more like the child she was. I shook my head, expecting an outburst. I sucked in my breath, preparing myself for a battle that seemed to have no end, only intermissions. "Our new place is way too small for that television. We can only take the stuff we really need," I said firmly. "When I get a good job, we can move into a bigger, better place. We'll get the big-screen TV back then."

I was surprised and pleased to see a smile slowly creeping onto Juliet's face. "Um, Mommy—*"Mommy?"*—"can I ask you something else?" Her voice was a whimper, something I had not heard from her since she was in diapers. "You mean we won't let the Goodwill man take everything?" she asked, her hardness softening right before my eyes.

"What is it?" I asked, rubbing the back of my aching neck. Other parts of my body were bothering me, too. However, my feet felt more firmly grounded than ever before.

"Another man is coming to take the big television and some of our other stuff to storage," I said gently. It was an even bigger surprise to me when Juliet strolled over and wrapped her arms around my waist.

"I do love you, Mama," she told me. "And I hope you still love me."

Unable to speak, I hugged my child and kissed the side of her face.

According to my new babysitter, Helen's daddy had developed Alzheimer's and had to go into a nursing home. I think that had a lot to do with Mrs. Daniels not sending the law after me for the mess Helen got herself into. Helen's brother and his wife must have been keeping Helen on a short leash because I never saw her come or go from the house next door again.

But Helen's mother was still angry with me. She didn't speak to me in public. But she rolled her eyes at me every chance she got. When she realized I was moving, she parked herself on her front porch steps and shaded her eyes with a newspaper. She watched until I'd hauled out the last item. Before I drove off, I gave the old bat one last look, hoping she'd at least offer a smile or a wave.

But she didn't, and I couldn't blame her.

The building that my children and I moved into was not as shabby as some of the others on the block. I was pleased to see several eager young security guards, decked out in nicely pressed beige uniforms, patrolling the apartment complex.

"You won't have to worry about none of that loud-ass rap music blastin' day and night or no break-ins around here no more. People wanna act a fool, they better be ready to move or go to jail." That's what the apartment manager had told me when I'd applied for the apartment. With no job, I had to show him my welfare documents before he'd let me sign a lease.

I had already decided that I would only be as friendly to my new neighbors as I had to be to keep from making enemies. There was a young woman across the hall from us. She was only twenty and already had four kids and no man. Ruth Anne Porter had dismissed four useless lovers, who'd each left her with a baby, and returned to school. Every time I saw her, she had a toddler in one arm and a load of books in the other.

"I wouldn't wash clothes in this buildin' if I was you," Ruth Anne advised me a week after I'd moved to the neighborhood.

It made me feel good to see a woman in her predicament working so hard to improve her life—without involving herself with a man like Clyde Brooks.

"Ruth Anne, I've seen some of the thugs around here, and I can imagine what they'd do if they caught a woman alone in a laundry room," I said. I was immediately sorry for making such a comment. One of the things I had promised myself was I would stop being so quick to judge people just because they lived in a run-down neighborhood. Especially now that I was part of that same environment.

"Oh, I didn't mean nothin' like that. These boys around here ain't that bad. Some of 'em even go to church, work, don't do nothin' but smoke a few joints, drink a little bit.

What I meant was, them machines always breakin' down and keepin' your quarters. There's another washhouse two blocks down the street, next door to that 7-Eleven."

"Oh, thanks," I mumbled contritely.

I took the kids with me to the Laundromat down the street from my apartment that evening. Each of us carried a basket of clothes. "Mama, why don't you sit down and let us do the wash. You must be tired after all you've done lately," Juliet told me. She motioned me to a chair along the side of the wall. A blind man could see how tired I was. And without my makeup, wigs, weaves, and all that shit I used to wear when I was turning tricks, I looked as tired as I felt. But looking like a frump didn't seem to bother me anymore. Juliet's changing attitude deserved my attention more than my appearance.

I had my head down, reading a newspaper somebody else had left on the chair next to me, when I heard a woman's voice call my name.

"Rockelle, is that you?" It was a gentle voice.

I looked up and almost fainted. It was my mother. She was wearing a crisp white blouse and a dark skirt. Her hair looked so nice, I couldn't tell if it was hers or a wig.

"Mama." My voice sounded like a croak, so I coughed to clear it before I continued. "Hello, Mama."

"You look good, child. I'm glad to see you," my mother said, slowly moving away.

"Mom, wait." I rose, keeping an eye on the kids at the other end of the floor dumping clothes into the machines. "Uh, how have you been?"

My mother, looking as tired as she always did, froze in her tracks with a look of bewilderment on her face. "I'll make it, I guess. Just workin' hard like always."

"The boys? Daddy? Is everybody doing all right?"

"The boys are doin' fine. Sid works for FedEx and just

got him a house in Sacramento. Carl just moved back in with me to help me get over my hip surgery."

"Oh. And Daddy? Is he well?" What I meant was, "is he working?" but I couldn't bring myself to say it. I was in no position to look down on anybody these days.

My mother dropped her head. "There was a virus goin' 'round, your daddy caught it, and he died two months ago."

I blinked hard to hold back tears that were long overdue.

"Bye . . . Rocky." Mama started walking off again. "I'll let you get on about your business."

"Mama, I live down the street now." With a tongue that felt as heavy as a bowl of cement I said, "Maybe you can come by soon? I'm sure the kids would love to get to know you." After almost thirty years, the blackness that I'd carried in my heart seemed lighter. I knew it was going to be hard for me to put all of my ugly behavior toward my mother and the rest of my family completely behind me, but I'd just taken a huge step. And it felt good.

A suspicious look slid across my mother's face like a shadow. "You want me to come to your place?"

I nodded then I beckoned to the kids. Juliet looked puzzled, the boys looked confused, but they all rushed over and stood next to me. They lined up like little toy soldiers as I introduced them to their grandmother.

With the suspicious look on her face fading, Mama finally smiled, revealing teeth that were just as crooked and discolored as ever. But now it didn't seem to matter. "Write me down your address and telephone number," she told me.

I started grinning so hard my lip cracked.

# Chapter 42

# MEGAN O'ROURKE

"Miss Meg, your mama gave me your telephone number and told me you said to call."

"Effie, I'm sorry I wasn't able to make it to Clyde's funeral. I-I've . . ."

"Child, you ain't got to explain nothin' to me. Your mama already told me about your husband runnin' out on you. And with both your kids out of the house, you must be right fidgety, too." Effie snorted and muttered under her breath. "But it was a nice service for Clyde anyway. Even though we couldn't, you know, let 'em open up the casket, with the way that gun went off in his face . . ." Effie's voice faded to a weak whisper.

"Effie, I know you aren't doin' so well. And, it's not going to be easy for you to take care of Keisha with Clyde gone now."

"Oh, you ain't got to worry none about my baby. My brother Moses that came out here for Clyde's funeral, he wants me to go back with him to Meridian, Mississippi."

"Yes, I know. Mom told me that's what you were planning to do. I was wondering about your plans for Keisha."

Effie cleared her throat. "Miss Meg, don't take this the wrong way now, but what do you care about that child? After all these years, you ain't never even come out here to visit her. And she such a lovely child, sweetest disposition in the world."

"I didn't even know until a few months ago that she was in California. All this time, I thought she was with your relatives in Mississippi, like we'd agreed before she was even born. And, I didn't know about her . . ." I couldn't bring myself to continue.

"About her bein' ill-formed?"

"Excuse me?"

"She got physical problems. But that ain't stopped Keisha from bein' happy. Shoot. She done even had a few boyfriends!"

I laughed. A hot flash covered my face like a blanket, almost smothering the life out of me. On top of everything else, menopause had crept up on me. I was an old woman at forty-five. "I'm glad to hear that. Uh, I would like to see her before you leave for Mississippi."

"Now, Miss Meg, like I said, don't take this the wrong way. The girl just lost her daddy, and she already got enough problems, just tryin' to get from one day to the next. She ain't never knowed much of nothin' about you; matter of fact, she had thought you died birthin' her. I just got Clyde to tell her the truth a few years ago. The last thing I want is for Keisha to be gettin' even more upset by havin' you bargin' into her life, tryin' to ease your conscience."

"Effie, Keisha is my daughter, you know. And it's time that I did the right thing by her." I was so proud of myself, my chest felt like it was going to split open.

"With all due respect, Miss Meg, you ain't thought nothin' about that 'til now. You didn't never call me up to try to find out nothin' about the girl," Effie scoffed. "And, why that is, I don't know, and I don't wanna know. If you think you gwine to up and take that child away, I got news for you. I'll get all over the television news; I'll go up to Jesse Jackson, the NAACP. I'll do whatever I have to do to take care of my business. Clyde left a right smart piece of money with me so don't think I can't get me a lawyer. Sister Borden knows Johnnie Cochran's whole family. I ain't scared of you!"

"Effie, please calm down. I didn't mean to upset you. I would never do anything to hurt you or Keisha. All I want to do now is help."

"Help? *You* want to help *me?* I don't need no help from you! You White folks ain't got a lick of sense. It's y'all's help that got us into slavery. And because of y'all's help, we ain't too much better off now. Naw! I don't need no help from you. Hold on, let me go get my pills." I waited for Effie to return. "I don't need your help!" she wailed, choking on her pills as she tried to chew and talk at the same time.

"I think you do. Effie, you are not a young woman, and you are not well. You've said so yourself. I don't want to take Keisha away from you. I just want you and her to know that I am here to do whatever is necessary to keep Keisha's life comfortable. I've talked it over with my mother and the kids. There's plenty of room in my house if you ever need a place to send Keisha when, if, uh, something happens to you, and you can no longer care for her. Heather is quite anxious to meet the sister she's always wanted . . ."

I could hear the angry old woman breathing through her mouth.

"Well . . . what about that husband of yours? Your mama done told me, so I know all about him thinkin' his shit don't stink, dissin' anybody who ain't White. If he was to want to come back to you, he ain't gwine to take too kindly to you havin' your half-Black daughter livin' in the same house with him."

"Robert won't be returning," I announced, clearing my throat and blinking hard. Robert had filed for divorce and moved into a condo in Sausalito. He had only been back to the house on Steiner once since the hotel incident, and that was to pack up his belongings. I couldn't decide which was worse, his setting up a date with a woman to pay her to have sex with him, or me being that woman. I had no intention of revealing what happened that night in the hotel to anyone, and I doubted if Robert would.

"Oh. Well, you don't need no man nohow. After a while, they ain't nothin' but trouble anyway. I loved my grandson, Miss Meg, and I probably won't never know what really happened between him and that Lula gal, but Clyde had to be up in that apartment doin' somethin' he ain't had no business doin'. And it was *his* gun that killed him. That Mexican gal, Ester, she and Clyde was like brother and sister. She seen the whole thing, and she ain't got no reason to lie. I tried and tried to tell that boy how to treat folks . . ."

"Effie, you sound so tired."

"I am tired. You'd be tired, too, if you had to go through all I go through. I declare, I wonder where God be at these days. All these years I been prayin' and prayin', and God ain't heard me yet! He ain't never done nothin' for me."

"Yes, He did, Effie. He sent me to help you," I said gently, surprised at myself for sounding so philosophical.

Several moments passed before Effie replied. "Miss Meg, did you mean what you said about takin' Keisha in when I, uh, you know, become unable. Like when I die. The few folks I got left, they said they'd look after my baby when I'm gone, but talk is cheap. Takin' care of a child like Keisha would be a double burden, and I don't know just how much longer I'm gwine to be around to do it." Effie paused and laughed. "My doctor is even surprised that I'm still around. With my weak heart and all."

"Effie, you will never have to worry about someone taking care of Keisha. I will see to it."

I had a commitment to keep, and I planned to do just that. There had to be a reason for things to turn out the way they did.

Clyde's death was the beginning of a new life for me and my daughter Keisha.

# Chapter 43

# ESTER SANCHEZ

I really don't know what's going to happen now. To Lula I mean. Me and Manny put our money together, and then Rockelle gave us some. We paid the bail money for Lula to get out of jail until they take her to court and shit. We talked to a bunch of lawyers. If they are as smart as lawyers are supposed to be, Lula ain't got nothing to worry about. She didn't mean to shoot Clyde. I know she didn't because I seen the whole thing. To be honest, nobody knows whose finger was the one that actually pulled the trigger. Clyde and Lula was both holding that damn gun when it went off.

Right now Lula is staying with me and Manny at his place, sleeping on the couch I hate so much. Her big lesbian sister, her stepsister I mean, she and that girlfriend of hers, they're coming out here soon. They said they would not leave here without Lula. But Lula told me she wasn't going no place.

"You are so lucky to have family who cares about you," I told Lula.

"Verna and Odessa have always been there for me. I can

always count on them," Lula said to me, still with that sad look on her face that had been there since she shot Clyde.

"Don't forget you got a lot more than me. You got a daddy back there in Mississippi, them twin brothers, you got that man Richard, too." As soon as the words *man* and *Richard* bounced off my lips, Lula rolled her eyes and looked at me like I grew horns on the top of my head. She didn't think that Richard was going to hang with her, until she straightened out the mess she was in.

"I don't want to involve Richard," Lula told me. Finally she gave me a smile. "I've shared enough with him. He don't need this, too."

"Don't you think you should let him decide that? At least give him that chance. You need all the friends you can get right now. You got too much on your mind."

One of the things on Lula's mind was Clyde's daughter, Keisha. My mind, too, for that matter. I'd known Clyde's daughter and her problems a lot longer than Lula. Old Lady Effie had to be a hundred and three years old. Even if Clyde was still alive, that old crone couldn't go on helping him take care of Keisha. Even if she had ten nurses coming to the house to help her out.

Last Friday when I went to visit Effie, the White woman Clyde had Keisha by was there. Megan. I don't know what Clyde seen in her, other than money and a piece of tail. But I ain't seen a man yet who didn't act a fool over a blonde.

"Do you think that White woman will help take good care of Keisha?" I asked Lula. I handed Lula a beer and poured some milk for myself.

"She will, Ester," Lula said. She gave me a real thoughtful look, and a sad smile. "I know she will."

# Chapter 44

# ROSALEE PITTMAN

It had been six months since I left California. I missed the warm sunshine that used to stream in through my bedroom window and wake me up every morning. I missed the palm trees and the orange trees that stood in front of my old apartment building like security guards. I wasn't happy being back in Detroit. But I knew I'd made the right decision.

I liked my apartment. Even as lonely and gloomy as it was. It fit the way I felt most of the time. And though it was clean and cheap, had free cable, and to my surprise, was ignored by the local burglars, it was nothing to write home about. There were cracks and dents in the hardwood floors and the walls were so thin I could hear the Japanese man next door farting up a storm. I could also hear the landlord's gay son and his lover fucking the hell out each other every night. My kitchen faucet dripped all the time, and I had to turn the shower on and off with a bent fork. The elderly landlord was a nice enough man, until I needed something, then he would make himself scarce. When I had a problem in my place that he didn't take care of right away, I didn't pay rent until he did. And, being a man, the landlord flirted with me until I told him I was gay, too.

I lived near public transportation, a mini-mall, a Kentucky Fried Chicken, and the furniture store where I worked five days a week as a receptionist. I made less money there in a week than I used to make in a day when I worked for Clyde.

I had a few new female friends, so I did have a social life. But I had not even been out for a cup of coffee with a man, even though I got asked out all the time. Mr. Bob, the funny old trick we'd had so much fun with, was the last man with whom I'd slept.

I hadn't planned on ever calling or writing to Lula or any of the other girls to see how they were doing. I wanted to put all of that behind me. So I don't know what made me want to call them. I guess it was because I had been thinking about old Mr. Bob.

The number for Lula and Ester had been disconnected. I got the same response when I called their cellular phone numbers. I didn't have the nerve to call Clyde. He was the last person in the world I ever wanted to talk to again.

When my curiosity got the best of me, I dialed Rockelle's number. It had been disconnected, too, but the recorded message gave out her new telephone number. She answered right away.

"Rockelle, it's Rosalee."

Rockelle let out a scream. I held my breath until she composed herself. "My God, girl! Are you all right? Where are you?"

"I'm fine. I'm back in Detroit," I said with caution and a stiff tone. At this point, I didn't care if she told Clyde. Rockelle and I had never been that close. Other than to discuss business, I had rarely called her up or visited her house, and she had never encouraged anything else from me.

"What about you? You doin' okay?" I asked, sincerely hoping that she was.

"Yes, I'm fine, too. This is such a nice surprise. I never thought I'd hear from you again, Rosalee."

"Well, I never thought I'd be callin' out there. I tried to call Lula and Ester. Did they move?"

"Yes, they did. Oh, girl. A lot has happened since you left." Rockelle sounded tired and old, just like I felt.

"Are you all still workin' for Clyde?"

"Uh, hold on. Let me run close my door. The kids don't need to hear any of this." Rockelle returned within seconds, out of breath. "Clyde's dead," she announced in a flat voice.

"What?" I gasped and had to sit on my bed to keep from falling. "What did you say?"

Rockelle started talking in a slow, low voice. "He got in Lula's face one night, waving that gun of his, and it went off. It was an accident, though." Rockelle let out a hollow breath. "The D.A. was real nice. Ester was Lula's witness, and she backed up her story. She got off."

"Is Lula still out there? What about Ester?"

"Lula's still out here, but she's out of the business. So is Ester. Ester's living with some Mexican dude, and they just had a little baby girl. How is your mother?"

I rolled my eyes and let out a sharp cackle. "That grumpy old sister is doin' a hell of a lot better than I expected. Oh, she put up a big fuss when I talked about movin' back here, but I got her on that plane anyway. She's sharin' a nice little apartment with another senior citizen. She even had the nerve to get her a man."

"I don't know what this world is coming to. Your mama had me convinced that she had one foot in the grave and the other foot on a banana peel. You have got to be kidding! Now she's got a man."

"Uh-huh. And he's one smooth-talkin' old brother. He gets a pension check *and* a monthly check from Uncle Sam for some army accident, and he owns a nice house. The only reason Mama won't marry him—he's asked her umpteen times—is she don't want to give up her freedom. So she says." I laughed. It hurt my throat, my chest, and my head when I laughed, but that didn't stop me. I laughed some more.

It was hard to believe that Mama was the same person she'd been a few years earlier. She hadn't mentioned Miss Pearl and that so-called curse since we'd left California. When she wasn't running back and forth to church or to some bingo game with her hot new companion, she took trips over to the casinos in Canada. The month before she'd visited her cousins in Georgia.

"What about you, girl? How's your love life?"

"Don't ask." I sighed, rolling my eyes.

"Oh. I guess things didn't work out with your husband, huh?"

It took me a moment to respond. "No," I said, unable to hide my sadness. "Things didn't work out the way I hoped they would. I love that man with all my heart, and I always will. I'd do anything to have Sammy back. But . . . he's got a woman, and I ain't tryin' to go there. He said he ain't even comin' in my apartment because he knows if he did, he wouldn't be able to keep his hands off me."

"I'm sorry, Rosalee. I really am."

"He's a good man. He got this apartment for me, and we are still friends. I *made* him take a key, and I told him that if he ever changes his mind, he can walk right on in and I'll be ready for him."

"You go, girl!" Rockelle squealed.

A few moments of silence passed before we spoke again.

"So Clyde is dead," I muttered. "What about his daughter? Who's takin' care of her? His grandmother was lookin' like she was ready to go meet her Maker the last time I saw her."

"And she did," Rockelle said with a heavy voice.

"Oh?"

"Old Miss Effie died a month after Clyde was buried. She had a massive heart attack *and* a stroke while she was sitting up in church. Everybody said it was Clyde's death that really killed her. That White woman Clyde had Keisha by, she packed up Keisha and moved her into her house that same day."

"Damn. There sure has been a lot goin' on since I left. Well, I'm glad I was able to catch up with you. It is so good to hear your voice. And your kids? How are they doin'? Is that retarded girl babysittin' for you again?"

Rockelle let out a deep groan. "No. I gave up the house on Joost Street and moved back to Hunter's Point."

I felt truly sorry for Rockelle. To think that she had tried so hard to live an upscale lifestyle, only to end up right back where she started. It had to be a nightmare for her. "Well, I'm happy to hear that you're doin' all right."

"I don't know about all that. I have a nightmare every now and then about Clyde getting killed. I always thought that something crazy was going to happen sooner or later." Rockelle sniffed and lowered her voice. "Rosalee, I know it's too late, but I apologize for not being better friends with you. I know there were times I acted like such a snob, but I'd like to think that I've grown since then. And I don't mean my hips." Rockelle laughed. "Which, by the way, are still growing."

"Don't feel bad about what you didn't do on my account. I didn't try that hard to be closer friends with you, either. But I did like you. And, we all did have some good times every now and then. Remember all the money we blew in Vegas and Reno, and shopping in Beverly Hills?"

"Uh-huh. In spite of what we did to get that money. Listen, I'd love to talk more, but I was getting ready for a date when you called."

"You still *datin'*? I thought you said . . ."

"Not the kind of date you're thinking about," Rockelle said, laughing. "I met this guy at work. I work at the post office now. Anyway, Leon is a mail carrier."

"That's nice, Rocky. I'm glad to hear you and Ester got somebody," I said, not even trying to hide my gloom. "Maybe there's hope for Lula and me."

"Oh, didn't I tell you? Lula did hook up with somebody. A bus driver. Things are shaky between them right now, though. She keeps trying to push him away, but he wants to be there for her."

My sadness felt like it had doubled. "That's nice, Rocky. Can I call you again sometime? Just to say hello."

"I'd like that, Rosalee. I'd like that a lot. Bye now."

As sad as I was, I was glad I had called. Though I felt terrible about Clyde being dead and Lula having to live with what she did for the rest of her life, I was glad to hear that the girls were doing so well. I just couldn't imagine Ester raising a baby and Rockelle seeming so humble. But then again, there were a lot of things about myself that I couldn't imagine either. So what did I know?

I was already tired and sleepy, even before I'd called Rockelle. But after all the heavy shit she'd dumped on me like a load of rocks, I felt twice as tired and sleepy. I didn't feel like wrestling with that fork to turn on my shower, so I took a bird bath in my stained bathroom sink. After a glass of wine, I fell asleep on my couch, a used but comfortable piece of junk I'd picked up at a flea market.

I didn't sleep long, though. I almost rolled to the floor when I felt my hair being tugged. Before I turned over and opened my eyes, I expected to see the ghost of Annie Mae, my playmate back in Georgia who used to pull my hair, before and after her death. But this time I was wrong.

It was my husband.

# Chapter 45

# LULA HAWKINS-RICE

Richard said he didn't mind me keeping Bo's name, too. "You can hold on to whatever part of your past you wanna hold on to, Lula. You my wife now, and all I care about is our future."

The day after we got married in Reno in the same tacky little chapel where I'd married Bo, we returned to San Francisco. A week later I started a new job at the California Department of Motor Vehicles. I was assigned the same boring job I'd done at the Department of Motor Vehicles in Mississippi! The pay wasn't that great, but with me and Richard both working, we were able to move into a nice two-bedroom apartment out near the beach.

I had used all the money that I had left from the hundreds of tricks I'd performed on new furniture, a new car for us to get around in, and baby clothes. My son was due any day.

After I'd been cleared of all charges for shooting Clyde, I went to visit my daddy, and we had a nice reunion. My pathetic stepmother, Etta, had been nicer to me than she'd ever been before in my life. That alone made the trip worthwhile. I even visited my mother's parents. I hadn't seen them since my mother's death, and even though they'd changed, I would have known them anywhere.

"Lula, don't you be a stranger. You keep in touch, and remember you always got a home to come back to," my elderly grandfather told me. "This new husband of yours, Richard *Rice*—he any relation to Jerry Rice, the ballplayer? I smell money!"

"I don't think so, Grandpa," I said, laughing.

If I didn't have Richard to go back to in California, I probably would have stayed in Mississippi. I didn't realize how important family was until then. But Richard was my family. He came first in my life. I had learned that from Rosalee's foolishness. If she hadn't left her husband to run off with her manipulative mother, she would have avoided a lot of pain and suffering.

I spent the rest of that day enjoying my grandparents' company and laughing about some of the stupid shit my mother used to do. Some of the same things I'd done, but I didn't go there with that. Not with my grandparents. I would only discuss my sordid activities in San Francisco with the people who'd shared it with me, and I didn't plan to do it that much. I wanted to get over it as soon as I could. But that wasn't going to be easy. Clyde was a hard person to forget. I prayed that he was resting in peace. He had suffered a lot, too. He'd grown up without a mother and had to raise a severely handicapped child. Those were things I wouldn't wish on my worst enemy. I prayed for Keisha every night. I planned to visit her one day so I could tell her just how sorry I was for taking her daddy away from her. I prayed she would forgive me.

I spent the last few nights of my visit to Mississippi with Verna and Odessa.

"You ever think about Larry?" Verna asked.

"Larry who?" I laughed because now that's all Larry Holmes meant to me. Something to laugh about.

Sex had a whole new meaning in my life, too. It wasn't something to laugh about like Larry, but it no longer caused trouble in my life. And that was a good thing because Richard couldn't keep his hands off me.

Ester and Manny, and their daughter Lulita (Little Lula), had moved to Mexico City the month before. I missed her, but she called me all the time. I planned to visit her after I had my baby. She was pregnant again and happier than she'd ever been. She'd landed a job working for an organization that located homes for abandoned kids. That didn't mean she was "living happily every after." None of us probably ever would. Ester and Manny didn't have enough money to afford a place of their own yet. They lived in a cramped house with ten of his relatives and had to sleep on a dirt floor. And Manny was having some problems with his health because of a bullet lodged in his back from a street fight during his reckless years.

And even though I had Richard and a new baby on the way, my life was not a bowl of cherries, either. But it could have been a lot worse. We could have all been arrested or killed by deranged tricks. And I could have gone to jail for a very long time for killing Clyde.

I'd had lunch with Rockelle the day before at a little sidewalk café in North Beach. Her relationship with the mailman didn't work out, but she'd hooked up with a clever detective who had been investigating a murder in her building. He helped her track down her deadbeat husband. With all the back child support she got from that fool, she was able to move into a better neighborhood. I was real happy to hear that she had moved her mother in with her.

"I heard from Rosalee again last Monday," Rockelle told

me, munching on some lettuce. I was real happy to see that she'd lost forty pounds. "She and Sammy just had a little boy."

I got so misty-eyed I couldn't even finish my lunch. I hadn't spoken to Rosalee since she left California.

"Do you think she'd mind if you gave me her telephone number? I'd like to chat with her again, too," I said, stirring my bowl of clam chowder with my spoon.

"And I'm sure she'd like to chat with you again, too," Rockelle told me. "But if I were you, I wouldn't bring up . . . you know."

"The tricks?" I asked.

Rockelle dropped her eyes and nodded. "Yeah," she muttered.

"Uh, do you still read a lot of books?"

"Every day," Rockelle said cheerfully, giving me a thoughtful look. I'd never seen her looking as relaxed as she did at that moment. "You know, somebody ought to write a book about us. Me, you, Ester, Rosalee. And even Helen and Megan. Maybe if other stupid females read about all the dumb shit we did, they'd learn something."

"It would take somebody like Stephen King to tell our strange story," I said, laughing.

Just thinking about Clyde, Mr. Bob, Fat Freddie, and all the other *hundreds* of men we'd slept with for money made a sharp pain shoot through my stomach. And it didn't stop there.

My son was born later that night. I named him Richard.

# Chapter 1

My husband was the *last* man in town that the people in our close-knit circle of friends expected to have an affair. Why he didn't cheat was as much of a mystery to me as it was to them. When I mentioned to one of my female friends that I was married to a man who didn't cheat, her only question was, "What's wrong with him?"

It saddened me to hear that some people thought that there was something wrong with a man who didn't cheat on his wife.

"There is nothing wrong with my husband. He's as normal as any other man," I told that friend.

"Ha! If that's the case, he's *not* normal," that friend told me.

Maybe she was right. If it was normal for a man to cheat, then Pee Wee was not normal.

Despite the fact that I had cheated on my husband just a few months ago (yes, *I'd* cheated, but I'll get to that later) and had accused him of being unfaithful on numerous occasions, I knew in my heart that he had not slept with another woman since he married me. However, one of my concerns was the other women who were dying to get their hands on him.

"If you ever break up with Pee Wee, send him to me," another female friend had jokingly suggested. "He's perfect."

When I told my mother what my friend had said, she told me, "Girl, as brazen and desperate as women are these days, I'd be worried if I were you."

Even after my mother's comment, I didn't worry or complain because I felt secure and comfortable. Looking back on it now, I realize I was too comfortable. That was my first mistake. I had a ringside seat in the eye of a major hurricane, but I was so comfortable I didn't realize that until it was too late.

The day that Pee Wee, my "perfect" husband, abruptly and cruelly left me for another woman had started out like any other day. It was the middle of March, and still a little too cold for my tastes. I'd been a resident of Ohio for over forty years by this time, and I still hadn't adjusted to the weather. When I was a child growing up in Florida, I used to run around naked in our front yard in March. Kids doing such a thing in Ohio, in March, was unheard of.

I had crawled out of bed during the night and turned up the thermostat. When the weather was nice enough, Pee Wee slept in the nude, and I usually slept in something very skimpy. Right after dinner the night before, he had slid into a pair of flannel pajamas. I'd wiggled into a pair of purple thong panties, a matching Wonderbra, and a snug cotton nightgown. I'd slid my freshly pedicured feet into a pair of nylon socks. Large pink sponge rollers covered every inch of my head, individually wrapped around my thick, recently dyed black hair. A rose-scented, wrinkle-busting, white gel, one of the many weapons that I used to fight Father Time, covered my face. We looked like we were made up for a Halloween party, but it had been a night of raw passion. I had peeled off my socks and that snug gown like a stripper. He'd helped me remove everything else. Within minutes I had his handprints on parts of my body that hadn't been touched since my last physical exam. And I had assumed positions that I hadn't been in since I gave birth to my daughter. Afterward, I fell asleep in his arms. But when I opened my eyes the next morning, I was in bed alone.

Pee Wee had already left the house by the time I got up and made it downstairs to the kitchen. That was odd, but it wasn't that big of a deal because he didn't do it that often. He usually waited for me to fix his favorite breakfast: grits, biscuits, scrambled eggs with green bell peppers mixed in, and beef bacon. And when I didn't get up in time to cook, he strapped on an apron and did it. The last time he had prepared breakfast, he had served it to me in bed.

For some reason, Pee Wee had not made breakfast this particular morning. He'd left the small clock radio on the kitchen counter on to some rap station (how many people listened to rap music this early in the morning?) and a mess on the kitchen table, which included the morning newspaper folded with the pages out of order, his empty coffee cup, a Krispy Kreme donut box, and an ashtray with the remnants of a thick marijuana cigarette piled up in it. I made a mental note to scold him about leaving a roach in plain view. It was hard enough trying to hide certain things and activities from our inquisitive eleven-year-old daughter, Charlotte, not to mention nosy relatives and friends who dropped in at the most inconvenient times. One day my mother went snooping through my bedroom closet and stumbled across an XXX-rated VHS tape that I often watched with Pee Wee when our sex life needed a shot in the arm. She took me aside and quoted Scripture nonstop for twenty minutes. By the time she got through with me, I felt like I knew every harlot in the Bible personally. She'd "excused" Pee Wee and "reminded" me that men were too weak, stupid, and horny to know better.

Pee Wee and I had shared a good laugh over that. Our life together was so idyllic at times that my meddlesome mother's antics and crude comments didn't bother us. I had the best of both worlds. He was not just my husband; he was also my best friend.

In spite of all my shortcomings and flaws, I looked at matters of the heart from a realistic point of view. I knew that no man, or woman, was perfect, and that anybody could make a mistake. Me jumping into bed with that low-down, funky, black devil that I got involved with last year was one of the biggest mistakes I'd ever made in my entire life. It had been such an intense and passionate affair that it had me acting like a fool. I had done things for him that I had never done to please a man. I'd told lies to be with him. And I'd given him money. It had begun gradually, but when I realized I was "paying" for some dick, I got real concerned because that went against everything I believed in. When I refused to continue paying for my pleasure, the relationship ended in a violent confrontation. Luckily, I had escaped uninjured—at least physically. But I had "paid" a very high price for my mistake. I was so disgusted with myself that for a long time it was hard for me to look in a mirror without flinching.

My husband had reluctantly forgiven me, and we had moved on. "Annette, you ain't the first woman to cheat, and you won't be the last. I'll get over what you done . . . I guess," he told me, cracking a weak smile to hide some of the pain that I'd caused.

I could not have been more repentant and humble if they'd revised the Bible and included a psalm in my honor. "Honey, I swear to God, something like this will never happen again," I assured him, with reconstructive ideas about how I was going to repair my marriage swimming around in my head.

Once that was behind us, I began to focus on the only intimate relationship that mattered to me now. But I was no fool. I knew that if *I* could fall into the deep black hole of infidelity, anybody could. However, since it was usually the man who acted a fool and got involved in an affair, it was more important for me to focus on what my husband might or might not do. I believed that if he ever did cheat on me, I had to look at the situation from an overall point of view: Would I be better off without this man? Does he no longer love me? Is he worth fighting for? Is this marriage dead? Has he become such a slimy devil that he is no longer good enough for me anyway?

Had any of that been the case, the bombshell that my husband dropped in my lap this morning wouldn't have caused so much damage. Because when he informed me that he was having an affair, I could not have been more stunned if somebody had told me that the Easter Bunny was a pimp.

He had committed the granddaddy of indiscretions: a torrid, ongoing, "I'd rather be with her than you," sexual relationship with a woman whom I had called my friend. To me, that was the worst kind of affair. If I couldn't trust my husband and a woman I called my friend, who could I trust?

To make matters even worse, I was probably the last person in our circle to hear about his affair!